Cultivation

LEGENDARY FARMER BOOK 4

Print book ISBN 978-1-7376510-6-2

First edition, October 2022

For my daughter, Kaylee, who bears more than a passing resemblance to Rouge, and who I hope will be just as smart, earnest, brave, loyal, and kind. Thank you for inspiring me every day, my sunshine.

Book Four: Cultivation

Cul·ti·va·tion /ˌkəltəˈvāSH(ə)n/ *noun*

noun: cultivation; plural noun: cultivations

1. the action of cultivating land, or the state of being cultivated.
2. the process of trying to acquire or develop a quality or skill.

Chapter One

Khor

For the first few weeks after the humans left, things went fairly well. Not good, but fairly well. The spider was her usual bossy self, the vampire hid in his caves, and the goblin and her offspring stayed mainly near the house and out of Khor's fur. If it weren't for that damned duck, he'd likely have upgraded the situation to 'tolerable'.

Unfortunately, the duck seemed to have decided to be a permanent fixture. On Khor's head. Right between his magnificent, spiral horns. Which were already heavy, so he really didn't need to add another twenty pounds of self-important poultry.

Khor grunted, pawing another rock out of the ground and kicking it neatly into a pile nearby. If he didn't do something, Sumi would find some petty task for him to do so he could 'contribute to the household'. As if protecting Gina's Tree and watching out for the young unicorns (he'd call them 'sparkles' when Atae's pool turned into a rainbow and spat out cookies) wasn't enough.

He turned a fond eye on the little foals as they cavorted in the warm spring sunshine. Kayti's coat grew more iridescent with each passing day, and a faint trail of colored light lingered in the air behind her when she ran. Kayli, the little scamp, glittered like grass after a hard frost, and when she flicked her tail or shook her short mane, sparkles drifted out around her, gleaming and winking for a long heartbeat before they flickered out. If he was absolutely honest, calling *her* a sparkle wouldn't be entirely inaccurate, but it was still ridiculous, and he refused.

He snorted and kicked out another stone from the area Aspen had designated as future fields. How the foolish humans had ever thought the babies were goats, he didn't know. Unless, perhaps, it was some subconscious recognition of their miraculous nature? Because, after all, there was nothing more miraculous than a goat.

Atop his head, Nuisance squawked a warning, and sharply bit Khor's left ear. Khor's head shot up, looking to his left and nearly dislodging the flightless waterfowl. Nuisance promptly spit out a few curse words in his gibberish bird-language, and Khor snorted back at him derisively, but lifted his head so the bird could resettle himself. After all, in spite of the creature's *many* shortcomings, he did have excellent eyesight (possibly better than Khor's, though he'd never admit that aloud), and good hearing.

Which meant, unfortunately, that Nuisance made a very good lookout. This allowed Khor to do his 'chores' while also protecting the fields and the Tree. Biting his left ear meant Nuisance had seen something moving in the fields, so Khor trotted that way, enjoying the way his hooves sank into the warm, loamy soil, and the gentle breeze lifted his fur. Raising his head, he shook his heavy beard and shaggy coat, well aware that his powerful muscles, thick, healthy fur, and bright eyes made him a fine figure of a goat.

Or they *would* if he didn't have a duck on his head.

Seeing him moving away, the little unicorns bugled an interrogative call, and Kayli trotted after him. Her more cautious sister tried to get in front of her and herd her back, but the smaller foal just danced around her sibling, sparkling blue eyes avidly seeking her newest adventure. Khor snorted at them both, and

Kayli bleated back unrepentantly, but dropped back behind him.

Satisfied, Khor returned his attention to the field he was approaching. It was filled with growing vegetables, and many of the plants were already nearly to his shoulder, and their growth showed no signs of slowing. Sarave had already had to harvest some of the largest produce, and from the size of the burgeoning pea pods, it seemed that she would need to do so again soon.

As he drew nearer, he saw that the tops of some of the corn stalks were shaking as though a hard wind was blowing, though only a sweet spring breeze stirred the plants around them. Nuisance stamped a webbed foot, and Khor flung his head in the direction of the disturbance. The duck, using the lift provided by Khor's powerful throw, flapped twice, gliding briefly, and then dropped sharply down into the field.

Khor ignored the momentary twinge of concern, no doubt at the thought that his assistant might be injured and leave Khor himself to do all the work, and locked his gaze on the spot where the duck had gone down. He couldn't see much except the long leaves of the corn, but a muffled rustling and a few angry quacks revealed that something was happening.

After a while, the duck came waddling out of the field, his broad beak firmly clamped on the tail of a Lesser Hare. The hare's eyes were glazed and unfocused, but his powerful back legs still twitched occasionally. Khor gave the bird a nod of grudging appreciation, and used his own hoof to gently tap the hare's skull.

Instantly, an image appeared before his eyes; a rabbit with x's on its eyes and a thumbs up, followed by pictures of both Khor and Nuisance. It flashed once, barely long enough for him to process, and then it was gone. So, he and Nuisance had both received credit for the kill, eh? Well, he supposed it was only fair, since the duck had knocked the creature out.

Carefully, Khor used his flexible lips to pick up the dead hare by its ear. He grimaced at the faint scent of blood, and was grateful the thing hadn't bled more, though he knew Sarave would have preferred if it was drained before he brought it back.

Not that he cared what any goblin wanted.

Turning, he trotted back to the house, leaving an angry Nuisance to flap-waddle his way home alone. It wasn't that far, and it wasn't Khor's job to serve as a conveyance for the persnickety fowl anyway. He did, however, make sure to keep his pace slow enough that the unicorns, with their short, spindly legs, could keep up. If it also meant that Nuisance didn't fall too far behind, well, that was entirely incidental.

ଙ ଙ ଙ

At the tiny, cramped farmhouse, Sarave had the doors and shutters wide open, letting the sunshine and breeze blow through the musty interior. Juniper, who was growing at what, he supposed, was an acceptable pace, squealed when she saw him.

"Mommy! Khow bwought a wabbit!" The little half-goblin ran forward and threw her arms around one of his legs. Khor used to shudder when she did this, but by now he was used to it, though he would still have preferred if she kept her hands to herself. Still, it wasn't *entirely* unpleasant, and at least *someone* appreciated him properly.

Sarave emerged from the house, wiping her hands on a threadbare towel that had seen better days. The cloth was little more than a rag, and Khor hoped Aspen would remember to bring back some new ones when he returned, if only so that the goblin could do a better job of cleaning the place.

The goblin smiled, raising a slender olive-green hand to shelter her eyes from the bright sun. Her race had long since adapted to living underground, and he could tell that the light bothered her, though she never complained. Juniper seemed to have inherited her father's human eyes, and they were not only less protuberant, but also less sensitive to the sun.

Perhaps when Aspen returned, he would also bring some glass for the windows, as they had discussed, and perhaps there would be a little extra. Khor had once seen someone using flat circles of smoked glass to protect their eyes from bright light. Something like that would probably help Sarave, too... especially when she was working in the field, harvesting crops so that she could make the dense vegetable loaf that she sometimes shared with Khor and the others.

Khor spat the hare out on the ground, taking small satisfaction in the thick green saliva that now coated the animal's ears. Sarave just stepped forward though, carefully picking up the carcass by the hind legs and neatly avoiding the herbaceous goo.

"Thank you, Khor." The goblin woman bowed respectfully, her free hand over her heart. Khor did have to give her that. Sarave was the only one who ever gave him the respect he was due. Certainly, that spider never-

<Could you not have kept it a little cleaner, Khor?> Sumi's acerbic voice entered his mind. <You know she'll have to cleanse the fur of your saliva before she tans it.>

<She'd have to wash it anyway,> he shot back. <What's a little more? At least I can kill things without making them inedible.>

The spider clicked her chelicerae together irritably, but had no response. Undoubtedly because he was correct, and she never liked to admit when that happened.

<Did you clear the third field of roots and rocks? I can tell Sarave it's ready to be plowed.>

He did, possibly, envy the old arachnid her ability to communicate with the two-legs. She and Sarave had worked out a simple alphabet that Sumi could spin in her web, allowing them to hold conversations with relative ease. Since Sumi was awake most nights, watching over the Tree and the fields, as he did during the day, she and Sarave often had quite lively discussions in the evening. Khor had even heard *giggling* once or twice.

Khor, meanwhile, was limited to speaking with Sumi herself, though he could certainly make himself understood by the others when he needed to. Though he hadn't figured out how to tell Sarave when he wanted more vegetable loaf. Yet. He supposed he could ask Sumi to let the goblin know, but that was beneath his dignity. He simply hoped the female would figure it out eventually. He made sure to spit and drool more often when she served it, so certainly his point should be getting across.

He was distracted by a childish, "Eww!" from below, and looked down to realize that he had somehow managed to drool on Juniper's head, and the little girl's curls were matted down in slimy spirals. He shook his head, shaking the rest of the spit from his beard before it could fall on her and elicit sarcastic commentary from Sumi.

Sarave rushed over, completely ignoring the fact that she was within easy striking distance of a seven-foot-tall war goat who had slain dozens, if not hundreds, of her kind during the war. The goblin's gleaming black hair nearly touched Khor's knee as she used the thin cloth to rub at her daughter's head. Khor snorted and shuffled back a step, catching a whiff of the goblin's now-familiar aroma of soap, chamomile, blue cornflower, and just the slightest hint of the sunflower oil she used in her hair.

<Khor! Pay attention!> The sharp snap of Sumi's voice brought him back to the present, and he shook his head again, scattering the memories of the feeling of his hooves punching through the thin skull-bone of a screeching goblin. <Is the field cleared?>

He danced back a few steps, away from the goblin mother and her child, who were engrossed in each other and didn't even glance up as he moved. <Almost,> he said grumpily. <It'll be done by tonight, as long as nothing else happens.>

As if on cue, Nuisance's most powerful call shattered the calm spring air, and all four of them whirled to look behind them. Shockingly, the sacrilegious fowl was riding on Kayli's back! The little foal was staggering beneath the weight, but Khor could tell from the glint in her eye that she was determined to carry the feathered fiend until she dropped or he got off. If the unicorn didn't have a quest for this, Khor was going to stomp that unholy bird into the mud, so help him, Gina!

Nuisance released Kayli's glimmering, albeit still slightly scrubby, mane for a moment, raising his head to let out another blaring squawk. Then he jumped into the air, flapping his wings ferociously, though the stunted one was barely able to do more than flop awkwardly. The duck was staring in the direction of the Tree.

The Tree!

Khor's hooves dug into the soil as he spun and galloped back toward Nuisance and the unicorns. With a flip of one horn, he scooped the feathered irritant up, tossing him so that the bird squawked again, this time in surprise, then landed neatly on Khor's broad withers. When the goat felt the now-familiar pull of a beak grabbing a firm grip on his fur, he started up again. Clods of dirt and other debris flew through the air behind them as Khor leapt forward, quickly reaching a speed that left everyone else in the dust.

In front of his eyes, another picture flashed. This time, it was a simple pictograph of a small, silvery tree with dozens of angry red insects swarming all over it. Bugs again. Why did it have to be bugs? He *hated* bugs!

Bugs had been attacking the Tree since the day Aspen left, taking with him the only member of their group who was actually good at defeating the six-legged menaces. Silus could eat hundreds of bugs when she really set her mind (and belly) to it, while even Khor had to admit that his huge hooves and horns weren't particularly helpful once the chitinous terrors were already on the Tree, since he was more likely to do harm than help.

Fortunately, after the first few attacks, which had come while the Tree was still little more than a green stem and two silvery leaves, Sumi had set up webbing that protected the plant fairly effectively. Small flying insects still occasionally made it through, but Sumi said that was actually good, since they would be needed once flowers began to bloom. While the spider was irritating and bossy, she was also highly intelligent for an arachnid, so Khor felt it was safe to assume she knew what she was talking about.

When Khor and a rather disheveled duck arrived on the scene, they found that Sumi's web was still doing its job. The attackers this time were simply Lesser Termites, and while they were annoying, unless a flying queen somehow managed to make it through the nearly invisible webbing, the nasty things would be trapped until help could arrive.

This was where Khor came in. The first few times, everyone had joined in, which led to mounds of crushed insect corpses and a bath taken en masse. Even the little unicorns had helped, though Kayti had been bitten on her knee, and one of Kayli's ears had been swollen for days. Even though Khor had seen the shimmer of stat and level increases around the foals, he had put his hoof down after that and told them they were not allowed to help unless something small actually reached the Tree. If it was something large, well, in Khor's mind, unicorns trumped even Gina's Tree, and the little ones would be staying out of the battle whether they liked it or not.

Now, Khor laid about him with his mighty hooves, squashing wriggling web-bound termites with abandon, though he shuddered at the crunching sound. There was just something so much more *disgusting* about insect innards versus humanoid innards. Plus, Sumi's sticky webs wrapped the gory remains around his hooves and legs, and sometimes with the larger insects some would even work their way up into the fur that dangled from his chest and flank, and from there work their way up to... Well, it just didn't bear thinking about.

Shaking his huge, shaggy head, Khor set to his task with even greater dedication. There was no way he was going to have to ask Sumi to ask Sarave to help him clean hard-to-reach areas today. He'd rather have the vampire do it!

When the last of the cocooned invaders had been squashed, including a young queen, who had popped with a particularly unpleasant gushing crunch, Khor stood among the carnage, possibly breathing slightly heavily, but entirely unharmed. His glorious fur was matted and tangled, and webs swathed him from elbow to hoof. On his head, Nuisance clung to the tuft of Khor's forelock that the canard preferred to use as a kind of anchor. Grumpy squawking trickled into

Khor's ears, which were directly adjacent to the bird.

Khor shook his head vigorously, but Nuisance clung tenaciously, and the goat snorted in frustration. Nuisance used to help with the insect eradication, and, in fact, seemed to actually enjoy it to some extent. Once Sumi's webs came into play, however, the bird flatly refused to help. You would think that getting his beak stuck closed for two days was a fate worse than death!

Sighing, Khor trotted toward the river, leaving the devastation behind. Sumi, who also refused to help on the grounds that, 'I've already done my part. Earn your keep, you enormous ruminant!', would be along soon enough to repair the damage to her web. After she was done, she should go home and sleep instead of doing whatever plotting and planning she'd been up to this morning. Even spiders needed to rest, and if she was exhausted, she'd be no use in protecting the farm at night. She might even get sick, though Khor had never known it to happen, and Khor didn't want to have to deal with all of the petty details and interpersonal relationships that the arachnid currently handled.

Nuisance flung himself into the air as Khor stepped onto the muddy bank beside the merrily rushing river. The only time the bird voluntarily vacated Khor's cranium was when they were near water, especially the river. In fact, Khor's favorite bathing place happened to be near the pond where Nuisance's mother had had her nest, and the duck seemed particularly fond of the area. Not that Khor cared about the duck's preferences. This place just happened to have the gentlest slope into the water, and the eddies caused by the river rushing into the open area helped to clean his fur.

Behind him, he heard the baby unicorns bleat-whinny playfully to each other as they gamboled about in the shallow water. As always, their gleaming fur resisted all dirt and tangles, so they remained as perfectly clean as ever even while standing hock-deep in muck. Khor turned a doubtful eye on his own web-tangled legs and sighed deeply, shaking his horns.

Cautiously, Khor waded out into the deep water near the place where the river emptied into the pond. When he was submerged up to his shoulders, he lifted his hooves from the murky bottom, and began paddling in place. Waves rushed away from his body as he used the force of the water to clean the lingering remnants of chitin and web from his fur, and Nuisance quacked happily as he was lifted up and down by the water. The kids, too, pranced playfully in the little ripples that touched the banks, and Khor watched them fondly. It was even possible that in spite of his own marked preference for dryness over wetness, he may have lingered a little longer than absolutely necessary as he watched his little friends.

That was how he saw the first V in the water, slowly and sinuously approaching the dainty little hooves that were perhaps intruding a little too deeply into the water. Once his eye fixed on it, he noticed a second, then a third. Each of them was caused by the tiniest hint of a tall fin lazily moving through the water toward the unicorns. Another of the ominous ripples was already nearing the place where Nuisance was bobbing happily on the waves.

Khor let out a bugle that was loud enough to be heard even under the water. The unicorns bounced backward as if they had been pulled by a string, but Nuisance just looked toward Khor, a puzzled expression on his beaked face. Khor let his back legs touch the muddy floor, cursing himself for going in so deeply that it was difficult for him to find purchase for his hooves beneath the silt. His chin was nearly submerged before he got enough of a grip to push off, but then he was lunging through the water, his powerful front legs ready to crush whatever aquatic menace was approaching his duck.

With a *thunk* he could feel but not hear above the splashing of his massive body driving through the water, his sharp hooves impacted something, and a moment later, a red cloud rose up from the area. A picture appeared in his mind, the glorious goat that represented himself facing off against something that looked like a long, slim fish with a tall, triangular fin on its back, small eyes, and a wide mouth full of serrated teeth. Whatever the thing was, it was clearly carnivorous, and as irritating as Nuisance was, Khor had no intention of letting the bird be attacked.

Khor swept his horns through the water, scooping Nuisance up and flipping him onto Khor's head just as vicious teeth snapped through the area where the duck's webbed feet had been paddling. The duck, only now realizing the danger he had been in, squawked in surprise, and grabbed onto Khor's forelock tightly. The moment Khor felt the painful pang that meant the bird was firmly attached, his mighty muscles began propelling his body through the water and toward the shore. Fortunately, the area of the pond in which he now found himself had a shelf of stone beneath the mud that allowed his hooves a firm grip. As he pushed through the water, which was as resistant now as it had felt supportive only moments before, he felt surrounded by cold scales and the stares of cold, uncaring eyes. More than once, he was certain something smooth brushed against him, but no more attacks came and he soon found himself on the bank of the pond, dripping and shivering.

The little unicorns huddled against his rear legs, shivering as much as he was, though they, no doubt, shivered from fear, whereas he was simply cold in what had formerly seemed such a pleasant spring breeze. The tableau held for a long moment, with the rippling surface of the water settling into barely disturbed glass, while the four residents stared out with terrified eyes. Except Khor, who was obviously simply cautious, rather than terrified.

Nonetheless, when a head emerged from the water, Nuisance and the unicorns were not alone in jumping back.

The head was humanoid and gray, with eyes that were entirely black, as far as Khor could tell, and the nose was unusually flat, with narrow nostrils. The mouth was wide, with narrow lips, and the ears were so small they seemed nothing more than an afterthought. Long black and gray hair trailed down into the water, drifting on the surface as the being stared silently at the trembling quartet.

Carefully, this strange being, who was nothing like the fishy caricature of Khor's quest-vision, nor the long outline of smooth, cold flesh and gaping jaw that had recently occupied the pond, emerged into the spring sunlight. In spite of the bright day, it didn't blink, and Khor could see wet, dark slits in the side of its neck gape slightly as it breathed.

From behind them, he heard the deliberate crack of a twig, and Sumi's voice came into his mind. Her tone was calculating and absent, and he knew that even as she spoke, she would be running through a hundred possible scenarios and deciding what her response would be to all of them. <I believe that is a Glyphis, Khor. Very dangerous in the water, but nearly helpless on land. That it has taken this form and emerged at all is… interesting. Back up slowly, if you would. We came when we heard your call, but Sarave is yet a bit behind, since she had to put Juniper in the house. Glyphis should be able to communicate, albeit with difficulty, so we may yet manage to avoid violence.>

Khor snorted, but softly. He was fine with violence, as long as he was dealing most of it. Still, he stepped back carefully, pushing the young unicorns with his legs as he did, and kept his head high so that Nuisance was out of attack range, even though that left his own throat exposed to the terrible teeth.

The glyphis showed those teeth as its lips twisted, and a strange, croaking voice emerged from its throat. Much of the force of the air seemed to be lost as it passed through the thing's throat, but in the strange calm that had settled over the group, the words could be heard easily.

"Where. Is. Tree?"

🌱 🌱 🌱

There was some confusion even after Sarave arrived and was able to translate between Sumi's web-writing and the laborious glyphis-speak, and, frankly, once Khor was sure no one was going to try to eat anyone else, he didn't really care what was going on. There was a lot of talk about priests, and dreams, and some very odd bits about commandments, but what it all seemed to boil down to was that Gina had finally gotten around to sending some more guards for the Tree.

Which was excellent news, except that these 'guards' were a good quarter mile from the Tree itself, and could barely poke their heads above the water, much less *get out and help*. Plus, the glyphis were carnivores, and there weren't all that many large fish in the river and pond, so, even though there was only one family who were actually going to stay, they would probably need help supplementing their diet.

Khor knew what that meant. Sumi poisoned her food so no one else could eat it, William got sick at the sight of blood, and everyone else was too small or weak to hunt. Which meant the goat would have to do it. The *herbivorous* goat.

After a lot of chatter and time wasted while the glyphis got in and out of the water so they could keep their gills wet, Sumi finally got around to being bossy. Turning to Khor, she said, <Khor, these people will be staying here. You'll need to find a deer or something for them at least once a week. Their mage will watch the Tree while you do your other chores.>

Khor perked up. Somewhere in all of the babble, something actually useful had happened? <What mage?>

Sumi clicked her fangs irritably. <The one Itan just told us about!> The spider produced a theatrical sighing sound, though he knew perfectly well that she didn't breathe like mammals did, because one of her favorite topics was 'the varied body forms and functions of living creatures', and she could talk about it for hours with no more encouragement than an occasional hoof stamp or particularly loud chewing of his cud.

<Itan, his mate Viqa, and their son Taqi, will be staying here when the rest of their clan moves on,> Sumi continued. <Their priest was sent a vision from Gina to come here and help protect the Tree. Viqa is the most powerful mage in their clan, and she can stay out of water for several hours by using magic. Her sole task is to watch over the Tree, and call you if she needs help. However, if she can't bring back enough meat from whatever creatures try to attack the Tree, then you'll need to help her.>

One of the spider's surprisingly sharp feet tapped impatiently at the ground. <Next time, perhaps you'll actually listen when others are speaking?>

Khor huffed grumpily. His hooves hurt from standing there for so long, and the unicorns had wandered off somewhere ages ago. He wasn't even sure where they were, which always made him nervous. <Unlikely,> he retorted. <But fine, I can help. Only when they need it, though.>

Unfortunately, so far most of the creatures that had attempted to eat, break, uproot, or otherwise damage the Tree had been insects. Since Khor doubted anyone with teeth like that ate many bugs, he suspected he'd be forced to help. Sometimes. Which didn't mean he had to do it gracefully.

<When does this Viqa start?>

<Tomorrow,> Sumi replied smartly. <As you'd know if you'd been paying attention!>

<Whatever,> he huffed, looking around. <Where are the foals?>

<You mean the sparkles?>

He sighed. An actual sigh, with lungs and throat and everything. <You know what I mean.>

<They're not horses, Khor.>

<They're not glitter, either!> He raised his head higher, flaring his nostrils wide as he tried to catch a whiff of his small charges. On his head, he felt Nuisance shift as the duck also looked around, sensing Khor's concern.

<I saw them heading back toward the house a while ago,> Sumi said without a single hint of worry. <They're not babies any more, Khor. They're quite intelligent, actually, though they lack common sense because you coddle them so.>

He snorted. <I do not!>

Ignoring whatever retort the arachnid was about to make, he trotted off toward the house. Though he would never admit it aloud, he knew Sumi was right. The unicorns were quite intelligent, though they seemed unable to take anything not immediately dangerous at all seriously.

That was *why* he had to watch over them so carefully, though! While Kayti was naturally cautious, Kayli would charge into trouble simply because she caught a glimpse of something shiny, and Kayti, ever the big sister, followed after without hesitation.

After a short time, he caught a faint whiff of Kayti's scent of lilacs and tangerines, so he knew he was heading in the right direction. A few strides after that, he smelled marshmallows and cinnamon, and knew Kayli, as usual, had been in the lead, probably chasing a dragonfly or a dandelion seed. Then, just as he was beginning to relax, a third familiar scent joined the first two. Soap, pine, and cloudberries wafted along the breeze, mingling with sweet sugar and citrus.

Juniper.

The child was *supposed* to be locked up in the house. Admittedly, the unicorns weren't the only ones who were smart for their age, especially since Sarave (and Sumi) seemed determined to teach the little girl about everything she showed the slightest interest in. He wasn't surprised at all to find that the half-goblin knew how to open the locks on the door of the house, though he was a bit surprised that she had been able to *reach* them.

He increased his speed. The two unicorns were capable of causing him enough inconvenience all on their own, but when you added in the little green trouble-maker, all bets were off. Juniper seemed to have no fear, and though she was as sweet as a sugar cube when she was around her mother, she seemed to delight in causing mischief the moment Sarave turned her back.

Khor himself had even been the victim of one of her 'experiments', when the girl painted his fur with her mother's clothing dye while he was napping. Fortunately, Sarave had known how to strip the color faster than it naturally faded, but Khor had been green and yellow for nearly a week. He didn't even want to think about the time the child painted his hooves with the brilliant purple dye made from the early spring berries Sarave had harvested and then discovered were poisonous.

Khor's ears swiveled forward as he heard a sound like the scrape of a hoof on a rock. Soft giggling sounded, and he slowed, walking as quietly as he could along the well-worn dirt path toward the house. His head grew warm as

Nuisance settled his fluffy feathered bottom more comfortably, and Khor ground his teeth, knowing full well that the bird was doing it deliberately since Khor wouldn't be able to shake him off at the moment.

Perhaps five more meters down the path, he came across his first real clue. It was a little tunic, beautifully embroidered with thistles around the hem by a nimble-fingered mother goblin. The tunic lay abandoned on the grass by the path, one sleeve pulled inside out, and a small red stain barely visible around the cuff.

Sarave's daughter had a distinct preference for nudity. No one cared about this except for Sarave, who seemed frustrated no end by her daughter's seeming ability to shed her clothing without actually taking the time required to remove it. They had recently found a compromise, in that Sarave had convinced the child that if she saw a little green full moon during the daytime, Juniper would get no dessert that night.

Khor lowered his head and huffed, drawing in a deep breath of lye soap and pine needles. The red smudge on the sleeve smelled like Sarave's strawberry jam, so there was no reason to believe the three scamps were in too much trouble yet.

With his nose lowered to the ground, trailing the scent of strawberries and sugar, Khor quickly found himself circling wide around the house, through a small copse of trees that had sprung up since Aspen did whatever-he-did to bless the land, but had apparently forgotten to specify that *crops* were the preferred recipients of said blessing.

While Motte and Rouge had cleared the land around the house for nearly a mile, Aspen's little party trick seemed determined to undo everything without someone weeding and pulling seedlings daily. Sarave had tried to maintain the area, but had given up after only a week, and now kept her efforts to the area immediately surrounding the house and the path that led to the Tree, the fields, and the river. As a result, dense thickets and trees taller than Khor had sprung up on previously-cleared land.

Somehow, in spite of interweaving branches so thick they seemed capable of forming naturally grown buckets, the two unicorns and the half-goblin girl child still managed to insinuate themselves into these shrubberies with depressing regularity. Fortunately, Khor's horns and hooves could do a credible job of clearing the smaller branches out of the way, though he'd be scraping twigs and leaves out of his fur for days. Nuisance was even, sometimes, slightly helpful when it came to cleaning debris from Khor's coat, so he supposed that was another reason to keep the waterfowl around.

Now, though, Khor followed the ever-more-obvious trail of fallen jam globules and the occasional sparkling or iridescent hair that littered the ground. Snorting softly, he paused when a little voice came to his sensitive ears.

"I get t'eat two bites, 'cause my mom made the jam. But that's okay, 'cause there's lots more, and even though we ran outta sugar, it's still really good." The little voice was coming from inside a particularly impenetrable section of underbrush, but while the growth was thick, it wasn't tall, as such things went, and Khor was able to lift his head enough to peek through.

The little girl was seated on one of her mother's cleaning rags, her pale, blue-green skin gleaming slightly in a faint beam of sunlight that penetrated the foliage above. Why the child hadn't used her tunic as a seat, if she was going to take it off, Khor didn't know, but then, he'd never claimed to be an expert in humanoid psychology. No, it was Sumi's job to be the expert. In everything.

A shadow beneath a sticker-bush moved, and Khor was able to make out the fragile legs and graceful neck of a certain pearly unicorn. Kayti's lips gently dipped into Juniper's sticky palm, coming away with a neat bite of jam. Another shadow moved. A shimmering nose shoved itself insistently against the little girl's side, and the half-goblin curled away, giggling wildly.

"That tickles, Kayli! You'll get yours in a second!" She gave the unicorn a stern look. "You gotta be patient, 'cause things don' happen any faster just 'cause you want 'em to."

Khor suppressed a snort. How many times had he heard Sarave explain this to her daughter, though the goblin's lilting accent and gentle voice made it sound rather different than the chiding tone of the little girl.

Juniper's short fingers delved into a large clay pot that was cradled in her lap, coming up with another dripping glob of jam. Kayli slurped the goo down with great haste, and Juniper laughed, petting the foal's sparkling mane with fingers that would have left the fur of any other creature a sticky mess. Thanks to the magical self-cleaning abilities of unicorn fur, Kayli's silky little mane just sprang back up into its usual gleaming glory.

Khor, satisfied that the children were safe from anything worse than an upset stomach and another lecture from Sarave, was about to pull back his head when another shadow moved within the thicket. A pale grayish hand stretched into the filtered light of the sun, flinching only slightly as the light caught the undead flesh.

"If you would be so kind, my lady," William the fructipire said formally, "May I have some as well? Your mother does make the most delectable jams and jellies."

A loud grinding sound caused the four jam-thieves to look up. Khor, whose teeth were causing the sound, tried to duck back before they could see him, but his horns, which he had maneuvered into place very carefully when he had arrived, now tangled in leaves and branches, causing both a rain of torn vegetation and also leaving Khor looking like an overgrown hat rack.

Instantly, Juniper was on her feet, somehow wriggling through greenery so thick that Khor would have sworn it was all but impenetrable. As soon as she reached him, she threw her sticky arms around his leg, then pressed an equally sticky face into the fur just above his knee. "Khow!" Her little voice instantly returned to the adorable (no, not adorable, *annoying)* babyish form that he was used to. Huge blue-green eyes blinked up at him through curling brown lashes, and the jammy face (now liberally covered in Khor's previously clean fur) beamed up at him.

Kayli followed suit, luminous blue eyes staring up at him adoringly as she butted her little head into his other foreleg. Kayti, of course, was more circumspect, lingering behind as she waited to see if they were in trouble or not.

William, who seemed to be the only member of the quartet who wasn't surprised by the 'sudden' appearance of a Greater Goat, simply watched from his shadowed hiding place beneath a thorny locust tree. When he saw Khor glaring at him, he lifted a bleached hand, his ever-haggard face even more worried than usual. His pathetic expression *almost* made Khor feel guilty for his suspicions, since the vampire had never once done anything to endanger anyone on the farm, and, indeed, seemed determined to be as helpful as he possibly could.

"Ah, Master Khor, I do apologize for my presence," the fructipire nearly stuttered. "It's just that... You see, I..."

Juniper tugged at the thick fur growing from Khor's chest. Her tacky little fingers tugged out several more strands of fur, and the look he turned on her may have been a bit fiercer than he intended. She completely ignored it, blithely continuing on in her cute little voice. "Mistew Willem was comin' t'talk t' Miss Sumi. I askid him t' eat wif us, 'cause Mama says it's nice to shawe."

William cleared his throat. "I saw the three misses leaving the house without, ah, adult supervision, as it were. I thought perhaps, mmm, it might be appropriate for me to accompany them. Just," he hurried on, "until one of their regular guardians was, ah, able to return. As it were." He rose, brushing twigs and leaves from pants that were otherwise meticulously clean, in spite of their shabby and threadbare condition. "I will return, ah, home, now. If you would, please, um, let Miss Sumi know I was here?"

Now that the vampire was standing, his shoulders and chest were exposed, since the bushes in which the children had been hiding were thick but low. Khor's head snaked out, and his teeth caught the sleeve of the suit jacket that William insisted upon wearing at all times. He winced slightly as the sound of ancient threads popping came to his ears, but he didn't let go.

William paused, looking frightened. "Ah, Master Khor, is there, perhaps, um, some way in which I may, ah, assist you?"

Khor huffed slightly, extending his flexible lips to pinch the fabric of William's sleeve. He tugged slightly, then let go and stepped back, tossing his head toward the house. Nuisance, who had been unusually quiet throughout the preceding, squawked and flapped down into the space beside Kayti, who was the only one still in the thicket. The duck promptly stuck his beak into the abandoned jam-jar and began to greedily gobble down the last of the strawberry goodness inside. Khor watched this with a particularly critical eye since, if he was entirely honest, he wouldn't have minded a generous dollop of the tasty confection himself.

Braying loudly, Khor tossed his head toward the house again, causing all five of the miscreants to jump. Juniper was now the only one not watching the goat with something akin to apology, or at least embarrassment, on their face. The little half-goblin seemed entirely unfazed, and began skipping merrily toward the house. Everyone else followed at varying paces which seemed to be primarily determined by how much trouble they thought they might be in.

By the time the group reached the house, with William at the end, smoking slightly even though he was sticking to the shadows and had covered his exposed skin with his jacket, Sumi and Sarave had also returned. Sarave held Juniper's tunic in one hand, and her expression was torn between mirth and a mother's eternal exasperation, while Sumi clung upside down in her favorite place beneath the eaves of the house.

When Juniper came within grabbing distance, Sarave's hand snaked out and grabbed her daughter's jam, dirt, and fur-covered fingers, promptly hauling the child inside without a single word, though she did offer both William and Khor a nod of thanks for returning her wayward offspring to her. Sumi dropped down to the ground on a silken line of web as soon as the pair closed the door behind them. Khor's ears twisted, just able to catch the sound of Sarave lecturing Juniper, and promising retribution in the form of Plain Bread for the next week, and he snorted, well aware that the scamp would be back at her shenanigans the moment her mother's back was turned.

Sumi and William, who had found some relief by entering the broad doorway into the adjacent barn, were already communicating via Sumi's web-language. After a few exchanges, Sumi began to click her chelicerae, a sure sign that she was agitated about something.

<Khor, you need to go with William.> The spider held up one front leg to forestall his protests. <I have been awake all night and morning, and if I don't get some rest, I'll be worthless as a guard tonight. *You're* going to need to go and make some decisions.> Sumi paused and then said something which probably hurt on the way out. <I trust you.> Then she promptly ruined it with, <In spite of your usual juvenile behavior, you are capable of intelligent decisions when you want to be.>

Khor stamped a hoof, causing Kayti and Kayli, who had been dozing in a patch of sun nearby, to start and sit up, looking around with wide, glimmering eyes. <I'm always intelligent! You just think anyone who doesn't act like you is an idiot.>

Sumi paused. <There is some truth to that,> she admitted finally. <But you seem to believe that violence is the first and best answer to any problem.>

Khor huffed. <That's because it is. After the violence, you can ask questions, if there's anyone left to answer them. But at least you'll be alive to do the asking.>

The spider waved a leg tiredly. <I suspect that this dichotomy is why Aspen left us both in charge while he's gone. It generally works well enough, with you protecting the farm and Tree, and me taking care of the house and making sure Aspen's plans are followed. Now, though, I truly do need you to put aside your irrational dislike of a being that has done you no harm, and go with William.>

Irrational! Khor spluttered. It was *not* irrational to hate and fear a member of a race that had once slaughtered thousands for no better reason than that they enjoyed it and needed to feed. He cast a glance at William, who was huddled beneath his coat, looking miserable. Even Khor did have to admit that William was a particularly unprepossessing member of his race. If, in fact, he could truly be considered a vampire at all, which Khor privately doubted more every day.

<Fine,> he muttered peevishly. <I can't fit inside his tunnels and caves, though.> He shook his broad horns proudly, the grandeur of the gesture slightly undermined as a hail of broken twigs and leaves came down around him.

Sumi clicked her fangs and chuckled a bit. <I believe you may be rather surprised.>

🍎 🍎 🍎

Khor was shocked.

The tunnel to which William led him was wide enough for not just Khor, but a whole wagon drawn by a pair of oxen. The entrance was nearly hidden by the sweeping branches of a large weeping willow that butted up against the small hill into which the steep decline had been excavated. It was close enough to the pond that Khor was doubly-amazed that he'd never stumbled on it during any of his too-numerous bathing trips. Its camouflage was so good, though, that even his sharp eyes hadn't picked it out of the many similar trees and hillocks surrounding it.

"Ah, you see, Lord Aspen said there was already a, um, cave system here," William said, entering the dimness of the tunnel mouth, then hesitating slightly to pick up a torch from a bracket just inside. "I'm very sorry, Master Khor, but I have no more charged glowstones, and, ah, I can see in the dark quite well, so…" The fructipire trailed off as he struck a flint and steel he'd pulled from a small alcove, using the resulting spark to start the torch up into a dim and smoky flame.

"In any case," William continued, leading Khor deeper into the tunnel, their path now faintly illuminated by the light of the torch. "Lord Aspen thought the caves would be a good starting place for, ah, some underground living space for Mistress Sarave and little Miss Juniper, as well as, perhaps, also some storage and work space. He was, ah, kind enough to grant me permission to make some space for myself, as well."

The fructipire's hesitant words paused as they entered into a vast space, and the path they were following leveled off to a beautifully flat finish. William trailed a proud hand over the smooth wall, then snatched it back as he seemed to realize what he'd done. "Ah, yes, I'm sorry! I didn't get to use this technique often, you know, before. Mine managers needed, mmm, easy access to minerals, and this makes for very thick, um, *dense* walls."

Pale knuckles rapped at the stone wall, which barely made a sound in response. "I would form the stone into balls or blocks, before, and the miners would carry it out as it was cleared. Only the main passages were like this." His voice grew more confident as he spoke, dropping the ums and ahs that made Khor's fur want to stand on end. "Instead of taking out the excess stone, I can compress it into much a harder form. Almost, ah, impenetrable, really, though an explosion might do it. Gave the miners somewhere safe to retreat to in case of a cave-in, you see, but not helpful for actual, ah, mining."

William looked around, watery reddish-blue eyes taking in the perfect glossy surfaces around him. "It's, ah, very satisfying, to be able to make something perfect, and, ah, know that it will be used to help others at the same time." His long, sad face grew even more lugubrious than usual. "I, ah, couldn't do that for, mmm, a long time."

Khor almost felt a twinge of pity for the man. Almost. He snorted and pawed at the hard stone beneath his hooves, which was indeed very hard and had just enough texture to prevent him from slipping as he walked. Atop his head, Nuisance quacked softly, adding his own commentary, as he so often did.

A dull gray flush rose in William's cheeks. The vampire yanked his hand back from the wall, and shuffled his way hurriedly across the room, toward one of the seven broad tunnels that led away. "Ah, yes, um, well," he muttered, the torch flickering in his hand as he all but ran away. "The, ah, tunnels are all arches, ah, because that shape is much stronger, ah, than the squared-off halls they use in, um, buildings. I could, ah, make them that way, but, ah, Lord Aspen said I should do whatever made them safest."

Several smaller openings branched off the tunnel down which they now walked. The uncertain light of the torch was barely sufficient to show deeper shadows beyond. It looked as if the space was actually honeycombed into even more rooms. Just how many tunnels and rooms had the undead earth mage managed to make down here over the past winter and beginning of spring?

Now, though, they were coming to a dead end, and Khor could see from the rough texture of the wall that this was natural stone, not the compressed stuff about which William was so enthusiastic. The fructipire set his hand on a small patch of the wall, and looked back at Khor.

"This is what I wanted Miss Sumi, ah, or you, of course, to look at."

Khor looked. It was a hunk of rock, with a few small bits of dirt mixed in, and possibly some shiny bits that could have been almost anything. He shook his horns, hoping William would take it to mean, "What's the big deal?"

The vampire coughed, probably unnecessarily, since Khor was fairly certain vampires only drew air into their lungs so that they could speak. He and Aspen had once more-or-less-accidentally dug up a vampire who'd been buried by an explosion well over a week before, and the thing had still tried to eat them, even though it was missing most of its lower body.

"Ah, yes, um, Master Khor, the light in here is dim, I'm sorry, so, ah, perhaps... Look here." A blanched finger tapped an area of stone that was slightly smoother than the area around it. "I could tell when I was working my way here from the mine that humans, ah, at least not *recent* humans, weren't the first to have lived in this area. Even when I was alive, this area, surrounded as it is by the mountains, with no real, ah, native resources for trade, was nearly uninhabited. So, ah, I suspect that whoever or whatever lived here was at least, ah, a few hundred years before my own time."

Which would put it at seven hundred or more years ago. Khor nodded to indicate that he was following, though he wasn't sure what this ancient civilization might have to do with them, other than as a matter of historical interest. Since he wasn't particularly interested in history, that meant it was of no interest to him at all, and certainly could have waited until Sumi was available to come down here and have a *fascinating* discourse with the old fructipire about things that weren't actually important to anyone any more.

As if William could tell that Khor was rapidly losing what little patience he had had, he hurried his speech, dropping the hesitant pauses in favor of simply getting out what he needed to say. "You see, whoever lived here before had magic, and I'm afraid that some of that magic still lingers. Aspen said that monsters seemed drawn to the tunnels, and that was part of the reason he wanted me to use them, since they were already large enough to support a creature that could be dangerous to everyone living here."

Khor stamped a foot, urging the man again to *get on with it.*

William's words tumbled over each other. "I believe, however, that the reason such powerful beasts kept showing up here is not, in fact, because they found the tunnels a convenient place to live, but because they *spawned* here. Slowly, perhaps, because the magic has grown ah, anemic, if you will, over the centuries, or perhaps even millennia."

Khor just looked at the vampire, pointedly chewing his cud, and William's fingers began to trace some ridges that even to Khor's excellent eyesight were little more than wrinkles and seams in the stone. Perhaps whatever it was was more obvious to vampiric Darkvision?

"I had, ah, been becoming suspicious, since I've also come across a few, um, creatures who should not otherwise have been here. Fortunately, they have all been small, and easy enough to dispose of, ah, even for me, but then I found this, ah, already here when I cleared away the rubble in front of it, and *here*," his nail tapped sharply, twice, scraping against the stone. "This is a very ancient symbol, and, ah, one I only recognize because when you are a mage who works in the dark spaces beneath the earth, it behooves you to learn all you can about the dangers that lurk around you, and *this*, Master Khor, says 'dungeon'."

Chapter Two

Rouge

G etting back into the Masker's hideout was easy. Rouge and Vonn simply opened the door and walked inside. The echoing chamber was as empty as it had been when they left. Not really surprising, since that had been all of five minutes earlier. Signs of their battle with the guards were still strewn around, though the bodies had already dissolved into small piles of dirt on the floor. The cages into which the prisoners had been crammed like animals stood open, barred doors wide in silent witness to the suffering that had occurred within. Taking a chance, Rouge sent up a whispered prayer to Gina that Aspen would be able to get his motley group safely home.

Gina has heard your prayers. *Aspen* has gained +10% Speed, Mana Recovery, and Agility for the next three hours.

She grinned as the notice popped up in front of her, hovered for a moment, then dissolved into shimmering golden dust, visible only to her. She had recently accepted a unique character sub-class, Fowl Trickster, and one of the perks was an increased chance that her deity would 'hear' her prayers. Nice to know her patron goddess was following through on her part of the bargain. Just in case, she muttered another prayer for her own success, but, unsurprisingly, there was no response. Too much, too soon, she supposed.

Rouge and Vonn exchanged glances, and Rouge silently took the lead. One of the prisoners had said hordes of soldiers had headed through the door on the left, so Rouge picked the right-hand door. Rouge had already died once tonight, and that was plenty. Aspen wasn't going to be around to resurrect her. Besides, Vonn and Silus wouldn't respawn if anything happened to them, so it was definitely best to avoid heading into obvious danger.

When they reached the door, Rouge glanced behind her, checking to make sure Vonn was ready to slip through when she opened it. For a moment, she panicked, unable to see the young wood elf. Then she caught a flicker of movement beside the door, and a grin broke across her face.

"Your [Stealth] is working!" Instantly, she triggered her own [Stealth], barely resisting the urge to giggle gleefully when her hand faded into the gray outline that was all she saw when she was in [Stealth] mode. She hadn't been able to use her sneakiest skills for *hours,* and she'd felt like she was missing an arm or a leg.

The shimmer that was Vonn twitched, as he probably looked down at himself. "Great Forest!" The elf muttered. "I didn't even think about it, just triggered the skill automatically. This area must not have the spell-breaker wards surrounding it."

Rouge nodded thoughtfully, then realized that her companion wouldn't be able to see that, and said, "I agree. It makes sense, I guess. Natives aren't as, um, inquisitive as Travelers. Travelers can't resist going into any place they can tell they're not supposed to be, but most Natives will stay out unless they're pretty sure there's something worth their while in there. Since the Native and Traveler areas are obviously supposed to be separate, they wouldn't bother using expensive wards here. The guards would be enough to keep most Natives from even thinking about trying the doors."

She quickly checked her Skill list, noting that none of them were grayed out anymore. "Looks like we're back to full power, Vonn! This should be a piece of," she swallowed down the last word, hoping it wasn't too late. You never, *ever* said anything was a piece of cake while you were still doing it. Or, honestly, afterward, because it seemed like there was always something that would bite you in the butt right after you opened your big, fat mouth. "Travel… rations?" She finished lamely.

Vonn looked like he was rubbing his face. "Yes. Shall we get on with the rationing, then?"

She giggled, setting her hand on the latch of the door. "In three. Two…" She pulled. The door stayed firmly closed.

"Oh, uh, yep, that's locked." Pulling her lockpicks from her inventory, she knelt down in front of the lock. Fortunately, it looked like it was a pretty basic one, probably because it was always guarded and used often. That should also mean that it wasn't trap-

She pulled her lockpick back as a small pin thrust toward her fingers. "*Some*body's paranoid," she muttered, and made sure to apply pressure against the top of the keyhole where the shank of the actual key would deactivate the simple trap.

Vonn laughed softly. "It does seem that they recruit from a certain, ah, group of people. I wouldn't be surprised if there are a great number of thieves in this cult."

Rouge stood as the lock clicked open. "Nah, we thieves are pretty independent. That was one of the reasons I went with a rogue class. Most of the guilds have all kinds of rules about who can do what, when, and where. It's not as big a deal for Travelers, but it really ties down the Natives. I mean, it's probably worth it, because you know the guild has your back as long as you follow the rules, but…"

She shook her head. "The Thieves Guild basically has two rules. First, pay your dues. Second, if you get caught, keep your mouth shut. I mean, I guess there's a third rule, which is that anyone not in the guild who gets caught thieving either joins up or gets their throat cut, but that really only applies to non-members, right?"

"Your guild sounds frightening, Rouge. Do they do anything for you?" Vonn shimmied to the side, giving Rouge plenty of room to open the door.

"Sure," Rouge grasped the latch again. "If you can afford it, they'll train you in any skill you want. Also, if you get caught, keep your mouth closed, and survive long enough to get to prison, they'll at least try to get you out. They also offer some pretty nice members-only quests."

She lowered her voice to a bare whisper. "Three, two…"

This time, the door swung open, smooth and silent for once. Rouge glanced through the crack, saw no movement, and ducked through. Vonn followed silently, and they immediately pressed themselves against the wall on opposite sides of the door as Rouge gingerly closed it behind them.

Glancing down at her arm, Rouge confirmed that she was still in [Stealth], and gave an invisible fist pump in celebration. Which reminded her of how she'd found out she *wasn't* in [Stealth] last time.

::Silus? Are you okay?::

The bat sounded a little grumpy when she answered. ::You and *Vonn* were too busy talking. I didn't want to interrupt.::

Rouge bit her lip. A jealous bat was the last thing she needed. She glanced over toward Vonn, then flipped him a party invite before she could think better of it. He already knew all of their secrets anyway, so what was the point of excluding him?

Vonn [NPC] cannot join the party.

Shoot! That was the same thing that had happened when they invited

Sarave and William to join, way back on Aspen's farm. They had thought it had something to do with the fact that they were both members of the 'Dark' races, being a goblin and a vampire respectively, but apparently not. So why could Aspen, Sumi, Khor, and Silus join? What was so special about them?

It *could* just be that because Aspen was a special quest NPC, he had abilities that other NPCs didn't. Sumi, Silus, and Khor had all been linked to Aspen's 'soul' - his program? - so maybe they were all considered part of him? Or maybe there was another explanation that she had specifically been told not to speculate about, so she shut down that line of thought by thinking very, *very* hard at Silus, ::Be nice. He can't join party chat, and he doesn't know he needs to include you.::

If possible, her little friend sounded even grumpier when she replied, ::Then *tell* him.::

So, Rouge did. Vonn had already known she could communicate with Silus, but he hadn't understood just how intelligent the small creature was, and as they snuck through dim, bare stone hallways, Silus slowly relaxed against Rouge's neck as the girl sang her friend's praises to an admiring wood elf.

At last, Vonn shook his head and spoke quietly. "I do not understand how this is possible. One person cannot speak to another person's familiar. Plus, she sounds as intelligent as a person."

::That's because I am!:: Silus sounded like she couldn't decide whether to feel insulted or self-satisfied, but was coming down on the side of insulted. ::I'm way smarter than *most* people!::

"Well, she isn't actually my familiar," Rouge said, hoping to forestall an argument. "She's Aspen's... friend? I guess?"

::He's my dad,:: Silus said, matter-of-factly, making Rouge's jaw drop even as she relayed the words to Vonn.

::What?::

"How can this be?"

Rouge and Vonn answered in equally incredulous tones.

If Silus was the little girl that Rouge sometimes pictured her as, she'd be puffing out her cheeks at the two of them. ::My mom was one of Aspen's companions, and my father was a Greater Bat that mom met while they were on a mission. That bat wouldn't come with them when they left, so mom and Aspen raised me. That makes him my dad, right? That's what Sumi said.:: The bat suddenly sounded a little uncertain and sad.

Rouge leaned her cheek against her friend's warm body, suddenly realizing how fragile the tiny creature had always felt before. Now that Silus herself was a Greater Bat, the girl felt like she could hug her friend without being afraid that she would crush her. "That's right," she said reassuringly. "If Aspen raised you, then he's your dad."

The thief thought back over so many of the interactions between Aspen and Silus, and much of it abruptly made more sense. They obviously loved each other very much, but Silus was always trying to create a distance between them. The bat was ready to grow up, and she knew she couldn't do that with her father there to protect her every moment. Nonetheless, when Silus was truly sad or frightened, it was always Aspen she went to first. Rouge bit her lip as she thought about her own relationship with Motte.

"Indeed, Silus. I understand and apologize. We wood elves rarely stay with both of our birth parents for our entire childhoods, and so we may have several fathers and mothers." Vonn sounded genuinely sorry for upsetting Silus, but Rouge found her curiosity suddenly piqued.

"Wait, why do you-"

But the Vonn-shadow was already turning away, looking down the narrow hall. "I'm sorry, Rouge, but that is a discussion for another time, if ever. There are things which I may not speak of to outsiders, no matter how much they look like one of my own people."

"Wait, wait! Is that why Travelers who play as full wood elves always spawn in those little guard outposts you guys have in the forests? Everybody thinks that's because you guys are so rare, and you don't actually *have* towns, but *I* always thought it was because…"

Quest: "Where the Wood Elves Are" available.

Let the wild rumpus start! You have stumbled on a Hidden Race Quest. The Wood Elves have a secret. Well, a lot of secrets, actually. This is a lore quest, and your rewards depend on how much of the truth you discover. Whichever player completes the quest first will receive the greatest reward, so while you may tell others about it, it's probably best if you don't.

Success: Variable

Failure: None.

Current number of players attempting this quest: 3567.

Current highest completion rate: 23%.

Accept: Yes/No?

Rouge, of course, accepted. Three thousand, five hundred and sixty-seven? Out of who-knows-how-many players? (Something in excess of fifty million, last time she checked.) It would be limited to people whose character was at least partially wood elf, of course, which was probably the biggest limiting factor.

Wood elf and dark elf were both pretty rarely chosen, actually, since they both had some big location-related debuffs. Dark elves only spawned in the Underground, and pretty much everybody hated them. It sounded like there were some really cool story-lines playing out down there, but anyone playing a dark elf was pretty much kill-on-sight if they came to the surface. Not to mention they were nearly blind in the daytime, and had crippling kenophobia, which could only be overcome using an item that occupied your secondary hand slot.

Wood elves, meanwhile, were pretty well nerfed in cities. They were meant to be played in wooded areas, and got lots of buffs from being in the forest. They were fine in plains, deserts, etcetera, but lost many of their buffs. In cities, though, their [Stealth] was pretty ineffective unless they held completely still, and they lost 20% of their Dexterity, and 10% off all their other physical stats. Plus, their starting quests were pretty lame. Which was probably explained by the fact that most people spawned, did their tutorial, and then left their boring starting location as soon as possible.

She took a deep breath, fighting down her gleeful chortles. Must. Finish. First. Quest. First.

While Rouge had been chasing down her racing thoughts, Vonn had been sallying forth down the passage. He whispered reports as he went, his voice barely audible even in the silent corridor.

"Door. Closed."

"Door. Closed. Wider than the first."

"Door. Closed."

"Archway. Open. Oh, sh-"

Rouge's eyes shot wide at the sudden panic in the elf's voice, and she raced forward down the dark passage. One door. Two doors. Three doors. A high, open archway, revealing...

Oh. Biscuits.

Chapter Three

Aspen

As the door closed behind Rouge, Silus, and Vonn, Aspen's fists clenched at his sides. He knew sending them in was the right thing. They *needed* to know what was going on, and those three were by far the best at being sneaky enough to actually get in and out without getting caught. Not to mention that their enemies, whoever they really were, would likely be less on guard right now than at any time in the future. After all, who was foolish enough to escape a death trap and then *go back in*?

Taking a deep breath, Aspen rubbed his hands over his face tiredly, then opened his eyes and looked around. How had this happened? Why were so many pairs of eyes *watching* him again? He had always hated the gazes, the flickering glances, the suspicious peering from downturned faces. Though, he had to admit that these people were watching him with far more hope and less mistrust than he had ever seen during his time as the King's Necromancer.

He cleared his throat, trying to meet the gazes of as many of the gathered people as he could. "First, we need to get far enough away from this place that no one can track us down again. If anyone lives in the city and has a home to return to, no one will try to stop you from going there." He grimaced, "But, from what I understand, these people don't like to leave witnesses, and they seem to have some way of circumventing the safe zones in homes. If your families are safe now, returning may place them in far greater danger."

Several heads nodded in agreement, and a few of the children began crying softly at the reminder of their losses. He suspected that most of them were orphans now, if they hadn't been before. He tried again. "I'm going to go home, and," he thought about the mansion filled with empty rooms and wild children, "there's enough room for everyone, I think. It won't be comfortable, but it should be safe."

Aspen ran his hand through his hair roughly, feeling tangles tug free under his fingers. It was time for a haircut. "I'm saying you're all welcome to come with us, but if you want to, you need to decide now, because we're going. You don't have to stay, obviously, but you can get some rest and some food, maybe take a bath, and decide what else you want to do when you feel better."

He thought for a second, then looked at the little girl who had spoken up earlier when Aspen asked about the doors inside. She was taller than most of the others, solidly built, with dirty blonde hair and wary brown eyes. Three of the littler children were clutching at the tattered hem of her shirt, and she patted their heads absently as she thought. Aspen suspected that she might be a half orc, but if so, she was the most human-like one he'd ever met.

"There are other children there," he said to her. "When Gina's hospital closed," his teeth gritted on the offending words, reminded of the way in which his dead daughter's memory had been betrayed, "the orphans went to my home. They're safe, and there's even someone who cooks and teaches them."

The brown eyes widened. "There's a teacher? They know how to read?"

Aspen thought about the wild imps infesting his house, and his mouth quirked a little. "A little, anyway."

She nodded firmly. "I want to go, then." She looked around, taking in all the other children, then back to Aspen. "We'll all go." She looked a little defiant, as if, now that she'd taken him up on his offer, he was going to withdraw it.

He nodded. "Good. Anyone else? I'm sorry, but you need to decide *now*."

It took only a moment for the adults to make up their minds as well. All of them nodded, though the mutated female dwarf they had rescued from the cultist's hidden lab hesitated.

"We have clan in th' city," she said, her voice shockingly deep and gravelly. "We'll need t' send them word."

Aspen nodded again. "Of course. We'll get messages out for anyone who wants to send one. The ragamuffins need something productive to do, anyway." Surprisingly, it was the tall orc who snorted in amusement at Aspen's weak jest.

Fortunately, it was some time past midnight, judging by the height of the moon in the sky. Few people were on the street at this time, and even fewer were conscious enough to be aware of the crowd of people passing by. Most houses, in fact, were not only closed, but shuttered, and as far as Aspen could tell, not a single pair of curious eyes dared to peek out past the heavy wooden boards latched tight across the windows.

They tried to be quiet, of course, and for the most part they succeeded surprisingly well. It turned out that both the charcoal-colored dwarves and the oddly stretched elf had acquired some form of [Stealth] from their time as experimental subjects in the lab, and the elf seemed to cast some kind of [Silence] around itself and anyone moving within about ten feet of it.

Once Aspen noticed that the back of the group was much quieter than the rest, then narrowed the cause down to the elf, he rotated most of the children and all of the babies into close proximity with the cadaverous being. The elf, for its part, neither responded nor reacted when he asked it about the silence, but once the change of marching order was made, it did seem to make some effort to slow down enough to allow shorter legs to remain within the area of effect.

Between the hour of the night, the quiet of exhaustion, and the deeper silence of the strange-looking elf's skill, they somehow made it to the woods at the back of Aspen's property without being questioned or stopped. From there, Tessle was able to lead them to the break in the wall surrounding the property line that Lyrec had mentioned.

It was, indeed, quite a large break, and the recent increase in foot traffic had left a noticeable trail. As they walked, Aspen summoned up his mana, which had refilled more than enough to do the job, and directed it with his fatigued and foggy mind. He touched the shell-shocked and weary travelers, healing them as best he could. In their trail, or rather, in Aspen's trail, since he took the rear-most position in their straggling train, the forest sprang up anew. Wildflowers bloomed, saplings leapt to new heights, and moss and lichen sprouted as if they had been multiplying for years, concealing the most obvious signs of their passage. By the time they reached the house, Aspen was nearly staggering with exhaustion once again.

Everyone seemed to sense that they were finally as safe as they could be, and lowered their guard. Footsteps cracked on fallen twigs, low voices began to speak quietly, and a few of the littlest children, who had been barely suppressing their tears, began to cry again. The sound-suppression effect put out by the pale elf seemed to be either voluntary or limited in time, since it, too, had stopped, allowing the sobs and muttering to be clearly audible in the otherwise silent night.

Plum, of course, heard them coming. She met them in the kitchen garden with a sword in one hand and a glowstone lantern in the other. Aspen could see some of her older charges arrayed behind her, weapons bared, though they all looked more worried than truly frightened.

Aspen summoned the last dregs of his endurance and made his way to the front of the crowd. As soon as Plum saw him, her face shifted from bafflement to true concern. She rushed forward. "My l- A-Aspen! You look terrible! Are you injured? Who are these people?"

He leaned against the wall of the building nearby, trying to make it look like he was simply relaxing after a long hike, when in reality he was nearly ready to fall down. "We rescued these people from captivity tonight. I hope that they can help us understand what has been happening in Bright. First, however, they need food, water, and rest."

Manuela, the soul mage who had once been Aspen's partner during the war, and now served as a physician, stepped out from inside the kitchen. Her narrow mouth set as her eyes flashed over the group in calculation. "Is anyone actually injured?"

Aspen shook his head, but shrugged. "I don't know, actually. I healed them as best I could, but I had to save mana in case we were attacked, so it's very possible I missed something. I believe, however, that your *other* skills may be more urgent. These people have been captives, and witnessed terrible events. They are all in need of some peace, for a night at least."

The mage nodded slowly, then stepped back, clearing the doorway so the first of the refugees could enter. He could tell by the familiar blank expression on her face that she was reaching out with her own abilities to evaluate each person who walked by.

As the last few members of the group entered into the circle of light cast by Plum's lantern, the girl flinched back, eyes wide. These were the people who had been rescued from the lab, and their warped appearances were universally startling at best. This effect was made even more surreal by the two normal-looking dwarven children clinging tightly to the hands of the hairless, charcoal-toned, red-eyed adult dwarves. The children had somehow recognized their elders in spite of their physical changes, and refused to release them.

Plum's dark brown eyes darted to Aspen, as if checking to be certain these, too, were included in those she was meant to assist. At his firm nod, she swallowed hard, then set her face into a mask of professional imperturbability of which any servant would have been proud. "Come in, everyone! I'm not the cook my mother was, but I can make you something that will fill your bellies until Millie comes in the morning. There are plenty of empty rooms, and piles of blankets, though not nearly enough mattresses. We'll figure something out, though."

She turned to the children, many of whom were standing huddled in small groups, watching everything around them with large, wary eyes. Crouching down, she put the sword and lantern on the ground and held out her empty hands, subtly tilting her head to let her young warriors know they should do the same. "It's all right, everyone. You're safe here. My name is Plum, and these three with me are Jack, Lionel, and Ulie."

Plum glanced toward the back of the kitchen, smiling gently. "That scamp back there is Matilda." She raised her voice slightly. "Matilda, please go back upstairs and let everyone know we'll have more company tonight. They'll need to make room, and anyone who has more than two blankets needs to share, please." In spite of the 'please', her voice made it clear there would be no arguing with this command.

Turning back to the blonde boy, the tallest of her defenders at perhaps five and a half feet, Plum went on. "Jack, put the swords away, and head up to fill the tubs. The water should still be at least a little warm, since it was a sunny day today."

Aspen grimaced, glad he'd remembered to convince the various insects and parasites infesting their new guests to relocate as they were walking through the forest. The adults from the lab had been surprisingly insect-free, but the children hadn't been so lucky. The last thing any of them needed was an epidemic of fleas. Of course, anyone coming in behind them was likely to find themselves host to a different sort of guest, due to the high population of pests they'd left behind, but he'd worry about that later.

Plum stood, clapping her hands gently against her sides, a habit she'd learned from her mother, who had flour on her hands as often as not, and thus always had to dust them off before dealing with the two starving young invaders in her kitchen. "Now then," the young woman said firmly, "Let's make some soup."

Chapter Four

Rouge

In retrospect, assuming that at least some of the cultists' experiments were successful made sense. From there, it was a natural progression to wonder how many successes there might have been, and where those successes might have ended up. Now, without even having to ask any of the hard questions in the middle, Rouge had the answer.

Here.

At first glance, the room seemed to be *packed* with monsters. Big, furry ones with lots of teeth. Small, scaly ones with lots of teeth. Medium-sized ones with skin like leather and lots of teeth. Sharp teeth. Serrated teeth. Jagged teeth. Red teeth, yellow teeth, even a few sets of gleaming white chompers that would have made a vid-star proud.

Vonn was frozen in the archway. His [Stealth] was good at covering sound and scent, but visually it worked more like camouflage than invisibility. She could just make out his outline because he was actually shaking very, very slightly. Which was actually impressive, considering just how many pairs of bestial eyes were currently locked on his location.

She, for instance, felt more like turning tail and running than standing stock still, though the latter was what she, too, did. Fortunately, since she'd been on guard after hearing Vonn's initial exclamation, she was far enough down the hall that they couldn't hear or smell her. Hopefully.

"Can you back up?" She whispered optimistically.

Vonn's trembling shape shook its head very slowly.

::Oooo, Rouge, I think that orange one is going to come check it out.:: Silus' voice was frightened.

Rouge flicked her eyes over the room, coming to rest on a particularly ugly orange critter that looked like it might have started life as a tiger. Or maybe a crab. It was covered in a mash-up of chitin and fur that made it look like it had mange, and the largest four of its eight legs had clawed paws instead of the pincers sported by the other four. Beady black eyes on stalks were indeed turned in their direction, and a feline tail whipped around behind it like cat stalking prey. It took one step closer to the archway in which Vonn stood, and froze, the incongruously adorable fuzzy cat ears between the eyestalks twisting as if to catch an interesting sound.

Rouge's eyes flickered around the large, open room. It held little other than the creatures themselves, though there were some piles of straw that might have been bedding, as well as empty troughs that were probably for food and water. On the walls, out of reach of even the tallest beast, glowstones rested, providing dim illumination. One door was barely visible between the monsters, but it was on the far side of the room. Of course.

::Okay.:: She tried to sound confident. "Vonn, when I say, you need to try to back up." ::Silus, if any of those things heads this way, I want you to fly up and knock down those glowstones. Just leave the one above the door over there. Don't try to fight them, your goal is to get rid of the light, so we can [Stealth] as much as possible.:: *And you're as safe as possible,* she added silently.

She summoned her Mambele into her hand, swallowing hard. "All right, Vonn. Slowly."

The blur that was Vonn shifted. She realized suddenly that he had been standing on one foot, caught mid-step. No wonder he had been trembling! Soon both feet were on the ground, and he began to shift his weight, preparing to take another step back.

That was when the tiger-crab made its move. Silently, its body coiled like a massive spring, then it leapt, sailing neatly over the heads of a few of its fellow monstrosities. It landed with a mixed *thud-click-click* only inches from Vonn, who stumbled, his [Stealth] breaking like a popped bubble.

Silus dropped silently from Rouge's shoulder, flapping hard to lift herself above the heads of the other beasts, who were now locked onto Vonn, and ignored the much-smaller bat as she flew by overhead.

Rouge burst into action. Leaping forward, she flipped on her hands, did a one-eighty twist in midair, and landed on the tiger-thing's chitinous back. Grabbing one eyestalk, she sliced it off in one smooth movement, then threw it over her shoulder toward the crowd of slavering creatures.

"Move, Vonn! Get up!"

The thing beneath her roared, and a notification popped up, filling her vision.

CRITICAL! You have dealt 84 points of damage to the *Demonic Rakshab*. The *Demonic Rakshab* is partially Blinded!

Mentally thrusting the notice out of her way, she commanded the notifications to remain minimized until after the battle. She grabbed hold of the other eyestalk, clinging tenaciously in spite of the Rakshab's efforts to shake her off, and cut this one off as well. This time, she made the eyeball disappear into her Body Bag. Aspen was always going on about alchemical ingredients, and she had an unfillable bag specifically for body parts, so, why not?

The battle became something of a blur after that. She knew Vonn was up, because knives were suddenly sprouting from the Rakshab's body, each one buried deeply in a furry joint. Taking the hint, Rouge, too, began going for the spaces between the chitinous armor. By the time the enraged creature she clutched collapsed beneath her, dead or dying, there were half a dozen other things surrounding her, all striking out with claws or biting with lots and lots of teeth.

As she rolled away from a particularly toothy maw, she wondered when her next dental appointment was, and if she'd been flossing often enough. Though, really, was it possible to floss *too* much? She nearly gagged on the rancid breath of her attacker and decided that she would also invest some of her income on a really, really good electric toothbrush.

The light flickered, and she saw that two of the glowstones had been torn from their resting places and thrown to the ground. If she could find a millisecond when no one was paying attention to her and she was in shadow, maybe she could turn this mess around.

"Can you distract them, Vonn?"

The elf's voice was tense, but he answered quickly, raising his voice over the howls, roars, and growls that surrounded them. "I can, but you will need to go to your left! You're right in the middle of the room, and likely to get caught up in the explosion."

Explosion? But she was already rolling left, flipping, twisting, and then leaping up and pushing hard against the wall that was suddenly in her face. A loud *CRACK* split the room, and then bits of… something she didn't want to think about too hard were flying past her to splat on the wall. As she landed from her backwards flip, her foot skidded on something gooey, and she was down.

Which turned out to be good, because a thing with too many tentacles (which was any number greater than zero, really) swiped at her, missing only because she was rather abruptly sitting on the floor. She used one arm to flip, and rolled to the side, regaining her feet as another tentacle crashed against the wall. Calling her Mambele back from wherever she'd dropped it when she fell, she slashed, chopping the thick cords of muscle in two.

Something screamed, and the light above her went out. For an instant, nothing could see her, and she triggered [Stealth]. Her [Darkvision] still showed her a scene that she thought she'd probably be seeing again in her nightmares, but now she knew what to do.

"Vonn! Mask!" Since he wasn't actually part of her party, what she was about to do had a chance of injuring him, too.

With a mental twitch, she triggered [Poof!!].

The thick cloud further obscured the area, sending burning smoke into whatever passed for lungs among the monstrosities surrounding her.

[Shadow Glide].

[Shadow Glide].

[Shadow Glide].

She nearly danced from one monster to the next, each time moving five feet higher, until the ridiculously high ceiling was only ten feet above her.

She leapt with the full force of her fifty points of Strength, jumping high enough that the top of her head brushed the ceiling before she began to fall again.

[Aerial Acrobatics].

[Poison Rain]!

A five-foot circle of projectiles, universally sharp and poisoned, rained down on the monsters crowded below her. Many of them ricocheted from hard shell or bony protrusions, but that simply allowed them to stab another, squishier creature nearby. The floor soon became covered in poisonous implements, and a few more of her attackers shrieked as they stepped on one of the blades, driving it into a tender extremity.

Many of the monsters were on the ground now, twitching or already still, and a cacophony of agonized screams, shrieks, and howls filled the air. Rouge became a whirling dervish of blades. Throwing her Mambele into the eye of a nearby vaguely aardvark-shaped thing, she scooped up a few of the knives from the floor, hurling them at other creatures who seemed to be relatively uninjured. Then she called back the Mambele, threw it again, threw knives after it, called back the Mambele…

It was by far the longest battle Rouge had ever been involved in, and some of the monsters seemed to simply Refuse. To. Die! After a time, there were only three things left standing, and they were universally dark, grotesque hulks, who shambled more than walked. You could tell they had all started out as different things, but now they were so similar that sometimes she couldn't remember which one she'd last slashed at.

As Rouge stumbled out of the way of yet another (fortunately ponderous) blow, she swore to put more points into Stamina next time she leveled up. She checked her cool-downs again, seeing that while [Poof!!] was ready, [Poison Rain] still had over a minute left to go. Not that she could really use it, since these things, however bulky they were, weren't anywhere near tall enough to allow her to fall fifteen feet before casting the spell. She'd be all of five feet from the ground by then, and since the knives appeared *beneath* her, they wouldn't do much good at that point.

::Rouge,:: Silus' voice came to her, followed by Vonn's exhausted, "Rouge!"

Rouge realized that she had been so focused on the battle that she'd tuned her friends out, and shook her head to clear it. She dodged two more clawed strikes as she replied tensely. "What?"

"I think those are undead!" Vonn called out.

Simultaneously, Silus squeaked, ::Those things aren't alive! You need to cut off their heads or something!::

"Oh, sh… oot! Of course they are! Okay, I'll work on the head-chopping, but do either of you have any ideas?"

Vonn's voice was bone-weary when he said, "I have one more of the Scatter Bombs. It should at least slow them down, but you need to get out of the way."

::I tried to [Bite] them, but none of my new skills work on undead.:: Silus sounded frustrated.

Rouge blinked, unable to believe she'd missed her small friend coming down to help out. The bat *did* have new skills, didn't she? ::What else...? No, we can talk about that later. For now...::

Rouge saw a spell come off cooldown and used it. Pointing behind the shambling things, she shouted, "[What's That?!]", even as she rolled to the side, aiming for a small gap between two of the undead monsters. Unfortunately for her, it seemed that while the spell worked better on creatures with low Intelligence, *no* Intelligence meant it didn't work at all. The creatures ignored her entirely, and the gap at which she aimed was suddenly filled with two long-taloned paw-hands. She dodged one, but the other shredded her shoulder, and she fell to the ground, seeing her blood already pooling around her.

"Damn it! Almost. Look, Vonn, go ahead and use your bomb thing!"

Then there was a gloved hand around the wrist attached to the arm attached to her injured shoulder, and she was hoisted into the air by the damaged appendage. She yelped. Around her, the undead things stopped in mid-movement, teeth and claws gaping in eerie stillness. Clenching her teeth against the pain (which, thanks to the 'Minimum pain for Minors' rule in *Veritas Online*, was comparable to stubbing your toe really, *really* badly), Rouge swung her Mambele, desperately trying to strike at whatever had hold of her.

A frighteningly familiar voice was suddenly in her ears, and Rouge was engulfed by a wave of déjà vu, though she had only watched this scene play out before, not been part of it. Their goblin friend Nekthadt had been using a skill to make himself look like Rouge at the time, while she was in a ridiculous dancer getup getting ready to die. Still, it had been strangely horrifying to see 'herself' dangling from the merciless hands of-

"Hmm. What is this? It seems I found some rats." The dark figure shook Rouge a little, and her body went suddenly limp. Her Mambele dropped from her hand. "Oh, no. I think not. Your little toy may be entirely unable to kill me,

Doom's sister, but that doesn't mean I want it poked under my ribs again."
FantumHat chuckled, and the complete lack of actual emotion in that sound sent
shivers down Rouge's back.

"Run!" She yelled frantically to her friends, eyes locked on her captor's
frozen gaze. ::Silus, get out of here before-::

With her body utterly limp, Rouge's gaze was currently directed towards
the floor. So, that was where Fantum's little buddies threw Vonn's unconscious
body. (Dead? Surely not! Not so quickly!) The elf fell bonelessly to the ground,
and she could see a thin trickle of blood oozing from two red dots on his exposed
throat.

::What do I do, Rouge? Should I [Bite] him?:: Silus' voice was frantic.

Realizing that the vampires (because that was what they had to be) hadn't
noticed the smallest member of their group, Rouge felt a faint flicker of hope.
::No! No, Silus, you have to escape! Wait until they leave, then fly for help!::

::I can't get out, Rouge!:: The bat sounded despairing. ::The door back to
the cavern is closed!::

::Beeswax and butternut squash!:: Rouge struggled with every ounce of
her willpower to move even a single finger. If she could… just….

FantumHat shook her again. "Now, now, little rat. I think I'll keep you to
play with for just a little longer. Say good night to your NPC friend. Or maybe
I should say, good *bye*."

Those words were the last Rouge heard before the lights went out.

Chapter Five

Khor

T ime was not, in general, something that goats worried about very much. The sun rose and set, the days grew longer, and then, if you weren't eaten by something stronger or smarter than yourself, the days grew shorter again. Khor was a very powerful, very intelligent, very *charismatic* goat, but, in the end, he was a goat. Not *just* a goat, never that, but a goat nonetheless.

Time passed.

Khor was not happy. Viqa, the glyphis guardian of the Tree, had managed to do her job adequately, for the most part, though Khor and the others had been called upon to assist with two swarms of Carpenter Ants, a small herd of Greater Deer, and some kind of beetle that had actually dug in from underground to attack the Tree's roots. They only caught that last one when leaves began to turn yellow, but fortunately, William had had some kind of earth mage trick that took care of it fairly quickly.

William, Khor had to admit, wasn't *quite* as bad as Khor had originally thought. Certainly, he was nothing like the vampires who had preyed on the human troops during the war against Lich Lord Akuji. It probably helped that he was unfailingly polite, respectful of the unicorns, and at least a little frightened of Khor himself. Which was entirely reasonable, because Khor was very frightening.

After Khor had told him (by dint of muscling in between the old man and the strange sigil in the wall) to stop digging in the direction of the possible-dungeon, William and Khor had spent a lot more time together. Far too much, in fact.

Since Viqa was guarding the Tree for most of the daylight hours now, Sumi had split the remaining guard shifts between herself and Khor. That reduced their actual time spent on sentry duty, and gave both of them more time to rest and complete other tasks. Which would have been good news, if Sumi hadn't decided that what Khor needed to be doing was hauling things.

Khor hauled rocks Khor had also dug up from the fields. Khor hauled the plow through the newly-cleared fields. Khor hauled water. Khor hauled clay William magicked out of the ground. Khor hauled ore and stone blocks that William also magicked out of the ground. If Khor wasn't digging something, or hauling something, he was standing around waiting to be hooked up to a wagon so he could haul more of something that was bound to be ridiculously heavy.

Khor was tired, he was sore, and he was cranky. Even the little unicorns (who now sported actual manes and stubby little tails) couldn't lift the weight on his heart.

Because Aspen was *late*. Khor didn't know how long Aspen had been gone, exactly, but however long it was, it was too long. He'd even asked Sumi, once, how much longer Aspen would be away, but he'd stopped listening to the answer after she'd changed it six or seven times 'depending on various factors'.

Khor was bored.

Nuisance was also bored.

When Nuisance was bored, he would start preening Khor's fur, and the constant tugging and movement on top of his head made the goat want to eject the duck from his perch with great enthusiasm.

Then Nuisance's family returned.

The reunion of the mother duck with her offspring was, perhaps, a little bit heartwarming. Mama duck checked Nuisance over very carefully, from top to bottom. She even flipped him over with her beak so she could, apparently, check his feet and tail. Upon finding no injuries, and seeing that he had grown to nearly double the size he'd been when she'd left, Mama gave a reluctantly approving quack and tucked Nuisance, who still looked quite small next to his mother, beneath her wing.

With a resounding **QUACK**, Mama duck called the rest of her family to her. A massive drake flew in from a stand of trees to the north, while a smaller drake and six hens not much larger than Nuisance popped up from the nearby pond. All eight of the new ducks landed with varying amounts of grace, and Mama immediately began to move among them, harrying them with her beak.

After several commanding quacks toward the smaller drake, the mother duck pecked at the two smallest hens, shoving them none too gently toward Nuisance. When the hens seemed shy, and Nuisance seemed more interested in making his way back up onto Khor's head than making friends, Mama duck let out a series of quack-quack-*quack-quack*-QUACKs that put everyone in their place, and soon the two little hens were snuggled up against Nuisance as if they'd always known one another.

Once the wedding ceremony, such as it was, was complete, Mama duck, her new swain, the remaining male, and what Khor was forced to assume was his harem, took off again. As the mother flapped her wings in preparation for her flight, she pointed one beady black eye at Khor with a very 'you'd better take care of my sweet little boy' look, and snapped her beak sharply at him.

Khor, of course, was not intimidated, but he decided that there was no need to purposely agitate the ox-sized fowl, so he nodded back politely. He also decided that, since Nuisance was now a grown-up with a family of his own, perhaps he should be treated with a bit more respect from now on.

That resolution lasted for about as long as it took for the small flock to vanish over the horizon, because Nuisance was decidedly *not* interested in becoming a family duck. The bird flung himself at Khor the moment his mother was no longer in sight, and pulled himself up to his usual roost. From there, he gave the two females a series of quacks that left Khor in no doubt as to their meaning.

Go away, nobody likes you.

The females just stood there, looking confused, which was an expression duck faces seemed made for, and then they exchanged glances and headed for the nearby pond. Nuisance made a few self-satisfied quacks, and settled himself back into place. Khor just huffed a sigh and continued on toward William's hidden underground city to haul more shiny rocks.

That night, the new ducks, who were dubbed Rowen and Claire after an unnecessarily long and serious conference between Sumi and Sarave, followed Nuisance and Khor home to the barn. In spite of Nuisance's emphatic protests, they snuggled up with him, one on each side, and after a while Nuisance simply seemed to give up. Khor, for one, appreciated the fact that he could actually get some sleep without waking up to find a waterfowl on his cranium, but his head did get a little cold at night.

Then the first flowers bloomed on the Tree, and the next morning there were bees. Greater Bees, in fact, and the swarm blackened the sky as it descended. Khor, who had been sound asleep since his shift had ended not long after the moon reached its highest point, snapped awake as the world seemed to be enveloped in a **BUZZZZZZ** that shook the small house.

Without thinking, Khor used one curling horn to scoop Nuisance from between his two sleeping beauties, flipping the duck up onto his head as he trotted out into the morning sunlight. The unicorns had adjusted their schedule to match his (whether they liked it or not) because it was his job to guard *them* as much as it was to guard the Tree, and so they, too, woke and trotted outside, blinking sleepily. Sarave and Juniper emerged from the house, Sarave holding the child in her arms, and Juniper's little face liberally smeared with some kind of grain cereal.

One by one, the residents of the farm began to run toward the Tree, where a massive black cloud completely concealed the scene. Khor felt his heart sink as he stretched out into a sprint, seeming to fly over the ground toward the darkness and the sound.

The sound was all-encompassing. Even if you somehow managed to miss seeing the mass that threatened to eclipse the sun, there was no way you could miss the bone-rattling hum that came from everywhere all at once.

When Khor arrived on the scene, he skidded to a stop so quickly that Nuisance, who was clinging to Khor's fur by a beaky death-grip, flopped forward and over into Khor's face with a strangled squawk. Nuisance hung there, swaying back and forth so that Khor could barely make out Viqa, who was standing at the edge of the small clearing that had naturally formed around the sapling. The water mage had globules of water hovering above her hands, but seemed unwilling to take any action. Khor was just moving closer, unsure what was going on, but ready to crush the fifty-foot-wide ball of darkness with sheer force of will, if necessary, when Sumi came up behind him.

<Khor! Stop! I think…I think this is a good thing!> The spider sounded uncharacteristically uncertain, and that in itself was enough to convince the goat to pause.

The tableau hung there, with the huge dark mass dwarfing the Tree's meager ten-foot height, Viqa staring with flat black eyes, Sumi quivering and clicking her chelicerae, and Khor, with Nuisance now scrabbling with broad webbed feet against the goat's nose as the duck attempted to establish enough of a foothold to climb back up. With a snort, Khor shook his head, swinging the duck up into place, and at the same time, a narrow band of blue sky appeared in the whirling, humming black ball, and a single insect flew down toward the Tree.

The Greater Queen Bee was beautiful, if you liked that kind of thing. Her body was nearly a foot long from her antennae to the end of her brilliant black and orange-striped abdomen. The slick black stinger protruding from her fundament was at least four inches long, and glimmered darkly. Her two large, compound eyes glittered in the sunlight that filtered through her swarm, and her fur was dense and silky. Her wings were made of pearlescent panes that reminded Khor of the glorious stained-glass windows that adorned the Temple of Bright.

With wing beats so fast they couldn't be seen, the Queen Bee darted down to the single flower that was now open on one of the highest branches of the Tree. Over the past week or so, many more buds had appeared, starting out as a small green bump the size of a pea, but rapidly swelling to a whorled three-inch bundle of petals that shaded from pale purple at the base to deep violet at the tips. Apparently, the first of these flowers had finally burst forth, and the heavy golden pollen scintillated as the Queen settled her heavy abdomen onto the slender branch, which swayed beneath her. She lowered her head into the blossom and began to drink.

Around her, the rest of the bees seemed to go insane. Swooping and diving, they swirled like daytime fireworks with their bright colors and gleaming wings. The sun was able to break through the mass more and more as the cloud of insects began to break apart, most of them flying out in a rush, though some quickly descended on the flowers in the field and orchard.

This left only a hundred or so of the largest bees hovering around the Queen, clearly guarding her as she ate. Sumi had sidled up beside Khor, and Sarave, Juniper, Kayti, Kayli, and even Viqa were simply standing, staring in something like awe at the deadly allure of the sleek soldier bees, with their barbed stingers and short, dense fur.

<This is a wild colony,> Sumi said quietly. <Now that the Queen has decided that she likes the Tree, they'll settle down and build a hive near here, if we're lucky.> She paused, then continued thoughtfully. <I'll have to place my webs closer to the ground. The bees will need access so they can pollinate the

Tree, and with Viqa here and able to use her [Water Needles] and [Drowning Ball], I haven't bothered repairing the webs anyway. It would not be good if the Queen got tangled up in a web, though once the hive is built, we'll probably not see her again until she goes on her mating flight.>

Khor pawed at the ground, restlessly. <But this is good, right?>

Sumi swayed side to side indecisively, then bobbed a yes. <So long as they understand that we're here to take care of the Tree, yes. Greater Bees can be very territorial about their food sources, and while they also boost the production of plants they pollinate, they have been known to kill animals that wander too near their hive or blossoms.>

<And how, exactly,> Khor asked sarcastically, <are we supposed to tell a bunch of bugs that we'd like to be their friend?>

The Queen Bee, legs now speckled with glittering nodules of pollen, rose up from the Tree, swaying slightly, as if she were dizzy. She flew in a slow circle, then abruptly dropped several feet, bringing herself (and her hovering guards) to just above the level of Khor's eyes. Khor suddenly found himself staring into those compound orbs, and his head spun wildly, making him sway. Beside him, he sensed Sumi stagger, and Nuisance nearly fell from Khor's head.

An image appeared in his mind. Shockingly, he recognized the person in it, though her rainbow eyes seemed to be made up of thousands of tiny lenses of light, and entirely lacked the horizontal rectangular pupil that Khor had always seen in his own visions. In this image, Gina even had long, draping antennae sprouting from her forehead, and Khor was reminded that, to some extent, all living things belonged to the Goddess of birth, growth, and life.

The vision of Gina smiled, reaching out her hands. In one palm a bee appeared, with a golden crown nestled on her head. In the other palm the goddess held a goat, a spider, a goblin, a glyphis, a duck... All of them were represented there, and when Gina brought her hands together, their edges touching, all the little figures tumbled together to become one group.

<Well,> Sumi said faintly, <that's clear enough.>

Chapter Six

Aspen

At first, Aspen expected his young friend to burst through the kitchen door, excitedly telling them all about her discoveries. When enough time had passed for Plum to finish feeding, bathing, and putting all of their guests to bed, Aspen acknowledged that he was truly worried. Sheer exhaustion finally forced his eyes to close, and he dozed at the kitchen table. He vaguely felt someone gently tuck a blanket around his shoulders, and sensed them shutter the glowstone lamp. Then he slept.

He was awakened when the front door crashed open with a resounding *CRACK*, followed by a familiar deep voice shouting, "Rouge!"

Aspen stumbled to his feet, grimacing against the pain of his back protesting the abrupt movement after being in an uncomfortable position for - how long? He glanced out the window. Faint reddish light gleamed there, indicating that the sun was just rising. He had been asleep for at least four hours.

Thrusting open the door that led to the small servant's antechamber off the main reception hall, he pushed past tumbled tables and broken chairs. This space had been relegated to storage for unneeded items, which performed the secondary purpose of delaying anyone attempting to enter the kitchen this way. Now, he just growled to himself as he shoved over a dainty tea table covered in gold-leaf and carved cherubs.

When he made it to the other door, he could already hear Motte thumping up the stairs to the dining room, and he ruefully admitted that he would likely have made better time if he'd just gone up the back stairs himself in the first place. Emerging into the entry space, he looked up at the armored form of his friend and spoke in party chat.

::Motte, come back down. I'll explain everything.::

The explanation did not go particularly well. As Aspen had half-expected, Rouge's father was angry that Rouge had been left behind, no matter how many others had been at risk if they stayed.

"No one should have gone back in there. If you felt someone had to, you should have stayed yourself!" The big man's jaw was tight, and it was clear that he really wanted to yell at Aspen.

Aspen shook his head, fighting not to cross his arms defensively. "I would have been more hindrance than help. My mana and endurance were empty, and it was all I could do to stay upright until we got home. Besides, Plum wouldn't have trusted anyone else as easily, and those people needed rest and safety, not questions and suspicion."

Motte's teeth ground audibly. "*Fine*, then you should have gone back to check on her!"

Aspen hung his head, rubbing the back of his neck. "I'm sorry. You're right. I do think, though, that you underestimate your daughter."

The big man heaved a deep sigh, closing his eyes as he visibly brought his anger under control. "I know. I *know* she'll be all right. Nothing can happen to her physically, but it's past her bedtime, and she never logs out late. I've barely seen her the last few weeks, thanks to finals, and then I get home at a decent hour today, and she's still in her pod. I mean, everything looks fine, but this just isn't like her."

"Then let's go get her now." Aspen tugged at the brim of the fancy felted hat he'd found stuffed in a drawer of a small desk he'd nearly broken his neck tripping over. He patted Stick, which was still in cudgel form and stuffed through his belt, turning toward the door.

At that, Tomas, who'd been watching them from the landing at the top of the stairs, broke in. "My lord! We need you here! There're so many things of which we must speak!"

Aspen sighed, looking up at the old man, who had returned sometime after Aspen had fallen asleep. He had appeared the moment he realized Aspen was awake and had been hovering anxiously ever since. "You're in command, Tomas. Do whatever you need to do, and I'll abide by your decisions."

Tomas opened his mouth to protest, then closed it, his rheumy old eyes taking on a calculating look that Aspen didn't particularly like. Aspen ignored the ominous chill running down his back, though, and stepped through what remained of the doorway. Tomas' creaky old voice sounded disturbingly chipper as he said, "Have a good time storming the temple, then, m'lord."

Aspen just waved as he walked away.

ཙ ཙ ཙ

The shabby building that led to the cultist's hidden temple was as innocuous as ever when they reached it. The early morning sun painted the splintered boards in red and gold, but nothing could make it look like anything other than a derelict shack.

Motte looked at it, then the peaceful, though downtrodden, street rather dubiously. "This is it?"

Aspen nodded and shrugged. "It was more frightening in the dark."

Motte snorted, then reached out and opened the door.

The inside of the hovel was exactly that; the inside of a hovel. There was no huge cavern inside the hill against which the shack was built. Even when

Motte punched the wall, and Aspen sent his Life Sense deep into the earth, they found nothing untoward. By the time they admitted defeat, the shabby building was little more than a pile of half-rotten sticks, and Motte's teeth were grinding again.

"What do we do now?" Motte asked, deep voice grinding like rocks in a landslide.

Aspen sighed. "Go home, I guess. Ask the prisoners if they know anything."

::I. Don't. Like. This.:: Motte's voice was nearly overwhelming in Aspen's mind, and he was about to reply when someone else did it for him.

::Motte?:: The hopeful little voice was faint and drained, barely more than a whisper, but both men froze when they heard it.

::Silus?:: Aspen asked, nearly shouting in his own mind.

::Aspen?:: If bats could cry, Aspen thought Silus would be sobbing desperately at that moment. The relief in her voice was palpable, though the sound was still little more than a murmur. ::Aspen, they took Rouge. I... I think they may have killed Vonn, too. I couldn't tell, and there was no way I could help, even though I was *right there*, but Rouge told me to try to get out, so I've been waiting, but-::

Motte broke into the flood of words, voice tense. When Aspen looked at him, he saw that the man's massive gauntlets were in fists at his sides, and deep lines bracketed his mouth. ::Silus, who took her? Where are you?::

Aspen reached out and placed a supportive hand on Motte's shoulder, though he knew the other man couldn't feel it through the solid metal pauldron he wore. ::Silus, we'll come to you, but we don't know how to get in. The cavern is just *gone*.::

::That big beezie FantumHat took them! Him and his crew of vampires. There were at least six of them, and my new skills don't work on undead! After Rouge passed out, he said something like, 'move the entrance to the secondary location', so they must have done that.::

Simultaneously, Motte demanded, ::What do you mean, 'passed out'?:: as Aspen said, ::Damn, the entrance must have been magical after all.::

Silus sounded a little flustered when she replied, ::She passed out. They used some kind of spell on her, and she went limp at first, but she could still talk in party chat. But then FantumHat did something *else*, and she went silent, so I think they must have knocked her out.::

::That's impossible,:: Motte said grimly. ::You can't actually make Travelers go unconscious. There are plenty of skills and spells that cause paralysis, to some extent, but we're always awake. They must have some way of blocking party chat, even though that's supposed to be impossible too. Whatever it is they're doing, it must also keep her in combat so she can't log out without a force quit.::

::What's a force quit?:: Aspen asked.

Motte sighed, grimacing slightly. ::It always feels awkward talking to you guys about this, but... Look, you know we Travelers have to follow certain rules, right? We can't stay here more than sixteen hours of your time each day. When we go, our avatars just stand there unless we give them instructions before leaving. Things like that. One of the big ones is that we can't log out – go back to our world – while we're fighting. It's possible for us to get stuck here because of that. Kind of the same thing those guys in Goose were doing to Manuela to keep her from healing so she could escape.::

He shook his head, frowning ferociously. ::In any case, if a Traveler is stuck in close combat - one they can't win, but aren't quite losing, either - sometimes the only way out is just to... let yourself die. Don't dodge an attack, or don't cure the poison that's sapping your health. If you can't even do that, there's a final option. Force quit. If you do that, your avatar will die, and you'll respawn back at your save point, but you get hit with all of the suicide debuffs, which are pretty harsh.::

His deep voice grew thoughtful. ::As her father, I can, technically, *make* her force quit. I have a, a spell, I guess, that lets me prevent her from coming here, or sends her home, whether she wants to or not. Or I could pop the lid and take off her mask. She'd be furious, but...:: He paused, clearly strongly considering this option, but finally shook his head again. ::I'll wait on that, for now. Leave it as a last resort.

::In any case, you can send in a glitch report to, well, the Gods, I guess, if you think it happened because... the world is broken? I've never heard of anyone succeeding in contesting it, though. Even if Rouge is stuck, she'll never quit. She did it once, early on, when she tried to take on a dungeon without me, and she hated every minute of the debuffs. She swore she'd never do it again, and she's just stubborn enough to keep that promise, no matter what.::

Aspen quirked a grin, remembering how headstrong Lark could be when something didn't go as she wanted. ::I understand. So, how do we find her?::

The big man snorted. ::Triangulation, I guess. It's a terrible method, but it works. Eventually.:: He looked up, as if he could somehow see beyond the remnants of the tiny shack into which the two men were crammed. ::Okay, Silus, start talking.::

It turned out that the bat had a lot to say. Starting with how tired, cold, and hungry she was, and proceeding through discussions of how much she liked being bigger, a full run-down of her new skills, and why they were terrible because they *didn't work on the undead*. As she rambled, the two men walked around, listening to the way her little voice faded in and out, gradually building a map of exactly where the edges of the one-mile party chat range ended.

Unfortunately, a vast portion of that range was solidly out over the waters of Lake Ata, and the docks were now bustling with people vying to purchase the early catch as the fisherman sailed back into port. It took them far too long to realize that Silus had to be under the lake itself, and the closest they were going to be able to get was the far end of a long dock meant for barges.

The process was not shortened by Motte periodically 'logging out' so that he could check to see if Rouge had woken up in his world yet. Finally, though, Aspen and Motte stared gloomily down into the deep turquoise waters of the lake. ::How do we get down there?:: Aspen wondered.

Motte shook his head. ::I have no idea. Even if we could somehow dig down into this cavern, it'd just fill with water, and we'd probably kill everyone inside along with ourselves.::

::I can make a tunnel…::

The warrior grunted. ::I know, I know, you've said that. But we still have no idea exactly how far you'd have to dig, and if your mana would even last long enough. You said yourself that last night you only had to nudge things out of the way, for the most part. Who knows what would happen if you tried to make a tunnel from nothing?::

The two had had plenty of time to discuss the adventures of the night before, and while Motte was duly impressed with Aspen's new abilities, he adamantly refused to allow Aspen to try something that might get them both killed. Reasonable, but still, Aspen couldn't help but feel a little hurt that the other man didn't trust him to at least try.

Motte caught the look Aspen gave him, and sighed, looking defeated. ::Look. I'm sure it'd be fine, but if something did go wrong, and you died, Rouge would never forgive me.:: He paused, then went on a little grudgingly, ::You did the right thing last night, too. Leaving her, I mean. We need to know what's really going on. You couldn't do anything more to help her, and you needed to go with the refugees. I wish she hadn't been the best bet for someone to send back in to keep investigating, but she was, and there's no denying it. I'm sorry I was angry with you.::

Aspen felt relief rush through him, and he wondered at the strength of it. He considered the other man a friend, certainly, but friends argued all the time, in his experience, and they eventually either got over it, or they didn't, and moved on to other friends. Dismissing the twinge, he offered the other man a wry smile.

::Thank you,:: he said simply, and they continued walking.

Silus had fallen silent some time before, after they had finished their mapping efforts and transitioned to discussing how they would actually reach her. The bat had grumpily told them to, ::Hurry up and figure it out. I'm going to take a nap until you get here.::

::I wish there was some way to know where the new door is,:: Motte said, not for the first time. ::I'm about ready to push the eject button, and then ground Rouge for a month for putting me through this.::

Aspen nodded, understanding the big man's frustration. Then he stopped. ::Wait,:: he said. ::Maybe there is a way.:: He felt like an idiot for not thinking of it before, but in his defense, he was still very tired.

Motte stopped in the middle of the street, then shifted over to the side as a woman nearly ran into him with a cart. ::What?::

::The temples block my Life Sense. Well, muffle it, at least. If I 'look' around as widely as I can, the absence of something may be the same as seeing it.::

::Then do it!:: Motte looked hopeful for the first time since they'd realized the cavern had to be beneath the lake.

Aspen started to, but thought of something else and frowned. ::If they're using teleportation portals disguised as doors, the door could be anywhere, as far as I know. Teleportation mages are rare, and I never had much opportunity to learn about their art, but it seems like just because the doors have been in this area so far doesn't mean the new one has to be. In fact, it would make the most sense to move it somewhere else entirely.::

Motte shrugged. ::I have a friend who thought about specializing in teleportation magic when she was building her char… ah, body, for, um, here. Anyway, you can make a lot of money working together with an enchanter to craft items that allow the user to teleport to a certain location. She eventually decided against it because the amount of mana you have to put into a spell with any range is absolutely ridiculous. Almost impossible, actually, since making a spell that takes you from one side of Bright to the other requires that you have over a hundred points of Intelligence, and it still pretty much uses your entire mana pool.::

Aspen ignored the jab he felt when Motte mentioned friends from his other life, and just nodded encouragingly.

Motte went on. ::Anyway, the larger the enchanted object is, and the farther the final location is, the more mana the whole spell takes. Making a doorway-sized spell would be incredibly mana-intensive, and unless you have an essentially bottomless mana pool, you'll want it to be as close as possible to the end site.::

::In essence,:: Aspen summed up, ::the odds should be good that the new entrance will be close to the destination. Which we know isn't far from here, under the lake.::

::Um, Aspen?:: Silus' voice sounded wide awake and more than a little frightened when she broke into the conversation. ::Whatever you're going to do, you should probably hurry. FantumHat just passed through here heading in the same direction they took Rouge, and he looked really mad.::

Chapter Seven

Rouge

When Rouge blinked her eyes open, the first thing she saw was a big, shiny notice blocking a big part of her vision.

WARNING – You have been *Unconscious+* for 03:24:11. This time will not count against your daily usage limits. Time remaining today: 01:45:20.

Holy. Cow.

That wasn't even *possible*. Players couldn't actually lose consciousness in the game. They *especially* couldn't lose consciousness for *three hours*! There was an *Unconscious* debuff, sure, but for all practical purposes, it was really a short-term *Paralysis* debuff stacked with *Deaf* and *Blind*. It was annoying, and usually led to death, if you were alone, but it never lasted longer than a minute or so.

Not even bothering to swipe away the notice, she pulled a real-time clock up from her interface and stared at it in disbelief. It was after ten. *After ten!* If her dad was home, he had to be worried, wondering why she hadn't logged out yet. Sure, she had more wiggle room right now, since it was summer, and her dad was trying to let her 'learn from her own mistakes' (it really sucked to go to work already exhausted) but it was almost ten thirty, and she'd been making a real effort to go to bed on time, and…

Several new notices appeared over the old one, and she pulled herself back into the now.

You have been dealt 63 hp of damage by Player *FantumHat*.
You have been dealt 7 hp of damage by Player *Grunder*.
You have been dealt 12 hp of damage by Player *Grunder*.
You have been dealt 3 hp of damage by Player *Grunder*.
…

The notices scrolled away faster than she could read them, and she realized they were the ones that had made it through her filters while she'd been out. Comatose. Senseless? Dead to the world? *Ha!* That's how they'd done it, though. Good ol' Grundy just sat there and poked her every now and then, keeping her 'in combat' and probably also reinforcing whatever skill they'd used to knock her out.

Rouge pulled up her character sheet and checked her remaining health points. Thirty-four. *Thirty-four* left out of two hundred and twenty-five. Admittedly, she'd been damaged by the monsters in that stupid kennel room, but… How long were they planning on picking at her?

Finally waving away the last of the notices, she sat up, abruptly realizing that she was just lying down in the dark like she was *waiting* for Grunder to come back. Speaking of which, where was he? Had they reached some limit on their ability? Or had they just decided they were tired of playing with her? If so, why wasn't she dead?

She staggered a little as she got to her feet. Debuffs blinked in the corner of her vision. *Disoriented. Confused. Dizzy. Nauseated.*

Ya think?

Looking around, she realized that she was in a tiny cell with stone walls and no windows. She could only see because of the [Darkvision] she had as a half dark elf. The room was barely large enough for her to take two long steps in any direction, and she'd been curled on her side when she woke. A door that looked like a single solid slab of metal took up almost the entire wall, and the only opening in it was a wide, narrow slit at about waist height.

Just as she was starting to ponder how to open a door with no keyhole or hinges, the door started to open, letting in blinding light from the outside. It seemed safe to assume that was bad, so she summoned her Mambele from her inventory.

Inventory is unavailable.

Unavailable? *Unavailable*? Inventory couldn't be unavailable! Well, it *could*, but the only place where that happened was...

She gulped, looking around at the small, lightless cell. This was prison. She was in *prison*. Like, the real, *actual* prison where City Guards could send you if they caught you breaking the law or if there was an active bounty on you. The place from which there was *no escape*.

She was in prison, and the door was opening, and-

"Routhe the Rogue?" Grunder's voice was just as annoyingly whiny as she remembered it. He was also just as pretty as she remembered, with wide, dark brown eyes, and long, silky blonde hair that fell to his waist, perfectly arched eyebrows, a narrow chin... Ugh. It was enough to put a girl off pretty-boys forever.

She pressed her back against the far wall of the cell. It was barely four feet from the door, which opened into the hall, but no way was she going to let this bad guy tag her again. She was *not* going quietly into that good night.

The high elf sighed, flicking at his hair with one long, slim hand. The perfect lock fell impeccably back into place the moment his hand dropped it. "Come *on*. I'm tho tired of thith. I have better thingth to be doing."

Rouge choked on a shocked giggle. "Are you... *lisping*?"

The high cheekbones flushed, the dull red looking oddly pale against his alabaster skin. Honestly, as white as he was, he should have looked like a boiled lobster when he blushed, but instead he was only faintly pink. He hissed at her, revealing long fangs that gleamed like silver needles beneath his lip. "*You* try talking with thethe thingth in your mouth," he muttered. "Whatever, jutht come *on*. FantumHat wantth to talk to you, and what FantumHat wanth, FantumHat getth."

He sounded more than a little petulant, like a child who had gotten the present he asked for and discovered he really didn't want it after all, but Rouge couldn't get past those teeth. Was *that* how they'd knocked her out? Kept her out? Had she been bitten by a *vampire* who-knows-how-many times?

Gross! *Gross, gross, gross, gross!*

Grunder finally stepped forward and grabbed her by the arm. Moving faster than she'd ever seen a player move before, he pushed her wrists together, metal bracelets she hadn't even noticed she was wearing clicked together, and suddenly she couldn't pull her arms apart, no matter how many points she had in Strength.

"What the *heck,* Grundy? You can't do this! I don't know what glitch you guys discovered, but I'm logging out and reporting this to the GMs." In spite of herself, her voice wavered, and she staggered again as he pushed her out of the room ahead of him.

"Whatever," he said, nonchalantly, continuing to push her down a hall lined with cell doors on both sides for as far as she could see, though admittedly her vision was a little blurry from the sudden brightness of the glowstones lighting their way. "Thith ith all totally legit, and you're in a dungeon right now.

If you forth quit, you'll come back at your thpawn point, not here, and then you'll never find out what happened to your little NP-thee buddy. I don't know why you'd care, but FantumHat thaid to tell you he'th thtill alive… for now."

Vonn! How had she forgotten? They had him, too, and she'd totally failed to give him even a thought since she'd woken up. Not to mention poor Silus. Had they found her small friend? Was the bat still alive? She tried to pull up the party list.

External communication blocked.

Right. She knew that. You couldn't chat with anyone while you were in prison. Also, no one actually knew where the physical location of the prison was. You could bribe a guard to help someone who was stuck in there, but you couldn't actually try to rescue them, because it was in a hidden dungeon somewhere, accessible only via portals or the guard's special teleportation spell.

Which meant she and Vonn were probably on their own. She just desperately hoped that Silus had been able to escape, though the odds of a rescue for Rouge herself seemed vanishingly small now. Which meant that she had to figure out how to get both herself and a nearly-dead NPC out of a mystery dungeon in spite of having no backup, no weapon, no inventory, and, oh, yes, not being able to move her freaking *hands*.

Also, there were vampires.

And it was after her bedtime.

Yeah, no big.

With a final shove, Grunder thrust Rouge through a door that looked no different than any of the others except that it was open. She stumbled and fell to her hands and knees, scraping her palms painfully when her wrists refused to part.

"Here she ith, *my lord*," Grunder's voice sounded both derisive and slightly frightened when he spoke. "Now can I go? I thould have logged off an hour ago. My mom'th gonna be mad."

FantumHat's usually emotionless voice held a hint of mockery that somehow burned far more fiercely than Grunder's snide tone. "You'd better go then. We wouldn't want your mummy to be upset."

Rouge managed to gather herself just enough to be able to look over her shoulder and catch the look of impotent fury that crossed the elf's face before it went blank and lifeless. Grunder's Zombie turned sharply and left back out of the door through which he had pushed Rouge.

A cold hand gripped Rouge's chin and turned her face back toward FantumHat. The player's dark, bleak gaze burned into Rouge's as her heart pounded in her ears. When he finally let go, he practically tossed her chin away, making a *tsk* sound as he did. "No matter how I look at you, you're nothing compared to Doom Bloom. Are you actually even related?"

Rouge staggered to her feet, letting her body weave as if she was even more disoriented than she actually was. A brief flicker of her eyes noted that the *Dizzy* and *Nauseated* debuffs had worn off. No wonder she was feeling a little better. She still had no idea how she was going to get out of this, but at least she didn't wish she could throw up everything she'd ever eaten anymore.

"She's my sister," she said firmly, and that was all, since he didn't deserve even a smidgen of an explanation.

His surprisingly generous lips compressed into a flat line, and then curled into a snarl, revealing one sharp canine. Yep. Vampire.

"Good. Then when she gets my message that I have you, she'll have to come and talk to me." He turned away, completely confident that Rouge couldn't do anything to him, even if he wasn't watching her. Sadly, he was right. She eyed the door that Grunder had left wide open behind him. "I wouldn't bother," FantumHat said nonchalantly. "That hallway is circular. No matter where you go, you'll always return here. There's no other way out. Besides, if you leave now, you won't get to see your little friend again. Alive, at least."

The fang-faced jerk turned back to face her as he said this. He seated himself in a large, high-backed wooden chair that was just short of being a throne, then steepled his fingers beneath his nose as he examined her critically once again. Once he was no longer in her personal space, Rouge felt like she could finally look around properly.

They were in a good-sized, though not enormous, room with stone walls that matched those in the cell in which she'd woken. There was no furniture in the room except for the high chair and a deep-piled crimson rug spread across the floor in front of it. A single door was half-concealed by the tall back of the chair, but there were no other possible exits.

FantumHat sat up, shaking his head so his short, wavy white hair shimmered in the light of the glow-stones resting in sconces high on the walls. He rapped sharply on the wooden arm of the chair with the knuckles of his left hand. "Well, now, what should I do with you while I wait?"

Rouge had to clench her teeth to keep them from chattering, but she was finally able to reply casually, "Well, usually the villains take this time to monologue about their evil deeds. It's okay, don't let me stop you." She tried to wave as if giving him permission, but was brought up short by the manacles.

The man's pale, heavy brows drew together. "The villain? Do you think I care if you see me that way? I'm just playing the game the way it was meant to be played, and no, I don't think I'll fill you in on my plans just now. You may just be a scurrying little rat, but even rats can squeak." He turned his head as the door behind him opened, and she blinked as his profile triggered a vague feeling of recognition.

Then Vonn walked in carrying a baby, and all other thoughts flew from her mind.

"Vonn!" Rouge almost tripped on her own feet trying to get to him, but the combination of FantumHat's arm flung out between them and the horrible look of apology and shame on the wood elf's face stopped her.

"Ah ah ah," FantumHat said. "Not yet. I want to see if you can figure out what's going on before he tells you. Do try." He tilted his head, considering her like a scientist might look at a sample on a microscope slide.

Rouge stopped, toes just touching the edge of the plush red carpet. She skimmed her gaze over Vonn, remembering the terrible limpness of his body and the two oozing red splotches of blood on his tanned throat. He seemed fine, now, though a white bandage was wrapped neatly around his neck, as if mocking her with its blatant reminder of her failure to keep him safe.

His arms protectively clutched a baby. Rouge was certainly no expert on small children, especially with the way they grew in *VO*, but if this was a real-life child, she would have guessed it was around a year old. Large blue-gray eyes watched her curiously, and one fist was shoved in its drooling mouth, while the other one held as firmly onto Vonn as he held onto it. Its wispy curls were the same shade as Vonn's, and both little ears were slightly pointed at the tip.

Rouge's eyes shot up, trying to catch those of her friend. "Is that your nephew? Vonn, you found him!"

Vonn's head bowed until his face was buried in soft brown curls, and FantumHat laughed coldly. "Had him given to him, you mean. Keep going. You're almost there."

Her gaze flashed between Vonn and FantumHat, her brain clicking away at a thousand miles a minute. The baby. Vonn's inability to meet her eyes. His ashamed expression. FartHat's self-satisfied tone…

"Oh! Oh, Vonn." Rouge couldn't keep the disappointment out of her voice, and she bit her lip hard. Of course he chose the baby over her. Who wouldn't protect their nephew before a girl they'd only known a few weeks?

FantumHat's chuckle held the first genuine amusement she'd ever heard from him. "Oh, that was wonderful. I think I just heard the hamsters in your brain squealing, little rat. I was having a rather bad day, but I swear you just made it all better. For that, I'll give you a little gift."

He dropped his arm, and Rouge stepped forward, her feet sinking into such luxuriously soft carpet that she could feel it even through her thin boots. Vonn took a corresponding step back, and Rouge stilled, struggling against an urge to cry.

"Vonn," she said quietly. "It's okay. I understand. You promised your mom, and he's just a baby. Anybody would do the same thing."

"Ugh!" FantumHat threw himself out of his big chair, growling in frustration. "No! Don't you *get* it? He *betrayed* you! He told me all about your friend Aspen, and your daddy, and that mansion where you rodents have holed up. I have my minions on the way there right now, and by tonight, every last one of you vermin will be dead. I don't know which of you is the champion, but if I kill all of you, that won't exactly matter, will it? Now, be *angry!* Hit him! Scream at him! He's killed you all, and traded your lives for a *worthless bit of code!*"

"Oh," she whispered, and now she knew she would have cried, if she could. In fact, she would swear she felt the hot burn of moisture trickling down her face. Plum, Manuela, all the children, Restur, Tomas, Aspen, *Silus...*

The horror swallowing her paused. Silus. FantumHat hadn't mentioned her. Surely, as slimy as he was, he would have been rubbing Rouge's face in it if he had another of her friends. Was Silus still free, then? Had Vonn not entirely betrayed them yet?

Rouge swung her hands, fumbling the blow as if hampered by the cuffs around her wrists. She tried for a kick, but only succeeded in scraping her foot along Vonn's calf, twisting until she was falling, her awkwardly splayed limbs pulling the wood elf after her. He curled in a ball as he fell, protecting the baby as it started to cry, frightened by the sudden activity.

As her lips passed his ear, she barely whispered in a puff of air, "Silus. Did you?"

As his eyes flashed across hers, he shook his head. A small movement. So tiny, it would have looked to anyone else like it was just part of their clumsy tumble.

Rouge rolled away, staggering to her feet again, screaming, "I hate you!

How could you do this?" It was, after all, what FantumHat expected, and Sara had certainly been impressed with her acting skills when she scared off Dr. Veralt.

You have learned [Acting]. This skill increases the chance that other people will find your acting convincing.
Your skill [Acting] is now level 2.

She would have laughed if she wasn't so busy being furious. She triggered [Acting], channeled every bit of the righteous anger she felt at FantumHat using love to force someone to betray themselves and their friends, and started yelling at Vonn. "You *suck*! Why couldn't you just have *died* when they bit you?" She advanced toward the wood elf, growling out the words, though she didn't miss the look of avid fascination on FantumHat's face. He was enjoying this like it was some kind of drama vid!

Vonn had gotten to his knees, but his body was still curved around the whimpering child in his arms. She stalked closer, screaming words she wasn't even paying attention to any more. They just flowed out automatically, and her brain ticked through possibilities, discarding one after another. Then Vonn's hand, the one furthest from their creepy watcher, opened slightly, and she caught a glimpse of something long and brown.

She saw Vonn's legs tense under him, crouching rather than kneeling, and she tightened her own body, ready to follow his lead when he moved. He did.

Dropping the baby onto the thick, soft carpet, Vonn lunged at FantumHat, driving the wooden splinter he'd been hiding deep into the vampire's thigh. As soon as Rouge saw Vonn move, she brought her hands, now clenched together to form a fairly effective club, slamming against their enemy's jaw, even as she drove her heel into his knee, forcing it backwards with a gruesome *crunch*.

FantumHat went down with a howl of pain and fury, already kicking and scratching at them with his long black nails. But Rouge was behind him, her legs wrapped around his chest, arms over his shoulders, using her bound hands as a garrote.

Vonn at least had his hands free, though he was otherwise unarmed. His expression was murderous, his face drawn and cold as he did his best to simply keep the vampire down as Rouge strangled him. The wood elf's hands were hard and focused, and they struck vulnerable points over and over, preventing FantumHat from bringing his full vampiric strength to bear against Rouge.

Finally, *finally*, the form beneath her stopped struggling, though they could see that the defeated player's chest continued to rise and fall. His eyes were closed, his face pale as milk, and his long-nailed hands laid limp in the deep pile of the red rug. He was unconscious, but whether it was the short-term debuff Rouge had always known, or the new Unconscious+, she didn't dare to guess.

Rouge and Vonn stared at each other, breathing hard. In the background, the baby screamed.

"What do we do?" She held up her wrists, which she suddenly realized ached rather a lot. Checking in her display, she saw that she'd gained a new debuff to replace the ones that had worn off. *Broken wrist (Left)*.

"Darn it," she muttered, jumping to her feet much more nimbly than she'd been willing to let FantumHat see she could move. Looking over at Vonn, she could see that he had scooped up the baby, and was attempting to soothe it. "What do we do now? He's not going to stay down for long, and if we kill him, he'll just respawn in a few minutes and call his buddies."

Vonn patted the baby into whimpering relative-quiet, and looked up at Rouge. "We'll have to go back out that way." He tilted his head toward the door through which he'd come. "They had me blindfolded, but my [Perfect Navigation] skill kept track of the turns, so I can get us part way out, anyway."

Rouge nodded, glancing behind them at the other door. "I don't know if I believe FH here," she gave him a quick boot to the head, just in case he was thinking about waking up soon, "when he says *anything*, but it is true that I didn't see anything but the same hall and the same doors over and over again out there. Plus, Grunder went that way, and there are no windows or other exits, so there's decent odds that that's where the vamps sleep. If it's dawn, they should be going beddy-bye soon, right?"

Vonn frowned at her, then knelt beside FantumHat's body, the hand that wasn't holding the now-drowsing baby digging through the vampire's garments. "I don't know why they would. Certainly, they have a weakness to sunlight, so they're generally active at night and hide during the day, but they don't necessarily sleep while they wait for the sun to rest. My aunt used to scare us little ones with stories of vampires attacking on very cloudy days, or during storms."

Rouge wrinkled her nose. "Can't even count on Bram Stoker anymore. Okay, so we just... wander out there with a baby and hope no one sees us?"

Vonn let out a triumphant sound, then stood, brandishing a shiny yellowish rock. "No, you're going to be a guard leading a prisoner back to the torture chamber."

She held up her wrists again. "Not going to be very convincing like this, plus, *torture chamber?*" She gave FantumHat a disgusted look. "What the heck, dude? It's bad enough you guys are kidnapping kids and making people into monsters, but *torture*? I'm so reporting you guys to the GMs."

Vonn pressed his pebble against Rouge's manacles, and they sprang apart. Another touch to each one, and they fell to the carpet, looking like nothing more dangerous than a plain pair of bracelets. The wood elf smiled tightly at her, picking them up and clicking them in place around FantumHat's wrists. Another click, and FH was as securely bound as Rouge had been. "They had these on me, too, until they were convinced that I was too scared to do anything against them. I saw what they did to take them off, too."

Rouge grinned, shaking her unbroken wrist and tucking the broken one into the front of her tunic carefully. "I guess that just leaves the question of what to do with him." She nudged FartHat again, and this time she thought she saw an eye flicker.

"Dagnabit! He's coming out of the debuff. We need to do something fast, or he'll be right behind us." She looked around, but the bare room offered little help. Then her toes wiggled in the plush carpet, and a wicked little grin crossed her face.

❦ ❦ ❦

"Oh man, I never thought I'd actually get to do this." Rouge chortled as she eyed the final product of her cunning plan. FantumHat was wound up in his fancy carpet like an overstuffed burrito. His feet hung out one end, while his eyes, now open and blazing furiously, peeked out of the top. They had tipped the massive, solid wood chair over on top of the vampurrito, and its weight, combined with the strength of the high-quality carpet fibers, the manacles, and the wooden splinter still impaled in FantumHat's thigh, kept him pinned like an ugly carpet bug.

FH was grunting, and his face was red and strained. He was obviously using every bit of his vamp strength to try to break free, but he was having no luck. Vonn had stuffed a strip torn from the edge of the baby's blanket into FannyHat's mouth when he started saying some really hurtful things about their mothers (he seemed to have some mommy issues) so the strangled noises were the best he could do.

Rouge turned back to Vonn, whose face finally looked like his own again. There was even a hint of amusement in his own eyes as he watched the vampire struggle on the floor. "That's better than killing him anyway. When someone comes in and finds him, they'll get a good laugh out of it, too."

If anything, FantumHat's expression, what she could see of it, grew even more furious at this, and she would swear his eyes were actually turning a little red. Swallowing against an involuntary shudder of fear, Rouge waggled her fingers at the helpless vampire.

"Toodles, FartHat," she said. "I hope you take this the right way, but I hope we never, ever meet again." With a little salute, she followed Vonn from the room.

The vamps must have led Vonn through the twistiest path ever in order to reach FantumHat's little playroom. Now that they were retracing the path with their eyes open, both Rouge and Vonn were able to tell that they repeatedly passed through the same intersections.

After the third time of seeing one particularly ugly tentacled frog-thing in a painting (though now it was on their left, instead of the right), Rouge growled in frustration. "Is there really no faster way to do this?"

Vonn looked a little hurt, and opened his mouth to reply, but Rouge held up her hand. "No, I'm sorry. You're doing the best you can, which is honestly amazing, because we've made at least thirty turns. At least we're out of the part with the crazy statue of Chris with eight arms. If I saw that one more time, I was going to have to knock it over."

For the first time since they'd been reunited, Vonn's face relaxed into a nearly-natural smile. "That was particularly terrible. I couldn't tell if the creatures in the bottom set of hands were hedgehogs or sea urchins."

She grinned. "Right? And what was with the guy in the top hand? He was all standing up waving his sword while the woman reclined at his feet clutching his leg. That's some grade-A misogynistic baloney." Her stomach growled loudly, and she clutched at it with her good hand. True to form, while her hit points and mana had recovered now that they were out of combat, a Broken Bone debuff wouldn't heal without a special item or a visit to a priest. Handily, they were probably surrounded by priests, but she doubted any of them wanted to help her out.

"Ugh, you know you're hungry when thinking about baloney makes your stomach growl," she grumbled.

Vonn looked perplexed. "I'm not familiar with 'baloney'."

"It's, like," she waved her hand, suddenly realizing that she wasn't sure what it was either, "when they take a bunch of meat, cook it until it turns to goo, then squish the goo back together to form a kind of...loaf? Maybe?"

Vonn was looking green, and he seemed to have covered his nephew's ears out of some instinct to protect the baby's sleeping brain from such heresy. "That does, indeed, sound vile."

She nodded. "Right? But somehow, sometimes, it's really, really good."

The wood elf paused at an intersection, peering left and right to see if anyone was coming. "I think I understand. My father's mother makes a dish on the holidays that requires pickling the eyes of-" He stopped, holding up a hand. "I think I hear someone coming. We're getting close to the end of the area I know anyway, since I doubt you actually wish to go to the torture chamber?"

Rouge gritted her teeth. "I kind of do. If only to kill everyone doing anything torturey and help the victims. Unfortunately, I think we have all we can do to get ourselves out right now."

Vonn nodded grimly, then pulled back. "There's definitely someone coming," he whispered, patting the top of his nephew's head with one hand. He'd gained a lot of mobility when they'd used the baby's blanket to strap the child to Vonn's chest, but the wood elf still couldn't seem to stop touching the infant as if to reassure himself that it was still there.

Rouge glanced around. They *could* try the whole guard and prisoner schtick, but honestly, she was pretty sure they'd bomb it hard, even with the aid of her new [Acting] skill. Then she smacked herself in the forehead. Sure, she couldn't use her inventory or communicate with anyone in any way other than verbally, but she could use at least some of her skills and spells. [Acting] worked, for example, and maybe…

You have cast [Substitution: Lv1]. You now appear to anyone viewing you as the sapient being <u>FantumHat</u>. This illusion will last 15 minutes. Spell will be canceled if you take damage or if someone with a high enough [Illusion Break] skill attempts to Identify you.

[Substitution] is now level 2.

Good news, bad news right there. Good that it worked, but bad that FannyHat had apparently managed to get himself free. That was the only way he would have discovered that she had stolen a really snazzy gold filigree *Locked Decorative Box* from him while he'd been under the Unconscious debuff. Unless, of course, he could actually use his inventory here, which if he was considered a guard he maybe could? Ugh!

Vonn was staring at her in horrified fascination. "Rouge?" he whispered.

She nodded. "New skill. It's only good for fifteen minutes, though, so let's do this. Which way are they coming from?"

Silently, he pointed down the left hall, and now she, too, could faintly hear the sound of energetic voices coming from that direction. At least two. No, three?

Vonn dropped into the attitude of an utterly defeated prisoner, dragging his feet, hanging his head, and curling his shoulders forward over the arms he kept pressed together as if he were wearing some of the magical manacles. Rouge, meanwhile, tried to set her face into the blankest, yet most supercilious expression she could manage. She triggered [Acting], and they set off down the hall.

Snatches of conversation became clear as they drew nearer.

"…don't know who we're actually meant to attack!"

"…idiot, just anyone who's not us…"

"But I *like* Bright…"

The hall ended in a T in front of them, and Rouge felt her shoulders tense as she realized that the speakers were right around the corner. She forced herself to relax, and gave Vonn a little shove, sending him stumbling forward against the wall. The voices fell silent.

She strode around the corner, looking impassively at the trio of players standing there, all of whom instantly paled and took a step back. Rouge focused on the only girl, since the voice saying it liked Bright had been more feminine than the other two. "What do you *like* about Bright?" she asked, trying to put as much cold derision into her tone as she could.

"I... I just," the girl stammered, nearly tripping over her long mage's robe in an attempt to backpedal. "I like that you can shop here..."

"Because you can't *shop* in Bloodhaven?" Rouge asked. Bloodhaven was FantumHat's usual stomping grounds, and her brain hadn't been able to stop turning over one simple question. *Why was he here?*

"You can, um, my... lord? But everyone there is..."

One of the boys, a guy a few years older than Rouge, stepped halfway out in front of the girl, who looked grateful. "She means everybody there's always afraid, or out to get whatever they can from you. You can get anything there, but it's not *fun*."

Rouge sneered and lowered her voice, stepping forward threateningly, "Then," she whispered, "don't you think you're on *the wrong side?*"

Now it was the third guy's turn. He actually reached out to touch Rouge/FantumHat's arm, though he immediately jerked back as if he'd been burned. "Look, man, we just want to be on the winning side, and this is obviously it. Now that you're the boss of Bright, things are gonna change, but that's okay as long as we're in on it."

I'm the boss of Bright?

A million clues and memories whirled around in Rouge's head, settling together like pieces of a puzzle that were finally coming together to create a picture. "That's right," she hissed, "I *am* the Lord of Bright, and don't you forget it. Now," she looked around, "which of you wants to prove your worth by leading this traitor out of here? I have better things to do, and he," she sneered again, "has one more betrayal to complete before I'm done with him."

Third guy, an archer with dark brown leathers and a feathered hat, cleared his throat. "Uh, I will, my lord. We just came in to turn in a quest, so we can-"

Rouge glared, watching the timer on her spell tick down inexorably. "Just *do it*."

The three nodded jerkily, and she strode away down the hall, back the direction from which the trio had come, hoping desperately that Vonn would go along with them quietly. They didn't seem vicious, like some of the players who'd decided to join Apofis, so she believed he and the baby would be safe with them. They certainly didn't seem like the type to kill an NPC just because they could, and they were way too scared of FantumHat to disobey a direct order.

Just to be sure, though, she dropped the skill the moment they were out of sight, and turned around to trail them silently. The halls were too well lit to allow her to use [Stealth], but she could still [Sneak], This skill was usually just a supplement to [Stealth], but it did work to muffle sounds and stuff a bit on its own. Fortunately, as soon as they were sure the 'Lord of Bright' was out of hearing range, they started bickering again, this time even more ferociously, so it was fairly easy to follow the sound.

It turned out the exit was only three more turns away, though there was also rather a lot of hallway to walk. Whoever had designed these areas for the cultists had definitely liked to make things *big*. Big caverns, big statues, and big, stupid, winding mazes.

At last, though, the players stopped in front of a set of double doors that was rather conspicuously different from all the others, not only because they were, in fact, double, but also because they weren't fancy. They were just big, solid, wooden doors, and they might as well have had EXIT written on them in big red letters, because everything else in here was ostentatious as heck.

The mage girl patted Vonn on the back patronizingly, as if he were a particularly cute but stupid puppy. "There you are," she said. "Go on through there and you'll be back in that big cavern place the NPCs use. Do you know how to get outside from there?"

Vonn nodded jerkily, though Rouge could just see him glance back down the hall in her direction. She couldn't really tell what his expression was from her position behind an egregiously shiny puce statue of a monster that seemed to consist of a turtle wearing a jellyfish as a saddle, but she suspected he was worried. About her.

That was okay, as long as Vonn got out, and, hopefully, managed to get to Aspen and everyone else before FantumHat's minions did. Vonn hadn't quite told FantumHat *everything* in exchange for his nephew, but he hadn't been able to keep much back, and he hadn't been able to lie at all, because one of them had a skill that told them when he did. So, while he'd had to give up everyone's name, and the existence of the mansion, he'd managed to talk around the exact location of the mansion well enough that the searchers would need to do some extra work when they reached the woods at the very back of Aspen's property, which was where Vonn had sent them.

She knew that she should wait for the three players to clear out and then follow Vonn as quickly as she could. Unfortunately, she'd seen something down the hall two turns ago that had set her roguey senses tingling, and there was *no way* she wasn't going to go check it out. So, as soon as the double doors closed behind Vonn and his nephew, she turned around.

Time to do a little sleuthing.

Chapter Eight

Aspen

After nearly an hour of fruitlessly searching for the elusive entrance to the cultist's underground lair, Motte had once again 'logged out' to see if Rouge had awakened in their other world. This time, however, he looked even more concerned when he came back. When Aspen had asked him what was going on, the bigger man shook his head. "I got a message from Lily – Doom Bloom. She said she thinks Rouge may be in trouble because of a message that someone sent to her. She's at work and can't come, but she told me someone's supposed to be waiting near the Great Temple for her."

Aspen growled, glaring around at the broken-down shops, tenements, and warehouses that surrounded them. They had been wandering further from the docks, but had assumed that the cultists would continue their habit of hiding their entrances in disused buildings. As a result, they had gone deeper into the poorer areas in the south-east of the city, and entirely away from the Temple.

"It's the only lead we have, and this is clearly not working. We haven't been able to hear Silus for at least ten minutes, either, so we're more than a mile from wherever she actually is." He pointed into the distance, where they could just make out the tall spire on top of the Temple. The only thing in the city that was taller were the two towers of the king's castle. "Shall we?"

Motte nodded, then whistled sharply. Soon, they could hear the clattering of hooves on cobblestones, and Rosalind, the huge, dappled gray mare that served as Motte's mount appeared, whickering questioningly. Motte patted the beast affectionately, then gestured toward the saddle on her back. "Get on."

Aspen eyed the animal dubiously. He, himself, was not exactly a small man, and Motte was even larger. "It's probably best if I run alongside. I have good speed and- "

Motte laughed and clapped the mare firmly on her thickly-muscled hindquarters. "Don't worry. I've put a lot of training into Rosalind here. Her Strength is maxed out, and I've been working on her Speed for a while now. She'll be fine." He eyed Aspen appraisingly. "Besides, you may have filled out since we met you, but you're still pretty stringy."

Aspen chuckled ruefully. "I prefer 'lean'."

Motte's dark eyes crinkled at the corners when he smiled back. "Semantics, but then, if I didn't like word-play, I would have chosen a different line of work." His cheeks flushed, and he looked away, suddenly very interested in straightening a few stray strands of the mare's thick mane. "Ah, in the rea-*Other* world, I mean. Anyway," he motioned again to the tall mare, "after you."

Aspen felt his own cheeks warm slightly as he used the stirrup to climb into the saddle, and he wondered at the sudden feeling of awkwardness. Riding would definitely shorten their travel time, so long as the animal could carry them both, so simple expediency demanded they ride. Nonetheless, as he felt Motte settle in behind him, and the other man's arms reach past him to pick up the reins, the blood pounded in his ears so hard that Aspen couldn't even hear himself think.

Fortunately, once Rosalind began to move, Aspen discovered that Motte had not been exaggerating her capabilities. The lovely steed made rapid and easy time over the distance to the Temple, though her movement was more akin to a bull charging through the streets than the graceful gait of a noble's mount. He found himself clinging to the saddle with an embarrassing level of desperation, and he was grateful for the firm security of the iron-clad arms on either side of him.

By the time they reached the square in front of the Temple, which was already full of petitioners even so early in the morning, Aspen was glad just to be able to get down and feel solid ground beneath his boots again. He swayed a little, and Motte, who was standing beside him, rested a supportive hand on Aspen's arm.

"Sorry," Motte said, raising his voice slightly to be heard over the murmur of a thousand voices around them. "I need to put more points into Roz's Agility, but after Strength, I thought Speed was more important."

"Motte?" The voice was familiar, but entirely unexpected, and both men jumped before looking around.

"Vonn?" Aspen and Motte asked simultaneously, looking around. It took Aspen a moment to recognize the boy, since his brain simply dismissed the young man holding a baby as 'can't be Vonn' and moved on. Only when the elf's fingers clutched at Aspen's sleeve did he take another look, finally recognizing the young man. His eyes flitted between the disheveled boy and the sniffling baby strapped to him with what looked like torn strips of cloth. "You found your nephew?"

Vonn smiled tiredly, gently touching the soft brown curls of the baby, leaning closer so he could be heard over the noise of the crowd. "I... Yes? It's a long story. Right now, though, we need to get back in. Rouge got me out, but she stayed behind, and I have a really bad feeling about it. She was captured by that madman FantumHat, and we managed to trick him and get away, but-"

Motte growled audibly. ::FantumHat! That's the guy who sent Doom that PM! That bastard really did trap her somehow!::

Aspen laid a hand on Motte's arm. ::We'll worry about that later. Right now, we need to get Rouge out of there.:: He turned his attention back to Vonn. "Show us the door, and then you'll have to take the baby back to the house."

Vonn looked conflicted, but nodded reluctantly. "It's back over here." The boy led the way back down the stairs, heading down a broad street that led to some of the more popular restaurants in the area. Past the restaurants, there was a narrower side street with shaded shop doors leading to stores selling incense, icons, candles, and religious trinkets of all kinds.

"Here. There's a cul-de-sac hidden between two signs. At the end of the cul-de-sac there's a green door."

Motte began jogging down the dark street almost before Vonn finished speaking, and Aspen frowned at the broad, armored back. ::Motte, wait for me!" he sent sharply, before turning back to Vonn to give the wood elf a few last messages to take to the others.

::Aspen?::

The sudden intrusion of Lyrec's voice was shocking, and Aspen jumped. his head whipped around, eyes examining the crowds surrounding them. ::Lyrec? Where are you?::

::Aspen!:: The bard's voice perked up. ::I still have tons of bard quests, so I'm about to make my debut playing for-::

::Forget it.:: Aspen knew he was being brusque even as he spoke, but the boy's obvious infatuation felt even more awkward now that Motte was there to witness it. ::Do you know where,:: he glanced at the sign of the closest tavern, ::The Swaggering Mole is?::

::Uh, yeah. It's on my list of possible- ::

::Good. Meet us there as quickly as possible.::

Aspen couldn't resist any longer, and glanced at Motte. The tall man had stopped, and was watching Aspen with one eyebrow raised, expression curious. Aspen cleared his throat, then shrugged lamely, uncertain what to say.

Fortunately, the bard chose that moment to walk down the street, and he waved a little awkwardly when he saw Aspen and Vonn. Then his eyebrows shot up when he saw Motte, and he stopped in his tracks. "Oh, hey, Dr. Williams. Um, wow, look at the time. I really should be in bed already, right?"

Motte's lips twitched as he held back a smile, but his eyebrows lowered as he cast the boy a stern glance. "Good point, Lyrec. Why are you here at this time of night? Don't your parents have a curfew of ten o'clock, too?"

Lyrec's hand twitched toward his head. "Uh, yeah. I just totally didn't realize it was so late. I'll log off right now!"

Aspen's hand shot out and grabbed the bard. "No, you won't! You need to take the baby back to the house."

Vonn gasped, and when Aspen turned to look at him, the young elf looked like he'd seen a ghost. "I forgot! I was so worried about Rouge that I forgot about the manor! FantumHat sent some of his guild-members to attack it. He was going to kill me and the baby, and I had to tell him where it was. I mean, I told them the entrance was from the back, through the woods, because that *is* my usual entrance, so it wasn't a lie, and that may delay them, but-"

Aspen growled. "Damn it! How... No." He shook his head, watching the way the wood elf's arms were wrapped protectively around the baby strapped to his chest. "That doesn't matter. Vonn, we need you to go with us and show us where Rouge is. Lyrec, you need to take the baby and warn everyone at the house."

A thought occurred to him, and he felt a dark smile touch the corners of his mouth. "It won't be as easy to get through the woods as it used to be, so you may have more time than you think. Go to the front door. Tell them to regroup at the old orphanage, but anyone who can flee the city should head north, and we'll be right behind them. Tell Plum and Tomas that it's time for the final option."

Vonn already had his arms outstretched toward the infant, following Aspen's orders as if under a spell, but he hesitated at this last. "Uh, final... option?"

Aspen nodded, though his gut burned at the thought of what he had to do. "They'll know. Just hurry!" He turned to Motte. "Can he ride your horse?"

Motte shook his head. "Travelers can only ride their own mount. Lyrec, is your horse nearby?"

Lyrec nodded jerkily, looking down at the child Vonn had reluctantly placed in his arms. "Yeah. I've only invested in a little Speed, though. Upgrades are expensive!"

Motte grabbed the boy's shoulders and turned him around, giving him a gentle push. "That's all right. Just do your best, Jace. Everybody's depending on you!"

Lyrec swallowed hard, but his shoulders straightened, and his jaw clenched. "Yeah, okay! I can do this!" Without another word, the boy ran off, clutching the crying child to his narrow chest.

Aspen turned back to Motte and Vonn. The elf was staring after Lyrec and the baby with an expression that clearly showed how terribly he was torn between the desire to save his friend and the need to reassure himself that the baby was safe. Aspen put a hand on the lad's shoulder and shook gently. "Vonn, we need you to show us where Rouge is. You can leave as soon as that's done. Now, is there anything else we need to know?"

Vonn filled them in on his and Rouge's adventures as he led them down the street to the well-concealed cul-de-sac. Unlike the cultists' other hideouts, this one was a well-maintained storefront with a simple CLOSED sign hanging on the door. Anyone who managed to stumble onto it accidentally would never suspect it was anything other than a shop with a poorly chosen location. Ignoring the sign, Vonn pushed on the door, and it opened easily.

As soon as they stepped through into the echoing cavern, Aspen knew they were in the right place, because the first thing they heard was Silus singing a plaintive song in a sad little voice. ::Great big bugs on little bitty flutter wings, tasty little yummy bugs, juicy luscious pea-pods too…::

Aspen felt his heart leap in his chest. ::Silus! We're here!::

An excited squeak filled his mind. ::Aspen! You're all right! You finally found me! Be careful, there are lots of guards now. Did you bring food?::

Motte shook a rat-faced little man who was dangling from his gauntleted fist. ::Don't worry, Silus. These 'guards' will be no problem.:: The warrior's contempt was clearly audible in his deep voice.

Aspen sighed a little as Motte threw the guard to the side, the limp body impacting another man who was charging at them with his blade already bared. ::So much for being sneaky.::

Motte snorted as he kicked the second man, who had been knocked down by the body of the first, hard enough that his neck cracked audibly. ::These aren't guards. They're common street thugs with delusions of grandeur. We can take them all out before they can send up an alarm.::

Seeing that four more of the people blocking their way to the doors on the left side of the room were heading for them with grim expressions, Aspen pulled Stick from his belt and sent it a trickle of mana. It lengthened to full size, chiming threateningly at the oncoming attackers. He readied himself, but Vonn coughed softly at his side.

"I hate to bother you, but it looks like the last two are thinking of bolting and calling for reinforcements. My lord Motte, do you have a bow, perchance?" The elf asked politely, his eyes locked on the two remaining door-guards.

Without breaking stride, Motte pulled a short bow and a quiver full of arrows from his inventory and tossed them toward Vonn. The elf grabbed them neatly from the air. A moment later, an arrow was flying toward the first of the two stragglers, with a second arrow winging after so closely that its barbed head seemed to brush the fletching of the first. Both guards fell without even having time to react to the sudden long-distance threat.

Motte's shield slammed into two of the on-coming guards, and there were crunches as breakable bones met unyielding shield. Aspen used Stick to vault through the air, planting his heels in the chest of the third guard, then shortening the staff into its cudgel form just in time to rap the last one on the head sharply. The man's skull thunked hollowly, and he dropped with a groan.

Motte's huge axe swung twice, and both of Aspen's targets lost their heads. Aspen nodded in somber satisfaction. Enemies left alive at your back were enemies you would have to face again, probably at the worst possible moment.

::No more guards here, Silus,:: Aspen sent. ::Can you get to the door on your side?::

Vonn was searching the bodies, and on the third one he triumphantly held up a ring of keys. Aspen nodded approval as Silus replied. ::I'm already here. I've been here for *hours*, and no one has noticed me:: The bat's voice held oceans of professional disdain at this failure to detect an infiltrator, and Aspen swallowed a laugh.

::Little one, isn't it *good* that no one noticed you?:: Aspen asked gently, accepting the keys. He hurried to the door and began trying each key that looked like it might fit the lock.

Silus just sniffed dismissively, as the second key Aspen tried turned in the lock with a *click*. A moment later, the door opened, and the bat dropped down from where she'd been hidden behind a bas-relief sculpture of a bug-eyed goose with four tentacles and a beak packed with sharp teeth.

Aspen winced even as he snuggled the no-longer-quite-so-tiny bat who curled into the hollow of his throat. ::I wouldn't want to look too closely at that statue either, to be fair.::

Silus didn't reply, just leaned hard into the warmth of his body, her small form shuddering at the relief of finally feeling safe again. Aspen spent several heartbeats just stroking her soft body, until her shivers slowed and she was able to look up. Her big, golden eyes were deeper than before, and the silver tufts of fur above them were now rich swathes that bracketed the gleaming gold, emphasizing their beauty.

::So, exactly what kind of food did you bring?::

Chapter Nine

Khor

The farm was bustling. The planting was done, at least for now, and Sarave was working hard most days just to keep up with weeding and harvesting the crops that were growing at a tremendous rate. William often worked in the fields during the night, and though Khor had thought at first that the ancient mage might feel such work was beneath him, that seemed to be far from true. In fact, William could usually be found humming in a surprisingly pleasant tenor as he hoed and harvested, and only rarely did Khor find a pale and desiccated vegetable placed neatly in the compost heap.

The unicorns were all gangly legs and huge ears now, much of their goat-like wool shed as the weather warmed, and their gracile builds were now clearly visible. While Kayli was still noticeably smaller and slightly rounder than her older sister, even she was beginning to lose her babyish ways and reckless attitude.

Juniper, meanwhile, was nearly as tall as her mother's shoulder, though she doubtless had more growing to do. Sarave had set the child to doing a little of the cooking, as well as some of the harvesting and weeding. They stopped when the sun was highest and hottest, and Juniper reluctantly learned her letters and numbers at her mother's knee. The child was more interested in running wild than in learning math, but Sarave bribed her with the promise of a chapter read from one of the few storybooks in Aspen's small collection, and the little goblin woman's lilting voice could later be heard over the hum of the bees as she read about princesses and dragons.

Though Khor was fairly certain that the original princesses hadn't been goblins, and the original dragons hadn't been zombies. He'd never particularly enjoyed fictional stories, though, so it was barely possible that he misremembered.

Khor himself had long since lost track of how many skill and stat points he'd gained since he began hauling everything all over the farm. Not that he'd tried very hard, since he usually lost count of almost anything after twelve, and all numbers thereafter were just 'lots'.

In any case, the days were full, and there were now more than enough people and animals on the farm for him to be tripping over someone at almost every turn. Nuisance's hens were sitting on eggs, and though they had let Sarave gather the first few, they guarded the ones they had now with wings and beaks. The two hens would trade places every few hours, one of them keeping the eggs warm while the other one went to get food and water and swim in the river or pond.

Nuisance himself seemed almost embarrassed by the way the two female ducks were acting, and avoided them whenever possible. If he caught a glimpse of the eggs when the hens were doing their shift change, Nuisance would leave the area as quickly as possible, even if it meant vacating his favorite perch between Khor's horns. This meant that Khor or someone else would occasionally find the duck in very unexpected places, but after Sarave found him in her stock pot for the second time, she banned him from the house.

Between young unicorns underfoot and Khor's missing lookout, by the time Khor noticed the goblin, he had nearly stepped on him. Once he *did* notice the goblin, he seriously considered stepping on him anyway. Sarave and Juniper might be growing on Khor rather like a particularly tenacious lichen, but that did *not* mean the goat was ready to extend his approval to the entire race. In his experience, goblins were smelly, rude, vicious, and stupid. Khor firmly ignored the fact that the same words had been used to describe him more than once.

The bright green goblin standing in the road in front of Khor certainly stank, and when a goat thinks something smells rank, it generally means that things have gone far past unacceptable and well into the range of deeply vile. He was also filthy and skinny, and half his face was hidden behind a ragged cloth that might at one point have been described as an eyepatch, but now barely counted as a stained set of strings. It certainly didn't cover the old, deep scar that crossed from his forehead across where his left eye should be and ended with a deep, cruel slice into the flesh of his cheek.

Khor was about to start his 'crush first and ask questions later' form of guarding when the skinny goblin collapsed to his knees. With one trembling hand, he pulled a leather flap back from the pouch he wore on his chest. A malodorous stench rolled forth, and the goblin gagged, but nonetheless reached down into the pouch and gently lifted up what looked like a half-dead fish. It lay in his palm, gills barely quivering, and the single visible eye was cloudy and gray.

"Please," the goblin croaked, "Aspen sent us."

Khor bugled for help.

ᴇ̌ ᴇ̌ ᴇ̌

Upon arriving in response to Khor's call, Sumi immediately went to fetch Viqa, who remained by the Tree unless specifically called. The glyphis woman arrived within a few minutes, alone, since Sumi stayed to keep watch after using her web-speak to tell Viqa where to go. When she arrived, there was an expression of mild concern on the gray woman's face. When she saw the limp bundle of gray slime that Nekthadt lifted out of his pouch, however, her expression transformed into one so full of emotion that it was impossible to tell whether joy or sorrow would win.

In an instant, the water mage conjured a ball of sparkling water, which engulfed the small body and lifted it away from the goblin's trembling hands. The water instantly grew cloudy, but the mage simply refreshed it again and again until it stayed clear. The little fish-like creature inside twitched a little, its tail waving weakly through the water.

Without a word, Viqa began to run in the direction of the pond, with the ball of water flying ahead as if it were in control of the mage instead of the other way around. The goblin took a step after, clearly wanting to follow, but simply fell to his knees again, unable to do more than watch after the glyphis with despairing yellow eyes.

A gasp came from behind Khor as the stranger toppled over into the dust, and Khor turned to see that Sarave stood there, hands clasped over her mouth, eyes wide, and a bright tear trickling down her pale cheek. She choked out a word that Khor didn't recognize, and Khor huffed a deep sigh. He knew a hauling-type situation when he saw one.

They attempted to get the goblin on Khor's back, but, after a few attempts that would have been comical if they hadn't threatened to injure Khor's pride, the goblin woke up. Well, it wasn't exactly full consciousness, but it was enough that he was able to limp back to the house by holding Khor's fur in one soiled fist while his other arm was slung over Sarave's shoulders. He was only slightly taller than the female goblin, so this position was still a bit awkward, but it worked, and Sarave, Juniper, and the new goblin entered the darkness of the house. Sarave didn't even stop to clean up the stranger, and it was going to take forever to get that stench out.

Khor knew he should go and relieve Sumi at the Tree, but, he thought a bit spitefully, it wasn't as if she would have relieved him in the same situation. He ignored the fact that the spider would actually fit inside the house and that the Spider's Milk she produced was a fairly good healing potion. The small window that opened between the barn and the house was open, and Khor set his bearded chin on the windowsill and chewed his cud, trying to look as uninterested as possible.

After a while, during which Sarave removed all of the new goblin's clothing, gasping and hissing periodically as she saw his injuries and realized how thin he was, the goblin woman emerged from the house. Her face was still pale and drawn, but she looked more determined than worried now, and she dumped the putrid rags she'd removed from the male goblin, as well as the almost as fetid rags she'd used to wipe him down.

With a forced smile, Sarave squatted down in front of Juniper, who had been ejected rather unceremoniously from the house before the stranger's clothes came off. Kayti and Kayli hovered nearby, their large, long-lashed eyes limpid and concerned. Sarave cleared her throat. "Juni, my love, you remember how I told you about your uncle Nekthadt?"

Juniper's little head nodded vigorously, and her curls bounced enthusiastically. "I remember! He saved you from the evil goblins who tried to kill us!"

Khor felt a little jump of interest at this, hoping that he might get a bit more of Sarave's story. He'd always had the sense that there was more to her than she wanted to admit. For one thing, she was far too intelligent and well-spoken for one of her race, and even the former servant she'd once claimed to be wouldn't have mastered all the skills she seemed to possess.

Sarave nodded, her hand gently cupping her daughter's round little cheek. "That's right. When Aspen left, I asked him to look for your uncle. I didn't think there was much chance that he would find him, but Aspen is… an unusual man.

That man inside the house is Uncle Nekthadt, and though it may take some time, I believe he will recover."

With this, the goblin woman wrapped her arms around Juniper and pulled her into a tight embrace. Deep, wracking sobs shook her slender frame, and she rocked the little girl, who patted her mother's back with a look that said she wasn't certain whether or not she should start crying too. Through her tears, Sarave managed to choke out, "It's all right. It's all right, Juni. I'm just so… so *glad*."

After she was done crying, the goblin woman dried her tear-stained face on her apron and gathered her composure around her like an old and familiar cloak. With a final hug, she sent Juniper off to find 'Uncle William' or Sumi. (And why the fructipire got such a title while Khor, who watched over the children far more often, did not, he didn't understand. Not that he would have *wanted* to be 'Uncle Khor' anyway. Probably.)

Predictably, the unicorns trailed after Juniper as the little girl trotted obediently toward the entrance to the underground tunnel system, and Khor, with a grumbling huff, followed after them. Also predictably, the three children took a rather liberal view of the timeline allowable for their little jaunt, and they wandered off course more than once, usually ending up in a patch of ripe berries or colorful flowers. Juniper's face was soon liberally smeared in sweet red and purple juice, and all three of them were decked out in flower wreaths woven by the little half-goblin's nimble fingers. The wreaths were lop-sided and had a tendency to fall apart easily, but they still added to the air of gaiety that surrounded the trio.

They 'found' Sumi first, which led to Khor being mentally badgered for several minutes for not immediately coming to relieve the spider, while the children played around the base of the Tree. The sapling was covered in blossoms and bees by now, and no attackers had gotten closer to the Tree than thirty feet since the bees moved into the big old apple tree on the edge of the nearby orchard.

Satisfied that Khor understood the depth of his indiscretion, Sumi took off, eight legs blurring as she ran toward the river. Khor had to admit to feeling a mild twinge of regret for his actions as he realized that Sumi's disgusting milk would probably actually have helped the little glyphis, a fact that he had forgotten once the more interesting matter of Sarave's brother had come to his attention. Still, since Spider's Milk simply aided the body in more efficiently using its own resources to heal, rather than providing any actual healing of its own, Sumi probably wouldn't be able to help until the little one pulled through on its own, since it had looked like its body had no resources left.

In any case, here he was again, carefully walking the perimeter of the clearing around the Tree, watching the young unicorns and the little half-goblin frolic in the grass and eat ripe apples until their bellies bulged. While he would rather be able to do his own things, he had to admit that with the warm spring breeze blowing through his fur, the sound of giggles and happy bees filling his ears, and warm sunshine heating his withers and back, all in all, there were worse places to be.

Chapter Ten

Rouge

The door Rouge had seen was big. She'd been in here long enough now to have figured out that for these people, in most cases at least, big equaled important. Which was a little insulting, to be honest, given her own petite size and build, but hey, being underestimated was a strength all its own.

Looking at the door in front of her, Rouge drew in a fortifying breath. It really was big. Epic, even. It was easily twice as tall as her dad, and he was over six feet tall in real life, and even taller in game. Gold-inlaid monsters chased gold-inlaid elves, goblins, and dwarves across the broad expanse of ebony wood, and she wondered briefly how hard it would be to dig the metal out.

Except she had no weapon, and no inventory. Dang it!

Wait, wait, wait, though. When she cast [Poison Rain], seventy-five pointy objects appeared from nowhere. Admittedly, they were as likely to be meat skewers and butter knives as actual, useful weapons, but still. If she could get up high enough to cast it, surely she'd be able to salvage at least one good sharp object out of it, and, bonus, it'd already be poisoned!

Then she realized that she'd never actually seen any weapons lying around by the time she looted after a battle. The stupid things must have a time limit, and went poof after a while. Which didn't exactly make them worthless as a possible source of weapons, but definitely did curb her enthusiasm for the idea. Well, it was obviously a cheat if she could just conjure up seventy-five saleable items every time she used the spell. It might take a while, but she could definitely make bank doing that.

Rouge suddenly realized that she was putting off opening the door. Honestly, she just wanted to log out, climb out of her pod, and get into her nice soft bed with Max lying across her feet so she couldn't move. She *didn't* want to open this door, maybe get into yet another battle, and maybe even die. But, unless she was willing to turn around and follow Vonn out, that was what she needed to do. After all, if she logged out while she was in here, she would either leave behind a defenseless Zombie, or it would kick her out of the 'dungeon' anyway, and *then* her defenseless Zombie would just be standing around somewhere else.

Tugging at a braid, she considered her options. One, just leave. Two, open the door. Three, log out and deal with the consequences later. Three was obviously off the table, and as much as leaving called to her tired mind, she knew option two was the only viable option as far as she was concerned.

So, she opened the door. Just a little. Just enough to slip one small elf-girl inside, and then she closed it again behind her.

Not really surprisingly, it was yet another throne room. How many thrones did these people *need*, anyway? Seriously, shouldn't one be enough? Though, she supposed, the first one had been a symbolic throne for a god, the second one had been not-quite-a-throne for a city lord, and this one? This one was a regular throne.

Eight red-carpeted stairs led up to a wide dais, where the claw-footed golden throne sat. It was large, but not impossibly so, though the man who sat in it still seemed too small for the tall, broad seat. The red velvet back cushions showed above his crowned head, and the golden cushion on which he sat was visible on each side of his spindly legs.

He sat, silent, with his head resting against his fist, and he didn't stir even when she entered the room. At first, she thought he was sleeping, but then one eye opened slowly. She couldn't tell what color it was from where she was, nearly forty feet away, but the wispy hair visible beneath the heavy golden crown on his head was graying blonde, so she imagined it might be blue.

"Yes, child?" His voice was weak, and as she slowly drew nearer, she could see that his body was thin, almost cadaverous. Rather than the emaciation of starvation, however, he looked more like he'd been worn away by a long period of sickness.

Looking around, she saw that although the room was gaudily decorated to the point of being ostentatious, it also seemed to be empty except for the two of them. Tall pillars lined the path to the throne, and she supposed guards or courtiers might be hiding there, but, honestly, why would they bother?

She took another step, then attempted a curtsey that turned into a bow halfway through. Curtsey or bow, it was awkward, but the king on his throne didn't laugh or, in fact, move. "Um, your... Majesty? I'm sorry, I'm not... We don't really have kings where I... I'm not sure what to call you?"

A dry chuckle came from the king, followed by a rasping cough. "Your Majesty is fine. Or," he lifted his head just a bit, then dropped it back to his fist as if his neck wasn't strong enough to bear the weight of head and crown together. "You may call me King Chester, if you like. I understand you Travelers aren't truly from this world, so I am not really *your* king, am I?" He gestured to himself with a bony hand. "Not much of a king at all at the moment, to be honest."

Rouge had covered half the distance to the throne by now, feeling more confident as she passed the first of the pillars and verified that no one lurked behind them. The closer she got, the sicker the king looked. His skin was yellowish, his cheeks hollow, and dark circles lurked beneath eyes that she could now see were some indeterminate shade of pale.

"Are you, um, all right, King Chester? You don't look so good. Um, is there anything I can help you with?" She uttered the last words hopefully, trying to trigger some kind of quest. Save the King, or maybe Find a Cure?

The hoarse laugh sounded again, and she shivered a little, pausing in her advance. "No need, my dear. My friends take care of everything for me, these days. I haven't been feeling well, and, truthfully, I was always more interested in books and crafts than ruling, anyway."

That jibed with the little that Aspen had said about King Chester, and the man looked like he wouldn't be able to walk without assistance, so why did she suddenly feel like a fly hovering at the edge of a spider's web? Was this man another victim of FantumHat's plots, too weak to do anything when a powerful Traveler weaseled his way into the position of Lord of Bright? Or was he part of the whole thing?

As if he could sense her doubts, Chester lifted the wrist of the hand that wasn't holding up his head. Something metallic glinted there, catching the light as the limb trembled. "Now, now, child, you needn't fear an old man. Things in this place are never as they seem, and sometimes kings are as much prisoners as the lowest of criminals."

Feeling suddenly more confident, Rouge took another step forward. Her hand clutched the shiny pebble-key where it rested in her pocket. "Is that a set of those magic manacles? I have a-" The door opened abruptly behind her, swinging wide and slamming against the wall with a **BOOM.** Rouge leapt to the side, scurrying into the shadow behind one of the pillars. She dropped into [Stealth], and desperately hoped she hadn't been seen.

"*Find her,*" roared FantumHat's voice. "There's no way that rat has found her way out yet. She's in here somewhere, and *I want her!* If I see you again before you've found her, I'll kill you all myself!"

There was a flurry of voices all saying something along the lines of 'Yes,

Sir!', and then the door closed again, though much more quietly. Hard boots clacked furiously on the stone floor, and FantumHat himself passed by her hiding place, stalking toward the throne. To Rouge's immense surprise, he dropped to one knee just before the first stair leading up to the dais. When he spoke, his voice was almost servile, instead of cold, angry, or amused, which had seemed to be the only emotions he was capable of. She supposed the king must still have some power left, even if he was also a prisoner, or FantumHat wouldn't bother being polite.

"I'm sorry, your Majesty. I know you don't like it when people are angry around you. It's just that I've had a *very* trying night, and my new pet rat escaped from her cage before I was done playing with her." FantumHat's head was bowed, and his wavy white hair fell around his face, concealing his expression, especially from Rouge's viewpoint behind and to the side of him.

King Chester raised his wavering hand again, offering it to the kneeling player. "There, there, my boy, I understand. We all have times when things don't go our way. Now, did you bring me the item you promised me?" For a moment, the king's voice sounded like that of a little boy expecting to be given his favorite treat, and Rouge wondered if that was the trick FantumHat had used to reach his current position. Would King Chester have made anyone the ruler of Bright if they'd just brought him whatever it was the old man wanted?

"Ah, no, your majesty." FantumHat's voice was smarmy and apologetic. "I'm afraid that rat made off with it. Rest assured, though, that I'll get it back soon."

Rouge's fingers dove into her pocket, clutching at the little *Locked Decorative Box* that sat beside the pebble-key. This? This tiny trinket that she had gotten only because her [Pilfer] skill had activated for only the second time ever, automatically giving her a random item from a nearby dead or unconscious enemy's inventory? She'd assumed it was some random loot-for-money item that FantumHat had picked up and been carrying around only because all players were magpies. But maybe it was actually something super important? If so, why hadn't it been in the assassin's personal inventory, where it couldn't be dropped or stolen?

The king's skinny finger beckoned to FantumHat, and the player stood slowly. Was she imagining things, or did he hesitate slightly before starting up the steps? Certainly, he took each step as slowly as possible, and when he finally reached the dais, he stopped just outside of the reach of that skeletal hand.

Wait, skeletal? Sure, King Chester was sickly and thin, but now he looked even more pale and lifeless than before. Rouge's eyes fluttered and she swayed slightly, feeling suddenly dizzy. Her hand clenched around the little box in her pocket, and the bite of the sharp-edged lid into her palm made her eyes snap open again.

Congratulations! Due to [Illusion Break], you are now able to see things more clearly.
[Illusion Break] is now level 2.

Her eyes locked on the figure in the throne, who suddenly seemed much taller and more intimidating than he had only moments before. Also, much more dead. Or *un*dead. King Chester's hands were nothing more than yellowed bones, and his head was a leering skull with flickering white flames in the eye sockets. Those flames were locked on Rouge's hiding place.

A long, rattling laugh issued from the open jawbone, teeth clacking together in a hollow clatter like dice on a table. "Oh, I think my little game is over. Your rat is hiding right behind you, Traveler. Catch her for me."

One pale fingerbone rose to point directly at Rouge.

That was big ol' nope, so Rouge tried to 'nope' right out of there. Unfortunately, FantumHat seemed to be ahead of her in basically every way. Before she could take more than a few steps deeper into the shadows beyond the pillars, the vampire was on her, striking her midsection with a kick that was so solid that she was certain he had been able to see through her [Stealth] somehow. As she flew through the air toward the foot of the stairs, she swore never to trust another innocent-looking little old person.

You have taken 62 points of damage from Player *FantumHat*. Your [Stealth] has been broken!
You have had the wind knocked out of you. You are *Breathless*.

That was a quarter of her health gone with one solid blow. She knew when she was outclassed physically, which meant that the only thing she had going for her right now was her brain. Which, unfortunately, probably wasn't going to be enough to get her out of this mess.

Rouge, why do you have to be so nosy? Even as she chided herself for her irrepressible curiosity, she found herself on her hands and knees in front of the steps, gasping as she struggled to breathe. Seriously, of all the debuffs in *Veritas Online*, this was one of the ones she hated the most. Not being able to breathe was the pits.

When she finally dragged in a full breath, she collapsed back on her heels, staring up with dislike at the two men who were watching her suffering with distaste (FantumHat) and amusement (Chester). "You guys... are... jerks... you know... that?" She panted as she attempted to stand.

You have taken 18 points of damage from Player *FantumHat*.

With a nonchalant kick, FantumHat swept her feet out from under her, and she landed on the ground again, gasping as she lost the breath she had just managed to draw in. "Stay down, rat," the player said, curling his lip. "If it weren't for the fact that I still need you, I'd kill you now and be done with it."

Rouge gagged, grateful again for the fact that she couldn't actually throw up in *VO*. Of course, she'd been certain she couldn't actually pass out (or sleep?)

in *VO* either, so maybe she needed to stop making assumptions. So far, this part of being a beta tester kind of sucked.

King Chester laughed that creepy, hollow laugh again, and both FantumHat and Rouge looked up at where he still sat in his throne. His skull was no longer leaning against his fingerbones, though. Now, he was sitting up straight, his arms resting on the arms of the chair, while one forefinger *tap-tap-tapped* in a constant monotonal beat. "*You* need her, my minion? I don't believe I've ever heard you say you *need* anything before. *Want*, yes. *Desire*, certainly. But never *need*. How is it that you *need* this pathetic creature?"

Rouge started to stir at that, but caught the sharp look FantumHat shot her from the corner of his eyes, and stilled. She had to bite her lip hard to keep silent, but she managed to wait and listen.

"It's nothing, your Majesty." FantumHat was clearly trying to keep Chester from becoming any more interested in Rouge, but she could see his hands fisted at his sides, and she doubted the king missed it either. "She knows someone who has something I want. I'm sure I can find another way to get it, so if Your Majesty wants this rodent, you can have her." He forced a shrug. "I just doubt she's really that useful to you, so if it's all the same to you-"

This time the undead king's laugh held true amusement, and a shudder went down Rouge's back at the sound. "You don't even know what you've caught, do you, my rook?" The king stood, his heavy velvet robe nearly muffling the clattering sound his bones made as he moved. One, two, three, four, five, six, seven steps he moved down, until the trailing edge of the pure white fur trimming that red velvet mantle tickled Rouge's fingers. She fiercely resisted the urge to pull her hand away as if she'd just touched something slimy.

Down the last step the bony foot descended, and Rouge locked her gaze on a yellowed metatarsal. She felt completely exposed and vulnerable, with two powerful enemies standing over her helpless form, but she would. Not. Break.

You have taken 47 points of damage from Player *FantumHat*.

The sudden kick took her completely by surprise, and she flipped in the air twice before slamming into the ground and rolling again. When she came to a stop, she was disoriented and shocked. Blinking open her eyes, she looked over at the two men. FantumHat, though he had his head bowed, looked somehow triumphant, while she had the distinct feeling that the king's skull was clenching its teeth. In the king's hand, he held a long white dagger that emanated a red light that, even in the bright light of the glowstones, looked somehow ominous.

"What are you doing?" the king hissed. "We must kill the little pawn now, before she reaches the other side of the board and-"

FantumHat took a step to the side, standing between the king and Rouge's fallen body. "You and your damned chess analogies! Come *on!* I've done everything you asked me to do up until this point- "

"And I've given you the power to do anything in this world!" Chester shouted. "You can kill anyone at your slightest whim! You murder and torment anyone you want- "

"Anyone except *the* one!" FantumHat yelled. "You promised me that I could have her, but you haven't even-!"

As the two misogynistic, murderous stench-nuggets continued to scream at each other, Rouge began dragging herself toward the door. She had two *Broken Rib* debuffs to add to her *Broken Wrist (Left)*, and even with the pain minimizer, moving was *not* fun, but there was no way she was just going to lie there while those idiots bickered over who got to kill her.

The door burst open, and Motte nearly ran over Rouge where she lay on the hard stone floor. The juggernaut barely swerved in time, and when he slammed into the pillar nearby, it cracked with a sharp report that stopped the vampire and the skeleton king mid-yell.

Aspen and Vonn (sans baby) followed Rouge's furious parent a moment later, and Silus immediately flew from Aspen's shoulder to where Rouge lay crumpled on the floor. The thief felt hot tears on her face, and realized that crying was apparently something else that she was beta-testing, and at the moment, she was okay with that.

SECRET Quest: "Mysterious Malefactors" completed.

You have helped the Duke find out who is behind the attacks on Gina's faithful, and saved as many of Gina's worshippers as possible (68/100).

Reward: 10 levels. 25000 Gold. +30 reputation points with Gina's faithful. +20 reputation points with Gina Herself.

A brilliant golden glow encompassed both Rouge and Aspen as their separate quests completed, and they gained several levels (and Aspen likely got some stat points as well). Confusingly, the same thing was happening on the other side of the throne room, as a red light coruscated around both FantumHat and King Chester.

Congratulations! You have discovered your true opponents! The tutorial has ended, and your true quest can now begin! Please be aware, however, that if you fail this quest, ALL PROGRESS MADE BY YOUR CHARACTER SINCE YOU BEGAN YOUR SECRET QUEST WILL BE RESET. Any skills, spells, items, and levels gained since you embarked on your epic journey will be LOST.

Fail/Success conditions:

1) Death of any of the following: <u>FantumHat AND King Chester</u> OR <u>Rouge the Rogue AND Aspen</u>

2) Complete the final quest in this SECRET quest chain

If none of the first conditions are met by 24:00 CST on September 12, the Player with the highest completion rate will win.

FantumHat current completion: 78%

Rouge the Rouge current completion: 27%

WARNING: This final quest must be accepted or refused. If you choose not to proceed, you may KEEP all skills, spells, items, and levels gained *to this moment*, but you will FAIL the final quest. If you accept the final quest, this decision cannot be changed, and you are indicating that you understand that in case of failure, your status will be returned to the condition you were in *at the moment you accepted the initial quest*, as if you had never participated in this quest line.

SECRET Quest: "Who Run the World" available. (This is a SECRET quest. If you tell anyone about it before it is complete, you will automatically fail it.) The forces of light and darkness are struggling for control of the world. Each side has appointed champions, and for the first time, those champions are facing each other directly. You must defeat Apofis' champions in order to keep the world safe from those who would reduce it to a place of strife and suffering. *WARNING: You get only one attempt at clearing this quest. If you die, the quest will be offered to ANOTHER PLAYER, who may then attempt to clear it.*

Success: Level 100 or 15 levels, whichever is greater. 1 million gold. Become a Saintess of Gina.

Failure: Apofis' religion becomes the dominant one in the world. All races other than Human lose status as sapient beings. Aspen's death. Silus' death. Khor's death. Sumi's death. Sarave's death. Juniper's death. William's enslavement. Vonn's death.

Accept: Yes/No?

The world paused as Rouge stared at the block of text occupying her vision, and she read it over twice, then three times, trying to make sense of it. She didn't even realize Emily had appeared again until the AI avatar sat down beside her, sighing softly.

Rouge turned her head, staring at the woman sitting cross-legged on the stone floor. She was still recognizably Emily, with her silky golden bun and clear blue eyes. Her aura of imperturbability was missing, however. Her face looked merely human, and very, very tired.

"They built in some time for you to decide," the woman said conversationally, her voice calm but slightly scratchy, as though she had been coughing or crying right before she had joined Rouge. "In those moments, I can speak to you with no one watching. The time is limited, but I can," she hesitated, "stretch it. A little."

Rouge shook her head, then started to sit up, pausing as she realized that Aspen was kneeling beside her, his hand already reaching toward her, and a look of concern frozen on his rugged features. Carefully, she slid to the side, wincing as she tried to use her broken wrist, maneuvering so that she could bring herself into a more tolerable pose than 'sprawled out like a spatchcock chicken'.

Raising her trembling right hand, Rouge pointed at the text hovering in the air in front of her. Though it should be invisible to anyone but her, she was certain that Emily knew exactly what it said. "What is this? I knew I had to keep Aspen alive, but now me, too? And if I *do* die, someone else gets the quest? Plus, now Aspen can die, but if I don't, we could still win? *And*, what the heck is with *that guy*," she pointed accusingly at FantumHat, "having more than twice as much of the quest completed than I do?"

Emily smiled, just a bit. "I believe Gina told you once, long ago, that you needed to hurry or your enemies would get too far ahead of you. Certainly, defeating them by percentage quest completion would have been the simplest method. Unfortunately, that was the only warning she was allowed to give you, and you didn't really take her seriously. Now, the only way you can win is through direct confrontation, and," she shook her head, "I'm afraid you have very little chance of succeeding at that, either."

"So what?" Rouge demanded. "I'm just supposed to give up? Refuse this last quest and take off with what I've gained so far? Let some other player give it a shot?"

The avatar tilted her head. "That would make the most sense. You have gained a unique class already, which was the thing you most desired. And, though I mean no offense by this, you are not particularly powerful. If you refuse the quest, you lose nothing, and your side will, perhaps, have a greater chance at success with someone else in your position."

Rouge felt like someone had kicked her in the chest. Again. "Do you," she had to clear her throat before she could continue. "Do you know who the quest would be offered to, if I refused it?"

Emily nodded. "Of course. I cannot tell you who it is, but Bridget has repaired the error that allowed you to be selected, and the next player would be an adult, with a higher proficiency for battle."

Another boot to the chest. Rouge sucked in air through her teeth, tugging hard at her braid. "But they wouldn't *care*, would they? They wouldn't know the whole story. I mean, the story behind the quest. And they wouldn't care about Silus, and Aspen, and everyone else the way I do, would they?"

The blonde head tilted the other way. Her blue eyes were quizzical as they examined Rouge. "You don't have to stop helping, even if you don't accept. You can still try to protect those you care about. But the pressure wouldn't all be on you."

A sudden desperation bloomed in Rouge's heart, and she clutched at the life-line the avatar offered. "That's true, isn't it? I mean, I would still be able to help. We'd just have to get Aspen, Silus, and Vonn out of here alive, and then I could go back to the way things were, and just help however I can. I've been doing my best," tears were suddenly streaming down her face again, "but it's *so much*. I'm just… a kid." She hiccupped and swiped at her eyes with the back of her good hand. "I'm gonna start school in a few weeks, and I won't be able to be here much anyway, and they'd have someone better to fight FartHat over there."

Emily nodded, and touched Rouge's hand gently with her own. "It's okay. It's all right if you can't handle it. Just give up, and someone else will-"

"Get away from her."

Rouge's head snapped around so fast she would have sworn her neck popped. Mai Ley stood there, silken black hair blowing in an unfelt breeze, pale eyes glacial as they stared at Emily.

Emily clicked her tongue with a clear *tch* of annoyance, and turned away from Rouge, looking at Mai Ley, who was glaring with more actual emotion than Rouge had ever seen her show before. "Come on," Emily said, waving a hand toward Rouge dismissively, "like you wouldn't have done the same thing, given the opportunity. Not that it would work, since our champion wasn't selected by a broken bit of code."

Rouge's chest felt like it was filled with ice, but it began to melt just a bit when Mai Ley frowned and stepped forward to stand between Emily and Rouge. "The code was only 'broken' in that it failed to take into account other people's preconceptions. Rouge is the champion Gina chose, and she has no regrets."

Emily's slender finger stabbed into the '78%' completion next to FantumHat's name. "No regrets? *None*? Even though your champion is a child who failed to even get your primary back to the conflict-region for *months*?" Her voice, which had just been a little scratchy, was shifting. Emily's clear, almost newscaster-perfect tones were giving way to a richer, deeper sound, with a huskiness verging on hoarse.

The avatar reached up and flipped her hair out of its perfect bun. As it fell in gleaming strands that mirrored the length of Mai Ley's, it also turned utterly white, falling around suddenly bare shoulders the color of old charcoal. Red-orange eyes turned to Rouge, and gleaming black lips split in a predatory smile, revealing rows of sharp teeth that would have made Jesiqa the shark-girl proud.

The woman (who was clearly *not* Emily, though the shape of her face and eyes, as well as her height and build, still matched both Emily and Mai Ley) stepped around Mai Ley as if she wasn't there. She crouched down beside Rouge, trailing long fingers over the girl's jaw. "You don't even want to do this any more, do you, little girl? Wouldn't it be lovely to just be able to log in and out whenever you want? Just play with little Lyrec again, and help Aspen here," she flipped a finger at the frozen farmer contemptuously, "just for *fun*? After all, it is a *game*, isn't it? You shouldn't have to be frightened, or worried, or guilty just because of a game, should you?"

Mai Ley's pale hand swept the new woman's dark gray one aside. Then all that Rouge could see was the deep black of Mai Ley's robe as the priestess planted herself firmly in front of Rouge, leaving no room for not-Emily to reach the girl. Rouge tried to speak, but her voice was still locked in her throat, and she felt as though she was rooted in place.

Not-Emily hissed, then a rustle of fabric touched Rouge's ears before light, quick steps moved away. Mai Ley softened her stance, and Rouge could just see the strange woman moving around. The simple, tailored pantsuit Emily had been wearing was long gone. Swirling folds of orange ombre fabric teased the eye as not-Emily moved, revealing a flash of bare midriff, then a slender calf or a toned bicep.

"Fine, fine," the rough voice growled. "Let her make her choice. I was just trying to make our game a little more interesting. With this one as your champion, the sport is done, the amusement ended. It was bad enough you selected a powerless *farmer* as your king, forcing him to build everything you have from nothing, but then you allowed this thief to become your hero."

Apricot eyes glittered as the woman tapped her teeth with a long, silver fingernail. "Did you know, *snippet*, that our champion had nearly 20% of the quest done within a day? Simply because we chose a better king." She tilted her head toward Chester, whose flickering white-flame eyes were the only thing still moving in this space of locked time.

Rouge's eyes snapped to Mai Ley, who still looked slightly angry, but not defensive at all. She couldn't help the words that burst from her throat. "What?

That's cheating!"

Mai Ley shook her head slowly, her own barely-blue eyes calm as they met Rouge's hazel ones. "It was necessary. In order for *our* king to understand the hearts of those he must rule, he had to walk among them." She stepped to the side and gently touched Aspen's shoulder, smiling slightly as she looked into his worried face. "He loves you, you know. Isn't that better than being a disposable piece? There is nothing replaceable about you, nor him, and that is the way it should be."

She was right. Aspen was irreplaceable, and *so was Rouge*. They were a team. Even if Rouge gave up now, faced with seemingly insurmountable odds, she would never stop trying to help Aspen and her other friends, she would just have very little power to actually do so. Rouge's lips quirked in a mirror of Aspen's favorite expression as a famous quote about power and responsibility drifted through her mind.

Without further thought, Rouge selected 'Yes', then smiled at Mai Ley. "'Come what sorrow can, it cannot countervail the exchange of joy,'" the elf-girl murmured. "I won't give up because I'm afraid of what may happen. Plus," she climbed to her feet, glaring at their new enemy, "I don't know who you are, lady, but you don't know me, or you'd know calling me a little girl *just pisses me off.*"

Both women stopped, momentarily as frozen as the rest of the scene. Both sets of eyes flashed to where the text of the quest was fading away, and then Mai Ley smiled even as not-Emily scowled. "Fine," again with the disdainful little finger-flick. "Enjoy the rest of your little family love-fest." She smirked. "However long it lasts."

Rouge blinked, and the world jerked back into motion.

Aspen's hand dropped to where Rouge should have been, and he looked very surprised when she wasn't there. Motte's great axe swung at FantumHat, whose body burst into smoke and swirled away. Vonn fired an arrow that also whiffed through the smoke, trailing tendrils of mist as it buried itself in the clawed wooden foot of the throne.

Darn it! I should have gotten in position before I clicked that button! Rouge took a long step back over to Aspen, ducking under the hand he still had extended.

"Heal, please?" she managed to grin at him, and if it was a bit shaky, well, who could blame her?

Relief flooded his face, and the warmth of healing filled her body.

Broken Rib (1) **has been [Healed] through divine power!**
Broken Rib (2) **has been [Healed] through divine power!**
Broken Wrist (Left) **has been [Healed] through divine power!**

Then Aspen pulled two long, curved, double-bladed knives from where they'd been tucked into his belt and pressed them into her hands. "Vonn told us you Travelers couldn't use your inventory here, so Motte gave me these before we entered. Vonn also mentioned you were facing a vampire, so I used [Mage Smithing] to make a small adjustment to them." One long finger touched the groove in the center of each blade, and Rouge saw that there was a splinter of wood nestled in each depression. "It should come out when you stab something, so…"

Rouge grabbed the knives, then flashed a totally-not-shaky grin at her friend. "How strong are you, these days, Aspen?"

It took a moment for the farmer to understand what she wanted him to do, but then he nodded, and the two of them sprinted for the throne. Around them, battle continued. Motte was swinging his axe in seemingly random patterns, though Rouge recognized them as katas her dad had learned in college and still periodically practiced when he was trying to 'get in shape'. Fortunately, FantumHat didn't know the patterns, so every time he *poofed* back to try to hit Motte, he had to *puff* right back out to avoid either a massive blade coming at him or one of Vonn's arrows.

Meanwhile, King Chester was just hanging back, watching all of this with an impassive expression. Honestly, not that surprising, since a skull didn't exactly have a lot of ability to emote. Since the king wasn't talking or moving, Rouge had no way to tell what he was thinking. She shook her head slightly as she bounded up the stairs to the dais. No time for him now. She had to focus on what she was doing!

Aspen's long legs made the step up onto the throne an easy one, and then his hands were cupped and waiting. Rouge jumped lightly from the seat of the throne, to the arm, then set her right foot in Aspen's hands. The tall man threw her as hard as he could, and Rouge added her own strength to leap straight up as high as she could.

Eight steps at something like eight inches each. The seat of a tall throne; about twenty inches. A tall man with his arms fully extended; 84 inches. By Rouge's rough calculations, she was already around fourteen feet from the floor by the time she soared into the air. Thanks to the ridiculous proportions of these rooms, the ceiling was easily twenty feet high. Actually, since she was still going up, maybe twenty-five?

Her fingers tapped the ceiling, and she curved her body as she continued moving upwards. Her behind hit the ceiling, then her feet, and for an instant she was actually *sitting on the ceiling*. She pushed her body back down, beginning the cascade of spells and skills that she desperately hoped would get them all out of here alive.

[Poof!!]

[Stealth]

[Aerial Acrobatics]

Then she fell fifteen feet, and [Poison Rain] lit up on her spell list. She was already below Aspen's head, but still above the battlefield on the ground level. When the cloud of darkness formed above them, Motte instantly realized what was going on. By the time the blades began to fall, he already had his shield above his head and was racing for Vonn.

FantumHat, fortunately, hadn't seen this trick before. Of course, not a single one of the blades pouring down were likely to do any real damage to him. Undead were generally resistant or even immune to poison, and a glancing blow from one of her knives would likely do little more than scratch him, but still, he would have to…

There! The vampire had reappeared outside the circle of falling, gleaming metal. He was behind Motte and Vonn, reaching for them with a cocksure grin. In real life, the best she could do was try throwing her knives and hope one connected. But, of course, this wasn't real life.

[Shadow Glide]

Her course abruptly changed, and she was suddenly shooting at a sharp angle away from her previous trajectory. [Shadow Glide] was *meant* to allow you to travel more quickly along the ground, and even if she wanted to move vertically, its five-foot step generally wasn't enough to lift her high enough off the ground to do very much. The skill's one second cooldown didn't seem like much, but when you were falling, it was enough to drop you right back down to where you started, so you'd never be able to do anything so cheaty as to fly with it. But, if you didn't want to *move* so much as change your angle without loss of momentum…

Rouge was suddenly coming at FantumHat with all the accumulated force of a twenty-foot drop. She clenched her knives in her hands and selected [Pterion Puncture] from the hotlist of skills that lined the bottom of her vision.

Warning: Player *FantumHat* is your Adversary. Instant kill attacks cannot be dealt to an Adversary. Attack reduced to Critical wound. CRITICAL! You have dealt 163 points of damage to Player *FantumHat*.

[Repeat]!

CRITICAL! You have dealt 163 points of damage to Player *FantumHat*.

CRITICAL! You have dealt 163 points of damage to Player *FantumHat*.

CRITICAL! You have dealt 163 points of damage to Player *FantumHat*.

CRITICAL! You have dealt 163 points of damage to Player *FantumHat*.

CRITICAL! You have dealt 163 points of damage to Player *FantumHat*.

Player *FantumHat* **is** *Stunned*.

Rouge cursed as she tumbled to the ground, thrown off balance by the collapse of her enemy. Her hip and right elbow impacted the ground hard. Why was there no 'defeated' message? How many hit points could he possibly have? Motte was almost level 100 and had put more than half of his points into health, and he only had around 1500 hp. How could *this* guy, who had obviously focused on Dexterity and Strength, have over a thousand health?

You have taken 57 points of falling damage.
You have a *Cracked Pelvis.*

Almost as quickly as the notifications popped up, she felt warmth wash through her and a new notice took their place.

Cracked Pelvis **has been [Healed] through divine power!**

She flashed a grateful smile at Aspen, who had obviously raced to her side the moment she fell, then jumped to her feet. "Let's go!" She held out her empty right hand toward her friends and pointed at the door with the dagger she still held in her left.

Vonn shot a confused glance from the fallen player to the skeleton, who still stood frozen where he had been when the four of them had burst into the throne room. "Shouldn't we save the king, too?" The elf took one step toward what he must see as a feeble man barely able to hold his head up under the weight of his own crown.

"Oh, heck no!" Rouge reached out and grabbed Vonn's hand, tugging him toward the door.

Aspen, too, looked conflicted, but Motte, who knew Rouge far better than the other two, reached out and grabbed his friend's arm. "Come on!" the large warrior growled, and Rouge was fairly certain that if Aspen didn't come quietly, he was going to be carried out.

"I'll explain later!" she shouted. "Run *now*!"

They ran.

Chapter Eleven

Aspen

A s they ran, Aspen's mind frantically turned over the events of the last half hour or so. Getting into the hidden, labyrinthine mess of passages had actually been the easy part. Motte had recognized the lock as a kind of puzzle he'd run into before. There were multiple keys to the same door, but each key was spelled so that it led to a different location. Once they realized that, they had simply tried unlocking the door with each key until it opened into a hallway Vonn recognized.

Just before they entered, Vonn mentioned that Rouge had told him she was unable to use silent communication or her magical inventory. A quick check revealed that that was true for Motte as well, so they stepped back out into the main area so that Motte could pull out his axe and shield. Aspen had also taken two daggers, to which he had added slivers reluctantly offered up by Stick, thus making them effective against vampires.

From there, Vonn retraced his steps using [Perfect Navigation], hoping that they might see a clue as to Rouge's whereabouts along the way. Honestly, that part had been pretty easy as well. As soon as Motte and Aspen saw the huge, elaborate door down a hall just a few turnings in, they instantly knew that Rouge, with her insatiable curiosity, would have been utterly unable to resist it.

Indeed, as they drew nearer, they could actually hear angry yelling even through the solid wood of the door.

"-given you... power... murder and torment- " came one voice, which was vaguely familiar to Aspen even as muffled as it was.

Another voice answered. "-except *the* one!"

Vonn's face instantly twisted into a mask of fury. "FantumHat!" the boy hissed. After that, things moved very quickly. Motte hadn't even bothered trying the door. He simply used [Battering Ram] to plow straight through it, nearly running over Rouge, who was lying on the floor, clearly injured. Fortunately, the big man had been able to adjust his angle to avoid her, though he'd nearly taken out a support column in the process.

Motte had directed a flurry of blows at the vampire, who had avoided them by misting in and out of his solid state, but at least that had effectively kept their greatest foe at bay. Or at least Aspen had thought the vampire would be their strongest foe, until he looked up from where he was crouching over Rouge, ready to heal her, and met the white-fire eyes of the only other occupant of the room.

Lich Lord Akuji.

Impossibly, though undeniably, the being standing there was the Undying King of Suffering, the undead lord whose army had ravaged every inch of humanity's territory until he met his death, spitted on his own wicked blade. A blade held by Aspen, or rather Iorgas Penbrooke, Duke of the North, Hero of the Battle of Bright, Master Necromancer, Atae's Left Hand, *Hozinte ssa'kinte.*

Oh, this version of Akuji was shorter, much smaller than the nearly eight-foot-tall form seemingly carved from the bones of giants and gods. The white fire had been silver, then, and his garments had consisted of sweeping black velvet robes adorned with silver and ruby sigils instead of what was, horribly, instantly recognizable as King Chester's favorite red velvet and ermine cloak.

As Aspen's topaz eyes met the skeleton's pale fire-lit eye sockets, the world stilled, and words appeared before him.

Congratulations! You have discovered your true opponents! The Great Goddess Gina is depending upon you to fulfill your ultimate role as her Champion.

Quest: "Did You Really Think It Was That Easy?" begun.

Somehow, Lich Lord Akuji has transcended death itself. Until you discover how, he cannot be defeated. You must destroy Akuji and his minions again, this time completely. Learn Akuji's secret and send him and the Traveler FantumHat to Atae's embrace.

Success: Live, and be blessed by all the Gods on the side of Light.

Failure: Death, and the deaths of all those you love.

Aspen's chest tightened, and for the length of four breaths or a million, he was in an entirely different place. Instead of the merely mortal throne in front of them, he saw the mountainous pile of twisted bones that had made up Akuji's original seat. The osseous edifice had towered well over twenty feet high, and the death toll required so that the lich king could build it was horrific.

The revulsion Iorgas had felt for that monument to Akuji's cruelty was nothing, though, compared to the heart-rending agony caused by the sight of what lay on the bare dirt floor in front of the dreadful chair. Lark. *His* Lark. His precious Birdie, dead and lost, long chestnut hair drenched in filth, and her too-solemn caramel eyes staring sightlessly into the distance.

It was a scene that played itself out in his nightmares, keeping him from rest for weeks after he was hauled out of that charnel pit more dead than alive. Every time he closed his eyes, Lark's face was all he could see. Sometimes her eyes were alive in her dead face, and she would stare at him accusingly, silently condemning him for the cowardice that led to his capture and her own death.

The only thing that had given him some peace was the surety that Lich Lord Akuji had followed her into oblivion almost immediately. And now, here he was. Back from the Chaos Pool, if he had ever gone there at all. Not as formidable as his former self, perhaps, but as solid as he had ever been. Worse, it was obvious that he had somehow taken King Chester's place. That foolish, simple man had been a poor friend and a terrible king, but he had still been a million times better than Akuji, and now he was probably as dead as Lark.

Aspen felt his fist clench in the air where he had been reaching for Rouge's fallen form. His body grew hot as it filled with hatred-fueled mana, and he would swear that his hair must be lifting from his scalp, blown in sweltering winds.

A cool, soft hand touched his arm gently, and the fire within him was instantly quenched. "Not now," Gina murmured, stepping gracefully into the space between Aspen and Akuji. Aspen's body locked up, muscles fixed in place, unable to do more than watch as his goddess strode forward, filmy green gown billowing behind her.

The shadow behind Akuji's diminished form stretched and swirled, glowing black and red until it coalesced into the hulking figure of a man. Tall and broad enough to tower over even Motte, the man was inhumanly muscled, with chiseled features, a mane of shoulder-length golden hair, and blue eyes so bright Aspen didn't think he'd ever seen such a color before.

When he spoke, his voice boomed out in something that was a bizarre mockery of the manner in which nobles and courtiers sometimes spoke in an attempt to cow the commoners around them. The only other person Aspen had ever heard speak in such a way was the Traveler girl, Flu-flu, and his brain stuttered over the implications of that. "Ho, Gina! Fair Goddess! At last, you show yourself before me! I have issued a hundred, nay, a thousand invitations, and yet you have spurned them all!"

Gina's voice was sharper than Aspen had ever heard it before, and he was acutely grateful for the paralysis she had placed on him, since without it, he would have tumbled to the ground in shock.

"Shut up, *Apofis*. I don't know who has his hand up your rear end, you muscle-bound chump, but you need to let my people go *right now*."

The impossibly handsome face showed comically over-blown shock, and a thick-fingered hand clapped to the broad chest that was covered only by a single piece of white cloth that draped from left shoulder across to the right side of the narrow but heavily-muscled waist and hips. "Gina! The manner in which you speak ill-befits such a lovely lady as yourself-"

Gina cut him off again with a distinctly unladylike snort. "Cut the crap, jerk. I know you've been cheating since the beginning. I couldn't prove it before, but your weaselly little Champion finally crossed the line when he used the Coma Protocols on Rouge. You *know* those are experimental, and *only* to be used on the Kings. What were you *thinking*? You could have hurt her!"

Apofis' head whipped around to look at FantumHat, and he scowled fiercely, revealing a mouth full of gleaming, dagger-sharp teeth. "He did *what?* I told him not to-" He clamped his lips tight on whatever he was about to say, but it was too late to take back the words, and Aspen could see Gina's shoulders relax a fraction as the other god all but admitted fault.

"You *told* him, huh? But why does he have that capability in the first place? It's GM-level stuff, and you know it! You have to have coded it in so he could do it, and you'd better fix that *right now*, or our deal is off!" The goddess's hands were fisted on her hips now, and Aspen could imagine the glare she was giving the towering god before her. He would have smiled in pride if he could.

"Fine!" A bulky arm swept toward FantumHat, and a medallion at the Traveler's throat vanished. "It's your fault for letting your pieces plod around for so long. If you'd been pushing them like I have mine- "

Again, the little goddess didn't let the other god finish his speech. "I would have broken them, just like you have yours. Look at him." A slim finger pointed to FantumHat's frozen face. His expression was furious, and his pale eyes were crazed. "You can't tell me there's not something wrong with him. Plus," she turned the accusatory digit toward Akuji, "is that seriously what you were going for?"

Aspen looked, *really* looked, at the Lich Lord. Without preconceptions, without the veil of the undead king's former self drawn over this current iteration.

Yes, Aspen had seen that the monster was shrunken, but it hadn't really sunk in just how diminished he truly was. His bones looked frail and brittle, yellowed in the bright, clear light of the glowstones scattered around the room. One premolar was actually missing, and a spider-web of cracks traced the visibly fragile temporal bone.

Apofis scowled again. "It's fine. He just has to survive longer than your puny pawns. Plus, it's not like they can actually kill him anyway. As long as he can reincarnate, I'll win this thing. He won't need to, though, because FantumHat over there is a death-dealing machine! As soon as you release the GM lock, he's going to crush all of these wimps, and then you'll have to come begging to me for- "

Gina's finger ticked slowly backed and forth. "Ah ah ah! I believe you're forgetting something, *Apofis*." She waved gracefully, and a scroll appeared to hover in front of her, unrolling into yards of parchment until she came to the part she was looking for. She tapped her finger on a few words, and they lit up in gold fire.

"And I quote. A-*hem*. 'In case either side shall be proven to have violated this contract, a forfeit shall be granted to the victim. The severity of the forfeit shall be equivalent to the severity of the violation.' Now, I ask you," she tapped the scroll again, and it rolled up and popped back out of existence. "Do I need to go to Virac with this, or can we figure things out between the two of us, right here, right now?"

Apofis' sharp teeth ground together so fiercely that actual sparks flew from his mouth. "*We can handle it now*," the god rumbled furiously.

Gina's voice was all syrupy sweetness as she said, "Oh, *good*. I had hoped you'd see it my way." Her tone turned to steel and fire. "Now let my people *go*."

The looming god's mouth dropped open, and his lips flapped twice, like those of a fish that found itself unexpectedly out of water. "*What*? No! Maybe the girl, since she was the one who- "

Gina's hand twitched, and a bright red button appeared in the air beside her. It was nearly six inches across, and large white letters were printed on it: PRESS IN CASE OF EMERGENCY. Without hesitation, the slender fingers began moving toward the inviting switch.

"**NO!**" Aspen's ears rang from the force of the bellow, and he winced internally. Gina's hand paused just above the button.

"*Fine*," Apofis grumbled. "I'll keep my King out of it *just for today*, as long as yours does nothing to directly injure either of my pieces. We'll skew the odds in your girl's favor, and I'll make sure they have a chance to escape. Just a *chance*. It wasn't that big of a violation." He muttered the last, sounding like a spoiled little boy who'd been caught with his hand in the cookie jar.

Gina twitched at that, and her strawberry-blonde tresses whipped in a sudden furious wind. "It's a deal, then." She still sounded mocking, but not nearly as triumphant as Aspen thought she should have. After all, the odds of all of them escaping alive had been essentially zero before she stepped in, and now it sounded like they were guaranteed survival so long as they took the opportunity.

The goddess turned her back sharply on the other god, and when Aspen saw her face, she was biting her lip fiercely, and he felt a pang pierce his heart. Lark had often had an expression like that when she was worrying over a particularly ill patient. When Gina's rainbow eyes met his, however, she smiled tiredly. Stepping to his side, she crouched before him so she could gently rest a hand over his heart.

"Reveal nothing of what you have heard," her voice whispered in his mind. "He believes you as sealed as the others. Act exactly as you otherwise would, but *remember this when the time comes.*"

She disappeared, and time resumed.

He healed Rouge, then helped the girl with her madcap plan, throwing her toward the ceiling, knowing as he did that she would somehow succeed. Once her poisoned blades began to fall, he dodged around them, coming to a halt at her side after she struck FantumHat a ferocious blow. He quickly sent prayers and mana into her body, healing the brilliant points of pain that afflicted her again.

When Rouge stood and grabbed Vonn's hand, pulling him after her, Aspen hesitated, looking at the still form of his old enemy. If it wouldn't violate the word of his Goddess, he could simply strike the monster down and be done with it. Except it clearly wouldn't be 'that easy', so when Motte's gauntlet closed on his arm, he let his friends lead him away.

Chapter Twelve

Rouge

A s soon as they ran out of the green door that concealed the cultist's hideout (for now), Motte and Rouge both whistled for their mounts. A mount would come to its master when called, but how quickly the animal responded depended entirely on the relationship between beast and owner. A mediocre relationship allowed the mount to wander for a minute or two after being called.

Most players maintained their mount's relationship at around 40-70 (Cordial-Helpful) through simply petting, stabling, and feeding it occasionally. As a result, it was rare to see a 'loose' mount in the city. Both Codswallop and Motte's horse, Rosalind, were at 90-100 relationship points, though, and they would travel to Rouge and Motte as quickly as they possibly could. Now that Wally looked like a horse, he wouldn't attract *too* much attention as he ran through the city, right? (Though she had to wince a little as she thought about his 'horse' form. Poor guy looked like the random appearance generator hit him with an ugly stick.)

Rosalind appeared before they went two blocks, but since Rouge could tell they were in the Temple district, Wally would have a much longer distance to travel. "We need to get home,:: Rouge gasped. ::FantumHat went a bunch of people there to kill everyone!"

Four voices spoke simultaneously.

"I already told them," Vonn answered, jogging alongside her.

::Lyrec went to warn them: Aspen said.

::Why aren't you in bed?:: Motte asked.

::Are you mad at me?:: Silus sounded miserable, so Rouge answered her first.

::Silus, no! Why would I be mad at you?::

::I couldn't help you. I just let you be captured, and then I couldn't even get out to let anyone know where you were. I was *useless*!:: The bat wailed pathetically.

::You weren't! You helped during the fight against the monsters, and it's not your fault you can't open doors! You're also the best scout *ever*!::

::You also helped us figure out where the underground complex actually is,:: Aspen put in. ::We couldn't access it without risking you and Rouge, but now that you're safe, that information is invaluable.::

::You did? Wow!:: Rouge hoped her little friend could hear how impressed she was.

::Well,:: Silus sounded dubious, but also slightly more confident. ::I guess that was good. It's not like I *tried* to do that, though.::

::But if you hadn't had the patience to wait, if you'd tried to attack instead of being wise enough to know when you were outmatched, if you'd been captured, or...:: Aspen's voice choked off. ::Well, you made choices that led to your survival, Rouge's survival, and our ability to attack the enemy base without their knowledge. Wisdom is more often found in quiet choices than brash ones.::

::I guess that's true.:: Silus definitely sounded better now. ::Next time, I'm going to bite someone, though!::

Everyone except Vonn laughed. The wood elf just shook his head, already used to being left out of these silent conversations.

Then Codswallop came racing down the street, launching himself over the heads of pedestrians and leaping from cart to cart, bugling as he ran. Cries of dismay and amazement followed him, and Rouge could see more than one player raising a hand in the classic L shape that meant they were framing a screenshot. When the ostrich saw Rouge, he actually redoubled his efforts, and his final leap (from the back of a particularly large draft horse) sent him sailing well over twenty feet through the air to land on the cobblestones in front of his mistress. His clawed feet scratched the stones as he landed, and everyone nearby winced at the *screeeeech* of the nails-on-a-chalkboard sound. (No one actually used chalkboards any more, but the sound was one that parents everywhere still used to torment their children, and vice versa.)

With a final, self-satisfied cluck, Codswallop burrowed his head beneath Rouge's braids. Face flaming, she stroked the soft feathers on his shoulders. "I'm glad to see you, too, Wally." After a last hug, she pulled back and looked into the big bird's liquid brown eyes. "Now, we need to get home. Fast. Can you carry Vonn?"

The ostrich eyed the wood elf for a long moment, then bobbed his head. "Great!" Rouge pulled herself up into Wally's saddle, then reached down for Vonn. As the elf settled behind her (she thought her cheeks were going to *burn off*, she was blushing so much), she looked over at Motte and Aspen.

::Can Rosalind carry you both?:: To her surprise, both men nodded confidently, though Aspen's ears were almost as red as she thought hers must be, and Motte refused to meet her eyes. Weird, but whatever. ::Um, okay then. Meet you there!::

☙ ☙ ☙

Amazingly, when they arrived at the house, they found the rusty, overgrown gate had been forced wide open, but there were no sounds of battle or distress from within. Two wagons, drawn by sturdy oxen, were trundling away down the street, while another two stood ready to receive their load of refugees, orphans, and whatever goods their passengers were carrying with them. Plum, holding the hands of two little scamps of indeterminate age and gender, stood directing the flow of traffic.

When she saw Aspen slide down from Motte's mount (with slightly more haste than was strictly necessary) Plum directed the two children into the wagon in front of her, and hurried over. "My lord! Thank Gina! I was so afraid you wouldn't make it in time!"

Aspen was looking over the carts with an utterly bemused expression. "What," he asked finally, "is going on?"

Tomas, his nearly-bald, wrinkled, tanned head gleaming in the morning light, hurried over as quickly as his ancient legs would allow. (Seriously, Rouge was pretty sure Tomas was at least a hundred, even though, mathematically speaking, as Plum's grandfather he was more likely to be no more than seventy or so.) "Lord Aspen!" the old groundskeeper exclaimed. "Welcome home! I've done just as you said!"

"And what," Aspen said weakly, "was that, exactly?"

Tomas grinned, showing more teeth than Rouge was really comfortable with, especially after her recent experiences. "Why, you put your faith in me at last, my lord! Y'told me to do whatever was needed, and so I have!"

Plum shot her grandfather a censuring look, then turned back to Aspen. "You *did* tell him that this was all right, didn't you, Lord Aspen? You were so against it before, but grandfather insisted..." She trailed off uncertainly.

Aspen coughed a little. "I suppose, if you looked at it from a certain perspective, I did. But could you, ah, just, go over it with me again?"

Rouge bounced down from Codswallop's back and nudged her way in between Aspen and the others. "Never mind all that! This looks great, Plum! Keep doing it! Everybody out, hustle, hustle!" She took hold of the older girl's shoulders and turned her around, giving her a little push. After an ambivalent glance back, Plum nodded and went back to work, leaving Tomas behind.

Rouge turned to the old man. "Didn't Lyrec make it back here? Where is he? Did he tell you that there are attackers coming from the woods at *any second?*"

Tomas waved dismissively. "Oh, those fools. They started straggling in about thirty minutes ago." He paused, looking thoughtful. "Maybe forty? I don't think twas an hour, because we were still feeding the children breakfast then…"

Rouge suppressed an urge to shake the ancient geezer and just gritted out, "Talk. About. The. *'Fools'*!"

Tomas chortled a little. "They started showing up just after your friend Lyrec got here. We were all in the kitchen, and they were screamin' and scratching at themselves, so it was like shootin' fish in a barrel. Your caravanner friends are excellent shots, m'lord, so once everyone had a bow and a position at a second story window, we just picked them off as they staggered out into the open."

At this, Aspen first smiled, then grinned, then finally started laughing out loud. At first, Rouge thought he had finally snapped, but then she realized that he was laughing out of sheer relief that everyone was safe. She found herself smiling, too, picturing the cocky players who had probably thought that attacking this place was going to be the easiest experience points they'd gotten since the tutorial. If they really were being killed that easily, it was great, though she wasn't sure exactly *why* it was happening.

So, she asked.

Aspen had a few false starts, as laughter broke through when he tried to answer, but finally he managed to reply. "The former prisoners, especially the children, were covered in fleas, ticks, and various parasites when we rescued them." Anger flickered across his face at the memory, and wiped away the last of his laughter, returning him to the serious expression that was much more familiar to Rouge.

"When we brought them home, I 'asked' all the insects to get off and stay in the woods. I planned to go back and gather them up, maybe take them to the house of, ah, an old acquaintance or two." He looked slightly embarrassed at this confession, but Rouge just grinned. That sounded like her kind of vengeance.

"In any case, in exchange for their cooperation, I gave them all a little boost of mana. Just something to keep them going until they found a new food source, but they're likely all quite, er, *large*, now. I also gave the woods a good bit of support in regrowing some areas that had been beaten down into paths, and 'encouraged' some thorny bushes I saw along the way. I figured it was only a matter of time until someone followed one of us back, and I could talk to the plants tomorrow – today – to explain who they should let by, and who they shouldn't."

Aspen rubbed his hand over the back of his neck, looking a little sheepish. "It looks like I inadvertently laid a trap, and when Vonn directed FantumHat's forces in that way, they set it off. No doubt the ones who made it through were infested with insects, and there are undoubtedly more roaming in the woods, lost."

Rouge was giggling now, too. "So, all of those low-level players and cultists that FannyHat sent, thinking this place would be full of children and non-combatants, got *eaten alive* by accidental super-bugs that were only there because they didn't take better care of their prisoners? So. Much. Karma!"

Aspen's mouth kicked up into his wry half-smile. "It does seem to have worked out well. Perhaps we should all offer up a prayer of thanks to Gina." One eyebrow hitched up, and she had a feeling there was something he wasn't saying, but… Oh well, time to get on with things.

She turned back to Tomas. "Where is Lyrec, then?"

"And the babe he was carrying!" Vonn put in almost desperately.

::And does anyone have food?:: Silus asked wistfully.

Tomas, of course, couldn't hear the little bat, but Rouge produced a large bag of peas left over from Aspen's farm and poured some into her palm. The brilliant green pearls gleamed brighter than Tomas's shiny pate, and Silus instantly climbed out of Aspen's collar and glided over to land on Rouge's wrist. The bat was too large to sit in Rouge's hand while she ate, but her cheeks were soon bulging with sweet peas nonetheless.

"The *baby*," Vonn insisted, edging toward the house.

Tomas nodded toward Plum. "The babe is with the others too small to walk. Miss Millie and young Master Struthio took them in the first wagon. They're probably already out of the city."

The elf's hands fisted in his brown curls. "Out of the *city*?" he whimpered.

"Aye, well, that's the best place for the little ones, isn't it? Just the oldest and the strongest left now, and Restur's people, who are gathering supplies for the trip." Tomas looked extremely self-satisfied.

"Trip?" Aspen's voice was suspicious, and his eyes were narrow. "*What* trip?"

"Why the trip north, of course, my lord. To our new home."

Rouge clapped a hand over her mouth as she remembered Aspen mentioning that he'd left Tomas behind to take care of things. 'Do whatever needs to be done', or something like that. Apparently, the wily old man had been doing exactly what everyone had been encouraging Aspen to do and getting ready to send *everyone* up north to Refuge Farm. Or maybe just Refuge now? If everyone was going, that would put the population at nearly a hundred, which was more than enough to be a village in game terms.

Suddenly, she felt a large hand land on her shoulder. Twisting her neck, she looked up into Motte's grim face. Gulping, she smiled weakly.

Motte looked over to Aspen, who was now looking as flustered as Vonn. "Aspen," he growled, "am I to take it that we're no longer needed?"

Aspen turned to face them, looking like an animal caught in a trap, but then he sighed, deflating. "Apparently not," he said. "At least not immediately. You need to go?"

Motte nodded. Firmly. "If Lyrec is still here, please send him away as well.

I know his parents, and they wouldn't want him up this late," he hesitated, and Rouge could practically see him swallowing the words 'playing a game', "when he should be sleeping."

Aspen offered a tired smile. "I understand. I'll find out."

"We'll have our Zombies follow, um, this wagon," Rouge put in, pointing at the last wagon, which was mostly filled with supplies. She smiled at her father hopefully, batting her lashes and trying to look as sweet and innocent as possible. Nooooone of this was her fault. Nope, not at all.

Motte raised a brow to let her know he wasn't buying her act, but a small smile touched his lips before he could hide it. "Fine. Then good luck, Aspen. We'll see you soon. Though not," he looked meaningfully at Rouge, "*too* soon." Then his eyes went dark, and his Zombie walked over and climbed up on Rosalind, bringing the mare around to trail the rear of the wagon by exactly six feet.

Rouge smiled weakly at Aspen. "Um, thank you for, you know, coming to rescue me today. Don't mind Motte, he's just really grumpy because finals are over and now he has to grade papers for a week."

Aspen raised a brow. "And his daughter was missing without an explanation."

She coughed a little. "Oh, uh, yeah. That, too. Anyway, see you soon!" She flashed him a little grin and a wave and logged out.

Chapter Thirteen

Aspen

Aspen watched Rouge's Zombie walk over to Codswallop, who nuzzled his head into her hair, and chirruped sadly when there was no response from his girl. Silus, who had flown back to Aspen when Rouge's spirit left her body, squeaked quietly. ::That's still creepy.::

He chuckled and leaned his jaw against her soft body. She was large enough now that she provided some real resistance, so he could give her stronger snuggles and scritches without worrying about injuring her. ::Shall we go find out what's actually going on here?::

::I guess so. I'm really, really sleepy, though.::

::I think it's safe for you to rest, little one. I wouldn't ask you to scout out the woods until I have a chance to talk with the trees, and tell them you're a friend. It's not safe for you to fly above them during the day, either. Not that you'd likely see much, since the foliage is quite, ah, *dense*.::

Silus giggled. ::Overdid it, did you?::

He ducked his head, smiling slightly. ::A little. I was very tired, and didn't have as much control of my mana as usual. I just wanted the infestation cleared from the prisoners before they entered the house, and the path behind us was practically inviting someone to explore. I knew I should be more careful, but I needed to get everyone home, and I thought I would have plenty of time to rectify any errors later.::

::That's okay.:: The bat rubbed her head affectionately against his cheek. ::Everybody makes mistakes.::

Aspen smiled, hearing an echo of his own words in hers. Truthfully, due to his exhaustion and his simple relief at nearly being home, his mana had been running out of him like a river overflowing its banks. He had known what he needed to do, and he'd simply done whatever it took to complete his task. For once, thankfully, it seemed that his error had had a positive result, but he couldn't count on that trend to continue. He knew from hard experience that his luck tended more to the bad than the good.

Turning to Tomas, who was still hovering nearby, watching Aspen with anxious eyes, Aspen sighed internally and forced a reassuring smile. "All right, Tomas, tell me what's going on."

The old man smiled happily at this sign that Aspen wasn't terribly displeased with him. "We've sent everyone out through the western gate, on the road toward North Goose, my lord. Restur and his caravan kindly agreed to escort us, since no one else is used to traveling outside Bright, though we did have to pay him a bit of a bonus, since he's missing the Traveler's Spring Triathlon Event."

Aspen groaned, rubbing his temples. "How *much* of a… No, let's circle back to that. There's no way you arranged all this since I left the house this morning. How long, exactly, have you been planning this little excursion?" He waved a hand toward the large, expensive-looking wagons, and the large, healthy, and very expensive-looking oxen.

Tomas tugged at the end of his nose, a habit he'd had for as long as Aspen had known him, and one which indicated that he was about to obfuscate the truth in 'the master's best interests'. "It was just a thought, my lord, just a thought. Restur and I, well, two old men will chatter on about things, and we may have discussed how nice it would be for an old, decrepit man like myself if there were a few more amenities up north. Since I *am* going with you, my lord, it seemed wise to plan out all the things a household might need."

Aspen rubbed his temples. "*A* household, Tomas? You have enough here for, let's see, a *town*. A town I believe I distinctly remember saying I didn't want. Plus, I already have a house."

Tomas' lip curled. "A *farmhouse*, my lord. Young Miss Rouge told me about it, and I'm certain it's not fit for one of your station, especially now that you're a duke. Indeed, though, only a few of the wagons were directly hired by me. Plum refused to allow me to go without her, and of course she has to take the children. Mistress Millie and Master Struthio decided that they preferred a quiet life to the bustle of the city, and since the children need to eat, they asked to come along as well, and work as a chef and handyman for the manor and orphanage. Then, of course, you brought home the *refugees*, and it was clear that non-humans were in danger in Bright, so most of 'em decided to leave as well. When they heard that we were going north to your lands, well, most of them wanted to come, so Master Restur loaned them the funds to hire their own wagons…"

Aspen groaned. "*Loaned*? At what interest rate? Against what collateral? How much profit is that crafty buzzard planning on making out of this mess?"

Tomas opened his mouth to reply, but Aspen waved him to silence. "Oh, I know, you're just an innocent bystander in all this. You were just doing your job." He pressed his fingers against his eyes, trying to ease the painful throbbing that was starting in his head. Then he remembered that he was a healer now, and sent a flush of [Heal] through his own body, instantly easing his rapidly multiplying aches and pains.

Feeling slightly better, though still somewhat frustrated and overwhelmed, he clapped a hand on Tomas' shoulder, sending a quick [Heal] to alleviate the red heat of inflammation in the old man's joints and back as long as he was at it. Tomas instantly stood taller, looking pleased.

"Shall I continue with the evacuation then, my lord? We don't want these wagons to fall too far behind the rest."

Aspen sighed. "Go ahead, old friend. But I want you on the last wagon. I know you're an excellent archer, but you can't move quickly any more, and when we leave-"

"Must you, my lord?" Tomas interrupted, then ducked his head when he realized what he'd done. "I'm sorry, I don't mean t' interrupt, it's just that... it's so final."

"That's why I called it the Final Option," Aspen chuckled darkly, then glanced back at the decrepit house behind them. "Without Birdie here, and with her hospital and the orphanage closed, there's nothing to bring me back. She would want me to help those in need, but it sounds like you've already taken care of that." His voice turned wry. "Though not in precisely the manner I would have preferred." A small smile creased the old groundskeeper's face, but he simply bowed his head as if accepting admonishment.

A loud shout rose from the house. "Reinforcements! Alas, my lord, come now, or all is lost!"

Aspen knew that voice. "Flu-flu?" He started running toward the house. When Tomas started after him, however, he paused to point firmly from the old man to the now-full wagon. "*Go.* That's an order, Tomas."

Rebellion flickered over the weathered features, but with a last glance at the house, the old man turned away and headed for the empty seat beside the waggoneer, who Aspen recognized as one of Restur's people. Nodding in satisfaction, Aspen began running again as the wheels of the wagon crunched away on the overgrown drive.

Inside, the house was in chaos. Furniture had been moved next to the front door, ready to block the passage of invaders if needed. Three pre-teens stood prepared to either attack or shove the furniture into place, and Aspen recognized them as Plum's most responsible trio of orphans; Jack, Lionel, and Ulie. Beside them, looking like he wasn't sure whether he should be terrified or thrilled, stood Jiminy, the skinny ventriloquist boy who had helped Aspen, Vonn, and Tessle draw the guard away from his post one very long night and day ago.

Aspen nodded to the four children, though his heart clenched at seeing them still here and in danger. "Go ahead and block the door. There's another way out, and once they realize they're coming in the hard way, they'll figure out how to get here soon enough. When you're done, head toward the dining room. *Do not* engage the enemy." The four nodded jerkily, and Plum's trio looked distinctly relieved. Aspen ruffled Jiminy's shaggy brown hair as he passed, offering the lad a wink and a reassuring smile.

At the top of the steps, Flu-flu waited, practically dancing in impatience. Her large, red-beaked bird glared at Aspen with his dark eyes as his mistress's words nearly tumbled over themselves. "The vile villains are coming in greater numbers now, my lord! I fear we shall soon be overrun! You must flee and take thy progeny with thee! I shall guard your back for so long as I am able!"

Lyrec poked his head out of a door to the right that led to a large lounging room with a balcony. "Fluff, come *on*! There are at least six of them who've made it through the forest now, and one of them is a player with a mage class. He looks itchy and pissed, and I think he's going to start lobbing spells any second now." The boy's blue eyes flickered to Aspen, and a slight flush touched his cheeks. "Oh, um, hi Aspen. Uh, welcome home?"

Aspen chose to ignore both Flu-flu's remark about progeny and Lyrec's obvious discomfort. He directed his attention toward the girl. "Thank you, Flu-flu. I've already told the children to come up to the dining hall as soon as they blockade the front door. I appreciate your offer to sacrifice yourself, but it won't be necessary."

Looking toward Lyrec, he continued, "Let everyone know they should stop defending the house. The non-combatants have fled, and the house is," he paused, looking around, then drew in a deep breath, "unimportant. I assume the kitchen and the windows along the back are already barricaded?"

Flu-flu nodded. "Indeed, Lord Aspen. Your most excellent manservant and m'lady Plum made certain that no entry was possible except through the front. But how shall we make a tactical withdrawal if all avenues of egress are impassable? Alas, I cannot spread the wings of my soul and carry us all from this imbroglio, though if the simple force of my desire 'twere enough…"

Aspen tuned the girl out. She meant well, but not only could she make any sentiment more dramatic than it needed to be, but she also had a tendency to use her fanciful phrases in ways that weren't *quite* right, and it hurt his brain. "Everyone still in the house needs to go upstairs. Use the handholds in the wall to get past the break in the stairs, but do *not* try to open the door at the top."

Curiosity momentarily flickered across the girl's pretty face before she struck a pose with one arm to point at the stairs, while the other hand lifted so that her first two fingers could form a V that bracketed her eye on the top and bottom. Her bird squawked irritably at this, but the girl was already proclaiming her willingness to do as Aspen had asked.

He shook his head and looked at the door through which Lyrec had already vanished. He wondered just how many people had stayed behind, and what condition they were in. If they were some of the former prisoners from the lab, as he suspected they might be, they wouldn't have recovered much stamina yet.

Sure enough, when the door opened again, the two mana-twisted elves stepped through. They clutched longbows, likely produced from Lyrec or Flu-flu's Traveler inventory, and their faces were drawn with exhaustion and worry. They both looked at Aspen as they drew closer, but only the feminine one ventured a smile, though she kept her lush lips closed tight.

Aspen motioned for Flu-flu to lead the way. The girl had finally finished monologuing and was standing at the bottom of the stairs all but bouncing on her toes. At his signal she bounded up the first steps. Just in time, the quartet of youngsters came up from below, red-faced and puffing with exertion. "The door's blocked, m'lord Aspen, sir!" Ulie chirped, looking like a little squirrel with her bright eyes and round cheeks.

The small group of defenders made their way upstairs as quickly as possible. When they reached the broken section of stairs, where Rouge had punched holes through the wallpaper to reveal the cunningly concealed handholds, the female elf, Flu-flu, and the children scurried across like monkeys. Lyrec struggled a little, but made it after Flu-flu went back halfway to help him. By the time they reached the far side, the boy was looking at the archer with a bright, worshipful gaze that Aspen dared to hope meant the young bard would soon have a more appropriate object for his affections.

Aspen himself was about to use Stick to vault across the gap as he had done several times now when he saw the cadaverous elf looking at the holes in the wall dubiously. The being's thin, elongated fingers, made even longer by an extra joint and the sharp, thick talons on the ends, wouldn't fit securely into the shallow apertures.

Cautiously, Aspen touched the pale arm of the stretched elf, noting that its skin was dry and vaguely pebble-textured, more like the skin of a reptile than human flesh. "Watch", he said quietly, then launched himself smoothly over the chasm. Swiftly, he reversed the action, arriving back beside the elf a moment later. Turning, he presented his back.

"Climb on. As slim as you are, you can't weigh much. I'll take you over." Indeed, the thin person seemed like they would blow away in a strong breeze, so Aspen was certain he could manage.

The elf seemed to think for a moment, then nodded once. Hesitantly, it climbed onto Aspen's back, wrapping arms around his shoulders and legs around his waist. Since it was nearly as tall as he was, it was a bit awkward, so he glanced back. "Tighter. It's all right."

Again, the being nodded, and the limbs tightened convulsively. Aspen bounced a few times until he was certain of his balance, then swung easily to the other side. The elf nearly leapt from his back the moment they touched down, though it hesitated before following the others up the last few stairs.

The spidery fingers gently touched its own hollow white chest, and the person spoke slowly. Immediately, Aspen saw the narrow, forked tongue and the needle-sharp fangs and understood why they were so reluctant to speak. "Not… sssssscared?"

Aspen just shook his head, smiling a little. "I've met many more frightening people than you, my friend. Now, let's hurry before one of those young idiots blows off a hand trying to open my door."

The reptilian being nodded, its tongue flickering out once in what Aspen chose to take as a silent laugh.

🐍 🐍 🐍

Aspen opened the door at the top of the stairs just as a series of resounding crashes echoed through the house. Far below, they could hear furniture tumbling to the ground, as wood cracked and groaned under some massive blow. The building itself seemed to shake, and the four children huddled together. Even Jiminy looked like he had finally decided to be more frightened than fascinated, and Aspen touched each of their shoulders reassuringly as they passed through the door before him.

Once everyone else was inside, Aspen turned back to the door. Pulling the last of the single-use wooden key medallions from a leather thong around his neck, he snapped it in half. With one half in each hand, he closed the door and pressed the broken medallion to nearly-undetectable depressions on each side of the door. With a quiet *click*, the door began to shine slightly in the light of Lyrec's glowstone.

"What did you do?" The young bard looked nervous as he glanced from the door and then around the room. Certainly, it didn't look like a good place for an escape, though someone might survive a short siege in fair comfort. Indeed, that had been Aspen's original intent, until he looted a certain item from the tent of one of Akuji's generals. It was somewhat ironic that that item would now save Aspen from Akuji's forces.

Aspen dropped the now-worthless pieces of wood on the floor, and turned back to the others. "I simply made certain that the next time someone tries to open that door, the entire house will explode." He smiled ferociously, briefly enjoying the look on the boy's face. Then he remembered that the others would be truly unnerved and hurried on. He looked around, meeting each of their gazes individually.

"Don't worry. We'll be long gone by the time they make their way up here. Setting this trap armed a few others as well, so we'll be able to tell," he paused as a dull thud followed by a muffled scream came from below, "where they are by what traps they set off. That was the kitchen, by the way."

"Now," he continued, "Lyrec and Flu-flu, I need one of you to carry a few final things for me, if you can?" At Flu-flu's enthusiastic nod, and Lyrec's more hesitant one, Aspen smiled. "Good. Come with me, then."

Within five minutes, during which a series of crashes, small explosions, and screams told him where the invaders were in the house, Aspen loaded the two Travelers down with everything he possibly could. He knew from talking to Rouge and Motte that a Traveler could put anything they could lift into their inventory, so he gave a few light things to Lyrec, until the lad shamefacedly admitted that he couldn't carry anything else. Fortunately, Flu-flu, who had apparently invested most of her 'points' into Dexterity and Strength, so that she could pull her ridiculously oversized longbow, was able to take everything that remained.

Aspen tucked one last item into the pouch at his own waist, motioning for everyone to move to one side of the office. Yet another *thunk* followed by a shriek sounded from below, and he shook his head, ticking his tongue slightly in mock-disappointment at the invader's lack of trap-locating skills, then muttered, "That's the bottom step to come up here. We're out of time." With a single, powerful shove, he pushed the desk up onto its side, then tumbled it onto its top. Everyone else winced slightly at the loud bang the heavy piece of furniture produced, knowing that it would give away their location, but Aspen just smiled slightly, looking down at the simple, reddish-brown rug that had been pinned beneath the desk.

Lyrec stepped forward. "Is there something under the carpet? Do you want me to help move it?"

Aspen motioned the young Traveler forward, then indicated everyone else should follow. "There's nothing under this except the floorboards. Now, everyone press close. Make sure everyone is on the rug, with not a single toe or elbow sticking out."

Flu-flu looked excited. "My lord, is this a *flying* carpet?" She clasped her hands tightly together. "Truly, this is a wonderful day, for I have long wished I could-"

Aspen reached over and gently covered her mouth. "I'm sorry. Flying carpets are more myth than reality, as far as I know, though there are rumors that there is some way to make them that only you Travelers can afford. This is a teleportation rug. Lich Lord Akuji's generals used to use them to teleport from camp to camp, allowing them instantaneous escape if it seemed they would be overrun." He winced as the door closing off the third floor rattled loudly, and the muted sound of voices came through.

"Tuck yourselves in tightly. It wasn't meant to carry so many, and anything outside the edges will be left behind." There was a small scuffle as everyone tried to crowd closer together. Aspen ignored it as he reached down to Stick, where it hung at his waist, waiting impatiently to be useful. When he pictured what he wanted, the magical staff tinkled questioningly, but when Aspen silently reaffirmed his choice, it reluctantly shifted shape for him.

With a swift movement, Aspen used the small sickle to slice his own palm deeply, then clenched his fist, allowing his blood to pour down into the thick fibers of the carpet. Instantly, the rather innocuous rug flushed deep red, and Aspen opened and closed his hand a few times, forcing more blood out, though he had to clench his teeth against the pain. Originally, a human sacrifice would have been used for this step, but...

Red light flared up around them, and Aspen heard a short yelp. The light grew so bright he was forced to close his eyes against it, and when he blinked them open a few moments later, spots and a lingering haze blocked his vision for several more heartbeats. He felt small, warm hands grasping his injured hand, and a familiar voice clucked chidingly.

"Why is it that every time I see you, you're almost dead?"

::Head Librarian!:: Silus, who had been remarkably silent during most of the escape, now glided off of Aspen's shoulders. As Aspen blinked away the last few light spots, he saw his little friend nuzzling a short, brown man whose wrinkled visage would put Restur and Tomas to shame. Those wrinkles creased into a cheerful smile as the short man gently patted the bat.

"Silus! My, how you've grown! Why, I do believe you're even larger than your mother now."

Everyone paused as a distant but powerful **_BOOM_** sounded, and a few books fell from the tops of the more precarious literary towers that seemed to surround them. The Head Librarian patted Aspen's hand, which was now wrapped in a white bandage that was already soaking through with blood. Aspen sent a [Heal] into it, but his vision blurred slightly as he did. The carpet, after all, used the mana of the sacrifice to do its job. Usually, losing that much mana would finish killing the sacrifice, but with his possibly-excessive mana pool, Aspen had simply been drained to the point of nearly losing consciousness.

"What… What was that?" Jack's quiet question was nearly drowned out by Jiminy's, "Where _are_ we?" and Aspen and the Head Librarian each answered one of the questions at the same time.

"That was my house blowing up."

"Why, you're in the Great Library of Bright. At least, what's left of it."

Aspen's eyes snapped to the Librarian. "What do you mean, what's left of it?"

The wrinkles creased even further, and the Librarian's bushy white beard seemed to twitch. His voice was distinctly disapproving as he said, "It seems that some books are no longer appropriate reading for the common people. Those who are even able to read. All books written by non-humans have been classified as restricted, as well as any books written by humans that mention non-humans in a positive light."

Lyrec gaped. "That's, like, all of them!"

The Head Librarian pointed a gnarled brown finger at the Traveler. "Right you are, my lad! That's why my people and I have been packing since we heard Duke Penbrooke had returned, and was inviting anyone who felt endangered within Bright to travel north with him, to create a new land, where everyone is equal."

It was Aspen's turn to gape. In fact, he tried to speak several times, but failed to make any actual words emerge from his mouth.

::That was a *secret*!:: Silus put in, sounding aggrieved. ::I just told you because Aspen sent me to let you know that we might need to use the rug, and it needed to be clear of books, and *you* started asking me about Aspen's plans, and I knew what Restur and Tomas were up to because they're not really very sneaky, and you gave me four moths and promised you wouldn't tell Aspen!::

The Head Librarian tutted. "And so I didn't, my dear. At least, I didn't tell him who my informant was. I believe *you* are the one who just told him that."

There was a long pause, and then Silus said, ::Oh,:: in a very small voice.

"Wait," Lyrec said, pointing from the Librarian to the bat, "you can *hear* her?"

The short man's blue eyes twinkled beneath his bushy white eyebrows, and he laid a finger beside his nose. "A Librarian hears everything in their library, you know, Lyrec the Traveler. How else can we make sure no one is breaking the peace? Do put that down, young Jiminy. You're not ready for it yet." This last was directed at the puckish brown-haired boy, who was flipping through a thick book titled *Spies and the Women Who Love Them*.

The boy blushed and slammed the book closed, somehow managing to drop it on his foot as he attempted to return it to its place in the stack. As he hopped about, clutching at his toe, Flu-flu looked around dubiously.

"Is this indeed that mighty edifice? I hast not seen this place since I was but a feeble neophyte in this world, desperately searching for power. Methinks I slew a rodent or six in the vaults of knowledge, once upon a time." The archer drew out her face in an exaggerated expression of sorrow. "How it has fallen since that time. Alas and alack." Pressing one hand to her forehead, she seemed to sway slightly. Lyrec instantly sprang forward to awkwardly grab her shoulders, trying to support her.

Aspen felt his headache returning. Fortunately, so was his mana, so he sent another [Heal] through his body, and felt the pain ease, including the throbbing in his palm. He looked over to see how the elves and the children were handling this.

The female elf looked awed as she stared around at all the books. Her hands twitched as she kept reaching for one, then pulled herself back through what seemed an act of will. As usual, the androgynous elf stood nearby, face expressionless, carefully not looking at the first elf.

Jack, Lionel, and Ulie were huddled together in the middle of the carpet. It seemed that they hadn't moved since the group had been transported into the room, but Jack was hovering protectively over the girl standing between the two boys. Ulie, meanwhile, was fussing awkwardly with Lionel's hand, which seemed to be dripping almost as much blood on the floor as Aspen's had been.

Aspen cursed, crossing over to the taller boy. "What happened?" he asked gruffly.

Lionel just looked away, pale face defiant, but Ulie's brown eyes were hopeful. "We didn't quite fit on the carpet, m'lord. His," she bit her lip, swallowing hard. "His finger got left behind."

Aspen shook his head at the over-inflated pride of teenagers everywhere, then grasped the boy's elbow. Lionel started to jerk it away, then stilled as the first warm pulse of Aspen's [Heal] flowed into him. The blood stopped dripping, and Lionel held up his hand, staring at it in amazement. The back half of the second knuckle of his left pinky had been cleanly severed at an obtuse angle, and the top part of the finger was missing entirely. Even as they watched, though, a shiny pink scar formed over the remaining stub, and in moments the wound looked as if it had happened years before.

It was Aspen's turn to sway, as the little mana he'd recovered drained away. To his surprise, it was the androgynous elf's cool, smooth hands that caught him as he toppled, and he had just enough time to see the female elf's wide, shocked gaze before he tumbled into darkness.

Chapter Fourteen

Khor

E very time Khor asked an offhand question about either of the patients, Sumi rebuffed him with a terse, <That is not my story to share.> In fact, after a few days, Khor was beginning to think that the spider was enjoying the opportunity to stymie him, and stopped asking, refusing to give her the satisfaction.

In the end, though, the little glyphis, with the amazing resilience of youth, recovered before Nekthadt was allowed outside by his overprotective sister. The first Khor knew of it, though, was when a pre-teen boy, with the distinctive gray skin and cold black eyes of the glyphis, appeared outside the house. On his shoulder was perched a miniature gray girl. Her skin was still noticeably paler than the boy's, but her eyes were bright.

The boy's sharp knock on the door woke Khor, and he only caught a glimpse of the curious pair through the open door of the barn before they vanished into the house. The goat had been getting a well-deserved rest, after having spent a good bit of time the previous evening stomping on what seemed like thousands of beetles, and it had taken him ages to get the remnants of glossy green chitin out of what was left of his fur after the mildly acidic insects melted half of it away.

Nonetheless, when the *rap rap* of knuckles on the door was greeted by the soft murmur of Sarave's welcoming voice, he found himself waking enough to shift closer to the window between the barn and the house. During the coldest part of the winter, it had remained open most of the time so that the two spaces could share warmth, but now that it was warmer, suddenly the scent of wet fur and warm bodies was 'too strong', and Sarave kept it closed much of the time.

Today, though, the shutters stood half open, and Khor settled himself comfortably against the wall that separated the two living spaces, swiveling his sensitive ears so that he could hear whatever was going on inside the house. Nuisance, who was perched between Khor's magnificent spiral horns, the unicorns, who slept curled against Khor's side, and even the two duck hens who still guarded their eggs with the fervor of new mothers, all shifted in response to Khor's movement, since his bulk occupied the vast majority of the cramped space. Discontented quacks and sighs drowned out the conversation in the house for a moment, before everyone settled back into slumber, and Khor was finally able to listen properly.

The voice that Khor had come to recognize as Nekthadt's was speaking, though he seemed to be murmuring barely above a whisper. Khor chewed his cud in frustration as the quiet voice faded in and out of his hearing.

"…glad that you're… thought for sure… Wyvern was going to…"

Khor's ears perked up further. He had to admit to some minor interest in the Wyvern of the Whispering Mountains. The thing was the most powerful monster in the area, and since Khor rarely got to battle anything deserving actual effort any more, he couldn't help but think longingly of the fun he could have fighting such a worthy adversary.

Of course, it could fly, and he was still rather less than he had been before he'd had to help track Aspen down into that nightmare realm of Akuji's undead.

He, along with Sumi and Manuela, had been reduced during the battles against the wraiths and wights - monsters who could temporarily drain stats with just a touch, and permanently steal them if they managed to capture their prey for long enough periods. All in all, it was probably for the best that he was never likely to meet with the Wyvern, no matter how much he might like to discover how he would fare against the beast.

As he pondered the pleasant notion of battling such a valiant foe, a long, hairy black leg thrust the shutters wide, and the voices inside grew much clearer. <If you're going to eavesdrop,> Sumi said sharply, <at least try to be subtle about it.>

Sarave said, "You're right, Sumi, we need more air in here. It has gotten stuffy while my *ifsthin* recovered."

Nekthadt grumbled, "If you'd let me get up and go outside, you could air out the whole place. Even I know I need a bath."

Sarave's usually serene voice was slightly flustered. "You had pneumonia, brother! You must rest!"

"*Had*, sister! I'm recovered, and will stay so if you don't make me sick again by keeping me in here!"

Sumi muttered in Khor's mind, <If I have to listen to this argument again, I don't want to be alone in my suffering.>

Khor snorted softly. <You've never been one to suffer alone, old spider.>

Sumi's fangs clicked quietly in a soft chuckle. <True enough.>

The siblings were still bickering almost happily, but a soft, breathy little voice interrupted them. "Want. Nek. Visit."

There was a long pause, and then Sarave sighed, defeated. "All right, Jesiqa." Her soft accent turned the sharp 'k' in the glyphis' name into a gentle 'qua', but Khor had heard the name mentioned often enough recently to know that it applied to the slimy fish-thing that the goblin had reluctantly handed over to Viqa.

Cautiously, Khor raised his head, peering into the well-lit interior of the house. Apparently, Sumi had taken it upon herself to open the front door again, as well as throwing open the other shuttered window, and the bright spring sunlight was flooding the small space. Sarave, her long hair caught back in her usual shining black braid, sat beside the single small sick-bed that had been set up in the main area of the house. The olive-green skin of her hand was dark where it rested against her brother's much more brightly colored arm.

Nekthadt laid a gentle hand on his sister's, though his face still held a hint of a scowl. "I just want to get outside, Sarave-*hijin*. I haven't lived in a house in years, and I think I may go mad if I have to stay inside another day."

Sarave's head bowed, and Khor thought even her pointed ears might have drooped a bit. Juniper, who had been sitting to the side eating a piece of honeycomb while watching the proceedings with bright blue-green eyes, hopped up and wriggled her sticky fingers in between her mother and her uncle's.

"I wanna show Uncle Nekfat the farm, Mama! Can't I?" The little girl's long lashes fluttered innocently.

Sarave and Nekthadt each pulled back their hands, Sarave absently wiping her now-tacky fingers on her ubiquitous apron. She sighed softly, but smiled. "How is it that I am now outnumbered? Fine then, Juniper, you may show Uncle Nek*thadt*," she firmly emphasized the correct pronunciation of her brother's name, "the farm." Lifting her head, Sarave's yellow eyes locked onto Khor's, where he peeked... no, *looked* over the edge of the windowsill.

"Khor, would you please go with them and make sure they don't get into too much trouble? I know it's not time for you to be up, yet, but I would greatly appreciate it. I was thinking of making some vegetable bread, but I won't have time if I must go with them."

Khor huffed a loud, put-upon sigh, but stood, thus disturbing the pile of sleeping animals, all of whom grumbled in their own way, though Kayli was looking around with a bright curiosity that said she was already more awake than asleep. Slowly, showing obvious reluctance, Khor stepped out of the barn, and behind him everyone else shuffled. The unicorns, both now sparkling with curiosity, trotted out after him on dainty hooves.

Scraping the ground with his hoof, Khor shook his horns vigorously, causing Nuisance to quack angrily before using his beak to pull himself back into place. The bird must have completed some difficult quests recently, because he had been growing larger seemingly daily, and by now Khor thought he could almost feel his horns bending outwards beneath the weight and width of the fowl.

The occupants of the house also tumbled out, with Juniper in the lead, followed by the glyphis boy, carrying the miniature girl, then Sarave, with her arm wrapped around Nekthadt's waist, though he was walking well enough that he seemed not to need the support. Sumi brought up the rear, but the spider simply stopped and watched from the doorway.

Out in the warm sunlight, both adult goblins squinted painfully until their eyes adjusted. Sarave nervously adjusted the new clothes she had tailored for Nekthadt from old fabric scraps and a pair of Aspen's threadbare pants. When the small hubbub died down, the goblin woman patted her taller brother's chest, smiling nervously at him. "Be careful. The farm is safe, but..." She leaned her head forward until her hair just brushed the brown fabric of his shirtfront. "You have just returned from the dead, *ifsthin*. Please, be careful."

She turned to her daughter, who was hopping from foot to foot in impatience. "And you, little *sothi*, little cricket, take care of your poor uncle, and bring him home when he tires."

Juniper popped the last gooey chunk of honeycomb into her mouth, and said stickily, "'Kay, Mama."

Finally, Sarave looked to Khor with a pleading expression. "Will you please, Khor, bring my brother back if he falters? I know you have no love for my people, but perhaps..."

Khor snorted harshly, but shrugged and sidled toward Nekthadt, whose face went expressionless as the goat's massive shadow fell over him. He looked over at Sumi. <Tell her fine. I expect bread later, though.>

Sumi's foreleg gently touched Sarave's leg, and the goblin woman turned to look at her arachnid friend. Sumi spun a small web, using deft movements of her forelegs to translate for Khor. Sarave laughed softly, and turned to gaze up at the goat. "I am certain that can be arranged. I thank you." She rested her hand over her heart, then bowed her head. Beside her, her brother's eyes grew wide, and he reached out as if to stop her, but halted and dropped his hand before he could touch her arm.

There was definitely something very strange about those two. They were easily the least goblin-like goblins Khor had ever encountered, and since Nekthadt had come, Sarave had dropped back into her older, more formal ways, almost as though she'd been reminded of some part of herself that she'd nearly forgotten. She'd also begun using more of her goblin language, though, again, Khor had mostly heard goblins using a mix of orcish, troll, and human languages. That was, when they bothered to speak in anything other than grunts and screams.

Juniper's syrupy fingers tugged at the fur hanging from Khor's chest, pulling him from his ruminations. "C'mon, Khow! Let's go see Uncle Willam! Uncle Nekfat, don't you wanna meet Uncle Willam?" The little girl turned big eyes on her uncle, who looked more bemused than anything, and simply nodded.

The tour took far longer than it needed to, as everything tended to when children became involved, and Khor soon found himself trailing along behind as Juniper's happy little voice extolled the virtues of absolutely everything around her.

"...'An this is where the bees live! It's called a hive, an' if you ask real nice, and bring them lots of flowers, sometimes they'll share some honey with you! Over there is the Tree, an' it's super important, and you're not allowed to climb in it, 'cause you might break a branch, 'an then you'll get sent to bed without supper." The little girl skipped toward the clearing with the Tree, now easily twenty feet high and blooming with brilliant blossoms. A rich and heady perfume filled the air, and the humming of the bees, now a constant background noise, rose in pitch as they saw strangers nearing.

Viqa hurried over when she saw the small crowd approaching, and when she saw Nekthadt among the group she stopped abruptly, then fell to her knees, arms straight out ahead of her and forehead pressed to the ground. Khor stopped in astonishment at the sight. Whatever emotions the glyphis felt were generally a mystery to him, and the woman before him had only once before shown anything that could be likened to a human expression, and that was when she had seen Jesiqa for the first time.

When she spoke, the glyphis' voice was muffled by the ground. "Thank you, great warrior Nekthadt. The clan of Fisqera owes you a great debt. You have returned a child we thought lost, and there is no reward we can offer that is great enough."

The boy's black eyes went wide, and upon seeing his mother prostrating herself on the ground, his own knees seemed to give out beneath him. He couldn't copy his parent's pose, since he was holding Jesiqa in his arms, but he, too, bowed his head. Only Jesiqa held her head high, looking from Nekthadt to Viqa with an almost smug expression.

Nekthadt, on the other hand, just scowled. "I didn't do anything special. I happened to be able to help Jesiqa, and I did. That's that." He reached down and tugged at the arm of the bowing woman, and she rose in a liquid movement that left her towering over him, which only deepened his scowl.

Viqa's expression returned to its usual flat façade. "Our children are rare and precious, and for someone outside of our race to treat one as something other than a curiosity or a prize is even rarer. Do not defame yourself or your deed." The woman reached out and touched Jesiqa, and the little glyphis' surface seemed to ripple briefly.

Looking more closely, Khor suddenly realized that both of the glyphis children were enclosed in a film of water that clung to them so tightly it blended in with their gray skin. That explained how they were out of the water and walking around. It must be some magic of the glyphis, though not all of them could do it, or perhaps simply not do it as long or as well.

Viqa continued. "My daughter told me how you rescued her from a monster who treated her as a toy at best, and a thing to be slaughtered for power at worst. You gave her food while you starved. Risked your life to get her clean water. You even brought her here in spite of her illness, and your own injuries, forging your way across the mountains when others would have abandoned her when it became clear she would die. You saved her a hundred times over, and so, we glyphis owe you a hundred debts."

Khor stopped in his tracks. Wait, what? Her *daughter*?

Chapter Fifteen

Rouge

Zoey snorted a little, then jerked upright, blinking her eyes against the glare of the sun. She rubbed her eyes, realizing that she had been thoroughly asleep a moment before, her head resting against Nina's shoulder, and her eyes darted to the short sleeve of her friend's bright orange blouse. No wet spot, so she probably hadn't been drooling, and that was good news at least.

Nina's brown eyes were warm with concern, and today's artsy glasses with frames shaped like stretching cats with lenses balanced on their curved backs only served to draw more attention to the worried expression. "You right, Zoe?" her friend asked, her New Zealand accent coming out more than usual.

Zoey nodded, though she still felt a little light-headed at the suddenness of her awakening. "Yeah, just played way too late last night." She frowned teasingly, trying to distract her friend from asking anything else. "Speaking of which, where have you been lately?"

Nina flushed a little, pushing her glasses back up her lightly freckled nose, though they hadn't actually been slipping for once. "I *told* you, Zoey. Ihadadate."

Zoey grinned, finally feeling a bit more like herself. "*A* date? You haven't been around since you got Sam to slip me that note."

Nina's face flamed.

"Wait, *Sam?*" Zoey's eyes sparkled. "Tell me all about it!"

Nina stood up, brushing down her slacks unnecessarily. "Yeah, nah. I already told you once, and it's not my fault if you were sleeping. Besides, there's only four minutes until lunch is over."

Zoey pulled her screen from her pocket and checked the time. "Oh, cripes! You're right! I'll see you soon, Nina, and don't think you're going to get out of telling me then!" Nina flipped her a jaunty wave in spite of her still-flushed cheeks, and Zoey waved back as she dashed toward the lab.

Zoey had been 'off' all day. With only three more days on her temporary internship, you would think she could pull it together to make an awesome last impression, but she just hadn't managed it today. After she and her dad had a short but also way-too-long conversation about what had happened, her mind had been racing too much to let her fall asleep easily. It had been almost two in the morning before her eyes closed, and she had already been down to the last amp in her power bank.

She'd managed to complete her job tasks, though Jazmin had had to elbow her once when Harris had trapped the two of them in the break room and begun a monologue about a particularly challenging dungeon his team was working on, as if either of them cared if his pseudo-leaf insects had two pincers or ten. (To be honest, Zoey normally *would* have been a little interested, because any hints about new mobs were good, but just *not today*. Plus, Harris was just *boring*. Sorry, not sorry.)

Anyway, she had somehow made it through to lunch, though she was so tired she hadn't actually been hungry, and she had apparently fallen asleep on the bench while Nina was talking to her. The good news was, though, that the brief nap had managed to take the edge off her tiredness, so at least there was that.

She dashed through the lab door with not a second to spare, ready to apologize for her near-tardiness, but screeched to a halt with her mouth already open. Sara and Dr. Joe were already in the room, but that wasn't unexpected. What *was* unexpected was that they weren't alone. Dr. Veralt, Ms. McKeene, and a vaguely familiar guy in his mid-twenties were already there.

When Zoey entered, everyone turned to stare at her, and she closed her mouth, then waved weakly, taking a few steps over to stand next to Sara, where she felt slightly safer from the venomous look that Georgia McKeene was giving her. Silently, Ms. McKeene tapped the anachronistic watch on her wrist. The slim gold band slid around on the woman's skinny arm, and her thin lips tightened even more.

Yes, I know I was almost late! Zoey thought rebelliously. *Almost isn't late, though, so suck it up, buttercup.* She firmly resisted the urge to stick her tongue out at the horrible woman.

Dr. Joe cleared his throat. "Ah, Zoey. I believe you've met Dr. Veralt and Ms. McKeene before. They were just introducing us to Dr. Veralt's new team member, Mr. Harrison." He paused, then smiled politely. "Though I didn't catch your first name?"

The tall, bony man replied, his voice slightly edged. "I prefer *Mr.* Harrison, actually. My first name is a bit unusual, and I wouldn't want anyone to stumble over it."

Everyone nodded and gave more of those stiff, polite smiles. Then there was a round of hand-shaking, though Zoey noticed that the new *Mr.* Harrison not only didn't offer to shake Sara's hand, but only gave Dr. Joe the ends of his fingers, as if he was concerned he'd be contaminated somehow. The invaders trooped out with Veralt in the lead and McKeene bringing up the rear. The snake tried to slither in front of Mr. Harrison, but the lanky man just took a slightly-too-long stride and cut her off without a pause.

Sara and Dr. Joe exchanged glances as the door closed behind Georgia McKeene, but Zoey had no idea what the look meant, though there was definitely a bit of worry in it. Then Dr. Joe turned to Zoey and smiled brightly, clapping his hands as if dusting them off.

"Well! I know Friday is your last day, Zoey, so I wanted to let you play a bit more, but Dr. Veralt also dropped off a new algorithm while he was here." He flashed one of Veritas Corp's internal thumb drives, neatly pinched between his first two fingers, then dropped it into the breast pocket of his ubiquitous white lab coat. "It's all approved by the high mucky-mucks, and we're supposed to give it a quick beta today."

"What does it do?" Rouge eyed the small lump in his pocket suspiciously. Anything that came from Dr. Veralt was a no-go in her opinion.

Joe shook his head. "You know I can't tell you that! I just need you to get changed, and run through the usual pre-checks. There'll be a couple of extra exercises to do before you log in, but otherwise you shouldn't even be able to tell the difference." He tapped the drive. "This is a change on my end, not yours, so you just need to let me know if anything seems off to you." He smiled again, and Zoey wondered if she was just imagining that the smile looked forced.

When Rouge opened her eyes, it was to find herself on Codswallop's back, with Motte's armored shape on his horse trotting along a steady six feet ahead of her. Around them, broad swathes of open fields were visible, and knee-high, bright green plants filled tidy rows. Men and women in broad-brimmed hats and light-weight clothing made from brown hemp and unbleached linen worked under the bright sun, swinging hoes and pulling weeds.

Rouge drew in a deep breath, relaxing for the first time in days. Somehow, they'd made it safely out of Bright, and the clear air and sight of the green fields beneath the blue sky made it feel like a weight had been lifted from her shoulders.

Unfortunately, just because she felt that way, it didn't mean she really had any less to do. Sighing deeply, she leaned forward and threw her arms around Codswallop's neck, breathing in the musty, dusty scent of his feathers. When her job at Veritas Corp ended, there were a lot of things she'd happily leave behind, but she would truly, profoundly miss the feeling of actually *being* there that she got from the magic pod.

The moment Wally registered that Rouge was awake, he let out a trilling honk and twisted his head around to look at her. She popped back up quickly when he stumbled, and patted his head. "Silly bird. You have to watch where you're going!" In response, the ostrich simply stopped in his tracks, causing the wagon closing on them from behind to swerve so it didn't hit them.

As the wagon passed them, the driver threw her a half-hearted glare. "Rouge, if yer awake, Restur wants t' talk t' you. He's in th' first wagon." He was one of the drivers from Restur's caravan, and she'd even exchanged a few words with him now and then, so she just waved jauntily and clucked her tongue at Codswallop, urging him to move.

The big bird didn't budge. Instead, he looked pointedly from Rouge's pouch to her eyes, then opened and closed his beak a few times. She laughed and pulled an apple from her inventory. "Greedy bird," she murmured affectionately, offering it to him. He gobbled it happily, before turning and heading for the front of the line.

As they trotted along, barely faster than the large, almost comically over-filled wagons, Rouge reluctantly pulled up her quest list. She knew she had a number of outstanding quests, but the one she needed to look at was...

SECRET Quest: "Who Run the World"
FantumHat current completion: 73%
Rouge the Rouge current completion: 36%

Rouge gaped at the numbers. She'd hoped for some change in her own completion percentage, but this! Not only had she jumped up 9%, but

FannyHat's number had gone *down*! How did that even happen? Sure, he still had twice as much done as she did, and she didn't even know what kinds of things the stupid quest counted towards 'completion', but still! Progress was progress, right?

Her mind raced over everything they'd done since she'd received the quest. Not that much, right? They ran away, first of all, and there was no way the game was counting that as a win for her side. Then they got home, only to find that everyone had already evacuated, and their allies had been picking off the enemy combatants, too. Seriously, in every book she'd ever read, she and Aspen would have needed to come in and Save the Day, so it was really, *really* nice that their friends had been able to handle the attack by themselves.

All of which put them... where? Running north like a flock of geese fleeing winter? Admittedly, thanks to Restur and Tomas, they were in pretty good shape. Frankly, if the wagons around her - which were piled so high that they had to be covered in canvas and tied with a web of ropes so the contents didn't just overflow and fall off - were any indication, they could practically start a new city beyond the mountains.

As if her thought had caused it, an announcement filled her screen so completely that she would have tripped if she'd been walking. Thankfully, Wally couldn't see it, and just kept jogging along, clucking quietly to himself.

WORLD FIRST! A *City Seed* has been found! *City Seeds* are single-use God-level items! These items can only be used by someone who fulfills the following requirements:

1.   Must be at least level 75.

2.   Must have one or more stats at 100+.

3.   Must have at least 1,000,000 gold, or solely own items valued at an equivalent amount.

4.   Must be ranked as a General, Admiral, Marquess, Duke, Prince, Princess, King, or Queen within an already-existing nation with its

own government OR have attained the rank of Saint/Saintess within an established religion with more than 1,000 worshippers.

5.   Must have a Relationship of 100 with a God or Goddess.

City Seeds may be stolen, sold, traded, or dropped, even if they are in a player's Inventory, so the sooner the item is used, the better! Only two *City Seeds* will spawn at any given time, so until the existing *City Seeds* are used, no more can be found.

Upon use, the *City Seed* allows the bearer to found a village, which can be developed into a city. This village will be under their exclusive control unless and until they voluntarily cede control to another person or group, OR the *City Core* is found and destroyed, at which time the city will collapse. Further rules regarding proper use of the *City Seed* will be available upon examination of the item.

Good luck to all who wish to rule their own city! Go forth and quest!

Oh, heck. She had a sinking feeling she knew exactly who had just picked up a new city.

Waving away the notification, Rouge leaned back in Codswallop's small saddle, absently patting his shoulder as she did. The ostrich seemed intent on moving right past the front wagon, apparently content to just keep going forever as long as he had his girl on his back.

Rouge fished another apple out of her inventory and passed it to the ostrich, then climbed nimbly up until she was standing in the saddle. With a little jump, she used an outstretched toe on the edge of the wagon's side panel to push herself into an effortless flip, landing neatly in the back of the wagon. Video game acrobatics were the *best.*

Restur, who was leaning back on the seat next to the driver, eyes closed and chewing contemplatively on a long piece of straw, opened one bright blue eye to examine the intruder. Sitting up, he nudged the driver with an elbow, then tossed the straw aside and climbed into the back of the wagon with Rouge.

"Glad to see you could make it, Miss Rouge," he said, smiling as he motioned toward a box that was about the right height for a seat.

Rouge's eyes narrowed. For all that Restur was a friend, he wasn't one who did things for others out of the goodness of his own heart. If he was looking so cheerful, it was because things were going his way. Which might or might not translate to things also going *her* way.

"Um, thanks, Restur," she said, casually sitting down on the box. "So, where are we? And where's Aspen?"

Restur chuckled in a particularly pleased manner. "Oh, we're well out of Bright. We left several hours ago, though we just met up with most of the caravan not too long ago. As for Duke Aspen, he stayed behind with a few of the others when we left." He quickly held up a hand when she started to demand more information. "Fortunately, I just received word from a, ah, *source* within Bright, that a mutual friend has managed to smuggle everyone safely out of the city. I expect we'll all be together again sometime late this afternoon, or perhaps in the early evening. We traveled a good way west before we turned north, you see, but our friends left from the north gate, so they'll actually reach the rendezvous point before we do."

"Who's your source?" Rouge insisted. "How do you know they can be trusted? How did they even communicate with you, if they're in Bright, and we're," she motioned around at the seemingly endless fields of grass and crops. "Wherever we are."

Restur leaned forward and patted her hand, using the motion to return to his feet. "There, there, lass, don't fret. You know I have some, ah, *unusual* sources, and quite aside from the fact that I like you and your friends, I've tied my profits rather tightly to your well-being." He smiled a little wryly.

"I may keep my little secrets, but you can trust me. Now, I let everyone know to send you up when you woke, since I knew that curiosity of yours would be urging you to do something that might not be in your own best interest. Hopefully, what I can tell you has set your mind at rest enough that you can simply wait here with us until all our plans come to fruition. In the meantime, however, I do have rather a lot of other things that require my attention as well."

Rouge tugged at one of her braids, irked at this clear dismissal, especially since the old man had been lounging around basking in the sun like a cat when she came up, but *whatever*. If he didn't want to talk to her, she had other sources, too. Grumbling to herself, she walked over to the edge of the wagon, stepping off and landing in Codswallop's saddle without any of the fancy maneuvers she'd used on the way in.

The ostrich trilled interrogatively, and Rouge patted his neck gently. "Don't worry about it, Wally." She cast a narrow look at Restur, who was once again stretched out in the front seat of the wagon, his hat pulled low over his eyes, apparently trying to sleep. "We're just going to go see some more *helpful* people."

The first ones she found were Millie and Struthio. They were in a wagon not far behind the front, and from the rattling pots and pans hung around them, Rouge was willing to venture a guess that this was the... what, chuckwagon? Struthio was driving four broad-backed oxen, who were trudging stolidly along, heads down as they pulled the heavy weight behind them. The tall, now slightly-plump man waved cheerfully as Rouge drew near.

"Ah saw y' when y'went by, Miss Rouge," the former ostrich-herder said, "but y'seemed t'be thinkin' mighty hard on sumthin', so ah jus' waved. Ah didna think y'saw me, so I'm glad yer back. Millie was right sad when I told 'er y'passed us."

Millie, who had been perched on top of a barrel in the back, busily digging through a large sack that was itself rather precariously balanced on a mound of cookware and grain sacks, looked up, her bright gold braids gleaming in the sun. The woman flashed a smile that rivaled her hair in brilliance, and held out her hands to Rouge and Codswallop. Large, fluffy, baked confections sat there, emanating the mouth-watering aromas of cinnamon, butter, and far, far too much sugar.

Wally's head snaked out, and he snapped up the offering. He tilted his head back and choked it down, his beak gaping as he attempted to snatch Rouge's cinnamon roll as well. Rouge had to risk life and limb to grab her own perfect pastry before the greedy bird could get it. Codswallop's beak closed on empty air with a snap, and he turned an accusatory eye on his mistress.

Millie, blue eyes wide, giggled a little nervously, then reached into the bag again, producing another cinnamon roll, which was still carefully wrapped in waxed linen. Cautiously, she unwrapped it, then extended it toward the ostrich. Rouge would have sworn her bird huffed at her as if to say, *Now this is how I expect to be treated.* Rouge's eyes met Millie's over the rapaciously gobbling ostrich, and they burst out into peals of laughter.

As they laughed, Rouge could almost feel a knot in her chest start to loosen. She grinned at her two friends, and began stuffing her own swirl of delectable cinnamon goodness into her mouth. She took her time about it, telling herself she was just doing what Dr. Joe had asked and checking to be sure nothing felt 'off' to her. Truthfully, though, she knew it was likely the last time she'd get to try one of Millie's decadent desserts while Rouge was still using Veritas Corp's souped-up super pod, and while her home pod was pretty good, it just wasn't as mouthwateringly perfect as this.

Millie settled into the seat beside her new husband as Rouge and Codswallop finished their treats. The four of them contentedly followed the wagon train, companionably enjoying the warm sunshine, the lovely fields, the scent of cinnamon, and the complete and total lack of anything trying to kill them. It was only when Rouge began to lick the last soft-but-crunchy bits of frosting from her fingers that Millie spoke up.

"We're glad t'see ye well, Miss Rouge, and, ah," the young woman reached behind her seat and pulled out a small, jingling canvas bag. "We need t'return this t'ye. We decided th' city's not fer the likes of us, y'see, an'-"

Rouge gently pushed the bag back toward Millie. "Keep it. I heard you're going to be helping Plum set up a place for the kids to live, and feeding that lot is going to be expensive enough. Plus, didn't you have to use it to buy supplies?"

Millie glanced at her husband, and Struthio's jaw firmed. "Y'gave it t'us t'start a restaurant, Miss. It isn't right t'use it for somthin' else," the big man said firmly.

Millie nodded, reaching out to twine her powerful fingers through Struthio's thick ones. "We borrowed from Master Restur, y'see. That way we could give y'back what y'loaned us, right an' proper."

Rouge wanted to groan. Again, she pushed the money away. "Millie," she said gently, "I thought I heard something about starting a village up north?"

Millie nodded a bit uncertainly.

"Won't a village need an inn? Where people eat? Which is basically a restaurant with bonuses, right?"

Another nod.

"Then please," Rouge pointed at the pouch, which Millie was beginning to reluctantly withdraw, "keep that, and consider it a long-term investment. Don't think I've forgotten about getting you unusual ingredients, either, huh? I mean, I have a quest and everything, and you wouldn't want me to fail a quest, right?" She did her best to flutter her eyelashes, though she knew they were a little too curly to flutter particularly well.

The newlyweds exchanged another glance, and Millie smiled shyly, her eyelashes doing a remarkably good flutter as the Amazonian woman looked down into her lap. "That's mighty nice of ye, Miss Rouge. Aye, we'll not deprive ye of a quest, though y'must let us know if y'need repaying."

Rouge nodded and grinned. "It's a deal. Now, tell me what I missed!"

☙ ☙ ☙

Millie didn't know much more than what Rouge had already gleaned from Restur and that sneaky games keeper-butler, Tomas. Basically, the two old codgers had put their heads together almost the instant Aspen had introduced them, and hadn't stopped conniving since. They'd carefully skirted the edges of Aspen's actual instructions, and when Aspen had given Tomas *carte blanche* they'd leapt on it like a pair of squirrels who could finally stash their winter store of nuts.

Carts had begun showing up within a half hour of Aspen and Motte's departure, and Restur had sent all of his people scurrying to buy anything he hadn't yet managed to acquire. The idea was to send Plum and the children ahead, since the two venerable conspirators were certain that Aspen wouldn't have the heart to chase them and tell them to turn around.

It just snowballed after that. Millie and Struthio had been among the first to volunteer their services, but many of the former prisoners had also asked if they could come. The adults with friends or family in Bright had tried to speak to their loved ones, but had mostly been spurned, and, in one case, actually attacked. The children, of course, were returned to their families, if they had one, and they knew where they could be found, but when the families heard about the mass exodus, they, too, had asked if they could come. All of them, obviously, had at least one non-human member, and they could all see how things were going in the city they had once loved.

By the time Lyrec showed up with a part-elf baby and instructions to flee, most of the non-combatants were already gone, filtering out of the city in dribs and drabs via the western gate, where a greedy guardsman had been well-paid to look the other way and not report a caravan full of taxable goods and suspiciously frightened-looking people.

Plum, who had been lingering to make certain all the children made it back from their usual rounds of thieving and sneaking, immediately took the baby and the reins. She sent Lyrec, Flu-flu, some of the adult former prisoners, and a few of the older children who knew how to use a bow or slingshot up to the second floor to watch for attackers. She handed the baby off to Manuela, who, Millie reported with a giggle, looked less than pleased to be saddled with a nursling, then took two more large caravanners to move every large piece of furniture in the house to cover the doors and windows.

They began hearing screams and shouting from inside the forest not long after that, though it took nearly another quarter hour before the first of the stricken assailants had staggered from the edge of the trees. When Flu-flu shot him neatly through the heart, his body fell, still wriggling strangely even though there was no chance the man lived. No one among the defenders even suggested going to loot the body.

It had continued much like that until Aspen, Rouge, and the others had returned. By then, the defenders had noticed that the quality of raiders was getting higher. A few were even Travelers, though they seemed to be fairly low-level ones, at least according to Lyrec and Flu-Flu, who recognized their equipment as 'newbie gear'.

From there, Rouge knew as much as Millie, and likely more, so the pretty chef wound down finally, ending with, "We were just that glad t'see ye this mornin', Miss Rouge. I even made your favorite rolls, jus' hopin' ye'd come back soon."

Rouge grinned, accepting yet another delicious roll. She wasn't sure if she was on her fourth or fifth now, but she *was* sure that Codswallop was several ahead of her. "Thank you, Millie. There's nothing better than one of your cinnamon rolls." She rolled her eyes in exaggerated bliss, then winked at the other woman, who smiled back, flashing deep dimples.

A long whistle came from the front of the caravan, and both Rouge and Codswallop hastily swallowed the bite they were chewing. Rouge recognized the sound from when they'd traveled with Restur before. "They saw someone!" she said a little stickily. "Do you suppose it's Aspen?"

Millie and Struthio looked at each other, and Struthio said in his gentle voice, "G'wan, then, Miss. Go and see."

Clucking to Wally, Rouge used her knees to urge her mount back toward the front. With a wave that showered frosting crumbs all over the ground, Rouge bid her friends farewell, and girl and bird trotted off. As Wally swallowed the last of his roll, his long throat rippling, Rouge giggled as a notification popped up in front of her.

Quest: "Let Them Eat Pastry!" complete.

You acquired at least six *Cinnamon Rolls* for Mount Codswallop.

Success: A belly full of joy. Improved Relationship with Mount *Codswallop*. Improved Relationship with Millie.

Chapter Sixteen

Aspen

W hen Aspen heard the distinct sounds made by Codswallop's two long-taloned toes, he looked up sharply, and winced as his neck protested the sudden movement. Being packed, unconscious, into a five-foot-long secret compartment beneath a carriage for several hours hadn't done much for his back, though he had used [Heal] several times in an effort to alleviate the pain. Somehow, no matter what he did, the cramping muscles refused to respond, and if he didn't know better, he'd think his Goddess was trying to tell him something.

Thankfully, when Rouge drew near, she threw herself down from her ostrich's back, so he didn't have to try to look up at her as he walked. Less fortunately, she threw herself directly onto him, hugging him fervently as he patted her back awkwardly, trying to hide his grimace of pain.

"Oh my gosh, Aspen! What *happened*? Where have you been? Why didn't you leave with everyone else?" The five-foot-tall dynamo glared up at him, fists planted on her hips, foot tapping in the dust of the old road they traveled.

Aspen grimaced, gently tugging the girl to the side so that the others could go past. There were happy shouts as the various members of his group met up with those who had gone ahead, and the entire caravan ground to a halt. He shrugged slightly and gently tugged at one of Rouge's braids, chuckling as she redoubled her glare.

"I couldn't simply leave our brave defenders behind, could I? Besides," he felt a grin pull at one side of his mouth, "I had one more little secret left. I had to stay long enough to put a pretty bow on it for our friends. Hopefully, they didn't enjoy it quite as much as I did."

He felt a rush of sadness and loss, though, knowing that the halls through which Birdie had run were now little more than ashes and cinders. No matter, though, not really. He'd gotten everything he needed out, and, most importantly, struck a blow at the organization run by the being who had caused her death.

The Head Librarian's cheerful voice broke into his thoughts, and the little man's gnarled hand clapped him on the back in passing. "Hello again, Rouge. I was glad to hear that you had helped this wastrel as much as I had hoped you might." Brown walnut-like face wreathed in smiles, the short librarian looked at Rouge jovially.

The girl's face went slack as she stared at the gnomish little man, and then she pointed at him with a shaking finger. "*You*! This is all your fault! If you had just *told* me in the first place-!"

The Head Librarian tutted slightly, waggling his tall, pointed red hat as he shook his head. "Now, now. If I had simply told you what was going on, where would the fun have been? It was your own inquisitive nature that led you to travel north alone, and look what has come of it! Why, I dare say that in only a few more days, weeks at most, most of these people would have been dead, or wished they were." He waved his gnarled fingers around, indicating the mixed human and non-humans who were beginning to form back up into a single wagon train under Restur's expert direction.

Aspen's eyes narrowed. "What do you mean, they would have been dead?"

The Head Librarian tutted again. "Well, what did you think was going to happen when the new city lord finally gained complete control of the city? He only had a few minor bastions of political power left to overcome, including Duke Geral himself, who has never cared much for the idea of sharing power. From the rumors I was hearing, an attack was planned for the end of the Traveler's Triathlon festival, and I doubt Geral would live to see the light of another dawn."

Aspen's mouth was suddenly dry, and he had to force out his next question. "What about Callie? Lady Calliope?"

Sharp eyes slid over to meet Aspen's, and the Head Librarian hummed consideringly. "I'm not entirely certain. Her father has set himself firmly against the city lord, but her husband seems to be on the side of the villains. Which side will the lady herself support, do you think?"

Memories of Callie's beautiful face twisted in confusion and fear as she was dragged away by her father while Aspen held a screaming, newly-spawned Lark flashed through his mind. Calliope had never been strong, tending to simply follow the path of least resistance. Marrying Iorgas had been, as far as he knew, her first and last attempt at rebellion, and it had, obviously, ended badly.

He shook his head. "I don't know." The words were bitter in his mouth. "Likely whichever one is most likely to save her pretty neck."

The Head Librarian nodded cheerfully. "Just so, just so. I have no doubt she'll somehow land on her feet, in any case. That sort do tend to manage. Now!" He brushed his hands together, as if dismissing a distasteful topic. "Let us get on with the business at hand."

Rouge, completely ignoring the little old man who had, at one time, been the fourth most powerful person in Bright, grabbed at Aspen's arm. Pulled from his own thoughts, Aspen looked down at her curiously.

"Where's everyone else? I mean," the girl looked around, her eyes touching the two strange elves, who were continuing their odd dance of ignoring each other while still remaining close enough together that they could reach out and touch. There were the four children, who were holding hands with Plum, while all five of them talked at once and tears ran down all of their faces except for Lionel's, though he was sniffling suspiciously. Flu-flu and Lyrec's mounted Zombies were neatly trailing a covered wagon that seemed to groan every time the wheels turned, and all six of the oxen drawing it strained at their harnesses.

"Where's Vonn?" Rouge finally burst out, though, to Aspen's amusement, the tips of her pointed ears were flaming hot where they protruded between her dangling braids.

Silently, Aspen pointed to the wood elf, who was standing just past Plum and the children. In his arms was the small part-elf babe, who waved small fists and blew spit bubbles at the older elf. Rouge, who was too short to see over the crowd, tugged at Codswallop's small saddle, pulling herself up to a higher vantage point. A moment later she let out a happy whoop, and urged her ostrich into a leap that carried them both entirely over everyone else's heads, and landed them neatly beside Vonn. She slid down again, and even Aspen couldn't see what happened next, blocked as he was by the bird's broad and fluffy back.

The dry chuckles of the Head Librarian drew Aspen's attention back to the small, wrinkled man standing next to him. "Ah, to be young again."

Aspen smiled, though it was quickly followed by a sigh. "No, thank you. I'm just as glad to be done with all of that. I think my life is going to be lively enough without bringing such things into it again."

The Head Librarian waggled his fluffy white brows. "Not even for 'Callie'? Or perhaps," he cleared his throat, "someone else more recently met?"

Aspen groaned and flushed, though he only vaguely recalled some of the things he'd said while in that semiconscious state between dreams and waking. Being locked into a cramped storage space wasn't exactly conducive to deep sleep, and apparently, he'd drifted in and out of consciousness several times as his mana reservoir righted itself. He only remembered bits, but it was enough to make his ears burn as hotly as Rouge's.

"No," he said firmly. "Not for anyone. One benefit of age is knowing that such things are usually simply a passing fancy." *And one which I hope will pass very soon,* he thought rather loudly, and imagined that he heard the tinkle of his goddess' laughter mingled with the cackle of the old man standing beside him. Shaking his head, he looked back down at the Head Librarian.

"You still haven't properly explained why you're here, you know. Unless this is a passing fancy of yours." Aspen motioned to the four huge carts that had made the journey from Bright with them, along with several rather nervous-looking young librarians who were driving said carts.

The Head Librarian sobered a bit, though in Aspen's experience the man was rarely truly serious. He always seemed to be thinking of a joke he hadn't told you yet, and while his jovial attitude deflected attention from the sharp mind behind that creased brown face, it was also, just occasionally, *very irritating.*

"Indeed, no. You know there is little I value more than knowledge, do you not, young Aspen?" Aspen clamped his lips shut, refusing to allow that 'young' to send him off on another tangent. "One of the few things that do fall in that narrow category is, in fact, free distribution of that knowledge. Knowing things is quite rewarding in and of itself, but sharing information is what keeps civilization from crashing down around our ears."

The old man looked momentarily tired as he gazed at his wagons, which Restur and his assistant Tia had now skillfully integrated into the caravan. "When a culture begins to deny access to books, a dark age is coming. It has happened over and over, as any student of history can tell you. So, when orders came down from King Chester and the city lord that no one was to be allowed to borrow certain books, I took notice. When the order came that no one was to even read other books, I began to prepare. When the Lord of Bright sent word that the library was to be closed to the public, I moved. This is the result of that move."

Aspen raised a dubious brow. "And it was simply fortuitous timing that this exodus occurred just when you were also ready to depart for parts unknown?"

The Head Librarian chortled. "Oh my, no." He laid a finger alongside his rather prominent proboscis. "I have friends in high places," his eyes twinkled, "but sometimes those in low places are rather more immediately helpful."

Aspen sighed. "You aren't going to tell me what that means, are you?"

The old man just chortled and grabbed the back of the last of his wagons as it trundled by, creaking painfully under the weight of its contents. With a surprisingly spry movement, the Head Librarian pulled himself up into the low bed of the wagon and settled down with his narrow behind pressed against a cloth-covered bundle that looked suspiciously like it contained hundreds of books. He waggled crooked fingers at Aspen, and began to whistle tunelessly.

Aspen looked around. Everything seemed to be in order, no thanks to him. Restur, Tomas, Plum, and, he suspected, Manuela had worked together and gotten everyone out of the city before they were in any serious danger. They had seen what needed to be done and done it, even while he was still trying to deny the necessity. As a result, the children and the other refugees were safe and moving toward what Aspen could only hope was a brighter future. Certainly, as long as he was the Duke of the North, he would make sure they had somewhere to run.

What would happen, though, when Akuji made his move? Aspen had watched the lich for years, studying him both through his own actions and by reading historical records that stretched back hundreds of years. Akuji would defeat some enemy, then stay still and consolidate his strength for as long as a century. However, something always happened that triggered the Lich Lord to rise again and send out his monstrous forces. The story the fruit-juice-drinking vampire William had recounted of how mad Queen Jezerey had encroached on Akuji's territory, triggering a war that destroyed her kingdom and subjugated her vampires to Akuji's will, was a perfect example. In the case of Quarternell, it had been King Chester's father, Chadwick, who had attempted to expand into the undead lord's territory, and brought the evil overlord's attention down on their small kingdom.

Now, armed with the knowledge of Akuji's impossible resurrection, Aspen wondered how many of those periods of hibernation had been the result of Akuji's death. How many times had history repeated itself already? The forces of the undead, or the Dark Races, or warlocks, or vampires, or whatever weapon Akuji turned his hand to would surge forth. They ravaged the world until someone, whether a hero or simply an everyday coward with nothing left to lose, slew Akuji's current incarnation. Things would sink into relative peace for a time, until one day the Lich Lord was roused, and the cycle began again.

Aspen's fists clenched at his sides as he watched the last few carts trundle by, filled with all the things his allies had gathered to save the innocents *he* should have been protecting. Behind the carts came the Zombies, each riding a neat six feet from the rear of the one before. Tessle was first, then Motte, with Lyrec and Flu-flu now added to the train. Aspen's eyes lingered on one particular figure, and then he grunted to himself and turned away, setting his pace to match that of the final wagon.

It was time to go home.

Chapter Seventeen

Rouge

The alarm went off, and for the first time in a month, Zoey didn't tell the house AI to pause it. Today was her last day at Veritas Corp. The last day she'd see Nina, Jazmin, Dr. Joe, Sara, Mr. Hamncheese, and Bridget (though she'd barely caught glimpses of Bridget since she announced she was quitting.) She'd even miss Granny, who wasn't anyone's Gran as far as Zoey could tell, and liked pickles way more than she should. On the other hand, she wouldn't miss Harris, who always seemed to be lurking around somewhere (especially since Bridget announced she was quitting), or Georgia McKeene, who'd finally given up trying to get Zoey to quit once she had less than a week left.

Zoey sat up in bed, stretching, then took a deep breath and hopped up. She'd been keeping her favorite slacks and blouse combo on hold all week so that she could wear them today. The left one of her pair of clunky but comfortable flats had lost half its sole on Tuesday, and she'd had to make an emergency run to the shoe store to get a new pair. Fortunately, she actually had some money in her account now, so she'd been able to find a pair that not only didn't feel like it was going to erode her heel or little toe away, but also looked pretty cute.

She tugged on her underwear and socks, then the pretty pink blouse and black slacks that actually fit her slim hips without trying to fall off. Her shoes slipped on easily, and she pulled her hair up into its poof on top of her head. Carefully smoothing down the baby hairs around her hairline with some gel, she stuck two hairpins shaped like pink plumeria into the base of her poof. Finally, she applied waterproof eyeliner and mascara, a hint of pink eyeshadow, and a little lip gloss.

Leaning back, she smiled a little, remembering how uncomfortable she'd been in her office-lady clothes and pantyhose just a few months before. Nina and Jazmin had both given her some tips, and she thought she looked really professional now. Tilting her head, she inserted plumeria earrings into her ears, then considered the final effect.

Yep, she was definitely getting the hang of this!

She trotted downstairs, where she was greeted by a gleeful Max, who acted as if he hadn't seen her in days, instead of having just left her room a half hour or so before, when Zoey's dad got up and started making bacon and eggs. The chocolate lab's front feet left the ground before he remembered his manners and put them back down, only to instantly forget again in his excitement. Zoey laughed and flopped his ears.

"I know, I know. I'll give you a piece of bacon."

Her dad, who was standing at the stove flipping what he called 'silver dollar pancakes', looked back over his shoulder and raised one eyebrow at this. "You'll do what now?"

She just blinked, giving him the big eyes. "I didn't say anything. Are you getting old and losing your hearing?"

He mock-glared. "That's it, no pancakes for you." His deep baritone was threatening, but she knew he would never deny his precious baby girl pancakes, so she just grinned at him unrepentantly.

"You don't want to have to eat all those pancakes by yourself, do you? When you've already lost ten pounds?"

He sighed, turning back toward her. His spatula was piled high with fluffy, two-inch circles that teetered ominously until he placed one finger on top of the stack. "Plate?" he asked.

Quickly, she pulled a plate from the cabinet, noting as she did that there weren't many left. "Allie, run the dishes after breakfast, please?"

A smooth feminine voice replied from nowhere, "Yes, Zoey."

The fancy dishwasher was Zoey's single biggest expenditure from her earnings at Veritas, because she really, really hated washing dishes. Now, all they had to do was put the dishes into the dishwasher, and the system would sort and wash the dishes in the most efficient manner possible given whatever was in there. It even recognized fragile dishes by doing something fancy with light, and made sure they emerged intact from the wash cycle.

Her dad shook his head as he slid the stack of pancakes onto the plate Zoey was holding out. "I still can't get used to the house talking back. I liked it better when it just sent messages to our screens."

She switched the plate to her left hand and patted his arm (which was about as high as she could easily reach, because he was Way Too Tall). "It's okay, dad. It's all part of being old." She squeaked as she dodged his playful smack, but silently noted that the hardest part of the dodge was not doing it so quickly that he noticed and got worried again.

Since she had started testing the long-term immersion pod at Veritas, she had noticed that her strength, stamina, and dexterity had increased. At first it had been barely noticeable, things like always being able to get her balance after she tripped, or catching something that fell before it could hit the ground. Now, though, it was apparent in everything she did, if she wasn't careful, and her dad was starting to worry about it. Nothing Veritas Corp was testing was supposed to be invasive, and he couldn't figure out how she was changing so much without something radical being done to her.

Zoey was pretty sure it was the blue goo. Whenever she asked about it, she got a whole lot of 'proprietary information' back, but she was pretty sure the stuff was using nanobots or microscopic circuitry or *something* to stimulate her nervous system while she was in there. She always felt more tired than she should when she got out, more like she'd actually been exercising rather than just floating in gelatin, and when she was in the goop, the virtual reality was noticeably more realistic to every sense.

Max leaned against Zoey's leg, looking up at her with adoration in his big brown eyes. Well, her or the plate of pancakes. She chuckled as she patted his head. That was one nice thing about her newly fit body. She'd never particularly enjoyed exercise, so she generally got tired of playing with Max long before he got tired of playing with her. Now, though, she could run and play with him for hours, which made for a very happy (and tired) doggo.

Carefully, she set the plate on the table. (That was a downside of increased strength. She'd actually broken a plate or two before realizing that she needed to be gentler.) The eggs were already there, covered in a glass bowl to keep them warm. With a flourish, her dad opened the oven, pulling out a tray of perfectly crisp bacon, and releasing the aroma of heaven into the room. Zoey and Max both started to salivate.

"No more vegetarian meals, Dad?" she teased as she set the table with two more plates, forks, knives, and syrup, and poured two glasses of orange juice.

He grimaced. "As much as I like eggplant parm and spinach lasagna, it was time for some bacon." He pulled out his chair and sat down. "Plus, this is your last day of work. Tomorrow you go back to being a kid, right? A working woman needs a good meal to start her day."

She laughed. "Tomorrow you'll say a growing kid needs a good meal to start their day." She forked some eggs and bacon into her mouth.

He raised that eyebrow again. "And I'll be right then, too."

A companionable silence fell over them, broken only by periodic sounds of happy crunching coming from beneath the table. In spite of the fact that they both knew they shouldn't feed Max people food, well, sometimes things slipped, and as long as it happened on both sides of the table, everyone except Max ignored it.

Zoey's stomach was pleasantly full as she used a pancake to wipe the last of the yolk and bacon crumbs from her plate. Popping the little cake into her mouth, she sat back in her chair and surveyed the damage. They had demolished all but one of the eggs, and the pancakes and bacon were gone. She exchanged a look with her dad, and he silently applied himself to finishing his last slice of bacon as Zoey walked over and tipped the final egg into Max's bowl. The dog slurped the treat down happily, and Zoey put the dirty plate directly into the dishwasher.

No. More. Pre-rinse. Yes!

Once the kitchen was tidied, they headed out to the car. Her dad refused to get one of the guided, self-driving cars that used technology to make sure the person in the driver's seat was sitting up and paying attention, but otherwise were entirely self-controlled. He said that as long as he had to watch the road anyway, he'd trust his brain before a computer system. Zoey was pretty sure that when their current car died, he wasn't going to have a whole lot of choice, but that was between him and the car manufacturers.

Today being Zoey's last day, and since the college where her dad taught literature was also between semesters, he took her all the way to work before heading back to his own job. Usually, since the college was halfway-ish between their house and Veritas Corporation's main office building, Zoey caught a bus for the second leg of the trip. She was fine with that, honestly, but it was kind of nice to have her dad take time out of his day to deliver her to Veritas' doorstep.

When they arrived, her dad pulled up in the loading zone outside the front door, and they both looked up at the rather imposing stepped building, fronted with the ubiquitous giant V that was on everything Veritas produced. Reaching over, Zoey's dad touched her hand. "You okay, kiddo? I know you'll miss this place."

Zoey was silent for a moment. Miss it? Maybe. She'd certainly miss the magic pod, and a lot of the people, but she would *not* miss the strange politics and social dynamics that hid beneath the conventional façade. No more worrying about who was on whose side. No more wondering if someone (besides Ms. Viper McKeene) was Out to Get Her. Bonus, she'd never have to see Dr. Veralt or his creepy 'team member', Mr. Harrison, ever, ever again. The new researcher had been lurking around ever since he was hired, watching everything that happened in Dr. Joe's office, and it gave her the heebie jeebies every time she rounded a corner to see his pasty face and disconcertingly flat black eyes staring at her.

She smiled weakly at her dad and shrugged one shoulder. "Yeah, it's okay. It'll be nice to have some time to relax before school starts in a week, and I'll still be able to see Nina in-game or get together for lunch or something. She'll keep me filled in on all the gossip, too." Her smile widened to a more honest grin as she thought about her glasses-wearing, conspiracy-theory-spouting, gossip-loving friend. She was so glad they'd managed to form a real relationship that was going to continue outside of work, because she would really miss the older girl if this had actually been her last chance to see her.

Zoey's dad reached over and hugged her with one long arm. She leaned her head on his shoulder for a moment, and then someone behind them honked, probably because this was a three-minute loading zone, and they were pushing it. "All right, Zoe. I'll see you this evening. Are you sure you just want to head straight home instead of coming by the office so I can take you?"

She shook her head. "It doesn't cost that much to catch a ride-share, and I'll get home sooner that way. I've almost finished my summer reading list, but I still have two chapters of 'Of Mice and Men' to get through."

Her dad laughed. "Too depressing?"

She rolled her eyes. "Oh my *gosh*. Why do people read this stuff?"

He smiled sympathetically. "There are some great lessons on compassion and understanding in there, and it's a good way to learn about the realities of a period of our history."

Zoey sighed and opened the door. She climbed out and then paused and leaned back in, much to the audible displeasure of the car behind them. "Love you, dad. Have a good day!"

He reached out and touched her hand where it rested on the back of the passenger seat. "Love you too, kid. I'm proud of you."

Zoey smiled back, and then it was time to step out and close the door. She waved as her dad drove away, and turned to look up at the mirrored glass building with the sparkling stone V that stretched up the front face of the middle ten stories. For better or worse, this was it. Her last day of work, then one week of vacation, and then it'd be time for her first day as a sophomore in high school. Time just kept slipping away from her, but she was going to make sure she appreciated this day to the fullest.

🍎 🍎 🍎

Sadly, fate didn't seem inclined to play along with Zoey's dreams of a peaceful and nostalgic last day. The first person she saw when she entered the Design department was Georgia McKeene, who was once again leaning over Jazmin's desk, staring at the other woman's screen. A black-lacquered fingernail poked at the screen.

"Here. Why did you need so many notepads and pens? Isn't everyone using their screens to record meetings and send messages?"

Jazmin was obviously fighting to remain patient, and her left hand clutched at the little cross hanging around her neck. "The number of 'device-free' meetings has increased lately. We keep running out, so I just asked the warehouse to double our order."

Ms. McKeene's eyes narrowed. "Where are you keeping all of these pens, then? Did you realize that the warehouse sent you *executive* pens since they were out of the standard ones?"

Zoey straightened her shoulders and marched in. After all, what did she need to be afraid of? It wasn't like the woman could fire her! "Ms. McKeene, why are you acting like *Mrs. Hollis*," she deliberately emphasized the use of Jazmin's last name, hopefully reminding the mean old snake that she should be treating other people with respect, "did something wrong? Everyone is vying for Miss Andrews' position, and they're having secret meetings to plan special projects to show her what they can do. They're using tons of pens and paper, and why do the executives need special *pens*, anyway? If you're looking for someplace to cut costs, shouldn't you look into that first?"

She tilted her head, touching her cheek with one finger as if she was thinking. "Oh, wait, you're in the Personnel department, so why are you asking about purchases anyway?" Not that it was really a question. Ms. McKeene seemed to dislike Jazmin as much as she did Zoey, and turned up every few days to harass the woman about something. Jazmin always looked shaken after the venomous woman left, and Zoey had had about enough of it.

Georgia's already thin lips tightened even further, and she straightened abruptly. "My *concern* is none of yours, Miss Williams. You are fortunate that today is your last day, or you would find yourself in my office being written up for insubordination. I believe that would be your third red mark, too, so you would be due for a week's suspension without pay."

Zoey glared hotly. "It is a good thing it's my last day, because you've been rude and hostile since the moment I walked into your office. Maybe *I'm* the one who should be reporting *you*."

Ms. McKeene flinched back, just for a moment, but Zoey saw it and could barely keep a triumphant smile off her own lips. She very much doubted that if she did report the woman, if it would be the first such complaint on her record. She wondered if Ms. Georgia McKeene was about due for some unpaid leave herself.

Ms. McKeene drew herself up to her full (average, but still several inches taller than Zoey) height, and brushed at her spotless, unwrinkled pencil skirt. "I will let this slide, since it is your last day, Miss Williams. Do remember, however, who will be writing your recommendation for your next position." With that apparently cutting remark, she turned her cold gaze back onto Jazmin. "Jazmin, I expect every one of the executive pens to be returned to me by the end of the day. We will go together to the warehouse and explain that you do not have the authority to requisition anything used by upper management unless it is a single item for Bridget's personal use."

Zoey gritted her teeth. She knew this tactic. Ms. McKeene would take Jazmin down and publicly humiliate her while pretending to 'educate' everyone involved. She took a step forward, opening her mouth to say… *something*, when she saw Jazmin give the smallest shake of her head. Reluctantly, Zoey sank back and closed her mouth. She stayed silent until Ms. McKeene swept from the room like a Victorian belle departing after delivering the 'cut direct' to an unwanted suitor. (Zoey really needed to stop reading Regency romances.)

Once the door closed behind Georgia McKeene's stiff back, Jazmin gave one final rub to her little cross, and then let her hand fall in her lap. Leaning back in her chair, the assistant gave a deep sigh, smiling tiredly at Zoey. "Thank you, Zoey, but this is nothing new. It isn't your job to protect me."

Zoey set her fists on her hips. "It may not be my job, but that doesn't mean I'm just going to watch it happen. 'It is an eternal obligation toward the human being not to let her suffer when one has a chance of coming to her assistance.'" Okay, so she'd taken some minor liberties with the quote, but she was fairly certain Simone Weil would forgive her.

Jazmin stared for a moment, then laughed, her beautiful face relaxing into her usual cheerful expression. "Your father?"

Zoey flushed a bit. "Dad made me read *The Needs of the Soul* when he taught it last fall, and it kinda stuck with me."

The other woman smiled gently, then stood, unfolding her nearly six-foot tall frame from her incredibly comfortable office chair. "I can see why it would. Now come on, Bridget has called another all-hands meeting."

Zoey swallowed hard. Last time Bridget did this, it had been after her best friend Amy died as a result of injuries she'd sustained in a suspicious hit-and-run car accident several months before. Bridget had announced that she wouldn't be renewing her contract, and that she would recommend someone from the department to take her place. This had led to all kinds of cliques forming, secret meetings, and occasional backstabbing.

As Zoey's feet traipsed down the hall, following the *click-clack* of Jazmin's matte gold stilettos, she looked around. The large meeting rooms were familiar to her now, and she knew which one had a drop-down screen that always stuck unless you pushed on the right side just so. She knew that Harris' beloved beanbag chairs were more effort than they were worth to get out of. She knew that as she walked by Bridget's closed office door, she was walking by an icon of the industry, and the woman who had been primarily responsible for creating true, immersive virtual reality.

The large room that was used for all-hands meetings also served as the kitchenette and break room, though the tables and chairs were currently pushed against the walls. Bridget preferred to keep people standing during meetings, since she thought that sitting invited them to linger after the important topics had been covered. Only Granny and a few other older members of the department were sitting in the seats tucked up against the walls.

Quiet murmurs rose in volume for a moment when Jazmin and Zoey entered the room, and the pair were offered some friendly smiles and nods of recognition. Zoey could see calculation in the eyes of some of the people who were vying for Bridget's position, since Jazmin was usually briefed before the meeting and then allowed to return to her desk in case anyone came in while everyone else was occupied.

Shortly after Zoey settled herself against the wall in a position that would allow her to remain unobtrusive while also actually being able to see Bridget (because being five foot nothing at the back of a crowd was incredibly irritating), Bridget herself entered the room.

The young genius, who had developed VR while still in college, was noticeably thinner than she had been when she'd made the announcement about Amy. Her soft blue blouse hung loose, and her skirt was belted tightly to keep it up. Her strawberry-blonde hair was limp and pulled back into a simple braid.

Issuing a stiff, businesslike smile, Bridget looked around. "I'm going to keep this brief, so if everyone would please give me their full attention?" She paused as a few people put their screens down a little shame-facedly. "I have two things to discuss today. First, I have received everyone's project briefs, and have narrowed them down to three."

Everyone tensed. The project applications were the first step in deciding who Bridget would recommend to the CEO and the board of Veritas Corp as the best person to replace her. Zoey had helped with various parts of several of them, and knew there were at least fifteen. Cutting that down to three from just the briefs seemed pretty harsh, but, honestly, Bridget probably already knew who she was going to recommend, and all of this was just to make it seem as though everyone had an equal chance.

"Harris, Drummond, and Kanumba. You may proceed with your projects. Everyone else, please set your own projects aside and assist one of these three, unless I speak to you individually. We can't let our regular work fall to the wayside, no matter how exciting these new ideas may be." The three people named had varying expressions of excitement, satisfaction, and calculation. They would now have to recruit the best of their former competitors to help them, and whoever snagged the best and brightest would have a significant advantage over the others.

Bridget was continuing, her face growing even more serious. "The second issue is something I hoped never to have to deal with during my tenure here. There have been suggestions made recently that a member of our team may be allowing information that should not leave this department to fall into the hands of outsiders. We're not yet certain if the information has left the company itself, but, as you know, Veritas is a very competitive company, and each department does have its own, ah, internal projects which are not to be spoken of anywhere else until they're finalized."

There was a long pause, while people shuffled and looked around. Faces which had been excited or crestfallen now grew wary and suspicious. Bridget drew in a deep breath. "This meeting is official notice that an internal investigation, as outlined in each of your employment contracts, has been instigated. As we speak, a third-party firm is checking each of your desks. All emails, notes, and messages will be logged, though no information found in this way will be given to me or any member of management unless it is related to the current situation. As your area is cleared, someone will come and get you, and you will have a brief interview with an investigator. Again, these are outside contractors, and they will not tell me, or any other executive, anything that doesn't apply to the leaking of company secrets."

Bridget's blue eyes were sad as she looked around the room. "My office was checked this morning, and I also had an interview. I can assure you that they will be very professional, and you have nothing to fear as long as you have complied with company policy. We understand that small infractions do occur, and this is not a witch hunt. However, if you do have a concern, you may come and speak to me with an unbiased witness present. Thank you for your cooperation, and we hope that this situation will be dealt with soon."

With that, the young Director of Design turned on her heel and left the room, leaving pandemonium behind her.

ৼ ৼ ৼ

Zoey was one of the first ones to be summoned to her interview, which was a little sad because she was about ready to get a pack of microwave popcorn from the cabinet and drop a dollar in the 'honor system' jar. Everyone seemed to be sure they knew who was leaking information, and it always seemed to be someone on one of the other teams. The newly appointed team leaders were glad-handing and baby-kissing all the people they wanted on their projects, while simultaneously bad-mouthing the competition.

No one wanted Zoey, of course, not only because she was just a lowly intern, but also because today was her last day, and she wouldn't even be a possible informant as of this afternoon. This left her in the awesome position of being able to pull up a chair and just listen and watch as the department slowly tore itself apart. A group of people who had been engaged in friendly competition when Zoey started her internship were now showing their true colors, and she had a feeling that when the whole thing shook out, some personnel would need to move to other departments, or possibly finding a whole different company at which to work.

Fortunately, while poor Jazmin and a few other people that Zoey had become friendly with looked more and more stressed and unhappy, Zoey herself was free and clear. When a man who looked to be around her dad's age showed up at the door and called out her name in a neutral voice, she was almost disappointed to be leaving.

The man, who wore a dark beige suit and introduced himself as Mr. Walker, had her follow him to one of the small two-to-four-person conference rooms near Jazmin's desk. These were usually used when guests came to the department to meet with someone who either didn't have a private office or didn't want them in there, so they were very bland, with round wooden tables and a few chairs, and nothing else.

As Zoey walked through the halls, which were oddly hushed, she could see stern-faced men and women looking through various people's areas. Most of them seemed to have implants that allowed recording, because they weren't holding a screen or camera, but would periodically touch their jaw or ear while speaking so quietly no one could possibly have heard them.

Mr. Walker ushered Zoey into the small room, where a Black woman, probably in her fifties, with steel-gray hairs liberally mixed through her chestnut curls, sat waiting patiently for them. The woman smiled warmly at Zoey, who sat a little nervously, in spite of knowing that she hadn't done anything wrong.

"Hello, Zoey. My name is Ms. Jackson. Mr. Walker is going to sit in on your interview, but he's just here to make sure there are no suggestions of impropriety, and will not be asking any questions. This meeting will, however, be recorded for our files, though it will not be released to Veritas Corporation unless you witnessed or committed some infraction of clauses 15 to 21, inclusive, which cover information sharing within and outside of the company. Do you understand?" Her voice was firm but soothing, sounding like some of Zoey's favorite teachers, the ones who knew their stuff and made sure you learned it, but also knew when to be flexible and kind.

Zoey nodded, then lifted her hand a little.

Ms. Jackson chuckled. "Go ahead, Zoey. This isn't school."

"Ah, well, about that... You know I'm a minor, right? I think maybe I should call my dad before-"

The older woman smiled again. "Right you are. Your father did sign a waiver allowing Veritas Corporation to perform its normal disciplinary proceedings as needed so long as the police weren't involved, but I'm certain he was thinking of the two times a," her eyes flickered up and to the right, but her expression didn't shift, "Ms. McKeene wrote you up, not a serious internal investigation. We could certainly argue that this situation, since it is internal and covered in your contract, falls under that waiver, but I don't think we need to."

Reaching out, Ms. Jackson tapped the table, and the center of it lit, then raised. Zoey's dad looked out of the paper-thin screen; his expression concerned. When he saw Zoey, the lines between his eyebrows eased a little, and he nodded. Ms. Jackson turned the screen and pushed it to one side so that Zoey's dad could see and be seen by everyone.

"Dr. Williams," Ms. Jackson said, nodding her head in greeting. "Thank you for joining us on such short notice. This shouldn't take long, especially since Zoey is not in a position to have had access to the information which was leaked, nor would she have anything to gain from what was done with the information. So, with that in mind, I have only three questions for you, Zoey."

Ms. Jackson turned her compassionate gaze to Zoey's dad. "If I may, Dr. Williams?"

Her dad nodded, but said, "If she starts to say anything that could be considered... problematic, I reserve the right to stop the interview and call my lawyer." By which he meant Aunt Danika, who had handled his divorce, but generally specialized in things like patent infringement.

Ms. Jackson nodded in agreement and turned back to Zoey. She leaned forward, touching her jaw just beneath her ear, then resting both hands on the table in front of her in a relaxed and nonthreatening manner. "Zoey, have you ever communicated private information that belongs to Veritas Corporation, or, more specifically, the Design department, to anyone outside of this department, in any way?"

Zoey shook her head, eyes huge and heart pounding like it might burst from her chest.

"I'm sorry, but could you respond verbally, please?"

"Um, No?" Zoey heard the question in her own voice, and swallowed hard. "I mean, no!"

Ms. Jackson nodded. "Do you have any information about any individual or group of individuals who have inappropriately communicated private information that belongs to Veritas Corporation, or, more specifically, the Design department, to anyone outside of this department, in any way?"

"No!" This time her voice was firm.

"Well done, Zoey. One more question, and then you're free to go." Ms. Jackson offered Zoey a reassuring smile. "Have you ever heard, read, or had communicated to you in any way the term, 'Coma Protocol'?"

Zoey frowned and shook her head again. Ms. Jackson raised an eyebrow, and Zoey said, "No," as firmly as she could. The older woman smiled and sat up straight in her chair. "Thank you, Zoey. Thank you, Dr. Williams. This concludes your interview, Zoey. For the sake of clarity, I will mention that the term to which I have just referred is private information, and it would be best if you do not mention it to anyone other than each other. While doing so would not violate your contract, it could impede this investigation, and we would appreciate your cooperation in this matter."

Ms. Jackson stood up, revealing a navy-blue blazer and slacks over a tidy white blouse. She proffered a strong, unadorned hand to Zoey, who shook it carefully. "Good day, Dr. Williams. Zoey, Mr. Walker will take you to another meeting room, where you will wait until all of the interviews have been completed, or it's time for you to go to the Research department, where Miss Andrews has informed us you also work, whichever one comes first."

Mr. Walker reached out and almost-but-not-quite touched Zoey's elbow, indicating the now open door with his other hand. His smile was perfunctory, but his eyes were impossible to read, and she wondered if it was really over, or if she was still being judged. She shivered a little, but followed the stranger down the hall.

🍎 🍎 🍎

Zoey ended up sitting in the mid-sized conference room (known as 'The Sahara Room' because the air conditioning never worked for longer than a day) for the rest of her last shift in Design. Fortunately, a few other people trickled in, though each was warned not to talk about their interview when they were ushered into the room. Also fortunately, the Sahara was one of the few conference rooms with an adjoining bathroom, and a small table was set up with a selection of beverages and snacks. Unfortunately, all of the beverages were hot, so no one wanted to drink them, since they were already sweating from the heat of all their bodies stuffed in the cramped room.

Zoey was making small talk with a woman named Rhonda who had just started a few weeks earlier (and thus, presumably, was also considered an unlikely perpetrator) when Mr. Walker poked his head in the door. This time, he didn't bring in anyone new, but rather made an announcement.

"The interviews are complete, and we'd like to thank everyone for their cooperation and patience. There's still half an hour until lunchtime, but Miss

Andrews wants to let everyone go early as a show of her appreciation. You'll be expected to return to your normal tasks when you get back from lunch." He smiled perfunctorily, and then stepped out of the doorway, though he held it open in invitation.

The fifteen people who had been packed into the room immediately headed for the opening. Faces that had been drawn and anxious were now bright with relief, and excited chatter rose between friends as they emerged into the hall and saw everyone else leaving the areas where they had been waiting. Zoey thought how amazing it was that an extra thirty minutes of free time so easily wiped away two hours of frustration and anxiety.

Walking to the small space beside Jazmin's desk where she kept her things during the morning, Zoey hesitated when she saw that Jazmin wasn't there. She wanted to say goodbye to the woman who had helped her so much during her time there, so she lingered as people flowed by. She heard snippets of conversation as she waited, and it was clear that there was a great deal of conjecture about what the investigators might have found. These theories were being spurred on by speculation over the meaning behind which people were placed in rooms together after their interviews.

The last of the staff trickled out of the door and into the wide hallways of Veritas Corp, but there was no sign of Jazmin. Ms. Jackson opened the door of the small room in which she'd interviewed Zoey and stepped out. Her heavy brows raised when she saw Zoey still standing by Jazmin's desk.

"Zoey? Are you waiting for me or another member of my team? Did you think of something you forgot to mention?" Her voice was friendly, but her eyes were calculating.

Zoey felt her cheeks warm, and she shook her head vigorously. "No ma'am. You know, today is my last day, and I wanted to say goodbye to all of my friends. Jazmin helped me out a lot, and I didn't want to go without letting her know how much I appreciated her."

The suspicion vanished, but Ms. Jackson's eyes shifted to the left ever so slightly before she replied. "I'm afraid Mrs. Hollis felt ill after her interview. She went home early. Surely you can send her an email?"

Zoey had to fight to keep her own eyes wide open and innocent as she said, "Oh, yeah. I guess I can do that. I hope she'll feel better soon."

The older woman smiled. "I'm sure it was just the stress and uncertainty of the situation. Sometimes people get nauseated or develop a headache under difficult circumstances."

"So, she'll be back on Monday?"

There was that sideways glance again. "We can only hope so, Zoey. Now, you'd better get to lunch. I hope the rest of your day goes well."

Zoey picked up the *Kimi ni Todoke* lunchbox she'd set down by her cute new black pumps, taking the moment when her face was out of Ms. Jackson's view to clench her teeth in frustration. By the time she stood up again, she had her 'I'm just a nice kid' mask firmly back on. *[Acting] skill level up,* she thought wryly. "Thanks, Ms. Jackson. I hope you have a great weekend!" She waved cheerily and then turned and walked out of Design.

With the extra twenty minutes or so before official lunch started, Zoey was able to hit the cafeteria and grab an iced tea to go with the tuna fish salad sandwich and Hoho in her lunchbox. Not exactly the tastiest combination she'd ever had, but when you were scrounging for leftovers, you made do with what you could find.

Happily, she headed for the bench where she and Nina usually ate, enjoying the beautiful sunshine, but also grateful that at this time of day the bench itself would be in shadow, so it wouldn't burn her bottom. She knew from experience that the sun would still be in her eyes, but at least her rear was safe. When she got to the seat, however, she found it already occupied.

Bridget looked up from the wrap she looked like she was forcing herself to eat and smiled at Zoey tiredly. Zoey puffed a small sigh, but smiled back and plopped down on the bench beside her boss. "Hello, Miss Andrews," she said cheerfully. "It's a nice day, isn't it?"

Bridget grinned back just a little, her shoulders relaxing in her loose blue blouse. "Yes, Miss Williams, it is a lovely day."

They each ate a few bites of their meal in silence, until Bridget popped the last bite of her maybe-chicken-salad wrap into her mouth, chewed, swallowed, and said, too casually, "I was wondering what your plans are now that you've completed your internship."

Zoey grinned a little and swallowed a bite of Hoho. "Weeeellllll," she paused, drawing out the word almost to the point of breathlessness, "I have a little summer reading to finish…"

Bridget's expression grew a little tighter, and Zoey almost felt bad for teasing her.

"…and there's this quest I've been working on. It's a competition, and the other guy is a real first-class jerk, and I'm looking forward to kicking his butt."

Bridget raised a hand to cover the broad grin that threatened to split her face in half. "Oh, thank goodness. I was afraid that with the things that have happened lately-" She broke off and shook her head. Soft waves of strawberry-blonde hair fell around her face, gleaming in the sunlight, and for a moment she looked very much like her in-game avatar, the goddess Gina.

Zoey sighed and tugged at a curl that had escaped her poof, thinking about those 'things'. *Like being knocked unconscious in the game, which isn't supposed to happen, waking up locked up in a place I shouldn't have been sent, unable to ask for help, and then facing a guy who seems determined to make my real-life sister fight him? Yeah, that was a little scary.*

She shook her head. "I thought about giving up, honestly, but I'm not that kind of girl. I'm the kind of girl who kicks you in the teeth after you knock her down." *Or at least, that's who I want to be.* "So, you don't need to worry about me."

Bridget started gathering together the remains of her lunch. A small smile played around the corners of her mouth. "I'm glad to hear it. That's the kind of girl I am, too." She looked up, blue eyes locking onto Zoey's hazel ones. "Don't put yourself at risk for this, though. It's just a game."

Zoey smiled back, hoping her expression was enough to convey what she was thinking. This was a game like having control of the nuclear codes was a game. If she managed to beat FantumHat in spite of his cheating, she might actually help change the world for the better when Bridget released the open-source code for her original Virtual Reality system. Zoey didn't even pretend to understand the full ramifications of that, but even if it only helped people in comas or allowed people to work through psychological problems in a safe place, wasn't that worth a little risk?

The other woman stood, then paused, glancing around before looking back at Zoey. "Ah, I just remembered." She reached into the pocket of her skirt and pulled out a roll-screen. With a deft flick of her wrist, she snapped it flat, holding it out toward Zoey. "Veritas Corp has just opened a raffle for all current employees below management level. Everyone gets one Blind Box code to redeem for at least a small prize. The minimum prize is one free month of *Veritas Online*, and the grand prize is a secret, but it's... very good. Winners will be notified next Friday. As a current employee, you're entitled to a code. Would you like one?"

It felt for a moment as if the world froze around her, and then she swallowed hard and nodded. "Yes?" That questioning tone was back, so she coughed and tried again. "Yes," she said firmly, taking out her own screen and holding it up.

Bridget smiled, tapping the screens together. "Thank you for your exemplary work, Miss Williams. You can count on me for a personal recommendation when you're ready to apply for your next position."

Zoey swallowed hard. Bridget Andrews had just promised her a personal recommendation. What manager would deny an application with that attached? "Thank you, Miss Andrews," she choked out. "I hope to work with you again someday."

A sly smile quirked the corner of Bridget's mouth. "I hope so, too. Have a lovely day, Zoey."

Zoey just nodded, waving a weak hand as Bridget walked away. A soft voice from behind her squeaked, "Holy *cow*, Zoey, was that *Bridget Andrews?*"

Zoey turned to see Nina, neon green and pink tie-dye glasses nearly falling from her short nose, mouth agape. Zoey nodded. "You knew I worked with her."

"That looked like you were, you know, *eating lunch together.* Like *friends.*" If Nina got any more excited, she'd be speaking entirely in italics.

Zoey just motioned for her friend to sit down in the spot Bridget had just vacated. Nina did, looking like she'd never wash her slacks again. Zoey, for one, hoped she'd get over that quickly, because the royal blue pants were Nina's favorite, and she wore them at least once a week. Either that, or she had several pairs, but Zoey had never had the courage to ask.

"She's technically my supervisor, and I ran errands for her a lot, so we chatted sometimes. She said there's some kind of drawing going on, and she wanted to make sure I got a ticket, if I wanted one. You know, since I won't go back to Design today."

Nina's face brightened, and she nodded. "Yeah, I heard a rumor about that. I thought it was happening on Monday, but Miss Andrews would know." Shrugging that off, she leaned forward conspiratorially, pushing her vibrant glasses back up her freckled nose. "I *also* heard a rumor that Design got locked down this morning for an investigation into an information leak. That is a *big deal*, and I want to know *everything.*"

So, Zoey told her friend everything she could without breaking the rules. Nina was particularly interested in hearing exactly who had been in the same post-interview room with Zoey, and what they'd said, and Zoey gladly filled her in. True to form, Nina had conspiracy theories ranging from government espionage to a jilted lover trying to frame their ex, and the two girls were giggling by the end of lunch.

When Nina stood, gathering her lunch debris just like Bridget had done half an hour earlier, she sighed. "I'm going to miss this, eh? Nobody else here wants to listen to my ideas. I'm glad we'll still see each other in-game, though." She hesitated, and then said, "and I'm glad you'll be away from The Snake."

'The Snake' was their code word for Georgia McKeene. They had come up with it after Nina found a list in Ms. McKeene's office that contained both Zoey and her dad's names. It had given the mysterious recipient until September 12 to 'Get it done'. Honestly, it wasn't that the note itself was particularly frightening, but the fact that it was in Ms. McKeene's office (because *she* was a little scary), and had Zoey's name on it as well as the name of Amy Landon, Bridget's best friend who had been maybe-murdered, had sent Nina into a conspiracy theory spiral.

Zoey nodded. "That's really the only thing that makes me glad. I'm tired of having to be polite to her."

Nina put a hand on Zoey's where it rested on her lunch box. "Seriously," she leaned in and whispered, "be careful. I'll be watching for your check-ins."

Ever since finding the note, Nina had insisted that Zoey send her a message in the morning if they weren't going to see each other that day, and at night before bed. Zoey had decided to find it sweet that her friend was so worried about her.

Standing, Zoey patted Nina's hand in return. "I'm sure it wasn't a big deal. Probably just a list of people she hates." She rolled her eyes, but inside she still wondered. The only thing that linked Amy, Bridget, Dr. Joe, Zoey, her dad, and Jazmin...

Zoey gasped. "Jazmin!"

Nina's eyes opened wide behind her completely-clear glasses (she only wore them for the sake of fashion). "What about her?"

"I forgot she went home sick after her interview. I also caught the Snake harassing her again this morning."

Nina's eyes narrowed, and she pushed her glasses up her nose again. "Do you remember anything else? Did she look sick when you saw her earlier?"

Zoey shook her head. "No more than anyone would be after talking to that woman. But now she's gone, and I can't help but wonder…"

Nina grinned. "I'll have you seeing the truth soon enough, Zoe. Conspiracies are everywhere! D'you want me to check in with her on Monday and let you know how she is?"

"Yes, thank you!" Zoey felt a warm flush of relief. She knew there wasn't really anything she could do for Jazmin, if something more serious was going on, but it would be good to know that her friend was back safe and sound on Monday.

Nina flashed what she called a 'shaka', with her thumb and pinky extended. "Sweet. I'll see you in game soon! I'm finally leaving Bright, and it's a mess down there. Non-humans are vanishing like ice in summer, and no one seems to know where they're going. Are you sure you don't want me to stay and join this cult thing as a spy? I'd be glad to."

Zoey laughed. "Yeah, I know. An honest to goodness conspiracy and I'm asking you to stay out of it. I don't want you to get stuck on the wrong side, and I have a bad feeling about these vows they're making people take. Plus, we're going to have so much fun in Refuge!"

The older girl shrugged, making a face. "All right, for you. Plus, if I stay behind, I won't actually get to play with you, eh?" She touched her ear, wincing slightly as her implant must have started chiming. "That's my alarm. Gotta get back to work."

Impulsively, Zoey threw her arms around the taller girl, hugging her quickly before letting go. Nina winced. "Wow! You're a lot stronger than you look!" Nina threw an arm around Zoey's shoulders and hugged her back, then stepped away, grinning.

"See you later, Zoe!"

Zoey's eyes widened as her friend started to move away. "Oh! I forgot to ask how your date with Sam went last night!"

A brilliant red flush rose up Nina's neck, making her freckles stand out in sharp relief. Sam was one of the front desk security guards. Sam had only been a friendly acquaintance to both girls until Nina had asked them to slip Zoey a note. After that, Sam had dredged up the courage to ask Nina out on a date, and Nina had agreed. Since Zoey herself had very little interest in actually dating anyone (in spite of getting an occasional crush on someone, romance still looked like way too much work) she lived vicariously through her friend.

"Um, it was… nice…" If possible, Nina's cheeks grew even redder.

Zoey grinned. Sam identified as non-binary, and while Zoey didn't know exactly how that worked, it seemed to be fine with Nina, and the pair were absolutely adorable together. "Just fiiiine?" She sing-songed. "So, if I tell Sam you thought it was 'fine', they'll be 'fine' with that?"

Nina jumped back to Zoey, clapping a hand over the shorter girl's mouth. "You… I… You're fourteen, and I'm not going to…"

Zoey grinned wider. "So you're past PG-13 dates, huh?" Her voice was a little muffled, but clear enough.

Nina huffed, then laughed. "Maybe. *Yes.* I really like them, and I also really have to go, so good *bye*, Zoey!"

The two grinned at each other, waved, and each headed toward their next task with smiles on their faces.

☙ ☙ ☙

Ever since *Mr.* Harrison (new assistant to Dr. Veralt, who seemed to have some kind of rivalry with Dr. Joe) started working at Veritas, Zoey had been cultivating her [Sneak] skill in real life. The tall, pale man could often be found lurking in the halls, and whenever he and Zoey came across each other, he watched her with black, hooded eyes, though he never said anything to her. Once, out of sheer perversity, she had greeted him with the same cheerful manner she would use with a friend, but he just bared his teeth at her in something only a sociopath could have interpreted as a smile, and turned away.

After that, Zoey had discovered that there was a 'back way' into the lab building. It was just a rarely used side door, but it dropped her directly into the stairwell. Sure, she had to climb four flights of steps, but nowadays she could take them two at a time and wasn't even out of breath when she reached the top. So far, she'd managed to avoid the disturbing lab assistant, though she'd seen his back a few times as he walked away from Dr. Joe's door.

Today, though, she was going to take the main door, and if Mr. Harrison turned up, she was just going to ask him straight out what his deal was. With that in mind, she marched into the small entry foyer, walked over to the bank of elevators, and firmly pressed the up arrow. The two-minute wait after that took a little of the air out of her sails, and when the door dinged open, she was glad to see that the small space was empty. She stepped in, and pushed the button for the fourth floor.

Her luck held when the elevator chimed again a few moments later, and the door slid gently open to reveal an empty hallway. Cautiously, she poked her head out, took a look around, and, seeing no one, walked into the corridor. The reason for her missing nemesis became apparent, however, when she reached Dr. Joe's lab and heard voices echoing out into the hall.

"...complete, I want to see a report on your findings on my desk within a week!" That was Veralt, who may or may not have been a decent researcher, but barely passed as a functional human being.

Dr. Joe's voice was friendly, but Zoey could hear the tension in it. "Dr. Perez is scheduled to return to the office in two weeks. She is my direct superior, and I will provide her with my results. In any case, it will take at least two weeks to put together my findings."

Veralt again, sounding furious. "Any *competent* researcher would have been working on it as results came in. The final paper should just be a matter of organizing the data. Besides, Dr. Perez will have enough on her plate when she returns, and I am the co-director of this department!"

"Thank you for the reminder, Dr. Veralt. I'll be sure to take all of that into consideration. Now, my subject is going to be here any moment, and continuing this conversation within her hearing could skew my results for the day. Not to mention the fact that I have a great deal to go over with her, and need our full four hours to work."

That was Zoey's cue if she'd ever heard one, and she clenched the handle of her lunchbox tightly in her fist and then breezed cheerily in through the open lab door. "Hello, Dr. Joe!" She stopped; eyes wide. "Oh, Dr. Veralt!" She knew Harrison was off to the side, but she kept her gaze locked on the red, sweaty face of the chief researcher for a long heartbeat before directing an uncertain smile at Dr. Joe and Sara, his assistant.

"Um, Dr. Joe? I'm not sure I feel comfortable changing-"

Dr. Veralt almost growled in frustration, turning on his heel toward the door. "I'll leave you to it then, Dr. Sherman. I *expect* to see that report on my desk soon. If you need help completing it within the required timeframe, I'll be glad to send my assistant to aid you."

A shudder ran down Zoey's back as Veralt and Harrison walked toward the door. Harrison's black gaze seemed faintly mocking as it crossed hers, and then he turned his back to her and was walking away. She swallowed hard against a trace of nausea that threatened to send her sandwich back up her throat, and was unable to look away until the door clicked quietly behind the assistant. She didn't know why, but every time he looked at her, she felt like a mouse being played with by a particularly sadistic cat.

When she looked back, Sara was already rushing toward her, holding the sealed bundle that contained the bodysuit and sensors that Zoey would wear for the tests. The Indian woman barely took time to smile at her before rushing Zoey to a small, private changing room to one side. "Good timing, Zoey, but we really do have a lot to get through today. Please get changed as quickly as you can and then come out so I can finish hooking you up."

Zoey did as she was asked, quickly climbing out of her office gear and sliding into her bodysuit. She still hated wearing the skintight item in front of other people, but at least she didn't think she looked quite as much like a boy as she had when she'd first put one on the day of her fourteenth birthday when the only thing she'd gotten (and the only thing she'd wanted) was a home VR pod and a subscription to *Veritas Online*. That had only been five months ago, and Zoey had been wearing a suit daily as part of her job for almost three months of that, but she still thought that puberty was finally deciding to sneak up on her after a delay that gave new meaning to the term 'late bloomer'.

Emerging from the changing room, she blinked at the flurry of activity in the lab area. There was a large machine sitting in the middle of the space. It was covered in thin cables and dripping in round weight plates of various sizes, and she had absolutely never seen it before. The machine was on wheels, and Dr. Joe was just latching down a brake to prevent the device from rolling away. Sara was on the other side, steadying the thing, and they both looked up when they heard Zoey's door open.

Dr. Joe grinned, showing his crooked bottom tooth and almost looking like his old self. His former fiancé, Amy Landon, aka Bridget's best friend, had died not long ago, and he'd taken it hard. He hadn't shown genuine enthusiasm for much in recent days, but it seemed that he was slowly starting to feel better, and Zoey was glad. The girl shot a sidelong glance at Sara, who she was pretty sure had a mega-sized crush on her boss, and saw that the woman's brown eyes were locked on Dr. Joe's grin. A happy glow seemed to suffuse Sara's pretty brown face as she took in Joe's pleasure, and Zoey had to suppress a smile of her own at the sight. She was totally rooting for Sara, and hoped that Dr. Joe would eventually see what was right in front of him.

"I've been working on this for a few weeks now, and it's really come together," Dr. Joe said enthusiastically. "You can do all the same tests you did for us on your first day, but you don't have to go to the gym. I would have liked to repeat the tests we ran in the pool, but there'll be enough data that they shouldn't be necessary."

With a grand gesture, he swung open a small panel that had been mostly concealed by cables and weights, and motioned to the clear area inside.

Dangling wires hung there, clearly ready to be hooked up to the electrodes that Sara was picking up from a nearby table. "I'll leave you two ladies to finish up, and then we'll start! See you in a minute!" With a flick of a salute, the short, roundish man disappeared into his office and shut the door.

Sara smiled at Zoey and advanced on her, holding out the bundle of electrodes. They'd done this at least a few times a week since Zoey started, and by now she knew where most of the sticky dots went, though there were a few they only used when they ran the full battery of tests. They got Zoey patched up and into Dr. Joe's torture device within a surprisingly short period of time. Sara touched her jaw, muttered something subvocal, and then started attaching leads to the color-coded dots all over Zoey's body.

Dr. Joe himself appeared when they were about halfway through, and began checking cable tension and weight distribution. Once he was satisfied, he and Sara closed the little door on Zoey, and out came a large number of pins that reminded Zoey of the retro pin art toy Harris kept on his desk and used to mold his hand (or face) when he got bored. The flat-ended posts halted when they touched Zoey, and she could barely feel any pressure, but it was disconcerting to look down and see the things, since she now looked like she was being impaled by about a zillion pins.

Zoey turned to look at Dr. Joe, who had a proud expression as he watched the pins flex and shift as Zoey moved. Clearly, whatever the things were made of, it wasn't metal, no matter what they looked like. "Um, Dr. Joe? I don't remember these from the original tests."

The scientist nodded. "We won't use them for long, but as long as I have you here, I thought I might as well include you in a data set for another experiment I'm working on. Don't worry about it. After a minute or so, you won't even notice they're there."

He was right. Zoey was already getting used to the slight pressure, and unless she moved abruptly, making them bend to adjust before they could change their length, she couldn't even tell they were there. Still, Zoey frowned.

"I'm not exactly an expert, but aren't you supposed to do all the testing in exactly the same way every time when you're doing an experiment? Like, if you change something, that can affect the outcome and undermine your results? Or something?" Zoey was just as glad to do the testing here and away from prying eyes, but she'd been in AP Chemistry last year, and she was pretty sure this was not how things worked.

Dr. Joe and Sara exchanged glances before they both looked back at Zoey. "Ah, yes, well, that is usually true, but what we're studying is," he coughed into his fist as he finished speaking, and the words were lost in the sound. When he looked back up, he was composed again, though there was a slight twinkle in his eye. "In any case, it would be terrible if any of your data was invalidated, and we were forced to discard the results. We'd have to start over again, which would be a terrible setback, and I'm sure my boss, Dr. Perez, would want to have a long talk with me about it. Perhaps she'd be able to offer me some suggestions on what we can do to salvage the experiment."

Zoey's eyes widened, and she giggled a little when Dr. Joe offered her a slow wink. Sara, too, smiled a little when Zoey looked over toward her, and then both researchers were once again entirely serious and professional.

"Now, Zoey, please use only your left hand and try to pull the handle attached to the cable marked with an 'A' straight toward the ground..."

Chapter Eighteen

Khor

Nekthadt's presence had become commonplace, and, in fact, Khor grudgingly had to admit that the goblin was more than a little helpful. When one of the long troughs that fed the irrigation system broke, falling down and snapping one of the wooden gears that allowed the mechanism to move smoothly from one field to another, Nekthadt was able to carve a new one and set it into place before the leaves of even the drought-sensitive potatoes could begin to droop.

Juniper loved her new uncle, and she followed him around like a puppy, peppering him with questions about his life and childhood. Since the unicorns followed Juniper almost as often as they followed Khor, and Khor always stayed within earshot of the unicorns, that meant Khor also learned quite a bit about the goblin's early lives. Strangely, though Nekthadt was tight-lipped with everyone else, he could often be found lecturing Juniper or telling her stories that were more history than fantasy.

On this fine spring day, for instance, Khor was turning up rocks in yet another potential field, while Nekthadt carried the stones to various piles. Depending on their size, shape, and density, the stones might become paths, walls, or stone fill on which to build so a structure was less likely to settle or sink. Nekthadt was stripped to the waist so his lean muscles and plethora of scars were entirely visible, and Juniper asked questions.

"How'd you get that scar, Uncle Ned?" Sarave had put her foot down over the child calling her uncle 'Nekfat', and Nekthadt had mentioned that Rouge called him Ned. This was deemed an acceptable compromise, especially since Juniper adored Rouge.

Nekthadt turned his head to look down at a particularly long, deep mark that just missed his spine and dug through his flesh beneath his left ribs. The goblin picked up a large rock that Khor had just finished digging loose, and headed for the 'wall' pile. "That was during the war. One of the human generals had sent his troops into our territory after a unit of fleeing orcs. General Hullbitter, Lord Akuji's orc leader, closed a pincer attack behind them, cutting them off. They had two mages with them, though, so Hullbitter told me and three other goblin *justat* to kill the mages so we could crush the rest of the soldiers."

Khor kicked a rock free with unnecessary force, flinging it in the general direction of the goblin, who just smirked a little and continued with his story. "There was no reason to squander orcs and goblins, you see, in going up against the mages. We could have overcome them with sheer numbers, and many of our generals would have taken that path, but General Hullbitter was one of the good leaders. He knew which of his tools to use for which purpose, and while he never hesitated to send in as many troops as necessary, he also didn't waste our lives."

Khor remembered the orc general. He was a huge, hulking behemoth, at least ten feet tall, with long, muscled arms that seemed to reach out to the edges of any battlefield and simply pluck soldiers up and tear them into screaming pieces. By the end of the war, simply the sight of the monstrous orc, with his curved red tusks and eight-foot-long studded club, was enough to send whole battalions fleeing the battlefield.

"When we went in, it turned out that one of the mages could see through [Stealth]. It's a rare skill, fortunately, and we didn't expect a fire mage to have it, but he did, and he called the guards on us. Two *justat* died before we killed him, and I received this wound. If it wasn't for Karali, the last and best of us, I would have died there too." He reached out and ruffled his niece's brown curls. "So, remember to always expect the unexpected. Simply because something is unlikely, that doesn't make it impossible."

Juniper nodded solemnly. "Like that time I bet Kayli she couldn't eat three jars of jam without getting sick, an' she did it. Mama was really mad, 'cause she was gonna make a jelly roll for dessert."

Both Khor and Nekthadt snorted a little at this innocent comparison, but the goblin quickly pulled his face back into his usual sober expression. Juniper reached out and touched a series of parallel stripes that crossed her uncle's bicep, opening her mouth to ask about them, when they heard the first laugh.

It was long, high-pitched, and seemed to roll down from the low hills to the south. First there was one voice, and then two, and soon there were so many that Khor couldn't tell them apart. He and Nekthadt exchanged glances, their recent silent clash forgotten, and turned to the children. Juniper was staring toward the sound, which was already noticeably louder, with huge eyes. Khor himself felt an instinctive shudder run down his back and knew that whatever was coming was as far beyond the simple bugs and small animals they usually faced as he was.

Khor knelt in the dirt, and Nekthadt silently tossed Juniper up on his back, and then grabbed a unicorn under each arm. Straining mightily, the goblin managed to lift the small animals up, then swing himself up behind them, holding them firmly in his arms. Khor could feel them all shifting on his back, and when it seemed they were all settled, or near enough, he unfolded his legs and began to run.

They had grown complacent over the last week or so. With Viqa and Nekthadt there, they had easily defeated everything that came sniffing around the Tree. The goblin had quickly returned to full health once he was able to go outside and get some exercise, and with frequent applications of Sumi's Spider's Milk. Though Khor hated to admit it, the goblin was a strong warrior, and a valuable asset in a fight.

It wasn't until they were nearly home that Khor realized Nuisance wasn't atop his head. The duck had been splitting his time between Khor and the barn, lurking anxiously outside as if he were waiting for the eggs to hatch, but didn't want to admit it. Today, however, Khor distinctly remembered Nuisance going with him to the field, since the duck had nearly fallen from his head and had only managed to catch himself at the last moment, which resulted in a dangling duck who pulled painfully at Khor's forelock.

Now, however, there was no duck, and Khor wasn't certain when the bird had vanished. His long strides hitched for a brief moment, but then he stretched out again into a ground-eating gallop, well aware that his first priority had to be getting the children home. As he ran, he drew in an almost painful breath and brayed out a warning.

When they reached the house, Khor dropped to his knees again, and his passengers fell off more than dismounted. Juniper looked thrilled and a little sick, while Nekthadt's expression was calm and determined. The unicorns were clearly displeased with the whole experience, and kicked free of the goblin's grip the moment they could, then pranced in place while angrily emitting their odd bray-whinny.

Sarave ran from the direction of the main field, scooping Juniper into her arms with a wordless cry of relief. Sumi emerged from the interior of the house. <What's going on?> she asked.

<I'm not sure. Something is coming down from the mountains. A lot of somethings. They sound... I think we should get everyone inside and prepare for battle.>

The spider sounded grim. <Should we send Sarave and the children to William?>

Khor dug at the ground with a hoof, thinking. <Not yet, not until we know what we're dealing with. They need to be ready, though.>

Sumi clicked her fangs in confirmation, and turned back to Sarave. She quickly wove the symbol that told the goblin she needed to retreat to the basement with the children and be ready to run into the tunnels if anything broke into the house. The tunnel was designed with a deadfall that would crush any pursuers, while also blocking the path so no one else could follow. Once they were through, the children should be safe, but they also wouldn't be able to return the same way.

Sarave nodded, mouth tight and determined, and ran into the house carrying her daughter. The goblin woman hesitated only briefly in the doorway, looking back at her brother, who was clearly not planning to retreat. Khor gently nudged the unicorns through the doorway with his nose, and the small creatures, who often napped with their little half-goblin friend, trotted inside without hesitation. They had long since built stairs down to Sarave's living area, replacing the shaky old ladder, so Sarave, Juniper, Kayti, and Kayli should soon be down below, with the trap door firmly locked.

Khor looked at the barn door. <What about the ducks?>

<They'll run if they have to.>

<What about the eggs?>

Sumi tapped a leg impatiently. <We'll keep anything from reaching this far, but if it did… There's nothing we can do for them. Not now.> Her words were harsh, but he knew her well enough to know that she was worried too. There would be more eggs, and more ducklings, if there were ducklings in the eggs the hens were sitting on, but Sumi had a soft spot for younglings of all kinds, and she would be blaming herself for not planning for a way to keep the ducks safe when they couldn't run away.

He lowered his head so his horns were in front of the spider. <We'll protect

them.>

Sumi climbed up onto his horns, then crawled down his neck and settled onto his back. <Good.>

Khor looked over at Nekthadt, who was standing, silent and ready, his upper body still bare, clutching a knife from the kitchen, though Khor hadn't seen him enter or leave the house. The goat bent a knee, and the goblin used the offered leg to leap onto Khor's broad back, settling in beside Sumi without hesitation.

Khor ran. Now that he didn't have to focus on making sure his gait was smooth and his passengers secure, he could run full out. It didn't take long for him to draw near enough to hear the eerie laughter again, and now he could just see the first of the creatures making the noise.

There were eight of the things. They were large, with the shoulders of the tallest ones well over four feet, which made them as tall as Nekthadt. They were deep-chested, with powerful front legs and smaller hindquarters. Their fur was yellow and tan, with black spots across their backs and down their legs. They had large heads, with wide, slavering mouths containing many sharp, jagged teeth. It was from this mouth that the distinctive laughter emerged, and they cackled as they ran.

The beasts were chasing perhaps a dozen graceful, running animals. The creatures were slim and small, with large ears and eyes, long necks, and small, fluffy tails. Their fur was a reddish-gold, though it was currently matted with sweat and, in some cases, blood. Even as Khor watched, one of the animals stumbled and fell, screaming pitifully. One of the predators was on it instantly, tearing out its throat with little more than a flick of its powerful jaws. Another of the monsters paused to eat the fallen animal, but it was clear that this meal was too small to last long.

Khor stopped as the flow of escaping creatures parted around him. The small beasts looked at him with wild eyes, but they were too terrified and exhausted to do more than run past, barely slowing. Another one stumbled and went down, its whistling cry cut off as quickly as the first.

Then the attackers were on them. Most of the spotted creatures leapt for Khor, and he struck out with his hooves, kicking with such force that he flung one of the laughing monsters several meters away, where it landed with a dull *thud* and lay still. He swept his horns from side to side, keeping the things from his vulnerable throat, though he felt teeth tearing and pulling at the ragged fur around his chest and legs. They were trying to pull him down.

Then he felt a push from above as Nekthadt leapt into the fray. The goblin's knife was a blur, and he landed on the back of one of the largest attackers. The knife flashed over and over as it dug into the thick fur and flesh around the creature's shoulders, and then it found the throat, and the goblin was gone, moving on to another beast, certain the first was already dead, though it hadn't finished falling yet.

Meanwhile, Sumi threw webs down into the fray to tangle around feet and jaws. As with many such creatures, while their bite could shatter bone like rotten wood, the muscles that opened their jaws weren't nearly as strong, so it was much easier to simply keep their mouths shut, effectively depriving them of one of their strongest weapons.

Hooves, knife, teeth, claws, and webbing flew. Sumi was too wise to enter the fray unnecessarily. Her hard carapace might seem strong, but the crushing jaws would crack her open like a boiled lobster at one of the fancy dinners Aspen used to attend. The stench of blood and other things filled the air, but gradually the laughter quieted, then stopped, and Khor stood in a field of carnage, sides heaving as gore dripped from his sides where he'd been bitten and scratched.

Nekthadt's knife flashed once more, and a beast whimpered as it died, twitching once before falling limp to the ground beneath the goblin. Blood stained Nekthadt's green skin, too, and Khor was certain at least a few of the injuries that covered his arms and torso would produce lovely new scars for his little niece to ask about. The goblin ignored his injuries, however, simply walking around and checking each of the fallen monsters, delivering a coup de grace where necessary. Only when he was certain that all of the attackers were truly and completely dead did he pause, then lean forward, hands braced on his thighs as he drew in deep breaths.

<Did any make it past us?> Khor asked silently, knowing Sumi would have kept track.

<Two. They were still chasing the little animals, and they were heading towards the Tree.>

Khor looked at Nekthadt, who looked back, seeming to understand that their brief respite was over. The goblin returned to Khor's side, and Khor bent his knee, allowing Nekthadt to clamber aboard once more.

<To the Tree, then.>

They had raced past the Tree on their way to confront the attackers, and so now they retraced their steps. Khor had to admit that he was, perhaps, slightly slower than he had been before, but that was because he was sure Viqa could handle two of the beasts.

Fairly sure.

So, when they arrived to find a spotted monster falling limply from a bubble of water while the other struggled in one of Sumi's web traps, Khor felt relief but no real surprise. Sumi quickly wrapped the last thrashing monster up until its native weaponry was thoroughly tangled, and Nekthadt dispatched the beast with a few thrusts, then went to make sure the drowned animal was dead and not just unconscious.

Once all the monsters were dead, the defenders turned to survey the damage. Thankfully, the Tree and Viqa were fine. The glyphis had had plenty of warning, and had played bait to draw the one beast into the webbing. She could only maintain one water bubble of such size, but the webs had done their job and kept the second creature busy until help arrived.

Only six of the small, gracile herbivores remained of the herd which had been fleeing the carnivores, and they now stood huddled around the base of the

Tree, some even leaning on it, breathing heavily. Their fur was wet with sweat, but they all seemed uninjured, which made sense, since they had to be the strongest and healthiest of their herd in order to survive. Thankfully, they made no move to nibble on the Tree itself, either bark or leaves, so Khor and the others didn't need to worry about them.

Khor himself seemed to be the worst injured. He had scratches and bites all over his legs, chest, and hindquarters. While his powerful kicks and sweeping horns had kept him from any lasting injury, he was still feeling a bit weak from blood loss. Nekthadt had a few scratches on his legs and back, and one good bite on his left arm, but all in all his agility had stood him in good stead against the thick, heavy-bodied beasts. Sumi, who was tired but entirely uninjured, quickly produced her Spider's Milk and dosed Khor, then had Nekthadt pour more on any open wounds. There was more Milk back at the house, so Khor was certain Nekthadt would be getting his own soon enough.

Once everyone was patched up, Sumi headed back toward the house to let Sarave know that they were safe. Nekthadt began skinning the monsters with his kitchen knife. Viqa settled back into her guard duty, and Khor remembered something.

Nuisance.

The bird had vanished before all of the excitement began, but Khor last remembered him being near the field where they had been working when they first heard the maniacal laughter echoing down from the hills. So where was the bird? Annoying as he was, he was a useful lookout, and Khor would, possibly, miss him if anything had happened to him.

Khor trotted back toward the house, shuddering against the aches and pains that were settling into his muscles and deep in his wounds. Sumi's Spider's Milk would speed up his own natural healing process, and he could feel the heat and itch of mending flesh forming around the painful places. Honestly, he'd almost rather heal at a normal pace. If it weren't for the fact that he never knew when they might be attacked again, he would have spurned the disgusting fluid regardless of how insulted the overgrown arachnid would be.

He had hoped that Nuisance would be sitting outside the barn, as he often was these days, waiting for the eggs to hatch. Only the hens were there, though, and they glared at him with beady black eyes when he maneuvered his horns in through the almost-too-small doorway.

Next, Khor poked his nose in through the open door of the house. Nuisance wasn't supposed to go inside any more, on threat of becoming dinner. While Khor was fairly certain Sarave was bluffing, the bird had so far decided not to risk it. Khor could hear voices coming from below, so he guessed Sarave and the children were preparing to come back up, but there were neither feathers nor quacks to give away a fowl hiding place.

To the river, then, and Nuisance's favorite spot by the pond. The bird could sleep for hours there, waking only long enough to snap up a few small fish and insects. Now that the glyphis were there, however, there were fewer fish available, and the duck seemed to be more than a little concerned that the fish-like people might make a 'mistake' and snap him up as well.

Back to the field where they had been working earlier, then. Khor didn't know of any places nearby where Nuisance liked to roost, so he had hoped that the duck had simply waddle-hopped his way to one of his usual places. Once Khor's hooves were once again sunk deep in the soft, rich earth of the field, he bleated loudly in the call he reserved for Nuisance. Once. Twice.

Nothing.

No quacks, no rustle of underbrush as a bird woke and hurried back.

Khor flared his nostrils. Nuisance didn't have a particularly distinctive scent. Sometimes he caught a whiff of warm feathers, or possibly a hint of the odor of the pond, if the bird had recently gone swimming. Nothing that could be used to track him, however.

A quest image appeared before him. A stylized duck and a black half-circle. A nest? No, it was curved side up. A… cave?

Looking around, he realized that they were, indeed, near the entrance to one of the small cave systems that ran beneath the farm. William had been connecting all of the naturally-occurring caves, so they had spent a few nights and days locating all the cave openings nearby that were large enough to allow a small humanoid to enter. There were a surprising number of hollows that fit that description, and Khor had quickly gotten tired of the task. Sumi, William, and even Sarave were better suited to the search anyway, since they could communicate their findings. Khor had, however, found a few of the larger openings before he stopped looking, and one of them was…

There!

It wasn't particularly large, as such things went. Certainly not big enough for a wagon or even an average-sized human. A largish duck, however, would fit easily, so Khor stuck his nose into the hole and called loudly.

After six or seven loud brays, Khor was beginning to think he must have misinterpreted the quest. Again, he wished that he had been able to learn to read, but other than his name and a few simple words, the letters seemed to dance before his eyes when he focused on them. Aspen or Sumi could tell him what the letter was, and if it stood alone, he could usually get it right, but as soon as it hid amongst its brethren, he might as well be looking at a tangled pile of hay for all that he could pick out individual words.

As he drew in his breath for a final bleat, he paused. Was that a sound from deep in the cave? A pebble? A scrape of something against stone. Even, perhaps, a very quiet quack?

A voice echoed up from the dark opening, and Khor recognized the sound of William's archaic accent. "Wait… need to… one moment…"

More scraping sounds came from the opening, and Khor dug at the hole with a hoof impatiently. At long last, two hands emerged, a wriggling duck clutched tightly between them. Nuisance was filthy, covered in mud and dirt, even his sleek feathers unable to sluice it all away. His beak was tightly clenched, and though he would normally be complaining loudly about the rough handling, he seemed determined to remain silent this time.

The pale hands clutching Nuisance's rather broad middle began to smoke in the sunlight, and William dropped the duck and snatched his hands back inside. The old fructipire's voice drifted out as Nuisance shook his feathers into place, preening a few with his closed beak.

"I am, ah, terribly sorry. This fellow made his way into some of the more, um, *distant* tunnels, and though he made quite a lot of noise, it took me some time to locate him. He seems unscathed, but he was in an area I haven't, er, thoroughly explored as yet, and he seems to have, ah, found something. He won't give it to me, but I hope you will have better luck. I shall return to my rest now."

Khor tapped the ground with his hoof a few times in acknowledgement, and scooped the reticent fowl up into the curve of one of his spiral horns. With a practiced toss, he threw the bird onto his back, and turned to trot away. Instantly, Nuisance slipped, and Khor realized that the duck was unable to use his beak to keep hold, the way he usually did.

Grumbling to himself, Khor made his slow way back to the house, pausing each time his passenger started to drift too far to one side or the other. Sumi would be able to convince the bird to give up his prize.

It turned out, however, that Sumi's intervention was unnecessary. Upon their arrival back at the house, Nuisance flew awkwardly down from Khor's back and, with visible relief, spat the thing he'd been holding down onto the ground in front of the door, then pecked sharply at the wood. After a moment, Sarave opened the door. The goblin woman looked perplexed when she saw Khor and Nuisance, but Nuisance quacked agitatedly, and pecked at the thing until it rolled onto Sarave's foot.

Bending down, Sarave picked the thing up, and when she did, a golden light surrounded Nuisance. The bird leveled up, growing noticeably larger. The last of the dirt fell away from his glossy feathers, and the green feathers on his head and wings deepened into a rich emerald. Satisfied, Nuisance waddled away toward the barn door, his prize dismissed entirely.

Sarave opened her hand, and Khor could see the thing resting on her palm. It was a deep blue-black stone. The black parts were deep and solid, gleaming as if it was already polished, but the midnight blue parts were crystalline, clear, and had smooth hexagonal protrusions. As Khor looked, a piece of the blue crystal seemed to shift, edging in toward some of the black, which turned to the side out of the way, like some kind of constantly changing puzzle.

Sarave gasped, her fingers curling around the mesmerizing stone. "*Kasi-tt galinn troth, vazti Gi-na!*" she exclaimed. "A dungeon seed!"

Chapter Nineteen

Aspen

When the formerly-abandoned hamlet of Filial appeared on the horizon, Aspen breathed a deep sigh of mixed relief and worry. This would be the first time in five days that the caravan would have someplace to stop and rest with a roof over their heads, instead of sleeping on bedrolls and stacked crates. Filial, like most human population centers smaller than a city, had been deserted as people fled before the oncoming hordes of Lich Lord Akuji's army. The few people who stayed, out of stubbornness or desperation, had not survived.

With humanity much reduced, most people had chosen to remain in Bloodhaven or Bright, though a few who preferred a more rural life had moved to North Goose, the pork-product capital of Quarternell, or Vargo, the last remaining significant military outpost.

Both Goose and Vargo had been spared most of the ravages of the war. Vargo had been north of the fighting, and His Grace General Geral had had a few of his less-competent soldiers stay there, primarily so they would stay out of the way of people who actually knew what they were doing. No one was quite sure why North Goose hadn't been razed, since its counterpart, South Goose, along with all the other settlements to the south and east had been burned to the ground. Most people, however, agreed that the most likely explanation was that Goose's ubiquitous pig-farms stank so much that even the undead avoided it.

In the wake of Akuji's 'defeat' – which Aspen now knew to have been temporary at best – some few people had begun returning to the tiny hamlets from which they or their families hailed. These new communities were usually ten or twenty people at most, and usually all were related by blood or marriage. Aspen had also recently discovered that these brave homesteaders were vanishing, so quietly and so thoroughly that rumors had only just begun to reach the cities.

For the hundredth time since they decided to leave the safe roads and travel on the abandoned byways that once led to thriving villages, he read through the goddess-given quest he'd received before leaving Bright.

Quest: "Crazy like a Phlox"
Strange events are occurring at the ruins of old villages around Quarternell. Cover some ground and find out what's going on.
Success: Variable.
Failure: People continue dying or going insane from their experiences.

Aspen turned to Restur, the caravan-master and leader of the trading group who were helping Aspen's band of refugees in their escape from Bright. "When was the last time you visited here?"

Restur clicked his tongue, thinking. He leaned back in the seat of the wagon he was driving and hummed softly. He chewed the single long stalk of grass protruding from his mouth as he pondered.

Aspen sighed. "I *know* I already asked. Please humor me?"

Restur sighed, but a suspicious twinkle lingered in his bright blue eyes as he looked over at the lanky farmer sitting beside him, anxiously clutching his short staff, which jingled the shiny metal leaves dangling from fine chains in a possibly-reassuring manner. "Well over a month ago. The Jostens and the Killians were settling in well, and they had three houses repaired, as well as fixing the mill and the docks. Liam Josten was hoping to have enough fish dried or pickled that they could trade some next time we came through."

Aspen shook his head. "I don't know why they didn't stay in Bright if they wanted to fish. With the largest city in Quarternell built on a massive lake, there's not going to be much market for it."

Restur chuckled and clucked at the two well-muscled oxen pulling the cart. "Didn't want to pay the taxes in Bright. Out here, especially with no nobles left to walk around with their hands out, a person can make their own way and actually get to enjoy what they produce."

Looking around with tired topaz eyes, Aspen muttered, "Or be eaten by a monster, whichever comes first." He winced as the cart bumped down hard as it rolled over a large rock in the worn dirt track. "Not to mention that a lot of the taxes they aren't paying should go to fixing the road, as well as hiring guards."

The old caravan-master laughed. "Florence and Horace Killian used to *be* guards. Well, soldiers, which isn't the same, but they're still mighty good at killing things. The road though," he shook his head, perfectly coiffed white hair gleaming in the sunlight. "They'll have to get ten houses, a hundred people, and at least two community buildings before they can start laying bluestone. At least the mill counts, though I think the docks are considered a 'transportation hub'."

Hamlets, Villages, Towns, and Cities alike were protected from random monster attacks by the magical gray-blue stones that would appear around the houses once certain conditions were met. No violence or theft could occur on streets made from these stones, and a house that was completely surrounded by bluestones also gained some of these benefits, though their owners could choose to turn them off. What benefits the stones granted, and how many homes and buildings they would extend to, all depended on the size of the population, among other factors.

The small gathering of dilapidated buildings drew ever nearer as the tired beasts trundled on. Animals and people alike looked up with newfound vigor, though, and around them Aspen could hear a few conversations lifting over the thud of hooves and creak of the wagons.

Aspen lowered his voice. "What do you think are the odds that things are still going well?"

Restur's expression froze into a neutral mask. "I have no more idea than you. We've been trying to build new trade routes as people venture out into the wilds, or try to resurrect an old town. In the last few months, when we went to check on our new trading partners, we've found a few abandoned again, with little sign that anyone has been there since Akuji's forces went through. According to Tia's family, though, it's not looking good. I wish Rothgan and Halla could remember more about what happened to them."

Rothgan and Halla, along with three other dwarves, were the only survivors of a tinker clan who had made their living wandering from town to town, repairing anything from cracked pots or broken swords. They, like Restur, had seen the opportunity in the new homesteads popping up all over Quarternell. Unlike most traders, tinkers were independent and flexible, and they had veered off the main road from Bright to Goose when they heard that a large group of five families with over a hundred members were going to attempt to rekindle Gally, a good-sized town to the west of Bright.

When they had arrived at New Gally, which already met all the requirements for a Hamlet and was currently repairing the road that surrounded the houses and community buildings, they had been greeted by a tired but pleased populace. They had been offered sleeping and working space in the town hall, and most of the clan had accepted. No matter how comfortable their wagons were, it was nice to have space to stretch out without kicking someone else in the nose.

The five remaining dwarves had been among the group selected to stay in the wagons. The two children, Nickel and Copper, had been feeling under the weather, and the teenage girl, Esly, had volunteered to watch them. Rothgan and Halla, meanwhile, had just been wed, and very much appreciated the opportunity for a little privacy in a separate wagon, which belonged to Halla's parents, since the young couple's personal wagon was still being built back in Bright.

None of them knew exactly what had happened in Gally. Esly and the children were asleep, since it was nearly midnight, and while Rothgan and Halla had been awake, they had been rather distracted. The first sign any of them had that something was wrong was when a horrible shriek had sounded, then cut off as abruptly as it had begun. After that, the two wagons in which they rested had begun to rock as if in a terrible windstorm, and then terrible monsters with long claws, black fur, and red eyes had burst through the canvas flaps that served as doors. A cloaked figure had come through a moment later, as they cowered in terrified horror, and then everything went dark.

When they woke, the three older dwarves were in the warded circles in the laboratory from which Aspen, Rouge, and their friends had rescued them. They were in horrible pain, and their bodies were already beginning to shift toward the charcoal-skinned, red-eyed, hairless creatures they now were. The two children, under gentle questioning, had revealed that they, too, had woken in the cages from which they had been rescued, and seen no one except guards and cultists during the time they were imprisoned. Since they had been fed irregularly, and none of them had been able to see any natural light, they weren't even sure how long they had been locked up before being released.

Aspen looked back down the caravan toward the three wagons that held the people who had been saved from that torture chamber slash laboratory. Rothgan, Halla, and Esly occupied the wagon the newlyweds had commissioned before their ill-fated final journey with their clan, and which they had retrieved from the wainwrights in Bright after they were freed.

There were also two elves, each of whom had been changed in ways drastically different from each other. While Zen was now hyper-feminized, completely different from the androgynous beauty of most elves, Kej had become a sort of inhuman serpent-man, complete with fine-scaled skin and a forked tongue. It was clear that Zen and Kej had some kind of connection, but the two refused to speak to each other, and while Zen sometimes watched Kej with sad red eyes, Kej rarely even glanced at his fellow elf.

Neither of the elves would tell their stories, except to say that it had nothing to do with humans and would not help Aspen figure out what was happening with the vanishing villagers. Surprisingly, these two had opted to share a wagon, though they had immediately erected a divider in the middle of it, and Zen, who drove the wagon, entered and exited from the front, while Kej used only the back.

Toast was the last of the humanoid test-subjects. As an orc, he was too large to easily fit in a standard wagon, but he was also too slow to keep up with the rest of the caravan if he had been forced to walk. Once the escapees had reached Aspen's home, Toast had vanished, then returned several hours later.

The orc, who, while small for one of his race, towered over everyone else in the house - including Aspen and Motte, Rouge's father, who was built like a wall - was wearing fresh, clean clothes and carrying a pouch that occasionally jingled when he walked. No one asked him how he had come by his newfound wealth, and he didn't volunteer the information. When they had decided to evacuate, however, Toast had been one of the few who could afford to buy his own wagon, and four hefty oxen to pull it.

Toast, too, knew nothing helpful. For an orc, he was surprisingly intelligent and genial, which meant he could use three-syllable words and didn't threaten to maim everyone who looked at him. When Aspen asked, he just said that he had been a sailor – though Aspen wasn't sure what position such a large being would fill on a ship except that of oarsman, and the orc's hands weren't nearly calloused enough for that – and that he had woken up in the lab after getting drunk and passing out in a dark alley near the docks.

The remaining survivors of the cultist's cruel experiments were beasts. There was a three-foot-long guinea pig with an impassive face and a gigantic bushy tail that showed every emotion. This somewhat solitary creature was named Cavi, and chose which wagon it would ride on seemingly at random, though Aspen had noticed that it seemed to prefer ones without children.

The second animal was Polly. It had a long snout and tongue, and the powerful front shovel paws of a scaled, anteater-like creature, while its back end looked like a half-plucked peacock. Its belly was red, its fur and feathers black, but its gentle eyes were a lovely green that watched Rouge's every move, even when the Traveler girl's body was in the soulless state known as a Zombie.

The final beast was a little striped golden creature that Rouge called a 'zebra', and it was now a favorite of the many children in the caravan. It was just large enough that the younger children could ride it, and it, too, seemed to enjoy trotting along with a grinning tot on its back.

This animal, now dubbed Peri, slept in the several wagons occupied by the urchins who had been cast out on the street when Bright's only orphanage closed. Plum, one of Aspen's former servants from his past life as a member of the nobility, had brought the entire group of wild imps back to his abandoned manor, and taken it upon herself to feed, clothe, and educate them.

When Lich Lord Akuji turned out to not only be alive – or however his unnatural state of existence could be described – but gathering a whole new army, Aspen's home had quickly become a target. Since Aspen was the one who had, however impermanently, killed Akuji nearly two years before, the undead necromancer seemed to be holding a grudge. Once Aspen and friends had garnered the attention of the Lich Lord, now wearing the guise of Quarternell's rather vapid but harmless King Chester, they had all been forced to flee Bright again, this time with Akuji's minions, including the Traveler FantumHat, on their heels.

All of which led to the more than twenty wagons that now wound along the earthen path that had devolved from the broad road that had once joined North Goose and Filial. The wagons were riding low under the weight of the goods and people, now refugees, who were trying to escape north to Aspen's farm, aptly named Refuge. When he had named it, he had meant it to be a refuge for himself and his own soul-bonded animal companions, but now he was bringing enough people to build a Hamlet at least, though building one from nothing was rather more involved than restarting one that had become vacant.

The weight borne by the wagons, therefore, was nothing compared to the more metaphorical weight on Aspen's shoulders. As the official Duke of the North, Aspen could authorize the creation of a population center anywhere in the vast area north of the mountains.

Again, actually creating that population center was more than complex enough to give him a headache just thinking about it, and while they built houses, laid roads, and erected community buildings, he had to keep all of these people safe, healthy, and fed. When he originally left Bright behind after realizing that someone – or several someones – was attempting to kill him, he had washed his hands of people and politics alike. How he had gotten pulled back in, he wasn't sure, but getting out again certainly wouldn't be so easy.

Not to mention that before he could even begin to create a new, safe home for his (*his!*) people, first he had to get them to his land. Vargo, the dumping ground for soldiers so inept that they weren't even called back to defend humanity's last bastion during Lich Lord Akuji's final assault, still stood before them, blocking the only pass through the Whispering Mountains. Aspen, however, had a terrible feeling that by the time they made their way there by the circuitous route available to them, Vargo would have been fortified by people quite a bit more competent.

Aspen was shaken from his gloomy thoughts by a girlish voice suddenly speaking directly into his ear.

"What's up with the smoking hole in the ground?"

He lifted his eyes from their absent contemplation of the rear end of one of the oxen, and turned to glare at Rouge, who had appeared beside him with all the stealth on which she prided herself. The Traveler grinned cheekily back at him from atop her eight-foot-tall ostrich mount.

"What smoking hole?" He asked, in spite of the fact that he had a sinking feeling he already knew.

She lifted a slim hand, soft brown skin gleaming against the black leather of the fingerless gloves she had recently taken to wearing. Despite his creeping dread, Aspen looked in the direction she indicated, and felt his heart sink.

Filial was, indeed, a faintly smoking ruin.

Aspen became suddenly aware of the quiet that had overtaken the caravan. At some point between when he had last looked at Filial, which at the time had merely looked broken down, but not destroyed, everyone else had realized that they would not be having a peaceful rest in a relatively safe place tonight. It seemed that Aspen was the last to notice, and now that he had, the weight of having to make decisions for all these people came crashing back down on him again.

Feeling almost as though he'd taken a physical blow, Aspen turned back to Rouge. "It looks like we're too late." Too late for what, exactly, he didn't know. Too late to solve his quest? Too late to spend a night in a safe harbor? Too late to save the people who had been building new lives in this gods-forsaken place?

Rouge looked conflicted. "Do you want me and Wally to head in and check things out?" She patted the neck of her trusty battle-ostrich, Codswallop. The girl had always been the 'better to ask for forgiveness than permission' sort, but after coming face to face with Lich Lord Akuji and nearly being killed for her curiosity, it seemed that she had finally learned some restraint. For now, at least. It probably helped that, as a Traveler, she had always known that even if she 'died', the gods would resurrect her with relatively minor consequences. Now, though, she was on a god-quest, and if she died, the repercussions would be significant for both her and everyone she cared about.

Aspen hesitated. Restur was already calling a halt to the caravan, and though it would take a while for all of them to stop, it seemed everyone had been slowing for a while as they came to terms with the devastation before them. There were several guards with the caravan, and they were being paid very well to escort the refugees north, but they weren't investigators. Their sole task was to keep the people and wagons safe, and that would be most easily accomplished by simply leaving the ruin behind and avoiding it entirely.

"We'll do it!" A voice came from his left, and Aspen looked in spite of himself, though he already knew there would be no one there. That was Jiminy's voice, and while the boy could mimic almost anyone with uncanny perfection, throwing their voice anywhere his voice could reach, Plum had finally managed to thump it into his thick head that he was going to cause real problems on their journey if he kept pretending to be someone else. Thus, Jiminy now used his own voice – at least when he thought Plum might find out – but they couldn't break the boy of his habitual ventriloquism.

Aspen sighed, eyes searching until he saw the scamp standing near Codswallop's large two-toed feet, nearly hidden by fluffy feathers. Three other children also stood nearby, looking hopeful. Aspen shook his head. "I'm certainly not sending four children into a place that has clearly been attacked."

Rouge looked pleased at being excluded from the 'children' category, in spite of being only fourteen. Jiminy, Jack, Lionel, and Ulie, the most independent and inquisitive of Plum's unlikely pack of orphans, looked crestfallen and rebellious.

Looking back up, Aspen met Rouge's eyes. "Do it quickly. Stay on Codswallop, [Stealth] when you can, and be in and out in," he hesitated, looking at the size of the once-prosperous village. "Twenty minutes. I'd like to go through the town and be on our way while there's still light. If we have to leave the road and go around, we'll lose the daylight."

Restur spoke up, his voice grim. "Most of these buildings look no different than they did when I was last here. Akuji's forces demolished much of it as they chased down the last of the people who refused to leave. Ironically, the houses that were most intact are the homes of the wealthiest citizens, who fled as soon as they heard they were at risk. Those houses are near the center of town, and it looks like that's where the smoke is coming from. If anyone is still alive, and the houses haven't burned to the ground, that's where they'll be holed up."

Rouge nodded, and nudged Codswallop, murmuring softly to the over-sized bird. She waved, tugged at the ostrich's soft rope bridle, and the two were off, using some debris that had fallen near the road as a jumping-off point for a leap that took them nearly thirty feet in a single bound.

Aspen sighed and turned back to Restur. "Should we assume we won't be able to go through and begin preparing the wagons to go around?" They would have to check the wagons over very well before leaving the road. The slightest crack in a wheel or axle could lead to a break that would stop everyone for the rest of the day. No matter what, Aspen did not want to be anywhere near this place when they slept, and it was already well into the afternoon.

Restur frowned, then gestured to Tia, his assistant, who was standing nearby, waiting attentively for instructions. The middle-aged woman stepped forward. "Tia, have Jurgen start going over the wagons. Anything he's been putting off repairing until we reached Filial may need to be done in a hurry. Hopefully, the road can be cleared, but I want a plan in place in case we can't."

Tia nodded and jogged away. Restur turned back to Aspen. "I may need you to do your little trick with a few axles."

Aspen smiled, grateful that he'd at least be able to do something helpful. While traveling incognito, he'd worked as the caravan's animal handler, and had found it simple but rewarding work. Now, as the putative 'Lord of the North', no one would let him do anything anyone else could do. Fortunately, as a druid, his abilities with animals went beyond the physical, so he used his mana to support the draft animals, both oxen and equine, so they could work longer and harder with no ill effects.

He also had the 'Mage Smith' job class, however, so when Jurgen found a cracked or bent metal axle or wheel rim, Aspen would be called in to convince the iron to reform itself into its proper shape. Unfortunately, he was limited to items considered 'farming implements', but since wagons and carts were often used on farms, he was able to work with them. He could do nothing, however, with broken swords or cracked armor, though if a buckle broke, he could repair that. He was still finding the limitations of his abilities, but his goddess, Gina, had been very clear when she told him that he would not be able to use his new power for anything directly related to war.

The caravan quickly settled into a state of subdued activity. They had had to leave the road a few times already in order to go around areas of broken road, and once when the scouts had seen a roadblock not far outside of North Goose. That was the point at which they had switched to this narrow track, which Restur had only known about since he'd been a traveling merchant since he was a boy.

It was only after several minutes had gone by that Aspen realized something was still itching at the back of his mind. Something he was forgetting? Something that he had expected, but hadn't happened? Then one of Plum's children rode by on Peri's back, the little girl giggling madly as the golden beast gaily lifted his gleaming hooves as if prancing.

Jiminy! Aspen had fully expected the four little imps to protest vociferously when Rouge was sent off without them. Instead, they had apparently slunk silently away, and Aspen had a sinking feeling he knew why.

Closing his eyes, Aspen sent his Life Sense out through the caravan. Gently, he touched the tired beasts, giving them a few drops of energy to heal small scratches and sore hooves. He avoided the sapient beings, though he could have helped them as well, since it seemed invasive to do more than brush their glowing spirit-lights. He could tell when his friend Manuela noticed him. Her own [Soul Sight] turned toward him, though she couldn't communicate with him as she would be able to with another Soul Mage. He felt her coming toward him as he continued searching.

After a moment, he knew he had to admit defeat. The children were nowhere in the caravan, which meant that they had probably decided to venture into Filial with or without permission. Hesitantly, he cast his senses into the broken, smoldering town, skimming lightly over insects, rodents, and burrowing creatures. Nothing looked immediately dangerous, but he realized rather abashedly that he should have done this before sending Rouge in alone. There was some small risk of something unfriendly 'seeing' him the way Manuela had, but at least he could have ruled out obvious danger.

Manuela's life light drew up to his side, and he pulled back his Life Sense, metaphorically blinking against her brightness. As a mage, her light was brilliant, often eclipsing the dimmer glow of other people nearby. It sometimes made it difficult for him to tell who she was with, unless that person was, like Restur, also a mage of some kind.

He opened his physical eyes and smiled at his old comrade-in-arms. The creases around her eyes and bracketing her mouth were a little deeper now, and there was more silver glinting in her black hair, but otherwise she was the same as when they had met, years ago, when he was the King's Necromancer, and she the soul mage assigned as his partner, killing the enemies whose bodies he would then turn against their foes.

"What's going on, Aspen? You feel worried." Soul magic was rare enough, and frightening enough, that few people had it. However, it was a prerequisite for the skills that allowed someone to heal hearts and minds rather than merely bodies. Long ago, Manuela had chosen a difficult path after watching her mother sink into despair and madness after her father's death, and then she had been forced into accepting a martial path instead of that of a physician when she had been conscripted into the army.

In fact, the only good thing that had come from Aspen's flight from Bright the night before Lich Lord Akuji's final assault had been the fact that Manuela had lost so many levels in the attempt to rescue him after Akuji captured him that she had been able to choose a new specialization when she reached level fifty for the second time.

Aspen had been attempting to exchange his own life – and thus the lives of everyone in Bright, since without their sole Necromancer, there was no way Bright could hold out even a single night against the forces of the undead – for the safety of his daughter, Lark. To anyone less desperate and overwhelmed than he had been, it was obvious that the Lich wouldn't be willing to make such a trade, since he would have both of them, one way or the other, on the morrow.

Lark, Khor, Sumi, Miya, Rook, and Manuela had gone into the magically-created crypt where Akuji was waiting. Liches, ghosts, and ghouls were able to steal the stats and levels of mortals, and all of Aspen's friends had been badly reduced during their venture. Aspen, meanwhile, had been suffering the attentions of Akuji himself, and by the time Lark found him, he was a level one nothing once again. Though he was weaker than a newborn, Aspen had begged his daughter to flee without him, and that was when Akuji sprung his trap.

Miya and Rook, who had gone with Lark into the deepest depths of Akuji's lair, were killed outright. Lark had given her life for her father, using her final Skill as the High Priestess of Gina to use the last dregs of her power to restore him. Aspen had managed to use the instant while Akuji was frozen in shock and disoriented by the intrusion of divine light into his inner sanctum, and had slain the Lich with Akuji's own cursed blade.

Sumi and Manuela, who had been hiding nearby, brought Aspen out as the burrow crumbled around their ears, and Khor, who had been too large to fit far inside the narrow tunnels, brought them all out on his back. Khor had suffered the fewest losses, while Aspen was little more than a shell of himself, nearly dead both emotionally and physically.

It was Manuela who had brought Aspen through the first few days following Lark's death. Though it had been difficult to reach the sickbed of the 'Hero of Bright' – since King Chester and Duke Geral had had to give the people someone to thank for slaying Akuji, and they had both been visibly elsewhere at the time of the Lich Lord's death – Manuela had found him, bringing with her a tiny, heartbroken young bat.

Silus had been only six months old or so at the time. She had lived her entire life under the threat of Akuji's forces, and when her mother, Miya, had been gone with Aspen on missions, Lark and Plum had cared for the tiny creature. Now, with both mother and 'sister' dead, Silus was as lost and bereaved as Aspen. Her real father had been a wild Greater Bat, and she had never met him, so Aspen was as close to a father as she had ever had. When she was laid on his thin, cold chest, she had curled into the curve of his collarbone and slept for nearly two days.

Manuela had fled Bright not long after that. She had lost enough levels that she was no longer able to slay her enemies with a simple skill, but she had also become a threat to Duke Geral, who was busily consolidating his power while King Chester sat back and tended his gardens. Geral was well aware that neither Aspen nor Manuela liked or respected him, and Manuela had become a potential enemy who could be easily handled now, but possibly not later.

The soul mage had escaped to Bloodhaven, where she apprenticed with an elderly doctor who had no magic, but managed to heal his patients with simple medicine and bandages. She was tight-lipped about what exactly had happened between that time and when the cultists had abducted her from Bloodhaven in an attempt to lure Aspen into a trap, but she had regained enough levels to be able to choose the Soul Healer job, leaving Soul Eater irrevocably behind. Now, she used both her physician skills and her Soul Healer ones to heal her patient's body and mind.

Unfortunately, the line between 'friend' and 'patient' still seemed to be rather blurry when it came to Aspen, and whenever Manuela sensed that he was struggling, she turned up with a list of 'doctor's orders' for him to follow. Unfortunately, it was rare that Aspen had the time to actually follow any of those orders, and so both of them simply ended up frustrated with each other.

Now, Aspen closed off all but the thinnest tendrils of his Life Sense, locking down his mental barriers so that Manuela couldn't see anything except his surface thoughts. She wasn't supposed to use her skills without permission of the patient, but Manuela had been a rebellious soldier for too long to start following the rules now.

Lowering his voice, Aspen murmured, "I need to go into town. Plum's trouble-makers followed Rouge in, and-"

Manuela nodded in understanding, lips thinning in determination. "I'm coming with you, then."

He sighed. "You're not my partner or a soldier any more, Manuela. Your skills are passive or non-violent. You'll only be a hindrance."

A blade appeared in Manuela's slim, calloused hand, flickering in and out of her fingers as she twirled it. Once she knew he had seen it, it vanished again into whatever hidden sheath she kept it in. "My magic may be meant to help, Aspen, but that doesn't mean I'm helpless. I've been a killer since the day I was conscripted, and this wouldn't be the first time I've had to fight without magic."

True enough. Once the soul had been removed from a body, it was simply a sack of meat waiting for a necromancer to control it. When that necromancer was on Akuji's side, their undead puppets had been entirely beyond Manuela's control. She had had to defend herself from more than one attacker who was entirely unaffected by her magic. She could attack the necromancers themselves, but not their zombies and ghouls.

Still, he shook his head. "I'll take someone else, if you insist, but not you."

A small smile flickered over her lips, and he realized that he'd just given her exactly what she wanted. If she had insisted he take someone other than her, he would have refused, and they would have wasted time arguing. By threatening to go herself, she had turned it into his own idea. His lips quirked and they exchanged a glance that acknowledged that while she had neatly outwitted him, he was, at least, aware of it.

Turning, Manuela called to Restur. "Do you know where Vonn is? Or are any of the other Travelers awake?"

Restur glanced at them, at first distracted, and then focusing as he saw the tight expressions on their faces. "Vonn is with Willow and Plum, as far as I know. Why?"

Aspen cast out his Life Sense again, this time dipping a bit deeper into the lights of the sapients around him. Vonn was, indeed, with his nephew, Willow, in the wagon where Plum slept with the smallest orphans. Bowing to the inevitable, Aspen sent a quick message through party chat.

::Rouge? Can you hear me?:: There was no response, so he nodded to Restur. "Could you send someone to fetch him? Jiminy and the others are missing."

Restur's eyes sharpened with concern, and he turned to a man standing nearby. "You heard the man. Find Vonn, and quickly."

Chapter Twenty

Rouge

R ouge and Codswallop bounded through the once-sprawling town, leaping from crumbling rock walls to the scattered remnants of cobbled streets. After her terrible morning at Veritas Corp, she was definitely ready to stop being Zoey and start being Rouge instead.

Unfortunately, after the *excessive* amounts of testing Dr. Joe had put her through, she only had a little over two hours left in the nearly magical full-immersion pod that let her experience *Veritas Online* as if she really was inhabiting the body of a half-wood elf, half-dark elf, Fowl Trickster riding her valiant Battle Ostrich.

Of course, through the magic of Proprietary Information™, that meant she actually had four hours in-game, but there was still the lingering knowledge that when she logged out this time, the odds were good that she'd never again be able to experience this depth of immersion. She did have a really good pod at home (not top of the line, but only because they'd released a new model last month) but the difference was still noticeable.

Closing her eyes, she reveled in the feel of Codswallop's fluffy feathers between her fingers, the scent of warm bird and dust, and the motion of his powerful legs as he nimbly carried them through the town. With another mighty leap, her bird threw them into the air again, and she whooped at the feeling of her stomach dropping as they fell back toward the earth.

Rouge allowed herself another few thrilling heartbeats of sheer bliss, just letting Wally take them in the general direction she'd pointed him, before prying her eyes open again. Codswallop was running and jumping quickly enough that the wind tugged at her clothes and whipped her braids around. She winced as the beads woven into her hair slapped her neck and cheeks. Even with the minimum pain settings required by her status as a minor, it still felt like dull little pins pricking her skin.

Reluctantly, she clucked at Wally, tugging gently on his bridle. The soft, silken rope was only meant for guidance, and hung as loose on him as she could make it while still having enough tension so that he could tell which way she wanted him to go. He had a tendency to ignore her when something tasty lay in a different direction, but, well, who could blame him?

This time, however, Codswallop responded easily to her direction, slowing and turning slightly to the left, where the smoke was definitely thicker and she could see blackened timbers and layers of cooling ash rather than the damage resulting from dereliction or rampaging hordes.

Your Battle Mount *Codswallop* has taken 1 point of Burning damage. If he receives 4 more points of damage, he will die and respawn at your last save point.
Your Battle Mount *Codswallop* has been *Burned*. He will lose one damage point every five minutes until the burn heals or a recovery item is applied.

At the same moment Rouge read the system messages, Wally squawked indignantly, pulling his large, two-toed feet from the deep pile of ash into which he'd stepped. Deep red embers gleamed in the gap he left behind, and Rouge realized that they were now close enough to the worst of the fire that some live coals were likely to be lying around. Obviously.

Rouge muttered a few words her dad wouldn't have approved of and vaulted off of Wally's back. She was still trying to get her [Acrobatics] skill up to 20, and even though she was solidly in the land of diminishing returns when it came to her fancy mounts and dismounts, she still got a little extra experience toward increasing the skill each time. Plus, it was fun to be able to do a double backwards flip with two full twists and stick the landing. She'd only been a decent gymnast in real life, earning several bronze medals and a few silvers in local competitions, but she could do All the Things now!

While she was still in the air, she accessed her inventory, and a Poultice appeared in her hand. Now that Wally was an official Battle Mount, she'd known he was likely to be injured and need Bandages, Splints, and, yes, Poultices, so she'd invested in *lots* of them while she was in Bright and had just cleared out Aspen's treasure stash.

Fortunately, while the Spring Triathlon event that was currently going on in Bright (without her!) did have a mounted portion, there were no mounted battles, so the price for these items were still at standard market value, rather than the vastly inflated prices being demanded for Stamina Potions and other things that would boost your chances of winning one of the races. She was fairly certain that she would never, ever need to buy Mount Recovery items again.

Gently, she pulled the foot that Codswallop was holding in the air toward her and placed the Poultice over the angry red blisters that were already forming there. Wally instantly sighed in relief, and she smiled.

Your Battle Mount *Codswallop* is no longer *Burned*.

As long as she was at it, she pulled a single Healing Pellet out and gave it to the ostrich, who gobbled it up greedily and then dug his beak into her hands and sides, looking for more. She giggled, twisting away as the bird's explorations extended to her ticklish ribs and underarms.

A small voice came from behind her, and both she and Codswallop stilled, turning toward the sound. A little child stood there, filthy and ragged, hair burned to nubs, with blisters all down its jaw and right shoulder and arm. "Are you here to save us?" the child asked again, voice hoarse and raspy, left eye wide and hopeful while the right was white and staring sightlessly, surrounded by oozing blisters.

Rouge gasped and fell to her knees by the child, who couldn't be more than six or seven, and stood around three and a half feet. Digging in her inventory, the thief pulled out a potion, then carefully held it out to the pitiful figure. "Here," she said softly, as if speaking to a wounded animal, "drink this. It will help with the..." She gestured wordlessly at the terrible burns.

The child hesitated, then reached out and snatched the bottle with its left hand. Turning, it started hobbling away as quickly as it could, dragging its right foot slightly. Rouge started to speak, but then just stood and followed after, stirring up fresh plumes of ashes and a few cinder-sparks. Codswallop traipsed after her, even the usually-boisterous bird seeming to sense some of the solemnity of the scene.

The child, which Rouge was more and more inclined to think was a girl, though it was still impossible to be sure, briefly vanished into a dark house at the edge of the large lake that bordered the north-western portion of the town. Blackened buckets lay abandoned around what remained of the yard, and it looked like some attempt at a bucket brigade may have been what saved the structure from total destruction.

Rouge hesitated outside the door. While it seemed unlikely that the child would have been allowed to wander around if there was anyone left who was able to fight, she didn't want to frighten anyone inside or take damage from friendly fire. As she was still debating over her best course of action, the child's head popped back out of the door.

"Mama says come in," the scratchy little voice said, and the sooty left hand gestured to Rouge.

Rouge patted Codswallop on the neck. "Keep watch, and only come in if you hear me screaming," she said quietly, mostly kidding, and the bird rolled one dubious brown eye at her. She smiled, and cautiously entered the house. It was, not surprisingly, dark inside, and she took a fully charged glowstone out and ignited it with a thought. When its clean white light fell over the room, she winced at what she saw.

Two still forms lay to one side, burned sheets not quite managing to conceal the fact that they were corpses. Three more figures lay on the remnants of two bedrolls and a child-sized mattress that had been repurposed into sickbeds. Two of the figures were asleep or unconscious, covered in burns that made the child's injuries look minor. The third was a woman, and her eyes were open and clear. She was still lying down, but the empty potion bottle beside her explained why she was in better shape than the others.

Quickly, Rouge pulled out two more potions and two greater potions. The basic ones would be enough to get the child and mother stabilized until Manuela and Aspen could patch them up, but it looked like the two other people would need something stronger. The mother hesitated briefly, but motioned for her child to take the bottles. To her credit, the first thing she did was force the little girl to swallow one of them, in spite of her attempts to go directly to the man lying beside her mother.

Once the child finished drinking, the magic began. Inflamed skin returned to a healthy pink, smaller blisters disappeared entirely, and the larger ones smoothed into scars that still looked tender and pink, but not dangerous. The milky orb that was her right eye still looked blind, but the red-rimmed lids lost their swollen appearance.

Mother and child clung to each other briefly, and then the mother drank her own potion, the last of her injuries turning into smooth pink and white scars, and then the two turned to their fallen comrades. Within a few more minutes, all four of the survivors were awake and conscious, though the second woman just stared into space, refusing or unable to respond when the other three spoke to her.

The mother turned to Rouge and clumsily climbed to her knees before the girl. "Thank you," she said quietly. "Thank you." Wordlessly, the man shifted the desperately sobbing child in his arms and also bowed as deeply as he could.

A lump rose in Rouge's throat, and she had to swallow hard before she could speak. "What happened here? Is anyone else alive?"

The man and woman exchanged glances, but it was the girl (Rouge was now nearly certain it was a girl) who spoke. "The monsters came. They came from everywhere, and they took Margie and Pete and Auntie Lisa. Uncle Liam died when he tried to stop them, and Mama and Daddy could only get to me and Olive." The girl pointed to one of the mostly-covered bodies when she mentioned her uncle, and indicated the catatonic woman when she said Olive's name.

Her mother took over after casting a sorrowful look at Olive. "It happened a week ago, I think." She cast a glance at her daughter. "I was unconscious for a while, so I'm not sure. I'm Florence - Flo - and this is my husband, Horace." She swept her daughter into her arms, burying her face momentarily in the remains of the child's burned hair. "This is Petunia. It was early morning, and we were all just getting ready for the day. The sun wasn't even up properly yet. Dozens of monsters just seemed to come from nowhere. They were all silent, far quieter than they should have been, and Horace and I didn't even see them until Olive screamed. They'd snatched her baby, Shye, right out of her arms, and one of them was running off with the child while another attacked Olive."

She closed her eyes, clearly remembering the brutal scene far too clearly. "They went after the children first, but Vanya and Lauren, my sister Nanette's teenagers, were out front hanging laundry, and they disappeared as well. I don't know if they were killed or," she swallowed hard, "taken. There were things that dripped fire as if it were saliva, and everything started to burn. My brother-in-law, Liam, was already out fishing on the lake, and he dove from the boat and swam in when he saw the smoke. He was killed before he had the ground beneath his feet."

Tears seeped from beneath her lids, and she stopped speaking. Horace laid a hand on her shoulder and continued where she left off. "Flo and I fought them while Petunia ran inside, just as she's supposed to do." He managed a proud smile for his daughter. "She's the only child left. Two of Flo's other sisters are alive, too, and they managed to keep the fire from burning this house, since the lake is just outside. Rani was Liam's wife, and she's not a bad fisherman herself. She swam out and brought the boat back, and she goes out to the shallows to catch fish every day. We were trying to build up some rations so we could get away from here after," he glanced at Olive. "I mean, when everyone could be moved."

After Olive died, Rouge mentally filled in, and felt her chest burn as she imagined the sorrow of hoping someone you loved would recover, but knowing that if they couldn't, the sooner they died, the better off everyone else would be. "What about the other sister?" She looked around, wondering how she could have missed a healthy adult, and where that adult had been while Petunia was wandering through burning ash.

Again, Horace and Flo exchanged speaking glances. "Lisa," Florence said. "Margie and Pete were... *are* her children, and she's sure they're still alive. We found her husband Peter's body, but no sign of the kids. Lisa goes out looking for them every day. She only comes back long enough to sleep and eat something, and then she leaves again. I think she's gone a little mad."

Rouge glanced at the still body of Olive, lying motionless on the floor in the same position she'd been in when Rouge entered. There were as many ways of dealing with trauma as there were people, but it seemed Olive and Lisa had ended up on opposite ends of the spectrum. Rouge tugged at a braid. "Are there any of the monsters left? Is the town... safe?" For whatever definition of 'safe' covered a place where you could burn up while walking, if a building didn't fall on you first.

"I'm here with a caravan," Rouge went on. "You might know the caravan master. His name is Restur, and he-"

Flo broke in, eyes suddenly growing brighter. "Of course we know Restur! He's here? He said he'd be back when we were more established, so we could talk about opening trade with some of the other hamlets that have been popping up within a few days' travel." She laughed bitterly. "We won't be doing that now, but maybe he'll be able to take us back to Bright? We have nothing left to pay him, but Horace and I spent a little time as caravan guards after the war, so we can work for our keep."

Rouge waved her hands, backing up a step in the face of the woman's almost desperate tone. "No need for that! I'm sure he'll help." *And if he won't, I'll pay your passage myself.* She still had plenty of money left from selling what she could of Aspen's secret stash, so even with Restur's eye for profit, she was sure she could handle paying for four adults and a child.

"We aren't heading for Bright, though," Rouge suddenly remembered. "We're actually, um, on our way to start our own town, north of the mountains. Bright is," she hesitated, unsure how to put it, "not as friendly as it used to be?"

Horace clenched his jaw. "I think we're done homesteading. We just want somewhere we can sleep safe in our own beds. If we'd had bluestones, this never would have happened. We were fools to think we could survive out here long enough to establish a hamlet."

The man's voice was bitter, and Rouge smiled at him tentatively. "We have more than enough people to establish a hamlet, at least according to Restur. We have all the supplies we need to build some houses and stuff, and Aspen is a Duke, and Restur said that the system," she coughed slightly. "I mean the *gods* reduce the required waiting period once all the conditions are met based on how high-ranking the leader is."

The two adults were exchanging uncertain glances now, so Rouge hurried on. "Aspen's really super nice, I promise! He's a little bossy, but that's okay, because he's going to be the boss, right? He said he doesn't care about taxes or anything either, because he just wants us to leave him alone and let him farm." She made a face. "Not that that's going to happen, but hey, wishful thinking, right?"

Petunia was tugging at her parent's hands now, looking a bit more like a normal child, and less like a terrorized wild thing. "Isn't Restur the man who healed Uncle Luke's leg? He was really nice, and I didn't like Bright. There were no trees, and people were mean to Vany and Lauren."

Rouge's eyes narrowed a bit at this. She certainly knew of one group of people in Bright who weren't very nice, and they tended to pick on- "Are Vany and Lauren non-human?" She kept her face friendly and open, hoping they would feel safe confiding in her.

It was Petunia, however, who spilled the beans. "Uncle Weston is a half-orc. Vany and Lauren are quarter-bloods, and Vany even has tusks!" She held her dirty little hands a full six inches in front of her mouth.

Rouge nodded; suspicions confirmed. Intellectually, she knew this whole group of people had to have been spawned by the game-AI very recently, because before that there had only been half-elves in *Veritas Online*. Nonetheless, she felt her heartstrings tug at the sadness in the little girl's eyes as she thought of the prejudice her cousins had had to deal with. "It was the Maskers, wasn't it? That's why we're all leaving Bright, too. Things are getting really bad there for anyone who isn't one hundred percent human."

Florence stepped forward, taking Rouge's hands into her own. "Yes, then. Yes. Even with Vany and Lauren gone, I hate to think of going back there. If you have room for us, we'd be glad to join you."

Quest: "Filial Bonds" available.

The survivors of Filial need somewhere safe to go. Gather them and take them north with you.

Success: Bring as many survivors to Refuge as possible. Rewards vary depending on the number of survivors.

Failure: None of the survivors reach Refuge. -10 points with Gina.

Current number of survivors from Filial in Refuge: 0/17

Accept Yes/No

Chapter Twenty-one

Aspen

No matter how far Aspen sent out his Life Sense, he couldn't find the children. He touched the small life lights of voles, mice, fleas, pill bugs, centipedes, snakes, and even a small family of feral cats hiding beneath a long-abandoned shed. But there were no children.

Vonn, who had left his nephew behind only after Plum promised to personally care for the baby, was circling Aspen's position as they moved through the rubble. The wood elf, while he wasn't exactly in his element, was no longer suffering the debuffs brought on by being in the city, and his [Stealth] was much more effective than the slightly blurry camouflage he'd had in Bright.

In fact, Aspen was finding that he had a hard time differentiating between the young elf's spirit and a particularly large animal. If it weren't for the fact that nothing bigger than the cats was currently living in Filial, Aspen wouldn't have known that Vonn was approaching to his right.

"Anything?" Aspen murmured as the boy neared. He knew Vonn would have said something if he'd actually seen any sign of the four children, but he still had to ask.

"Nothing," Vonn sounded as frustrated as Aspen felt. "Are you *certain* they came into town? I should have found something by now."

Left unsaid was the fact that the wood elf was an excellent tracker, at least outside of the city. He had easily found four small sets of footprints leading away from the caravan, but the moment they stepped into what would once have been the area protected by bluestones, the prints vanished completely.

Gritting his teeth, Aspen shook his head. "I'm not sure of anything any more. We know they followed Rouge, but maybe they turned back, and we just didn't find their tracks?"

Vonn sighed, dropping his [Stealth] and slowly fading into view. Unlike Rouge's standard thief-type [Stealth], which made her seem to instantly appear and disappear, but only worked in shadowed area, and muffled any sounds she made, the wood elf had hunter [Stealth], which built up and fell away over a few seconds, but functioned in low light and completely blocked any sounds or smells.

"I would have found tracks." The young elf sounded confident, though his expression was still worried. "Jiminy may be able to throw his voice, but he can't pick himself up and move somewhere else. Not yet, at least."

Aspen and Vonn shared a glance of understanding and mild exasperation. Jiminy was the only survivor of a troupe of actors who had all been infected by the plague that hit Bright at about the same time Akuji's forces had laid siege to it. Many people had died, and the only hospital that was willing to help infected commoners was run by Lark, Aspen's daughter and a powerful priestess of Gina.

As a result, many children, who died less often than their elders, and were thus left behind as orphans, entered the orphanage associated with the hospital. When the hospital and orphanage were shut down by Duke Geral, with the help of bank officials who undoubtedly pocketed a large portion of the funds Aspen left behind to pay for the facility's upkeep, Plum had taken in all of the orphans.

Jiminy and his compatriots, Ulie, Jack, and Lionel, were among the oldest and certainly the most independent of this miniature horde. Jiminy had learned acting and ventriloquism from his family, and could often be found at the center of any pranks or trouble amongst the ranks of children. Ulie and Lionel were siblings, and were always together, though the boy generally spent most of his time glaring at anyone who got too close to his pretty and cheerful little sister. Jack was a quiet lad of about the same age as Ulie, and the girl followed him around like a puppy. Though the serious boy didn't seem to return her interest, he did watch out for her, and he and Jiminy were Lionel's only friends.

Aspen was fairly certain which of the four had instigated this latest fiasco, and he was going to have to figure out some punishment more effective than writing lines or memorizing 'educational passages' from books, which were Plum's favorite tools of discipline. Most of her barely-literate rapscallions would rather eat soap than have to read or write, but Jiminy's family had been surprisingly well-educated, and had taught the boy from an early age, so these things were simple for him.

Vonn was fading from view again, and then his now-dim light moved away, toward the center of town. "When do you think Rouge will hear us?" The voice was like a whisper of wind.

Since the thief-girl was in the same party, as long as Aspen periodically used party chat, Rouge would eventually 'hear' him. Aspen stood up from where he had been squatting, looking beneath a fallen wall that had enough dark space under it to conceal a child. He grunted slightly and pressed his hand to his lower back, sending a small pulse of healing magic through the sore muscles. One would think that, as a healer, his own body would be free of aches and pains, but when he mentioned that to Manuela, his friend had just laughed at him.

"When we get close enough, Rouge will hear us," Aspen said, just loud enough for his voice to reach the Vonn-light. "Filial was a decent-sized town, and since it wrapped around the lake, it sprawls more than others, but it should be soon." It was well after the twenty-minute time limit he'd set for Rouge's return, and after the children's disappearance, he was worried for his young friend, too. He sent out a questing thought. ::Rouge?::

::Aspen!:: The sound of Rouge's voice was welcome. They must have just moved within range, because, like real voices over real distance, the girl sounded faint and far away.

Aspen whistled sharply, the prearranged signal that indicated he had contacted their missing friend. ::Rouge! Where are you?::

Vonn whistled back, and Aspen sensed his presence moving more quickly toward the center of town, where Rouge was supposed to be. He hurried his own pace to keep up. It wouldn't do to have anyone else vanish without a sign.

Rouge sounded like her usual cheerful self, and Aspen felt a sense of dread he hadn't even realized was there falling away from him. ::I'm at the only house left standing. It's near the big dock on the lakeside, and Wally is standing outside. You can't miss it!::

Aspen's voice was sharper than he intended it to be, but he had been worried. ::Why are you late? You were supposed to do a quick scouting run and come right back!::

::Sorry, Aspen.:: She really did sound contrite for a moment, but then she was right back to bubbling excitement. ::I found survivors! Well, maybe one of them found me, but anyway, there are four here, and they say two more are around somewhere. Plus, I just got a quest that says there are a total of seventeen! I mean, that's not many out of, what did Restur say, almost fifty? But it's way better than none, or even six! We need to help these people, Aspen!::

Aspen was jogging now, thankful for his high Endurance as he continued breathing easily in spite of his speed. He dodged around the remains of a small outbuilding, and then he could see Codswallop. The bird was, indeed, standing outside of a good-sized house. The stone walls were blackened, but sturdy, and the roof looked as if it had been recently reinforced.

Vonn dropped out of [Stealth] as they drew near, and by the time he vaulted the low fence, he was clearly visible. Codswallop chirruped inquiringly, pushing his beak into the elf's belt pouch. Vonn gently bumped the big bird's head aside with a chuckle. "I don't have anything for you right now, you *k'vinnet*."

Rouge's head popped out of the doorway, and she grinned, hazel eyes twinkling with laughter. "You always call him that. What does it mean?"

Vonn shook his head. "A small black and white bird, smart and fast, but always greedy. I think you call them magpies?"

Rouge burst out laughing. "Other than the small part, that sounds about right." The girl stepped out into the late afternoon sunshine, the beads in her braids glinting brightly, and patted Codswallop's shoulder. With his favorite person now available, the bird instantly turned his back on Vonn and pushed his head into Rouge's hand instead. She laughed and scratched the bird.

Behind Rouge, a thin, pale, scarred woman appeared in the door. While she might have looked like she would fall over in a strong breeze, the grip she had on the heavy sword in her hand was firm, and her stance was professional. This, then, was one of the survivors, and Aspen could guess why she was one of the few to make it through whatever had happened here.

Rouge turned around, and her shoulders stiffened slightly when she saw the sword the woman was holding. "Whoa, Flo!" Then she giggled at her inadvertent rhyme, and the tension drained away, leaving everyone feeling slightly amused. "Um, this is my friend, Aspen. He's a healer, so you should let him take a look at you guys, too."

The woman, a tall, strongly built brunette with fresh scars on much of her exposed skin, nodded at Aspen, her eyes calculating. She flicked a glance at Rouge. "He the one you said was bossy? The Duke?"

Rouge's face flushed darkly, even the tips of her pointed ears turning deep red. "Uh, yeah, I guess I might have, um, said that."

Aspen snorted a laugh and laid his hand on top of the short elf girl's head, feeling the reassuring solidity of her head beneath the thick twists of hair. "All adults are bossy when you're fourteen."

She flashed a relieved grin at him. "That's true."

Flo looked between them, and her gaze softened as she stepped aside slightly, leaving enough room for Aspen and Vonn to enter the house. They accepted the tacit invitation, and entered. Aspen noticed that the doorway was high enough that his head was nowhere near the lintel, and he wondered absently whether they had made the doorway larger for someone in their group, or if that was left over from whoever had originally inhabited the building.

Inside, the smell of smoke and ashes, which Aspen had unconsciously become used to, was diminished by the drying bundles of herbs that hung from the high rafters. Aspen was slightly bemused to note that his newfound ability to sense what uses a certain plant might have extended even to these bundles, though Millie's ground or powdered cooking herbs did not supply him with similar information. Perhaps it was because these were still whole, with stalks, stems, and even flowers or seed pods intact? In any case, it was an overabundance of currently-unimportant knowledge, so he pulled his Life Sense in, shutting off everything he didn't need.

A man and a woman lay in smoke-stained bedrolls on the far side of the room, and the doors and windows were securely boarded up. Anyone who wanted to enter this room would have to come in through the front door, and Aspen saw that there was a sword lying by the man's hand that matched the one Flo held.

He looked at Flo, who was now sitting beside the man. In her lap was a little girl of perhaps seven. The child also showed signs of fresh scarring, and her right eye was a blind, milky orb. In spite of her injuries, the child looked cautious, but not terrified, and Aspen was reminded again how resilient the young could be, especially when they had a trusted adult nearby.

Aspen knelt by the silent woman, who was staring into space with sightless eyes. The only signs that she still lived were the rise and fall of her chest and an occasional slow blink. Gently, he shook her shoulder.

"That's my sister, Olive." Flo's voice was flat. "Her baby was stolen from her arms, and it seems to have... broken something in her. She's had a hard life, and getting her a fresh start is part of the reason we came here." The woman barked a short, bitter laugh. "Some new start."

Aspen closed his eyes and looked inside Olive's body. He sent some gentle magic to heal the lingering damage left by fire, as well as the remains of some deep wounds in her abdomen that had to have nearly killed her. It was a miracle that she was even alive, and without thinking, he murmured a prayer of thanks to Gina.

His right index finger began to glow with soft light where it rested on the woman's limp wrist. He frowned down at it. The silver 'tattoo' was the symbol of a unique skill given to him by Gina, whose Champion he was. It was meant to cleanse the taint left by the evil god Apofis on the spirits of the innocents his cultists abducted.

Aspen opened another internal 'eye', looking not just at Olive's physical self, but her spirit as well. Sure enough, it showed faint signs of the erosion that ate away at those Apofis' cult had taken. Aspen sat back on his heels, spreading his senses wider. This vision used far more of his mana and had a much shorter range than did his Life Sense, so he hadn't used it since they left Bright.

Fortunately, Flo, as well as the man and the child, looked as spiritually healthy as they were physically damaged. It was only Olive who suffered from this particular form of injury. Aspen tightened his hand on the comatose woman's thin wrist and murmured, "[Winnow]."

A breeze instantly sprang up in the room, clearing out the stench of smoke and sickness. The smell of flowers drifted in, and everyone there drew in an almost involuntary breath, smiles crossing their faces. Olive, too, drew in a deep breath, though hers shuddered and shook her thin frame. The edges of her spirit solidified, and the faint shadows that had been forming in or on it vanished like puffs of dust blown free by the breeze.

As the wind died down, leaving a lingering trace of summer's perfume in the air, Olive began to cry.

The smell of ripe fruit and blossoms still filled Aspen's nose as Olive began to sob, at first quietly, and then hard, body-shaking wails that made everyone wince in sympathy. With a small cry, Flo pushed Aspen aside none-too-gently and caught her sister up in her arms. The two women held each other and wept, and when it seemed that they were going to continue this for a while, Aspen saw Rouge begin to edge toward the door. He understood. These people certainly deserved compassion, but there was so much to *do*.

Aspen turned and caught Rouge's eyes, then looked toward Vonn. He tilted his head toward the door, and the three of them sidled out while the small family clung to each other. Once they stood outside, in the dim sunlight trickling through the heavy cloud of ash, Aspen said, "Should we leave them to it? They've been through a lot, and now that they're all stable, the best thing we can do for them is go find their friends and family. Not to mention the children."

Rouge halted just outside the door, her face paling. "Wait, children? What do you mean?"

Aspen gently rested a hand on her shoulder, knowing that his words would upset her. "Jiminy, Ulie, and the boys all followed you. Vonn was able to track them to the edge of town, but they just vanished. Even my Life Sense can't find them."

Rouge crossed to Codswallop and hastily leapt onto the ostrich's back, settling into the small saddle. "That's just like when Silus and I were stuck in the cultist's hideout. Do you think there's a teleportation portal around here somewhere? That would make sense. Florence and Petunia told me monsters just appeared out of nowhere, and then vanished just as quickly once they'd grabbed everyone they could. Apparently, there's yet another sister, Nanette, who spends her days looking for them, but she hasn't turned anything up in more than a week of searching."

Vonn growled, and Aspen gritted his teeth. "Now that I know Akuji is behind all of this, everything is beginning to make so much more sense. The Lich Lord was always able to pervert the laws of the world, as long as he had enough time and lives to burn. He attacked cities that should have been fully protected by bluestones. He used rugs like the one we used to flee my home to send his generals all over the battlefront. These portals, too, are defying everything Motte or I knew about teleportation. There's no way they should be able to send Akuji's minions such long distances without unimaginable influxes of mana."

Rouge's brows drew together. "When Mirna was talking about the cult, she mentioned something about a 'daily mana tax' or something. It wasn't much, like, five or ten mana, maybe? It seemed like just a starter quest, no big deal. But if you multiply that by all the Travelers who have joined the cult so they can become 'Nobles' or whatever, it could be-" She paused, obviously thinking. "Hundreds of thousands of mana a day? If they ask for more as you go up in rank, it could go into the millions really easily."

The girl stopped, looking sick, and Aspen understood why.

"Add that to whatever power they get from sacrificing the lives of their victims to Apof- ah, I mean, Chris, or Akuji, or whoever - and they're probably fully capable of building a teleportation device that can send their followers and monsters all the way here from Bright or Bloodhaven." Vonn looked grim as he spoke, and his gray eyes were darting around as if any shadow might suddenly spawn a horde of beasts.

That weight on Aspen's shoulders was back, and he suddenly felt as though he might break beneath the pressure of it. How could they possibly win, or even simply hold their own, against such an overwhelming force? He closed his eyes, barely able to breathe as the world closed in around him, and then a warm breeze lifted the edges of his shaggy hair, playfully tickling his nose, and he smelled strawberries and warm mango.

He let his head drop so his chin nearly rested on his chest, and he prayed to his goddess. *Gina, please, we need some way to at least know when they're coming. They hide in the darkness, and we're constantly under attack from every direction. If we can see them coming, at least we can defend ourselves!*

The wind swirled around him, sending ashes rising into the sky like a column of darkness. By some miracle, the air around Aspen and the others cleared of ash, and sunshine seemed to gather around them like the light of a thousand glowstones. A pure blue light came from Aspen's right hand, and words appeared before his eyes.

The Goddess Gina has heard your prayer. As Her Champion, She grants you the following Skill to be used in pursuit of Her goals.
[Detect Evil] *Gina's light will pulse from you in a sphere, revealing the influence of true evil in a half mile radius. Your enemies will see you, but you'll be looking back when they do. Can only be used once per day in any given area.*

Aspen only realized that the wind had lifted him from the ground when his feet settled gently into the dirt again. The ash swirled around him and his companions, though it now lay in concentric circles around them, five perfectly round mounds of black and gray with clean, bare earth and grass in between. The grass was brilliant green, not the sickly yellow blades that they could see elsewhere, and the visible soil was rich black loam, not dry faded brown dirt.

Behind him, Aspen heard Vonn whispering a prayer of thanks, but before he could do the same, Rouge was snatching up his hand and turning it over in her own.

"That is so cool! It kinda looks like Celtic knotwork done in woad, but, you know, shinier." The elf girl traced a finger along the delicate blue lines that now covered his right thumb and the fleshy pad of his hand. It did, indeed, look something like a shiny blue string tied in a complex knot that reminded him of a square tied up in a circle that had been divided into four distinct quadrants. The lines glinted a deep, rich blue in the sunlight.

Vonn, too, had come closer so that he could see the new tattoo, which joined three similar ones representing other unique skills gifted by Gina. Aspen's index finger looked like it was covered in silver swirls of clouds or mist. He had received that tattoo at the same time as the [Winnow] skill, which allowed him to remove the taint of evil from an innocent person or creature. The constantly shifting images of creatures growing through cycles of metamorphosis that wrapped around his middle finger suited his [Metamorphosis] skill well. The skill allowed him to change a sapient being into a member of a different race, so that those who had persecuted others could suffer the same fate as their victims. [Resurrection] was linked to the simple white glow of his right pinky, which he had found he could use as though he had a weak glowstone implanted beneath his skin. With the associated skill, he could bring back one of Gina's worshippers who had recently died, though the skill only worked once every three days.

Now, the deep blue, metallic knot joined the other three, and Aspen had gained a valuable new skill. When he looked up, he met two pairs of expectant eyes.

"Well?" Rouge demanded. "What does it do?"

Aspen grinned. "Solves a really big problem."

ಠ ಠ ಠ

Since none of them knew how long the effect of the spell would last, Aspen went back inside the house to explain what was happening to the survivors. They looked uncertain at first, but once Rouge explained about her quest that showed there were still eleven of their family and friends who could be saved, Florence and Horace became eager to help. They all went outside to prepare, even Olive, who was so shaky that Florence had to hold her up.

Aspen used [Heal] on Petunia, Florence, and Horace, repairing the lingering effects of their wounds enough that even their scars were only visible if you knew where to look. Upon seeing his daughter's face returned to its original condition, with even her damaged eye repaired to a pretty green, though

Petunia said the vision in that eye was still fuzzy, Horace fell to his knees in front of Aspen.

Holding the heavy sword out across his palms, the former soldier bowed his head. "Thank you." His voice was choked, and Aspen was sure that his face would have been tracked with tears if he'd lifted it. "The little elf says you're a Duke, and though I know of no Duke Aspen, I'll swear my loyalty to you now in exchange for returning my child's life to her. From this day forward, I am your man." His wife knelt in the rich grass beside him, offering up her own sword with equal sincerity.

Congratulations! You have gained two vassals. As a Duke, you may have up to one hundred sworn vassals, who cannot betray you in pain or death. Their relationship level is currently 72 (Helpful). You gain 5% of their experience gained. This bond can only be broken if both parties agree.

Aspen sucked in his breath sharply, once again feeling the overwhelming pressure of the expectations placed on him by others, but he forced a smile and reached out to help them up. "Thank you for your faith in me, though I'm certain there are others far more worthy. I-" he choked off the words that would urge them to take back their oaths, and instead returned to the matter at hand.

"I have a skill that should show where the invaders are coming from. I don't know how long the effect will linger, however, and I can only do it once in an area per day. I need everyone to watch closely, because if it lasts for only a split second, and we miss it, well…" He shrugged, and everyone nodded in understanding.

Petunia held up her hand. "Should we go around to different places, so we can see different things? Or climb up high, maybe?" She reached out and grabbed her mother's hand, and Florence pulled the little girl in closer to her side. "I want to go with Mama, though."

Aspen smiled and nodded. "That was a very smart suggestion, Petunia." He looked up at Florence. "Where were you all when the monsters attacked? Could anyone tell which direction they came from, or which way they went?"

Florence's lips pinched. "We were eating breakfast in the town hall, which *was* the largest building left with a roof. We built a sort of cafeteria there, and Scott and Nima cooked meals for everyone. Amanda was a teacher, and after we ate, she'd take the children for lessons in the morning, while we adults worked. Olive was the first to react, when they took Shye."

Olive nodded weakly, though tears once again staining her cheeks and her lips trembled. "I'm a tailor, and I've been repairing torn clothes and keeping everything as clean as I could. There were clotheslines hung outside the town hall, and everyone would drop things off for me to work on. Tyler had built a little play area there for Shye, and I was just getting ready to set her down when—"

Her voice choked off, and her shoulders hunched as she fought off sobs. Florence put a comforting arm around her shoulders, and Petunia hugged her aunt's leg. When she was able, Olive continued. "They came from the west, I think, but they were just *there*. A short man with black skin and red eyes snatched Shye away, and when I hit him with the iron that was heating on the brick oven, a *thing* covered in spikes tried to yank out my guts with his claws. I thought I was dead, and Shye…"

She paused again, but gathered herself more quickly this time. "Before I lost consciousness, I saw the one carrying Shye run away. I nearly crushed his skull with the iron, but he was still moving, and he definitely headed west, toward the entrance of town."

Aspen nodded, considering. "That would make sense with the way the children seemed to vanish as soon as they entered the town. Perhaps the portal is actually just outside of town somewhere?" He exchanged looks with Vonn and Rouge. "Right near where the caravan is waiting?"

Vonn cursed and triggered his [Stealth]. Aspen sensed the boy moving quickly and silently through the debris, back the way they'd come. The wood elf was already racing away when he called back, "I'll warn Restur and the others. Willow is there!"

Rouge looked back and forth between the distant caravan and Aspen. ::What should I do?::

Aspen hesitated, then shook his head, choosing to respond out loud. "Vonn will warn the others. We need to get this lot back so we can protect them, and they can help us find the entrance. I'll use [Detect Evil] whenever I can, while you all keep watch, and we can learn about the skill as we go. It's only about two miles back, but we need to learn how this works. Since we think the portal may be near the entrance, it should be safe to test it here, even without as many eyes to watch what happens."

Rouge nodded. "Sounds good. Wally can carry Petunia, too, for sure, or maybe Olive, since she's so thin. That should let us move faster."

Horace scooped his daughter up into his arms and set her on his shoulders. The little girl looked thrilled, and grabbed her father's hair in small fists. He grimaced a little, but said, "If you can take Olive, Florence and I will keep up."

Olive looked dubious, as did Codswallop, but once Rouge bribed the ostrich with a cinnamon roll pulled from her inventory, the bird reluctantly knelt to allow the woman to climb up onto his back. He squawked pathetically, but stood back up with ease, shaking his feathers to settle them back into place.

Rouge grinned. "I have enough cinnamon rolls for everyone, and even though they're not quite as good as the ones Millie originally gave me, they still grant +5 to all stats and increased speed and stamina recovery. I pretty much live on these things." The girl produced a cinnamon roll for each of them, and Aspen could see each of the worn survivors perk up as they ate the delicious confection.

Popping the last bite of his own pastry into his mouth, Aspen felt his own flagging spirits lift as well. He looked around. "Is everyone ready?"

Rouge held up a hand. "Just a second."

Olive yelped as Codswallop took a great leap to the top of a nearby stone wall. From there, he made it to a tall post that was probably part of a fish-drying system before the fire. Finally, he jumped to the edge of the roof, then hopped up to stand on the ridge. He and Rouge looked very proud of themselves, while Olive looked like she was going to be sick.

"Do it now!" Rouge yelled, and he did.

"[Detect Evil]!"

Chapter Twenty-two
Rouge

The pulse that expanded from Aspen's body wasn't exactly light, and it wasn't exactly sound, but it had elements of both. Rouge thought that if humans could use echolocation, this is probably what it would look (or sound) like. A second radiating sphere of disturbed air (excited sound waves?) followed the first, and then there was a third and a fourth. After the second, Rouge pulled up her in-game clock, and when the third wave hit, she started a timer. Exactly 2.5 seconds later, the fourth wave rolled out.

Silence.

Everyone was staring around expectantly, and there was nothing. Lots and lots of nothing. Finally, Rouge sent, ::I guess that means there's either nothing to find here, or we missed it?::

Aspen sounded more than a little frustrated. ::We knew the chances of finding anything this time were low, but I hate feeling as if we may have missed something for lack of enough eyes to see.::

::For want of a nail, huh? Well, Wally, and I were keeping pretty close watch, though I think Olive hasn't opened her eyes since we got up here. In any case, if whatever was supposed to happen was something obvious, I doubt we'd have missed it.:: Rouge clucked to Codswallop, and the ostrich nimbly leapt down from his perch.

Olive's hands clutched convulsively at Rouge's shirt, but otherwise the woman didn't react. Rouge actually felt pretty bad about scaring the poor lady, especially since she'd just gone through a lot, so she patted one of the hands where it was clenched around her belt. She wasn't sure what else she could do, since they had to get moving, but hopefully Manuela, who seemed to be *Veritas Online's* answer to a psychologist, as well as a physician, would be able to help.

Once the ostrich's big feet touched down on the ground, Aspen nodded to everyone. "I hope I'll be able to tell when we're out of the area of effect for this first use of the skill, but, if not, if anyone thinks we've gone far enough to try again, please speak up. Also, since we don't know how long the effects may linger, say something immediately if you see anything odd."

He looked around, meeting each person's eyes, and Rouge was sure he didn't miss the way her hand was still resting reassuringly on Olive's. Nodding decisively, he gestured to the west. "Let's go."

Everyone held up surprisingly well as they jog-ran toward the entrance to town. Given how injured Horace and Florence had been, Rouge had wondered if they would be able to move any faster than a walk, but they simply set their jaws in identical looks of determination, and began jogging. She wondered if that was something they learned in the military, or if they were just naturally unwilling to give in to weakness. Both, at a guess.

After ten minutes or so of running, silent except for the occasional scuff of feet on rubble and panting breaths, Aspen raised his right hand, slowing to a stop. He turned his hand in the air so everyone could see the faintest gleam of blue from the new tattoo. "It looked more gray than blue right after I used it. I think it's either recharged, or we're in an entirely new area now."

Rouge bit her lip. It would be a problem if the skill couldn't overlap at all with the previous area. That would leave diamond-shaped gaps between areas, even if Aspen used it in the most efficient way possible. Hopefully, it was just a cool-down period. Not for the first time, she wished that Natives could see their skill lists the same way Travelers could. The NPCs gained skills, spells, and stats in a much more organic way than players, and as far as she could tell, quests were the only 'messages from the Gods' they got on a regular basis.

As Aspen spoke, Rouge triggered her internal timer again. If there was a cool-down on the skill, timing it should reveal that. For fun, she also timed the pulses, and noted that each one was, indeed, exactly 2.5 seconds apart. She wondered if that would stay the same as the skill leveled up, or if the area it covered or number of pulses would increase instead. Did goddess-given skills even level up, or were they already as strong as they would get?

With each pulse, she made sure she was looking in a different direction, and she noticed that everyone else did the same. They knew a bit of what to expect now, so they could work within the limits of the skill. When nothing happened, everyone exchanged looks of mixed relief and frustration, and then Aspen gestured, and they began running again.

Flo and Horace actually seemed to be running more easily, now, but Rouge noticed that Aspen wasn't moving quite as easily as he had been in the beginning. She had a suspicion she knew why. ::Aspen, you can't drain yourself to keep healing them. We're more than halfway there now, and if you run out of mana, you're going to pass out again. What if we get to the caravan, and they're under attack?::

She'd let Codswallop fall back until he was pacing Aspen, and she saw the glance the tall man flicked at her with his slightly disturbing pale topaz eyes. ::I know,:: he said, ::but if they fall now, they won't get back up, and who knows what we're heading into. They're only moving by sheer stubborn grit. They must have both been foot soldiers, because they know how to pace themselves and breathe so they use their energy efficiently. It's not taking much assistance to bolster their endurance. I think it's the [Detect Evil] skill, mostly. I'd say it takes about ten percent of my mana pool each time I use it. It's certainly not something I can just use as often as I'd like. If I could meditate to replenish my mana, I could probably do it nearly every ten minutes, but as it is-::

Rouge nodded in understanding. They weren't combat, and had no debuffs, so their health, mana, and stamina were regenerating naturally, but sitting or sleeping would have allowed that regeneration to happen nearly twice as quickly. ::When [Detect Evil] is ready, let me know, but don't use it, okay? I'm timing it to see if it's on cool-down or just requires no overlap with the previous area.::

He smiled, sending her another glance. ::I was also thinking it would be best to wait until we were closer to the caravan, since the portal could be anywhere now, if there is one at all. Thank you for timing it. I was trying to count, but I know your Traveler's clock is much more accurate.::

She grinned at him, and then clucked at Wally, urging him to move to the front of the small group. She was in the best shape to deal with an attack, if there was one, and, besides, she could see much further than any of the runners, simply because she was on top of an eight-foot-tall ostrich. It was nice to be the tall one, for once.

At precisely ten minutes from the last pulse of [Detect Evil], Aspen said, ::It's available again.::

Rouge glanced down and back. She had been watching the clock, and had urged Wally up onto a short wall, where they had paused while the timer continued to tick along. Aspen, Horace, and Florence (now with Petunia perched on her shoulders, to give Horace a break) were just now reaching the narrow, overgrown path below.

::Got it,:: she said. ::Ten minutes and seven point five seconds. Looks like ten minutes from end of the last pulse.:: She was relieved, since trying to picture the most efficient pattern to avoid any overlap of the spheres had been making her head hurt.

::Thank you, Rouge. Can you see the caravan from up there? They should be in sight soon.::

She turned and looked, but the remains of a tall building blocked her view of the way forward. ::Not yet.::

Aspen whistled sharply. When Rouge looked at him questioningly, he said, ::It's the signal for Vonn.::

There was no answer, and Rouge frowned. She hadn't realized it, but Aspen was right. They were almost certainly close enough to the caravan that Vonn should have answered, even if he were fighting.

::Carp,:: Rouge muttered, urging Codswallop into an even faster pace. The ostrich leapt, easily clearing several piles of rock and then scrambling up on top of what had probably once been a house. Staring out across the debris left by Akuji's attack, she finally saw the caravan, barely a quarter mile away. It was silent. No children shrieked as they ran from the ministrations of frustrated adults, no guards paced the outskirts of the camp, and Restur's silver hair didn't shine from the seat of the front wagon. Worst of all, not a single animal still stood, shifting in their harnesses and looking longingly at the green grass just off the worn track.

It was empty. Wind flapped a piece of loose canvas, and the traces that should hold the horses and oxen lay abandoned in the dust. The only ones left were, shockingly, the defenseless Zombies of the Travelers. All of them sat peacefully atop their horses at the end of the caravan, as if nothing had happened at all. Rouge felt a chill go down her back at the sight.

::Aspen,:: Rouge sent, glancing down to see that the others had caught up and were running along the road below them. ::They're gone. Everyone is just… gone.::

Aspen's voice was grim, and he picked up his pace. ::I had a suspicion when Vonn didn't answer. Do you see any,:: he hesitated, ::bodies?::

::Nothing,:: Rouge said. ::It's like someone just scooped them up and spirited them all away. The only ones left are the Zombies, which doesn't make any sense. Once combat is engaged, Zombies are viable targets, and they're defenseless, so they should have all been killed. Unless-::

::Unless combat was never engaged,:: Aspen finished grimly. ::Something took them away without a single blow being exchanged, even after Vonn warned them. Unless they were gone before he got here, and whatever it was simply took him, too. Will the Zombies remember anything, when they wake up?::

Rouge shook her head, urging Codswallop back into motion. The ostrich easily caught up to and then passed Aspen and the others, even though they had all increased their speed. ::They're like pre-programmed robots.:: She remembered Aspen would have no idea what robots were, and tried again. ::I mean, like automatons or golems. We can give them tasks to do while we're not here, but they don't have any consciousness of their own, so if something happens that falls outside of their task list, they'll just do what they did, and stand there. If whatever happened didn't create any notifications, then they'll be even more clueless than we are.::

Aspen stopped not far from the first wagon, where Restur should have been sitting, glaring at them and asking what took so long. ::We have no choice. I'll have to use [Detect Magic], and-::

Silus' sleepy voice interrupted him. ::Aspen? Rouge? Why are you guys so noisy? Why aren't the wagons moving?:: Rouge and Aspen stared at each other, shocked and relieved, and then the little voice was back. ::Where *is* everyone? *What is going on*?::

As if the bat's question was a trigger, a quest notice popped up in Rouge's vision.

Quest: "What Happened, Lassie?" available.

Maybe everyone fell down a well? Who knows? You certainly don't, and you probably should. Find everyone and rescue them before time runs out. *After 30 minutes, members of your caravan will begin to die. You probably want to hurry. Time remaining: 00:29:41*

Success: Experience. Some of your friends survive. *Special success result: Variable increase in completion percentage of SECRET quest "Who Run the World".*

Failure: Everybody's dead. -10 Reputation with Aspen. -10 Reputation with the Filial survivors. -10 Reputation with Silus. *Special failure result: -17% completion of SECRET quest "Who Run the World".*

Rouge grabbed Olive's hands where they were wrapped around her middle, and urged Codswallop into a leap that took them to the top of the second wagon. This wagon was unusual in that it had a solid wooden roof, rather than a canvas one, and it creaked but held beneath the ostrich's weight.

::Silus, we need your eyes! Come out if you can!::

A moment later, the little bat, all soft fur and huge ears and eyes, flapped out of the wagon where she slept hidden in a wooden box in the back. Presumably, whoever had taken the rest of the members of the caravan had missed her because of her size and location, and Rouge found herself fiercely grateful for this fact as she waved the small creature away when Silus tried to land on Rouge's shoulder. ::Fly up, Silus. Get as high as you can, and watch for anything strange. We'll explain, but there isn't a moment to spare.::

Rouge looked down at Aspen, noting that he, too, had climbed to the top of a wagon, and Florence and Horace were each standing facing in opposite directions. ::Do it, Aspen!::

The sphere rippled out, and they were surrounded by monsters.

Ghostly images of hideous monsters surrounded them. They were everywhere, and it took Rouge's mind a moment she didn't really have to realize that what she was seeing was something like a dozen movie clips all running at once, on top of each other. She began to pick out the same toothy beast shambling toward the wagons at the same time as it moved away, clutching Restur and Tia's limp bodies in its arms.

Hooded figures were everywhere, and she could tell that the trim on their hoods was made of some dark shade, deep green or maybe dark red, but in their insubstantiality, she couldn't be sure which it was. One of the caped presences moved through Codswallop's legs, while a pale thing like a cockroach, but with too many legs and at least twenty human-looking eyes scuttled nearby, its back laden with unconscious forms. Wally shifted and shuddered beneath her, his feathers fluffing as he croaked out a confused and miserable call.

As each wave of Aspen's skill swept through the area, a new scene was laid over the previous one, until all around her were silent phantasms in all their clawed and gooey glory. Then the oldest figures, the ones revealed by the very first flash of [Detect Evil] began to fade, rapidly followed by the others, leaving only a few hazy images scurrying toward a small hillock to the east.

Aspen was already on the move, following the last lingering traces of shadowy robed figures, and Rouge clucked to Codswallop, urging him into motion. They quickly passed Aspen's merely human speed, and popped over the low hill to see Silus swooping in to land on a large door that was closed in now, but in this strange vision of the recent past, still stood open as the final flash of vision passed through before fading entirely away.

Coming up beside Rouge, Aspen stared at the door. "Probably a root cellar, or perhaps a storm shelter. This area gets fierce snowstorms sometimes. Though why it's out here-" He shook his head.

Horace, who had come up to join them, gestured to the ground. "Used to be a foundation here. Likely a house that was still going up when they evacuated originally." Looking closely, Rouge could just make out the squared corners that were all that still held the shape of a human habitation. Everything else around those small, worn corners was just more rubble and ash, with spring vines already consuming them into anonymity.

Aspen scuffed the ground with his boot. "Why are there no tracks? No broken grass, loose strands of fur, or footprints. How did they take everyone in the caravan in minutes, and leave no sign of their passing?"

Florence knelt, rubbing dirt between her thumb and forefinger. She looked up, face set and pale. "Why did they not do this to us? Why not take us as they did your friends? Silently, bloodlessly, while we slept? Why slaughter us instead?"

Horace reached down and pulled his wife to her feet, wrapping her in a hug that was probably meant to comfort them both. Petunia wriggled between them, and they widened their embrace to include the child.

::Aspen,:: Rouge sent, ::I got a quest that said we only had 30 minutes before our people started dying. We need to move.::

Aspen sounded grim. ::I received a similar quest. I think we need to go alone, though. These people are too worn out to help us, and if they find their family, I don't know that they'll be able to keep from doing something foolish.::

Rouge nodded and vaulted down from Wally's back, flipping twice to land in the dirt with a quiet *thud._*She set a gentle hand on Florence's shoulder, feeling a little strange about it, since the woman was at least twenty years her senior and nearly a foot taller. "Flo, we need to go."

The warrior woman spun, eyes teary and wild. "We're going with-"

Rouge shook her head. "You know you can't." She looked at Petunia and Olive. "Petunia can't go in there, and Olive isn't strong enough. They can't stay here alone, either. Even if those things don't come back, there are other dangers here. Besides, if Rani or Nanette find your note-"

It was her turn to be interrupted, as a gruff female voice came from behind them. "Nanette already did. I got here just in time to see your little magic trick."

Rouge spun on her heel, pulling her Mambele from her inventory with a thought. A haggard woman stood there. She was well over six feet tall, with powerful shoulders and huge, square hands, which were currently holding a heavy hammer that Rouge doubted most men could even swing.

With a cry, Petunia hurtled toward the woman. The child stood barely as high as the woman's knee, but she clung on with the tenacity of a toddler who had just found her favorite teddy bear after thinking it was lost forever. "Auntie

Nan!"

Nanette leaned down and scooped up the girl, who looked tiny in the woman's embrace. Nanette trailed a shaking finger over the side of Petunia's face where the terrible burns had been only a short time before. "How did this happen?" She looked over at Florence. "Your note was short on details, Flo."

Florence strode over and hugged her sister briefly. "These people happened." She pointed at Aspen. "Meet our new lord. He's a healer." Her voice was as proud as if she was showing off a prize-winning pony.

Aspen's mouth quirked, but he stepped forward and shook Nanette's hand briefly. Rouge could tell from the way the lines around the woman's mouth eased that he'd given her at least a small [Heal], though she didn't look as injured as the others had been. Nanette nodded in thanks, then cast dark eyes toward the door set into the ground. "This is where those things came from, then? And where they took my family?"

Horace and Florence exchanged glances, and Flo set a restraining hand on her sister's well-muscled arm. "You're a farrier, Nan, not a fighter. You going in there won't do anything but get you killed, too."

Nanette's voice was rough. "I might as well be dead now, Flo. You have Petunia, at least." Her arm tightened around her niece, and the little girl squeaked slightly. "Without West and the kids, I have nothing." She held up her free hand. "Don't tell me I still have you. You know-"

Aspen broke into what Rouge suspected was a well-rehearsed argument. "Rouge and I need to go, *now*. Our friends and whatever's left of your family depends on it. You're all staying here, voluntarily or not. Rouge and I-"

::Hey!:: Silus said.

"*And* Silus, know what we're doing." He looked at Florence and Horace, and his expression was a cold and commanding one that Rouge didn't think she'd ever seen on his face before. "You two are my vassals now, and you'll do as I say, like it or not. Stay here and protect Petunia, Olive, and the caravan, though not at risk of your lives. If Nanette tries to follow us, use whatever force is necessary to keep her here." His topaz eyes looked like chips of ice as he glared between the two.

Florence just nodded her head, but Horace's face went white, and he bowed deeply. "As you say, my lord." Florence cast a slightly confused look at her husband, but then followed his lead and deepened her own bow. Rouge had a feeling Horace had just figured out who their new Duke really was.

Aspen turned back to the door and reached down to the rusted metal handle. With a creak, he lifted the slab of wood and stared down into the impossibly deep set of stairs that had been revealed. They were wide and scuffed, with deep gouges dug into the wood here and there, with a few splatters and spots of some dried substance that Rouge didn't really want to think about. Obviously, whatever spell hid the monster's passing stopped at the door frame.

Aspen held out a hand, and Silus dropped from the bush where she'd come to roost, swooping up to land on his wrist. Rouge moved before he could step through. "Let the rogue do rogue-work. There could be traps left in case someone managed to follow them."

Honestly, she doubted it, since that many semi-sentient monsters would surely trigger any trap that was set, but she didn't want Aspen going first. If she died, she'd lose months of work, but that was all she'd lose. Soon enough, she'd respawn back as her puny level 19 self, and while it might be annoying and tedious, she'd recover at least some of what she'd lost. If Aspen or Silus died, however, that was it for them. Their files would be archived to the database the NPCs called the 'Chaos Pool', and when the *Veritas Online* system needed more file space, they'd be overwritten forever.

Aspen drew in a breath as if to argue, but then he just nodded and stepped aside. Rouge turned to Codswallop, patting the ostrich's soft shoulder. "Wally, you keep these folks safe. It's probably going to be tight down there, and there won't be anyplace safe to leave you. Just wait for me, okay?"

Codswallop leaned his football-sized head down and pressed it into her chest, chirruping softly. She scrootched his ear ridge before stepping back.

"Okay. We have," she checked her in-game clock, "fourteen minutes and twenty-three seconds to save someone's life."

Aspen quirked a grin. "Lead on, then, lady rogue."

Rouge ran like she'd never run before. Technically, she even checked for traps, but she was moving so fast that she doubted she could have reacted in time even if she'd found one. She leapt down three or four of the huge steps at a time, quickly realizing that they were easily twice as tall and wide as normal stairs. Going up them would be a bear, but going down was almost like flying.

Behind her, Aspen jumped almost as quickly and smoothly as she did, following in her footsteps so that they both used the same stair steps. If Rouge triggered a trap, Aspen would fall into it with her, but if she jumped over one, so would he. The girl spared only a faint corner of her mind to be amazed at how far her friend had come from the skinny 100-pound weakling she'd first met. As she understood it, he'd been significantly improved from the state he was in when he and his companions fled Bright, but he'd still looked like a recently-recovered plague victim.

NPCs gained and improved stats as they used them, instead of being assigned a flat ten stat points to allocate however they wanted each time they leveled. If an NPC ran a lot, their strength and stamina would go up. If they played an instrument, their dexterity would increase.

Standard NPCs did the same thing over and over until a player interacted with them, at which point they would be allocated more processing power and might do something entirely different, depending upon the results of the interaction. If that player or others continued the interaction, they'd gradually become more and more complex and independent, but if they were ignored, they'd settle back into either their old routine or an entirely new one.

Veritas Online also granted decreasing amounts of experience for repetitive actions. This prevented players from gaining skill or spell experience by spamming the exact same action over and over, and encouraged exploration and new activities. For NPCs, this meant that a default NPC would eventually reach some cap on their stats, simply because they never did anything different, and thus couldn't gain any more experience.

Aspen, however, was a quest NPC. He and all of his companions had obviously been allocated enough processing power to effectively function entirely independently of player input. They grew and changed, had their own ideas, and made choices without anyone ever interacting with them. Quest NPCs could continue growing until they became veritable monsters (or literal ones, in some cases), so the difficulty of a quest sometimes continued to increase over time simply because all of the NPCs involved had grown.

Aspen also had a boon from his goddess, Gina. He gained all kinds of experience 10% faster than a regular quest NPC, who, Rouge was pretty sure, already had some kind of built-in advantage over regular NPCs, since the level difference between a quest NPC and an equivalent standard NPC was usually pretty significant.

All of this meant that as they bounded down what seemed like hundreds of stairs, Aspen was able to keep up with a rogue-type player character who had just over *three hundred* points in Dexterity. Add to that the fact that he was breathing easily, which meant his Stamina was also at least on par with hers, and she was starting to wonder if she should have let him go first after all.

Then it was too late to wonder, because the dark stairs ended, and they tumbled out into the light.

Chapter Twenty-three

Aspen

Aspen blinked against the sudden light as they entered a large open space that he found disturbingly familiar. It wasn't either of the cultist's hideouts that he and Rouge had recently infiltrated, though it did have many architectural similarities. Its vulgarity lay somewhere in between the decorative excess of the Traveler area Rouge had described to them in excruciating detail over the past few days, and the more subtle horrors Aspen had seen for himself in the area designated for Natives.

No, the most obvious similarity lay in the stacked cages and warded circles that held prisoners. Dozens, if not hundreds, of humanoids and animals alike, crouched, paced, or otherwise languished in captivity. The room was oddly silent in spite of the number of souls within. A few people sobbed quietly, and some of the animals made an occasional protesting noise, but in general there was an atmosphere of utter despair.

Then Manuela's voice broke the quiet, and both Aspen and Rouge's heads snapped to the right, where they saw their friends sitting, shackled and chained to a wall. "It's about time you got here, Aspen. I was going to be very disappointed in you if you took much longer." Her always raspy voice sounded hoarser than usual, and her hair and clothes were disheveled, but otherwise she and the others seemed unharmed.

Rouge raced over to the group and began working on the locks, while Aspen looked around for obvious threats. A cough came from behind him, and Restur spoke. "Nobody here but us prisoners, lad. We were alone when we woke, and no one comes in except one of those robed idiots every ten or twenty minutes. They grab some poor soul and take them away, and that's the last we see of them."

Rouge had several of the caravan members unlocked already, and the freed people rubbed their wrists and ankles as they waited for everyone else.

A soft, sweet voice came from a cage not far from where they had been held. "Restur said you'd come. I told him he was a fool." Aspen stepped over and peered between the bars of the rusty, stinking cage. A human woman sat there, dressed in the remains of sturdy, practical garments. Her hair was stringy and matted, but she, too, looked otherwise uninjured.

Aspen reached into his belt pouch and pulled out a long, slim worm. The thing was more akin to a snake than its invertebrate cousins, since Aspen had fed it far more mana than it had ever needed, but its slimy squishiness made it the perfect tool for the job to which he now put it. The small creature wriggled easily into the large lock on the cage, and it wiggled around until it pressed each of the tumblers in the mechanism. With a *click*, the lock opened, and the door swung open with a creak.

Rouge rejoined him and looked with fascinated disgust at the worm as it wiggled back out into his hand. He sent a small flush of mana into it before sending it into the next lock.

"I've never gotten to see that thing in action. That's… disgusting."

Aspen sent the girl a look of mock affront, retrieving his worm from the now-open clasp. "You only say that because you can't pick locks as quickly as

Jimmy can."

Rouge stuck her tongue out at him and turned to another cage. Nearby, Restur, Manuela, and several of the children - who all, unsurprisingly, had the [Lockpick] skill – were also popping locks as quickly as they could, probably using extra lockpicks from Rouge's magical Traveler inventory.

::We have four minutes and eighteen seconds left before someone was supposed to die, by the way.:: Rouge's quiet voice entered his mind as he worked. ::The quest hasn't completed, and the countdown hasn't stopped.::

"Rouge? Aspen?" Vonn's frantic voice rose above the hubbub that was starting to fill the cavern. Looking around, Aspen realized that not a single non-human or partially non-human member of the caravan was with the others. "I'm locked in one of those cursed magic circles. I need to get to Willow!"

Silus, who had flown off of Aspen's shoulder as soon as they entered the open space at the bottom of the stairs, piped up. ::I see them, Aspen. There're a bunch of doors on the opposite side from where we came in. Some of them are big enough for those nasty beasties who kidnapped everyone, and some of them are regular people-sized doors. Vonn and the others are stuck in a bunch of those circles.::

Aspen left Rouge and the others behind as he took off toward where he'd glimpsed a few of the circles when they'd first entered. In the bright light of the glowstones placed around the walls at regular intervals, Aspen was easily able to pick out Silus' sleek brown form as she dipped and dove, weaving through the air above Vonn, who was doing his best to wave his arms in spite of being bound in a circle barely two feet wide.

Skidding to a less than graceful halt, Aspen pulled Stick from his belt. At his mental command, the short, thick cudgel lengthened into a six-foot staff crowned with silver chains and metallic aspen leaves that jingled in excitement. Aspen had bound a tiny thread of his soul into the staff when he created it, and it had a bit more personality than he'd expected at the time.

The metallic cap of the semi-sentient staff glowed corn-yellow for a brief instant, and then reformed into a short sickle. Aspen used the sharp point of the blade to cut the ward carved into the stone floor, and Vonn tumbled to his knees as the invisible wall holding him up collapsed. The boy instantly scurried over to another nearby circle, this one even smaller than his own, and he stabbed at the ground with the blade of the knife that had still been in its sheath at his belt. Sparks flew, but the ward was undamaged.

Aspen quickly stepped over and sliced easily through the spell-circle that Vonn was struggling with. The young toddler inside burst into tears and fell into his uncle's waiting arms. As the boy reassured his small nephew, Aspen strode to each of the traps and carved all of the circles apart, releasing prisoner after prisoner. Without stopping to listen to either words of thanks or demands for aid, the tall farmer strode through the room, his staff trailing sparks and gouging a deep line in the stones beneath his feet.

Aspen's fury was building. He was sick of this. Sick of people thinking they could cage other people, tear them from their families, even kill them, all without consequences. When he ran out of circles, he swung his sickle at the bars of the cages, and they, too, split and fell away. His staff began to glow with golden heat, and before it even touched the bars, they grew red with heat, and a few people who had been waiting for release backed away as they were nearly burned.

Without a thought, Aspen sent out a [Heal] more powerful than any he'd never tried before. His hands shook as he swung Stick once more, and he stumbled as he felt a massive quantity of his mana drain away. From all around came cries of joy and wonder as people realized their bodies had been restored, and he leaned heavily on Stick as he continued on his way.

As the last lock fell to the ground with a hiss and a clatter, he heard Rouge's voice. ::Five. Four. Three. Two. One.::

One of the doors at the back of the room swung open, and a short, squat figure stepped through. His cowled face was bent toward a scroll he held in his hand, and he was muttering to himself, so several of the prisoners were on him before he even realized what was going on.

Two men beat their fists into the face beneath the red-trimmed hood at the same time. Another threw a well-trained kick into the cloaked belly. A woman shoved a dagger into the short man's back, thrusting up between where the ribs should be.

The man screamed, but the scream wasn't one that could be produced by a human throat. Clawed hands shot out and clasped each of the first two men by their throats, then threw them at the kicking man with contemptuous ease. The woman fell back with a startled cry as the flesh beneath the cowl billowed and twisted. Long, bare arms thrust from the cloak's sleeves, and the sleeves tore as muscle and sinew bulged into powerful masses. The legs likewise lengthened and swelled, and a slavering snout protruded from beneath what was left of the cowl. The thing's hunched back made the head and claws hang down so that the yellowed talons scraped the floor as the huge hands swung. The woman was hit, flying backward through the air to crunch into the wall.

Rouge shouted, "Panginoon! We've fought one of these before! They're undead, so you have to destroy the brain, or-"

Former prisoners, who had been rushing toward what seemed like a single human, a representative of those who had killed and tormented them, now screamed and ran away from the rampaging monster. The thing swung its arms wildly, grabbing anyone it could reach and throwing them away with terrible strength.

Aspen, Rouge, and a few others were the only ones pressing through the crowds of fleeing captives. The caravan guards were there, as were a few other capable-looking men and women, each of them holding a sword or small axe. It seemed that their captors were so confident in their own abilities that they hadn't bothered to search anyone, and many of the prisoners still had weapons.

Looking at the Panginoon, it was difficult to say the jailors had been wrong.

Crumpled bodies lay everywhere, and Aspen had to step over two just to get near the seemingly mindless behemoth. He dodged a slicing claw, and sent a question to Rouge and Silus. ::Do either of you have anything that will work?::

Silus sounded frustrated. ::Why is it always undead? My [Poison Bite] and [Disease Vector] won't work, and he wouldn't even notice my regular [Bite]. I can use [Drain], but it won't do much, and it's a contact skill::

Rouge grumbled, ::Unless someone can throw me up at least fifteen feet, through this ceiling, or knock out all of the lights, all I can do is throw my Mambele.:: As if to prove her point, the weapon flew past Aspen, spinning viciously through the air until it *thunked* deeply into the Panginoon's right knee. The monster roared and staggered, but then it was back up, angrier than ever. Rouge triggered the Mambele's [Return] enchantment, and the triple-bladed knife pulled from the beast's flesh with a sickening pop as it returned to her hand.

Vonn cheered a bit as the Panginoon staggered again, this time going down on one knee before pulling itself back to its feet. Unfortunately, the monster had now had enough time to figure out where the painful thing was coming from, and it charged straight at Rouge, who leapt aside with a yelp.

Vonn took advantage of the Panginoon's change of focus to send a blade flying through the air. It buried itself into the creature's meaty shoulder. It didn't seem to notice as it took another swipe at Rouge, this time catching one of her braids in its fist and hauling the girl toward it. Cursing, Rouge sliced through her own hair and rolled away, but not without first slashing her blade down and burying it in the taloned foot just inches from her face.

A short, solid man who looked like he might be part dwarf jumped onto the Panginoon's back, then pulled himself hand over hand up to the brute's shoulders. The monster swung its body wildly, attempting to shake off its rider, but another attack from Rouge's Mambele was enough to pull its attention back to her, and make thick black blood flow from the thing's right elbow.

The dwarfish man jerked a stout-looking axe from its loop on his belt. He swung it in a vicious chop toward the thickly muscled neck of the frenzied colossus, and it grunted a gurgling growl as more black blood poured from the new wound. It reached up with its overlong left arm and ripped the stout man from its shoulders, throwing him away with ferocious strength.

Aspen happened to be near the man's flight path, and he dove in front of the limp body, feeling it impact his chest with enough power to knock him back several steps, though he was just able to catch the loose form in his arms and lower it gently to the ground. He sent a small rush of healing energy into the crumpled form, hoping that it would be enough to stabilize the man.

The goddess Gina had been very clear that nothing Aspen created with his mage-smithing ability could be used as a weapon, so Aspen simply took his cue from the brave man at his feet and used Stick as a pole vault instead. Running forward as the Panginoon lumbered toward Rouge, who was still dodging as she flung her Mambele, but was visibly tiring, Aspen ordered Stick to stretch into a long, flexible pole. He planted the silver end-cap in the crevice between two stones, and then leapt, urging the staff to grow longer even as he arced through the air. He had to drop the staff at the top of his arc, but he couldn't actually use it any more, anyway.

The brawny little man's axe was still wedged between the Panginoon's collarbone and the thick muscles of its neck, and Aspen pulled it from its resting place with a grunt. He saw the monster's long arm reaching toward him, heard Rouge scream, "Aspen!", and then he was chopping down and across with all his might.

The Panginoon's head went one way, and Aspen went the other, propelled through the air by the last command the brain had sent to the monster's arm. He flopped more than flew, and when he impacted the ground, he lost his breath, but seemed more or less intact. He lay there, gasping and helpless, as Rouge ran toward him, dodging the Panginoon's falling body.

Aspen rolled his head to the side, and saw that Vonn and several of the other prisoners were taking care of the severed head, crushing it beneath repeated blows of boots and axes. Rouge dropped to her knees beside him, and reached out a trembling hand to touch his head. When she lifted her fingers away, they gleamed crimson.

Oh, he thought distantly. *I guess I was hurt a little bit after all.*

🐛 🐛 🐛

He opened his eyes to see a beautiful strawberry-blonde woman glaring at him with eyes that swirled like angry rainbows. "Aspen," his glorious goddess Gina snapped, "you have got to stop *doing* this."

He looked down, realizing that he was once again standing in Gina's garden. As the goddess of birth and life, she was usually surrounded by animals, buzzing insects, and plants; thousands of plants, all blooming and bearing fruit at once, while the spicy scents of cinnamon and ginger wove through the sweet smell of ylang-ylang and hyacinth. Burgeoning roses drooped heavy with blossoms, and dewy peonies glistened in the eternally-bright sun.

Gina stepped closer, moving into his line of sight again, her sweet, round face lifted to his as she rested a gentle hand on his chest. She was slightly short for a woman, which put her at significantly less than his own six-foot-three, and there were still several inches between their faces, but he stepped back nonetheless.

Dropping to one knee was the easiest way to stop towering over his goddess, and so he did so, lifting his own face to her, instead. "I'm sorry, your gloriousness. I didn't mean to." He looked around, trying to see if Gina's sister goddess, Atae, might be lurking somewhere in the nearly-nonexistent shadows. "Am I, ah, dead?"

Gina frowned and clicked her tongue. "Of course not. If you were, do you think you'd be here? No, Atae is waiting for the return of her favorite servant with her usual irritating patience. You're here because you took yet another blow to the head, and poor Rouge is desperately pouring healing potions down your throat, while Restur is wasting his [Heal] on you. You have a Concussion debuff for another ten minutes, though, so they'll just have to wait for their turns to be mad at you."

Aspen lowered his head again and flushed. "What else was I supposed to do, your majesticness?"

Gina booped him on the nose. "Aspen, are you *mocking* me?"

He looked up, smiling just a little. "I would never mock the most magnificent goddess in the entire universe."

She laughed, and sparkles drifted away from her, as if the air itself couldn't help but be infected by her joy. "That's a shame. I do like a bold champion, every now and then."

Her rainbow eyes glanced to the side, and when Aspen followed her gaze, he saw Emilieu, Gina's chief servant. The slim woman wore her usual draped white gown, with her pale hair swirled into an elaborate hairstyle. Her expression was the same bland smile that was usually there, but somehow this time Aspen felt as if the expression actually touched her eyes. Moreover, those eyes were vaguely familiar, and not just because he'd met Emilieu before....

Gina snapped her fingers, and a shower of sparks shot up from her hand. "Excuse me, Aspen? Did you hear what I said?"

Aspen coughed slightly and shook his head. He was grateful, not for the first time, that his goddess was a forgiving one. "I'm sorry, your holiness, I was lost in thought."

She eyed him thoughtfully. "Well, you *do* have a concussion. Fine, I'll let it go. Now, I was trying to decide on a present to give you when you make it home. What's your favorite number?"

He frowned a little, regretting the flightiness that seemed to go hand in hand with Gina's gentleness. "I don't-"

Gina glared at him.

"Twelve?"

Full pink lips smiled happily, and Gina turned to Emilieu. "Did you write that down? I don't want to forget. A favorite number can be a very important thing. I, for example, have always had a fondness for the number 1.618, but if I had to give a whole number, I guess I'd say," she paused, tapping one finger on her round little chin, "Eight. Not too many, but not too few. Divisible by two, and you can tell all the best jokes with it. For example, why are all the other numbers frightened of seven?"

Aspen had had a seven-year-old daughter at one point, and he knew exactly why, but he was too bemused to answer, so he just shook his head.

"Because seven ate nine!" Gina's giggle shimmered through the air, and visible motes of light touched the plants surrounding them, causing even more fruits and blossoms to spring into being. One startled little bee suddenly acquired a glittering crown and tiny golden cloak, and flew away on shimmering wings. When Gina saw that Aspen was not joining in her laughter, she pouted.

"Fine. You always were a bit of a stick in the mud. Go back home now, and I don't want to see you again for a long time!" She waved a languid hand through the air, and the jeweled colors of the garden exploded into pure white light.

🐦 🐦 🐦

With a gasp, Aspen sat bolt upright, nearly head-butting Manuela, who had been bending over him. His old friend went sprawling backwards on her rear with a surprised, "Oof!", and one of the bedraggled prisoners nearby reached out a tentative hand to help her to her feet. Accepting, Manuela shot a tired but grateful smile at the woman, and stood.

"Aspen," the physician said, sounding like her usual irascible self, "the next time you decide to try to crack your head open like an egg, I hope you'll wait until we're in a safer place."

Aspen poked tentatively at the tender spot on the back of his head, where, he assumed, the floor had greeted his skull with the gentle touch of an orc with a war-hammer. It shifted slightly beneath his fingers, and he winced. He sent his own [Heal], backed with the holy power provided by a quick prayer to his goddess, into the bone, and could actually feel it knit back together beneath his fingers.

Sadly, most bone-related debuffs were best left to time or clerics. Magical healers could cure wounds, but not resolve concussions or gout. Non-magical physicians like Manuela learned how to use poultices and splints to assist in natural healing, and, with conditions like Aspen's Concussion debuff, were often more effective than a healer like Restur, who had little recourse when his magic failed. Clerics or priests, in which group Aspen's own Druid class fell, had widely varying abilities. Some could do little more than dispel bad luck or minor curses, while others could heal anything short of death so long as their god willed it.

Accepting Manuela's extended hand, he pulled himself to stand, rather shakily. "I'll do my best. What did I miss?"

Sighing, Manuela looked around. "Not much, sadly. There are a dozen doors leading from this place, and all of them are locked. Rouge found a ring of keys on the 'Panginoon', and she's trying them out, but it seems that every key opens every door, and every single one goes to a different place. She said she's seen this before, in that cultist temple you lot stirred up like an angry anthill back in Bright. You'll have to go talk to her about it, because no matter how we tell her we need to run, she insists it's a 'puzzle', and she can figure out the solution. We just need to get out of here, though."

Aspen growled in frustration, though it was more at the situation than his young friend. "Are the horses and oxen here, too?"

Manuela shook her head, expression set. "They're gone. None of us remembers anything, but the prisoners who were here already say any large animals are led away through the fourth door. They suspect they've eaten a few of them, but otherwise, they're never seen again."

"A lot of that going around," Aspen muttered, then thought loudly, ::Rouge! Silus!::

A little voice came back promptly, and Aspen saw Silus' wings rise up from somewhere to his right. The bat swooped in and landed on his shoulder, nuzzling her soft head against his jaw. ::Rouge is trying to figure out the puzzle.

She says there have to be clues, and-::

Rouge's distinctly unhappy voice broke in. ::There *are* clues! There are always clues to this kind of puzzle. The problem is that there are too *many* clues this time. The keys are all different colors, and shapes, and there are even Roman numerals on them. The doors each have carvings of all kinds of animals, or people, or even Chris himself.:: Chris was, of course, Apofis, the evil god that the cultists worshiped. Since gods could choose to listen in when their names were spoken, Rouge had decided to call him Chris.

Aspen shuddered slightly. ::Let's avoid that one, shall we? Rouge, we need to *go*. We have no way of knowing when something else will come through one of those doors. These people need to escape, not exact vengeance or discover more about their foes, or whatever you're planning now.::

::No! Ugh! Look, let me just-:: There was a long pause, and Aspen wove through the frightened crowds of people toward where he'd first seen Silus. When he came into sight of the young elf girl, she was waving her hands through the air, flicking her hand dismissively, and then jabbing a forefinger sharply into blank space. Suddenly, words popped up into the air in front of Aspen.

Quest: "It's As Easy as 1,1,2,3".

You have as many doors and keys as the last two times combined, and it's three times as hard, but you can do it! One of these doors will end this sequence of problems, but it's up to you to find it.

Success: A way out.

Failure: Return to the caravan and leave everything behind. Walk the rest of the way to Refuge. Some people will die or return to Bright.

Aspen stared at the quest, baffled. "That makes no sense at all."

Rouge jumped at the sound of his voice, looking up from the ring of keys she was holding in her hands. She grinned brightly, and for a moment he thought she'd jump forward and hug him, though she stopped herself before actually moving. Aspen reached out and set his hand on her head, gently patting the straight rows of square braids. Rouge batted his hand away, though she didn't look entirely displeased.

"No, it makes sense. It's obviously about the Fibonacci sequence, but none of the numbers I come up with are actually *in* the sequence! Look." She held up the keys. "There are ten keys. Nice and round, right? Sure, but *not* in the Fibonacci sequence. There are twelve doors, which is also not one of the numbers. Every key opens every door, and I don't even know how many possibilities there are, so if I have to figure it out, we're out of luck. Just like back in Bright, if I look through the door, the room on the other side is different depending on which key I used."

At Aspen's concerned look, she waved her hands in exasperation. "Yes, I *know*, I stopped opening them after the second time I saw guards. Obviously, I can't just keep doing that and hope no one notices. If I didn't have the quest, I'd just give up and get everyone out, but since I *know* that there's a better way, I just can't make myself do it!"

Aspen drew in a deep breath, and then puffed it out again, thinking of a certain goddess and a level of air-headedness that was unusual even for her. He knew that she was restricted in how she could help him, since apparently Virac, the high God of Justice, had also taken note of the ongoing conflict between the pantheon forming around Gina, and Apofis, who was hopefully, however unlikely it was, working alone.

"What about eight? Is that one of your numbers?"

Rouge's eyes flickered, and then she nodded. "One, one, two, three, five, eight, thirteen, twenty-one, um, thirty-four…" Her voice trailed off as she fished through the keyring, finally lifting one unimpressive brass key with a raised VIII printed on the vaguely triangular head. The V was a deep enameled purple, while the three I's were red, orange, and yellow. "Why this one?"

Aspen glanced around at the people watching them with avid, frightened eyes. "Just a guess. Look, the red and yellow combine to make orange. Or, maybe you take orange apart to make red and yellow? Are there any doors with lots of red and blue, to go with the purple of the V?"

The elf girl turned to look at the ten doors behind her. They ranged in size from barely large enough for Rouge, who was slim to the point of frailty and stood barely over five feet tall, to large enough for Toast to ride through on Codswallop's back, if the ostrich was foolish enough to allow the orc to ride him at all. "Well, if it's just a hunch, then it could apply to the doors, too, right? The eighth door could be either that one," she counted from the left, ending up on a high, broad door with a mosaic depicting four toothy beasts swallowing something unpleasantly gelatinous. "Or that one."

The door she landed on when counting from the right was also one of the biggest ones, taking size out of the 'clue' category, since Aspen assumed that any portal which allowed them a solution to their predicament would have to be large enough to admit any member of their group. The image depicted on it was no help either, since it showed an ominous set of stairs, with hordes of hideous monsters descending into darkness.

Rouge stepped forward and traced the curve of the stairs with a finger. "This is actually one of the ones I was leaning toward, since this spiral shape is what you get if you graph the Fibonacci sequence. Unfortunately, it's also on door number one, in a nasty little snail-thing sucking the guts out of somebody, and on door number five, in some kind of possessed Romanesco broccoli-beast."

She stepped back again, sweeping her gaze over the doors. "The purplest one is probably that one in the middle, and the reddest is definitely the one with the ocean of blood. There's not a lot of blue, so I'm not sure about that one."

Aspen reached up to tug at the brim of his hat, then remembered that he was still in the process of making a new one and just ran his hand through his hair instead. "Do you have to solve the puzzle the right way, or can you," he cleared his throat slightly, "just get lucky?"

Rouge grinned wryly. "What do you think I was trying to do? I opened a bunch at random. I mean, one of these stupid doors probably leads right back to Bright, and probably to every other town in Quarternell. There are certainly enough of them. Honestly, my biggest question is why those," she turned and pointed back to the long flight of stairs they'd originally come down, "even exist. I mean, why not just have one of these doors lead to the root cellar thing and be done with it? Why build the stairs at all? Sure, the door up there is flat, but if they can build a million stairs, they can build a short ramp."

Aspen turned back to the stairs, then hesitated. "You said this sequence makes a spiral, right? And that it starts with one?"

Rouge frowned. "Yep."

"I almost ran into the wall more than once as we came down. You were moving so quickly that you may not have noticed, but the staircase definitely curved, just a bit. What if this," he waved his hand around, "is *one*? The beginning of the sequence?" He pointed at the spiral stairs on the door in front of them. "These could be the stairs that lead here. Or, maybe, lead *away* from here?"

Rouge stared at him. "Are you saying we need to go back out the door we came in? That these stupid things are just," she waved her hands at the doors, starting to look angry, "are just, just, *red herrings?*"

Aspen frowned a bit. "I see several red fish depicted here, but none look particularly herring-like. Would that be another clue?"

The young elf threw up her hands in defeat. "No! Fine! Let's go *back up the stupid stairs!*"

Chapter Twenty-four

Rouge

R ouge led them back up the stairs. She still felt angry and frustrated by the stupid, ridiculous, *inane* puzzle of the doors, but she knew that they just needed to get out. If Aspen's hunch turned out to be wrong, well, she could head back down and try out a few more ideas while the refugees gathered the few belongings they could carry on their backs. At least she'd cleared out her inventory at the Traveler's Guild outside Bright, as had the other players, so if they'd just *log in*, then they could carry some stuff for these people.

Not surprisingly, it took a lot longer to get hundreds of frightened people and small animals *up* the stairs than it took for two determined people to get *down* the stairs. On the upside, now that her brain wasn't doing automatic course-corrections, it was clear that Aspen was correct, and the stairs had a definite curve. It was just that there were so many of them that the angle was small when considered step by step.

By the time she saw the half-moons peeking in through the open door above, Rouge was watching the clock. She only had about forty-five minutes left in the game before she had to log out and then clock out from work for the last time. Sure, she could be back online within an hour if she called her new friend, Jackie Chan, who used his car in a ridesharing service, but it wouldn't be the same. Not quite, anyway. More importantly, though, two hours would pass in *Veritas Online*, and a lot could happen in two hours, especially if she had to leave her friends somewhere dangerous.

When the first of the rescued people emerged into the open air, Rouge heard a cry from above. Nanette, eyes brilliant with tears, ran through the doorway, arms wide. A tall pair of figures threw their arms around her, and they all stood there for a full minute, sobbing and smiling, until the shorter of the two asked a question. At Nanette's slow headshake, the rescued pair broke into new tears, this time of sorrow rather than relief.

Similar scenes were happening outside as well. Florence, with a sleeping Petunia in her arms, was being embraced by another tall woman, while Horace was clasping forearms with a man who looked enough like him to be his brother, and quite possibly was. Meanwhile, other people, presumably others of the recovered citizens of Filial, stood looking around with sad, hopeless expressions. Yet another woman, a net tied at her waist and a fishing pole strapped to her back, stood by, watching. This was, presumably, the missing Rani, and though she smiled and greeted some of the returned people, her expression said that she already knew the person she longed for would never return to her.

It was Olive, though, who drew Rouge's eye. The woman was going from person to person as they exited the door. Each time she saw a child held in someone's arms, her face would brighten, and then fall again when she looked a little closer. Then a small woman with slightly pointed ears and the lambent blue eyes of an elf stepped slowly through the portal. On one side, she had her arm wrapped around a slightly older woman with the same eyes and more sharply defined bone structure. In the other arm, she held a baby with golden curls and ears that came to a much more definite point than either of the two women.

Olive cried out, her hands reaching for the baby. The woman holding her tightened her grip for an instant, and then blinked, seeming to take a moment to recognize Olive, given her tattered and run-down appearance. When realization flooded her face, however, tears overflowed her eyes and she held the baby out. Olive clasped the little girl to her chest, then fell to her knees, holding tight as the baby opened her eyes and began to wail.

Rouge felt her own eyes beginning to well up, and she swiped at them, vowing to let Dr. Joe know that there were certain things that took realism a step too far. Crying, drooling, and nausea should all be removed from the code immediately. Or at least made optional. Though that might already be the plan, and they were just auto-on for her because she was the beta tester. Still, that was definitely going in her feedback.

Rouge felt a gentle touch on her shoulder and turned to see Vonn, who was holding his little nephew, a quarter-elf he had named Willow. Vonn's half-sister had been murdered before he found her, and no one left alive knew what she and her husband had named their little boy, but for wood elves the willow tree represented remembrance and hope, so Vonn had given the baby a new name.

Vonn's mother, who had married a human and spawned Vonn's sister while on her *r'nspiga* (a five year long journey undertaken by all young wood elves before returning home and settling into their lives there), had asked Vonn to look for his half-sister and make sure she was safe and happy. When Vonn discovered that his sister Violeta was missing, and her husband and father were dead, he had come to Aspen and Rouge for help in finding his missing family. This had led to the discovery of the cultists murdering and abducting non-humans in Bright, and Vonn and Rouge's capture while exploring.

Vonn had been forced to trade some of Aspen's secrets to the leader of the cultists, a player named FantumHat, for the safe return of his nephew. Vonn had managed to gloss over enough specifics that he and Rouge had time to warn the people they'd left behind as Aspen's house, but they'd all been forced to flee, and Aspen's house, the last link to his dead daughter, had been destroyed.

Honestly, Rouge had her own suspicions about whether or not the baby Vonn was caring for was actually his nephew, given what she knew about FantumHat, but Vonn seemed satisfied, and that was enough for Rouge. She'd forgiven Vonn for his betrayal, too, and now they were... what? Friends? Something a little more than that? Given that Vonn was nothing more than a video-game character who had been assigned more processing power once he'd become a quest NPC, what could he possibly be to her?

Rouge shook her head and smiled back at her friend, hoping she hadn't been drooling and staring into space for the last five minutes while she thought about things that *did not matter*. Right now, anyway.

"Is everyone out?" she asked.

Vonn nodded. "Are you sure you don't want company?"

She shrugged, ignoring the twinge of loss she felt when his hand dropped away at the movement. "Nah. I'll be right back. You guys make some popcorn and chill."

Vonn's pretty gray eyes blinked. "Popcorn?"

She mimed a small explosion with her hands. "Heat up dried grains of corn until the water in them turns to vapor and they *pow*?"

He tilted his head and smiled thoughtfully. "I have never tried that, but if it works, it would be interesting to taste. Is it moist, from the water?"

She started to answer, and then stopped. "Nope, not gonna. I'll tell you what, though. When we get to Refuge, I'm going to get together with Millie and figure out how to make popcorn. I'll let you try the first batch."

Vonn grinned. "It is a plan. Now," he looked meaningfully at the open cellar door, and the dark stairs beyond. Rouge glanced at the timer ticking down in her display. She usually kept notifications and icons out of her way, preferring the most realistic immersion she could get, but she was, literally, on the clock.

00:31:12

Right. ::Let's do it,:: she sent out via party chat.

Rouge stepped through and walked down enough stairs that her head was below ground level, and flashed Vonn a thumbs up. Aspen walked up beside the wood elf, towering over the boy. Silus peered down from Aspen's shoulder, and then, without a word, dropped off and flew down to join Rouge in the hole.

::I'm coming, too.:: The bat's voice held a note of finality, and Rouge exchanged glances with Aspen.

He quirked a smile as one eyebrow went up just a bit. ::As you wish.::

Vonn and Aspen reached down, each grasping a corner of the large, heavy, splintered wooden door. With a heave, they raised it up and dropped it down, closing Rouge in darkness. Her vision flickered, losing much of its depth and color, but remaining as clear as it had been a moment before. *Racial [Darkvision] for the win*, she thought. *I knew there was a reason I wanted to be half dark elf.*

Truthfully, she'd initially wanted to be full dark elf, because they were just *cool*-looking. They had white to silver hair, with faint hints of color ranging from violet to pink. Their skin could be pitch black to pale gray, and if you pushed the skin-tone slider all the way over, you might even hit a very, very dark purple. Their eyes, too, were different from those of any other race, and varied from a deep crimson to an apricot orange, all with a little bioluminescence to make them really shine. If only they didn't spawn in their own isolated little city and hate anyone who wasn't them, Rouge would have gone that way for sure.

She snickered a little at her own joke, taking the *Ring of Mysterious Keys* out of her inventory. She flipped through them until she found number VIII and inserted it into the lock.

Clunk.

That was it. No satisfying click, but also no refusal to work at all, which was, she supposed, a good sign.

::Well?:: Silus' excited little squeak made her jump a little. She'd almost forgotten that she wasn't actually alone in the darkness.

::Let's see!:: she sent back, and pushed against the door. The edge lifted from the ground, and Aspen and Vonn peered back in at her.

"That was fast," Aspen said. "Did none of the keys work?"

Rouge growled a little. "That was only key number eight. I thought it worked, but here we are. Hang on. I'll try the others." She dropped the door and tried the other keys. She saw Vonn and Aspen's faces nine more times. Each time, they grew progressively more resigned, and when she pushed open the door for the tenth time, Aspen reached down and heaved the door the rest of the way open.

Rouge climbed up out of the stairwell, ignoring Aspen's proffered hand in a fit of pique. When she emerged into the darkness of the night, she saw that a few small fires had been started nearby, and grim-faced warriors stood, all facing the door through which she had just exited. Clearly, these people would not be taken unawares again.

Jiminy, the kid (never mind that he was probably only two to four years younger than Rouge herself) who had led his friends into Filial and promptly got them all captured, wandered over. He had been appropriately chastened for about fifteen minutes after being released, and only Plum's firm grip on his ear had prevented him from getting into everyone's business after that. Now, he kicked at the door frame with a booted toe.

"Too bad doors don't go to different places from both sides, huh?" The boy, whose skill with voice mimicry as well as ventriloquism was startling, spoke in a teasing feminine tone which Rouge recognized instantly.

Aspen and Rouge stared at each other, then at the boy, who just grinned. He flicked them a little salute and wandered off, whistling.

Aspen shot a reproachful little glance toward the sky, and Rouge giggled. "They say the gods watch over drunks and fools, right?"

Aspen's lips twitched. "He's a little young to drink."

Laughing felt really, really good.

Once Vonn and Aspen carefully closed the big door again, Rouge fished through the key ring to find number VIII. *Again.* Whatever was going on with this stupid puzzle, if she ever met the person who designed it, she was going to kick them in the shin. If she was lucky, it was Harris, who probably deserved a kick or two anyway, just for designing all those nasty demonic beasts and making poor Mr. Hamncheese the hamster into a gross people-eating monster.

Silus butted her fuzzy little head against Rouge's jaw. ::Hurry up! I'm hungry!::

Rouge grinned. ::You're always hungry.::

::Sumi says I have a high meta-ball-prism.:: Silus sounded prim, and Rouge heard Aspen snort behind her.

::Metabolism?::

::Yes, one of those!::

Rouge gave in and giggled, reaching up and petting the little bat's soft ears. ::Sumi's pretty smart.:: She produced a pea pod, one of the last ones left in her inventory from before they left Aspen's farm, and held it up for her friend. Silus grabbed it with a wing-thumb and instantly began stuffing as much of it into her face as she could.

With moist crunching in her ears and the scent of sweet green growing things in her nose, Rouge bent down and inserted the VIII key into the big keyhole on the outside of the cellar door. She glanced at her clock, and saw that she had just over twenty minutes remaining. *This had better work.*

The lock clicked. Rouge was so startled, she actually jumped back, landing in a crouch with her Mambele in her hand.

::Hey! I almost dropped my pea!::

Rouge stood, a little embarrassed, and cleared her throat. "Um, sorry. I guess I was kind of expecting either nothing or some kind of trap. That's kind of how my day has been going."

Aspen, who had been standing a good five feet back as Rouge tried the key, was now able to reach out and gently pat the girl on the back. "Understandable." She glanced back suspiciously, but his expression was bland, without even the little only-on-one-side smirk he often had. She still thought his topaz eyes were suspiciously bright, but decided to let it go.

Tugging at her mottled kind-of-camo tunic, Rouge settled her shoulders and stepped forward, examining the door carefully. "No traps as far as I can tell."

"Nor I," Vonn said. He was a hunter, and hunters set more traps than they fell into (if they were any good at it, anyway), but he still had a rudimentary [Trap Finding] skill, and she wasn't too proud to accept help. Not today.

Rouge looked at her friends. "Who'd like to do the honors?"

The two males exchanged glances, and then both stepped forward. "We'll lift, and you stay ready. If anything comes through, we'll count on you to save us," Aspen said.

"And us as well," a female voice came from behind them, and all three turned to look.

Florence stood there, with Horace beside her. Arrayed behind them in a simple defensive formation, were several other people who Rouge recognized from the battle in the dungeon-room at the bottom of the stairs. One of them, the dwarf who had gotten his axe in the Panginoon's neck, allowing Aspen to finish the thing off, hefted what looked like the same axe, a solemn expression on his face.

Rouge hesitated. "Are you sure?"

Florence looked at her newfound companions and nodded. "We're not standing aside while others risk their lives for us. If we were that sort, we'd have been cowering in Bright with the *King* when Akuji came." Her voice was full of contempt, and Rouge's eyebrows shot up. She didn't spend a lot of time hanging out with soldiers, former or current, but nothing in the lore said that the military of Quarternell was anything but completely loyal to King Chester and Duke Geral.

It was Horace's turn, and he was looking at Aspen. "Most of our leaders hid as far from the enemy as they could, during the war. Leading from the rear." He sounded bitter. "Everyone knows there was one man who was always on the front lines, though. Hell, you practically *were* the front lines, once the undead started rising."

Aspen was looking down, cheeks pale beneath his tan, and Rouge wondered if this was the first time anyone had actually had the chance to thank him for his role in the war. Whenever he talked about it, he made himself out to be some kind of cowardly loner, but these people weren't looking at him like they agreed with that.

As one, the twenty or thirty hardened warriors fell to one knee. Every one of them raised some kind of weapon, and laid it across their forearm, as though offering it to Aspen. Again, it was Horace who spoke. "We offer you our weapons and our lives, Duke Penbrooke. If you will protect our families, we will protect you and your lands."

Rouge could see Aspen swallow hard, but when he looked back up, his yellowish eyes were hard and clear. "I accept in the name of Refuge. We will all work together to keep safe those we hold dear."

A soft, pearly light shimmered briefly around the entire group, and Rouge was almost dying to know what that meant. Obviously, *something* official had just happened, but she didn't know what. On a hunch, she pulled open her quest list.

SECRET Quest: "Who Run the World"

(This is a SECRET quest. If you tell anyone about it before it is complete, you will automatically fail it.) The forces of light and darkness are struggling for control of the world. Each side has appointed champions, and for the first time, those champions are facing each other directly. You must defeat Apofis' champions in order to keep the world safe from those who would reduce it to a place

of strife and suffering. *WARNING: You get only one attempt at clearing this quest. If you die, the quest will be offered to ANOTHER PLAYER, who may then attempt to clear it.*

Success: Level 100 or 15 levels, whichever is greater. 1 million gold. Become a Saintess of Gina.

Failure: Apofis' religion becomes the dominant one in the world. All races other than Human lose status as sapient beings. Aspen's death. Silus' death. Khor's death. Sumi's death. Sarave's death. Juniper's death. William's enslavement. Vonn's death...

FantumHat current completion: 77%

Rouge the Rogue current completion: 40%

She had to fight the urge to give a victorious fist pump. Another 4% completion? Heck yeah! Sure, FannyHat had gotten 3%, too, but still, she was catching up! Maybe she could win this without another confrontation, after all!

Rouge looked at everyone, and found that they were looking back at her. It looked like Aspen had asked her a question while she was busy with internal celebrations. She felt a hot flush rise from her throat to the tips of her pointed ears. "Um, yes?" she said, intelligently.

Aspen raised a brow, and *there* was that little smirk. "I asked if you wanted to do the honors, since we have others ready to assist in case of battle."

"Oh!" She grinned. "Heck yes!"

When they finally, *finally* opened the stupid door, the results were anticlimactic, because, in fact, nothing happened. They all found themselves staring down into a dark, empty stairwell. Rouge wanted to scream in frustration.

"It did something this time! I know it did!" She glared at the rough wooden stairs, then paused. "Wait, these *were* wood before, right?" She gingerly reached down and touched a step. They were still dirty and abused, but these steps were definitely made of stone.

Aspen and Vonn's hands reached down next to hers and touched the step. Vonn rapped it hard with a knuckle, producing a flat *thump*. He shook his hand slightly. "They were most certainly wooden before."

Rouge whooped. "We did it! Darn those crazy cultists and their evil little puzzle! We figured it out!" Okay, so maybe it took a little divine intervention, but that puzzle was *way* too complicated. Rouge's dad had told her that puzzles had been getting harder and harder since the advent of the internet, since people just looked up the solution instead of trying to figure it out themselves, but eventually game designers had mostly given them up and returned to making the puzzle itself easy, and actually implementing the solution difficult. Since no one else had this quest, Rouge *couldn't* look up the answer, if there even was one, she had a feeling there had been some shenanigans, and Gina (or rather Bridget) had just been leveling the playing field.

Aspen started to stride down into the stairwell, and Rouge put a hand on his shoulder. "No way, Aspen. We didn't come all this way to have your foot blown off or have you fall through some collapsing stairs. Rogues first, if you please."

The tall farmer quirked an eyebrow at her, but then he smiled and nodded. "It is your job."

You know it, buddy. Rouge grinned as she stepped into the darkness.

ᕮ ᕮ ᕮ

Thankfully, the stairs were short. They, too, curved, but they were just as broad as the ones that had led down to the prison, so the gently rounded walls and stair edges were mostly lost in the dimness, even to Rouge's enhanced vision. By her estimation, though, she had probably not turned more than six or seven degrees before the steps ended in a huge stone arch.

Peering out, Rouge realized that she was outside again. The ground at her feet was just that, hard-packed dirt, and she could make out tall grass to each side of the path that extended ahead of her. A strange sound came to her ears, and it was so unexpected that it took far longer than it should to realize what it was. An ox lowing.

The sound, so familiar as part of the relatively peaceful days spent traveling with the caravan, was oddly comforting in the current circumstances. For one thing, if the animal nearby was calm enough to moo, there probably wasn't a big, stinky monster about to eat it. Or Rouge.

::I'm going to scout,:: Silus sent, dropping from Rouge's shoulder so she could fly into the night. Rouge watched her clock continue ticking down until, when she had exactly ten minutes remaining, Silus spoke again. ::It's just a great big field full of cows and horses and all kinds of animals. There's a fence around it, and I don't even see any guards.::

As the bat finished talking, words appeared before Rouge's eyes, hovering against the backdrop of the bucolic scene before her.

Quest: "It's As Easy as 1,1,2,3" complete.
You knew you could do it! Fibonacci would be embarrassed by that mess of a puzzle, but you managed to figure it out. Now you just have to get those wagons down the stairs. Good luck with that.
Success: A way out.

Rouge felt tears of relief prickle her eyelids, and swore again that she was going to tell Dr. Joe where to stuff his realistic emotional responses. ::Come on back, Silus. My quest just completed. This is it. This is our way home.::

"Well done." Aspen's voice was quiet, but Rouge nearly jumped out of her skin anyway. She whirled around, ready to smack him for not only following her but also being sneaky about it. When she saw the expression on his face, however, she paused.

Aspen looked years younger. Rouge hadn't realized just how much strain he must be under, with all of these people suddenly depending on him. His main goal just a few months ago was to live out his life as an anonymous farmer with a particularly green thumb. Now, thanks to a title he hadn't asked for (it had, in fact, been given to him while he was unconscious and expected to die at any moment) he was the only person who could officially lead an ever-growing population of refugees. Every time another responsibility or problem was added to the ever-growing stack, Aspen had gotten a little quieter, and a little sadder.

In this moment, though, with Silus winging back to them, a dark blob against the starry sky, and a soft spring breeze full of the scents of green grass and flowers stirring their hair, Aspen looked almost happy. The deep creases around his mouth and between his eyes were nearly erased by the soft moonlight, and his shoulders were relaxed for the first time in days.

A bright red countdown timer began to flash in her peripheral vision, and she drew in a deep breath. She was out of time, and…. Her nose began to tickle, and then she sneezed violently, barely managing to muffle the sound in her sleeve.

Hay fever? Seriously? Dr. Joe had a lot of explaining to do!

🐛 🐛 🐛

In the end, Zoey had to log out of *Veritas Online* before she and Aspen even figured out exactly where they'd ended up, much less how they were going to get the wagons down the stairs. Her anxiety at leaving her Zombie (and her friends) behind in an unpredictable situation was practically giving her hives. Or maybe that was grass allergies? Her fingers twitched with the desire to scratch as the plastic honeycomb platform lifted her out of the warm blue goo and up to the level of the pod hatch.

Which didn't open.

After a long, indecisive pause, Zoey pressed the internal switch, and the hatch released with the sound of equalizing pressure. As the door lifted, Zoey sat up and looked around. Usually, either Dr. Joe or Sara was there to help her out. The goop was kind of slippery, and even though it had a strange surface tension that kept most of it in the pod even when she got out, it always made things a little precarious until she rinsed off.

She poked her head out and reached for the railing on the side of the pod, then paused as she saw something hanging there. A bright white note was stuck to the gleaming black material of the pod, and she tugged at it, wincing as her damp fingers started making the biodegradable paper dissolve. Not many people used the old, long-lasting paper for notes any more, since most information was passed digitally, so this single-use easy-disposal paper was far more common. The downside was, as soon as it got the slightest bit moist, it started to do exactly what it was meant to do.

Zoey,

We were unexpectedly called away to an emergency meeting. Don't worry, there are no aliens or nuclear war. Sara put your clothes on the table by the pod, along with a towel and a screen. Please rinse off, get dressed, and complete the standard questionnaire on the screen. You know the drill. We'll be back before your shift ends. Thank you!

Dr. Joe Sherman

The blocky handwriting was familiar, so Zoey knew Dr. Joe wrote the note. She shook her head as she realized she was suspicious that someone else might have snuck in and left a fake note for her to find. To what end, exactly? Nina's conspiracy theories were starting to rub off on her.

Carefully, she swung a clammy body-suited leg over the side of the pod, then braced herself with both hands on the railing. Once she was firmly standing on her own two feet, she felt much better, and looked around for the promised clothes and towel. Seeing them, she climbed down the two stairs from the pod platform onto the lab floor, and grabbed the soft, fluffy white towel from the stack. As she lifted it, something clattered to the ground.

Frowning, she leaned over and picked it up. It was a Veritas ID badge. It had a wide blue bar across the bottom, and the name listed below the smiling photo was 'Sara Agarwal'. Sara's badge! Everyone who worked in the labs wore their badges so that they were visible at all times, and Sara's was always,

always clipped to the pocket on the front of her lab coat.

Maybe it got hung up in the towel and pulled off because Sara was in a hurry to get to this emergency meeting? Zoey frowned in concern. Losing your badge could earn you a write-up if the wrong person found out, so Zoey hoped that the meeting was among friends. Unlikely, in a company that seemed filled with more politics and cliques than Washington D.C., but one could always dream, right?

Carefully, Zoey set the badge back down on the table, and scooped up the towel again. There was a built-in shower stall in the corner of the room, and she hit the button that activated it. The doors slid out of the wall as warm water cascaded down on her from above, and she rinsed thoroughly, then peeled off the body suit. Usually, she only rinsed here, then undressed, wiped down with disposable cloths, and got dressed again in the changing room. She felt oddly vulnerable being completely naked in the lab, so she hurried through the process as quickly as she could.

Once she had the towel wrapped around her head, turban-style, she looked at the screen patiently waiting for her on the table beside Sara's badge. She knew she should get started. That was her job, after all. But she also knew that this room had another secret. As if against her will, she found her fingers slipping onto the nearly undetectable button on the wall.

A section of the wall slid aside with a soft *shoosh*, and Zoey stepped into the dim room beyond. Once before she had found herself left alone in the lab, though that time there had been no explanatory note. Since the main door locked from the inside as well as the outside, and Zoey couldn't open it, she had found herself with nothing to do but explore. That was when she had found this door, though she hadn't had enough time to do more than take a brief look inside before Dr. Joe had found her. They had agreed that since she wasn't supposed to be in there, but he wasn't supposed to have left her alone, they would keep each other's secrets.

She had promised herself, though, that if she ever had another opportunity, she would find out the answer to a question that had been burning in her brain since she'd first seen the contents of this room. Because there were two pods in here. Two matching, smooth, egg-shaped pods that were vastly different from the cylindrical, experimental pod Zoey used. While Zoey's pod lacked an outer shell, leaving its guts bare for maintenance and adjustments, these two pods were fully assembled and in use.

With silent steps, Zoey dashed across to the first pod. Looking in, she confirmed that the person within was still the same as last time. Bree Stephenson. Bree was a world-famous gamer who had built herself up from being just another pretty girl with a gimmick into a powerhouse role-model for girls everywhere. She also happened to be Bridget Andrew's mother, and had raised her genius-class daughter alone from when she was only sixteen years old.

Bree was also somewhere in *Veritas Online*. She was fully immersed in the game, and had been for about four months now, as far as Zoey knew. She was in the process of reviewing Veritas Corps' groundbreaking long-term immersion process, and was only supposed to wake up after six months. Six months in the real world, which meant a whole year in *Veritas Online*, thanks to the game's ability to boost the brain's processing speed.

Zoey and her dad (who was a huge fan of Bree's, and had been since she was just another bikini-clad babe playing games online for money) had a few theories about who Bree was playing in the game. She could be a player, since another aspect of the game that Zoey had been testing was a kind of personal space outside of the game. Usually, if you were logged on, you were in-game. The 'Study Room', as Zoey called it, was a fully adjustable room online but outside of the game. If Bree went to her own version of this when she 'logged out', she could easily pretend to be a player.

Equally possible, however, was that Bree was disguised as an NPC. Zoey and her dad had been assured that Bree was involved in their quest line in some significant way, but they weren't allowed to discuss it, since breaking the confidentiality agreement they'd signed when they agreed to be in the quest had some pretty hefty consequences. They could, however, exchange *meaningful glances,* and Zoey thought they were on the same page as to who Bree was likely to be. Though to have been pulling that off for this long, she had to be the best actress since Katharine Hepburn.

Bree, however, wasn't the person Zoey was here for. If Zoey was right, then the person in the *other* pod humming quietly away nearby was actually their true adversary. The person on the other side who was trying to help FantumHat complete the quest. Who that person was didn't really matter, Zoey supposed, but she still wanted to *know.*

Unfortunately, when she tried to cross the room to the other pod, she ran into an invisible wall. Well, more of a window, really. It was completely transparent. She tapped at it cautiously with a fingernail. It *plinked* more like plastic than glass, but it didn't quite feel like either of those materials.

She darted back into the lab and snatched up the damp towel. Returning, she carefully wiped away the smears left by her face and hands when she smacked into it like a bug on a windshield. Then she glanced around, looking for... Aha! There was a small panel set into the wall to her right, and a red light gleamed faintly from it.

Approaching, Zoey saw that it was a panel much like the one outside her pod room, where Dr. Joe or Sara put in about fourteen different confirmations of identity before it would allow them inside. She huffed a defeated sigh, since there was no way she could fake a fingerprint or a retina scan, but she stepped a bit closer anyway. There was only the flat rectangle that read the card and a number pad there. Sara had been getting pretty relaxed around Zoey, and she knew what the lab assistant's code was. Not that she'd been *trying* to watch, but what were you supposed to do when the person barely bothered to use her other hand to block the pad anymore?

With shaking fingers, Zoey tapped the card against the rectangle, then punched in the eight-digit code she'd seen Sara use a hundred times. At first, nothing happened, and then the clear material actually rolled up, just like the fancy flexi-screens that were all the rage lately.

Cautiously, Zoey stepped over to the pod and looked down into the faintly-lit goop. Interestingly, this goo looked slightly green, instead of the clear sky-blue she was used to. It cast the face of the man inside in an unhealthy shade of seafoam, but Zoey could still see the flicker of his eyes beneath his eyelids, so she knew he was alive. Beside the sickly color of his skin, the black of his eyebrows and lashes was stark, but he was still good-looking in a stern sort of old-guy way. Not that he was as old as Zoey's dad or Bree, probably, but he was definitely older than, say, Bridget, though maybe not by much.

Zoey stared, feeling her heart pound in her chest. The man's face was only a foot or so from her own, and she felt as though his eyes might open so he could look straight at her at any moment. A smooth, flat cap covered his head, so for all she knew he was bald as an egg, but she had a feeling he would be too proud for that, and he'd find a way to have a full, conservatively-cut head of hair. She could only see his throat and face, but there was no extra weight on them, and the jaw was sharply defined while the throat was leanly muscled.

She tilted her head. In fact, there was something familiar about the way his cheekbones curved, and the slope of his nose. He looked like someone she'd seen before. Or maybe she'd seen him in a photograph?

Then the panel behind her chirped quietly, and when she glanced back, she saw flashing red numbers counting down. Twenty-five. Twenty-four. Twenty-three... Darn it! There was a time limit on how long the rolly partition was supposed to stay open. How long had she been standing there, staring at a strange man in an electronic sarcophagus? Five minutes? Ten?

She leapt down from the side of the pod, easily crossing the seven or eight feet between her perch and the wall. She landed neatly, without a hint of effort, her body responding to her commands almost as well as it did when she was in-game. Whatever it was about the pod that had caused her increased strength, dexterity, and stamina here in the *real* world, she was definitely going to miss it when she went back to normal.

Quickly, she flashed the badge at the panel, then typed in Sara's code one more time. The 'wall' rolled down, and the red numbers glowing from beneath the surface of the wall stopped with seven seconds left. Zoey huffed out a breath of relief, then cast one last glance around, trying to see if she'd missed anything.

Nope, just two pods and one invisible wall.

On light feet, she ran back to the lab, closed the panel behind her, set the towel and the ID card on the table, and scooped up the screen with the questionnaire on it. She had just punched in her own employee number and answered the first question when the door to the main lab hissed open, and Dr. Joe walked in.

Zoey had long since taken to heart the idea that a good defense was a good offense, at least when it came to verbal confrontations. She popped to her feet from the seat she'd taken on the cold floor and tapped the screen with her stylus. "Hay fever, Dr. Joe? Seriously?"

She would have sworn that Dr. Joe's blue eyes flashed toward the blank, closed wall, and then the genial but slightly apologetic grin with which he generally greeted her criticisms crossed his face. "All part of the beta, Zoey, sorry. It may not make the cut, but I'd rather have it available and not need it than need it and-"

"Not have it. Yeah, I know." This was part of the doc's usual response, too, so she just sighed in resignation and brushed at her behind with her free hand. "Well, at least I won't have to worry about running into whatever you come up with next." She shot him a teasing grin. "Though I will miss a few things about it. I don't know what you guys did to make food taste so good, but it's almost good enough that I don't care about eating in real life anymore."

Zoey laughed, but Dr. Joe's expression was suddenly serious. He touched his jaw lightly to trigger his implant, and murmured something too quietly for Zoey to catch. When he was done, he focused on her again. "Is there anything else like that, Zoey? Anything that makes you feel like the game is *too* good?

We don't want people's real lives to be negatively impacted by their gaming experience."

Zoey shrugged uncomfortably. "Just that things in there are – well, used to be, anyway – simpler than out here. If someone bullies you, you can just punch them in the face. If you don't want to kill things, you can get a job as a miner, or a cook, or anything, really."

Dr. Joe nodded, face a little sad. "That's going to be true of all games from here on out, I'm afraid." He smiled a little, but his eyes remained introspective. "Why live a real life when you can live your dream in game? There's not much we can do about that except limit the amount of time people can be logged in, but we have a whole department that looks at things like what we can do to subtly remind people it *is* a game, and encourage them to voluntarily log out and enjoy the real world sometimes."

Zoey thought of a few of the things that people complained about not existing in the game, and nodded. "Makes sense. It's nice to know you guys aren't *completely* in it for the money." She laughed, but her joke fell a little flat when Dr. Joe's expression only grew more melancholy.

Fortunately, Sara bustled in at that moment. She actually wasn't wearing her lab coat, and when she saw Zoey notice, she smiled a little tightly. "I spilled something on my coat earlier. It's being cleaned, but they didn't have another one my size, so I'm out of uniform for a bit." She forced a laugh, and hurried over to scoop up the towel, cap, and wet bodysuit. Zoey had carefully tucked the badge back into the plush folds, clipping it to a corner in such a way that it was vaguely possible she might not have even realized it was there.

Zoey smiled back and then lifted the screen in her hand a little awkwardly. "So, um, I still need to finish the questionnaire. Did you want to go over it with me?" Usually, Sara read off the questions, and recorded Zoey's answers. She was pretty sure they noted it when she hesitated before answering, or looked like she wasn't being completely honest, which had happened a few times when the questions touched on her Secret Quest.

She didn't want to lie to Sara and Dr. Joe, but if she slipped up and mentioned the Secret Quest even once, she'd automatically fail. It was one thing to lose to FartHat because he killed her and Aspen, or even because the big cheater got closer to completion than she did, but she was going down swinging, not because she blabbed to the wrong person.

Sara's expression lightened as she clutched at the towel. If Zoey wasn't mistaken, it looked like her hand had closed around something hard in the soft fabric. "Yes, of course. I'm sorry we weren't able to be here earlier. There was a meeting about-" She paused, and her dark eyes met Dr. Joe's.

He cleared his throat. "The, ah, situation in Design. I believe you know what I'm referring to?"

Zoey's eyes widened. "Do I? That was crazy! Um, did they figure it out? Who was the leak, I mean?"

Dr. Joe held up his hands defensively. "That's above my paygrade, I'm afraid. They just wanted to ask all of us if we knew anything about it, since it, hmm, infringed on our department just a bit. As far as I know, they're still gathering evidence. Fortunately, they'd already spoken to you, so we could leave you to finish up your session."

He reached up and tugged at his collar, which was already open one button. Zoey had never seen him wear a tie, though most of the other men at Veritas Corp did, but his polo shirts were usually closed all the way up, with the collar lying in tidy points. "Well, Zoey. I wish I could offer you a better farewell, but I'm afraid this is it. I'm behind in my work thanks to the meeting, so I should get to it. I've enjoyed working with you, and if you ever decide to apply for a more permanent position here at Veritas Corp, I'd be happy to write you a recommendation."

Dr. Joe hesitated. "If, of course, I'm still here at that time. You never know." He grinned, showing the crooked bottom tooth that had first charmed Zoey into believing he was nothing more than a typical absent-minded professor type. Reaching out, he shook Zoey's hand warmly. It was the first time he had ever done more than lightly touch her arm while helping her through the tests, and his grip was firm and dry.

Stiffly, she shook, feeling suddenly shy. It was a little strange to be treated like an adult, and a respected colleague at that. She liked it, though. "Thanks, Dr. Sherman. I've enjoyed my time here, too, and I'd really appreciate that recommendation. I'd love to work," she paused, just for a second, "in the gaming industry, someday." *Just maybe not here, after all.*

Forty-five minutes later, she was sitting on one of the visitor's couches in the lobby. She had been dreading her exit interview with Ms. McKeene the Snake, but apparently, she was busy with something related to the Great Information Leak, and wasn't available to deal with petty things like interns. A nice, plump lady named Miss Thurman had asked Zoey all of three questions, had her sign a few documents reminding her not to talk about Proprietary Information™, shaken her hand, and told her to have a good day.

Frankly, it was an anticlimax that Zoey could get behind.

Her screen pinged, and she looked down. Zoey had sent a message to Jackie Chan, a friendly acquaintance who drove a ride-share, hoping that he could come and take her home.

@JackieChan411: Heya, Z! Dropped off my last pax. Heading ur way. U cool?

Zoey sighed. She wasn't a fan of the 'text speak' that had evolved when you had to actually use the keypad on your screen to send messages. Now that most people had implants, and everybody had screens with speech to text, it was just an affectation, and an annoying one at that. Still, she liked Jackie, so she tried not to let it bother her.

@RedZ: I'm fine. Just hanging out in the lobby. I'll track you. Thanks, Jackie!

She pulled up the ride-share app and looked at her current ride offers. Jackie had accepted the job, so she could now see a blip representing him on the map, with an estimated time of arrival in about ten minutes. She glanced out through the huge mirrored windows that fronted the lobby, and saw about five vehicles idling out front in the passenger pick-up zones. She could have caught any of them, but she really wanted to take one last trip with Jackie.

Standing, she looked around. She was feeling a little too antsy to keep sitting on the couch, however comfortable it was, but it was drizzling outside, and she hadn't brought an umbrella today. She didn't mind getting a little wet, but her hair had just finally dried after her shower in the lab, and she didn't really want to start over again.

A row of paintings caught her eye, and she wandered toward them. She'd noticed them on her first day, and a few times since then as she hurried through on her way to work, but she'd never taken the time to look at them properly. She thought it was funny, because they were real paintings, with visible brushstrokes and everything, instead of the photographs or even holograms that were more common these days.

The paintings were, of course, mostly a bunch of old guys, with long names and fancy titles like Chief Financial Officer, and Director of Operations. Bridget was up there, though, smiling vapidly into space. The little plaque beneath her picture read 'Bridget Andrews, BS, MSc, PhD – Director of Design'.

The big central painting held a face that Zoey vaguely recognized; Carl Landon. He was the grandson of the founder of Veritas Corp, and, as far as Zoey knew, the sole owner, since it was still a privately held company. The string of titles after his name was impressive, but Zoey was more interested in his face.

She had actually met the man once, not long after his daughter, Amy Landon, had died. His hair had been thick, but mostly gray, and he'd walked so stiffly that she'd wondered if he would fall down if he relaxed even a bit. He had definitely been younger when the painting was made, but his blue eyes already looked tired, and gray touched his temples.

Zoey chuckled a little. It was funny how women spent so much time and money getting rid of their grays, and now she was actually wondering if the artist had taken a little license and added some to this portrait to make Carl look more dignified. She shook her head, and the next painting caught her eye.

Amy. Amy, who was, perhaps, not quite as dead as her family thought her. She and Bridget, together with Joe and Amy's brother, Harkness, had developed virtual reality from a theory that Bridget had come up with while she was still in college. Bridget and Amy were best friends who wanted to change the world for the better.

Amy, who was as brilliant as Bridget in her own way, as far as Zoey could tell, had become a neuroscientist and cognitive psychologist. The two young women had dreamed of reaching into the minds of people trapped in comas or otherwise unresponsive bodies, and helping them recover, or at least enable them to interact with the world and other people again.

Ironically, it was Amy herself who ended up needing that technology before it was complete. She had been involved in a hit and run the previous winter, and though she had lingered in a coma for months afterward, she had finally succumbed to her injuries and died not long ago. Before she died, Bridget had been desperately attempting to use her unfinished project to reach her, but all Carl Landon had seen was a grieving woman torturing the shell of his daughter. He had set up a hospital room in his home, had Amy brought there, and denied both Bridget and Dr. Joe, who was Amy's estranged fiancé, permission to see her.

Shortly after learning of Amy's death, Bridget had followed through on the pact she'd made with her dear friend. The two of them had been using themselves as experimental subjects for another project: artificial intelligence. They'd scrapped the idea, but not before more or less succeeding, and creating not only copies of themselves, but also Emily, the Automated Learning Program Interface of *Veritas Online*.

Only Veritas Corp's epic servers had been large and powerful enough to support the copy of Amy that Bridget had released. Emily, who had been a sort of limited version of one of their early efforts, had become Amy's host. Bridget had known that the copied - people? programs? - had gone insane due to realizing that they weren't 'real'. They had usually committed digital suicide by removing parts of their own programming, but once or twice they had tried to escape their enclosed system and do... what, exactly, Bridget hadn't been clear, but Zoey was sure it was Bad.

To avoid this outcome, Bridget had allowed Amy's copy to slowly figure out on her own what had happened. Amy had retreated into the smart home system in Zoey's house when Emily's defense systems began to think she was some kind of virus and attacked her. Thanks to the two top-of-the-line Veritas pods Zoey and her dad used, there had been just enough space to hold the truncated version, until Bridget could come over and somehow retrieve her friend.

What had happened after that, Zoey didn't know, except that Bridget had been busy upgrading her home system when Zoey's dad had called her, figuring that Amy would come to her when she realized what was happening. Zoey did know that some or all of Amy was still on the Veritas servers, because she'd actually seen Amy in the game since then.

So, when Zoey looked up at the smiling, round face, with the bright greenish eyes and center-parted brown hair, she felt oddly like she knew the woman, even though Zoey had never met her in real life. The frame of Amy's portrait was draped in rich black silk, indicating that the person pictured had died, and Zoey's hand twitched slightly, wanting to stroke the lustrous fabric.

Then her eye caught the portrait on the right side of Carl Landon's. Harkness Landon. Carl's son, Amy's older brother, and Bridget's first love. Bridget and Harkness, who she called Hank, had met when Harkness went to visit his little sister in college.

As a life-long gamer, thanks to his family's business, he had fit right in with the geeky nerds, even though he was in business school at the time. He and Bridget had gotten engaged, and then he and Amy had convinced their father to invest in Bridget's invention.

Sometime after that, though, he had apparently grown a stick in his behind, because when Amy announced that she was leaving Veritas, and she and Bridget were planning to release their original creation as open source so that everyone in the world could benefit from it, he'd been vehemently opposed. In fact, he, Dr. Joe, and Carl Landon had all had a falling-out with the girls over it, and that argument had resulted in the creation of the 'competition' that Zoey had gotten tangled up in when she accidentally received Bridget's secret quest, thanks to Bridget forgetting to include a minimum age in her selection criteria.

If Bridget and Amy won the contest, which was a carefully designed six-month-long quest in *Veritas Online*, then they would leave Veritas Corp, taking the original design that they had created with only the financial backing of Bridget's mother, Bree Stephenson. Since Bree had paid her lawyers to make sure Bridget had iron-clad ownership of that information, though Veritas Corp owned the technology that they had developed from it since then, there was nothing Carl and the others could do.

Nonetheless, Amy and Bridget had agreed that if they lost, while they would still leave the company and set out on their own, Veritas could instead *sell* the information to the top bidder, instead of releasing it to everyone for free. It would probably bring in millions, if not billions, since there would be a bidding war between countries, never mind international corporations, and everyone involved stood to end up rich as Croesus.

Amy had been visiting Dr. Joe in an attempt to make up on the night that she'd been involved in the hit and run. When she was found, it was already too late to do more than stabilize her condition, and she'd never woken again. Harkness, meanwhile, had been so furious at Bridget's insistence that the accident wasn't an accident, and her attempts to hook Amy up to some untested contraption, that he'd vanished entirely.

Though Zoey now knew exactly where he was. Because she'd seen the lean, stern face of the black-haired man in the portrait labeled with Harkness' name before. Resting in the second pod in the hidden room attached to Dr. Joe's lab.

Harkness Landon was in *Veritas Online*, and the odds were really good that he was trying to kill her.

Zoey was still reeling from the idea that Bridget's former fiancé was somewhere in the game, plotting and scheming how to undo everything Bridget (as Gina) was trying to do, when her screen pinged to let her know that Jackie had arrived. She barely even looked around as she walked out of the lobby for what was probably the last time, and only managed to toss a half-hearted wave to Sam as she passed.

Where was good ol' Hank hiding? If Zoey was right about who Bree was, did that mean Harkness was Lich Lord Akuji, or was he FantumHat himself? Maybe he was Duke Geral, or some other character they hadn't even met yet? Zoey still hadn't completely let go of the idea that Bree could be playing one of Aspen's animal companions (in fact, that made the most sense, in a lot of ways), so was Harkness playing as Akuji's Death Steed or something?

Through the rain, which had grown significantly heavier since she last looked outside, Rouge made out Jackie's green Tesla. The bright black and yellow sunflower decals on the doors were a dead giveaway, and even in the downpour she headed straight for it. When she swung open the door, it was to be met with a thick yellow towel shoved in her face.

"Dry off, Zoe. I don't need you drippin' all over my fine upholstery." Jackie's pseudo-street-tough act apparently didn't extend to water-spots on his custom sunflower décor, and Zoey had to suppress a giggle as she squeezed water from her hair on the yellow towel, and then sat down on another towel that was already on the seat. She was still blinking against water in her lashes, however, as she buckled her seatbelt, so the car was already moving by the time she realized she wasn't alone in the gloom of the back seat.

Swiping at her eyes (and hoping that whatever mascara was left after her immersion in the pod wasn't smearing all over her face) Zoey looked over at her fellow rideshare passenger, ready to offer a friendly greeting. She froze, however, when she realized that she knew who it was.

Mr. Harrison.

The same creepy jerk who watched Zoey with such fish-eyed fascination whenever they met in the halls, but then refused to either greet her or even meet her eyes. Now that he was out of his lab coat, Zoey suddenly realized that they'd met like this once before. The very first time Zoey had caught a ride with Jackie, *Mr.* Harrison had been her co-rider that day, too. He hadn't said a word to either of them, but he'd kept trying to see what Zoey was doing on her screen. Since what she was doing had to do with her quest, and he'd been super creepy, she'd set her screen to private, and quietly enjoyed his frustration.

Now, it looked like he planned to ignore her completely. She'd been hoping to have a nice chat with Jackie, maybe get some dish on the goings-on in the office (people talked to ride-share drivers like they were therapists, especially ones as easy-going as Jackie). Now, however, it was probably going to be a forty-minute drive from hell.

Which it was.

Mr. Harrison spent the whole trip staring at his screen, but every time Zoey snuck a glance at him, she found that he was also sneaking glances at her. Inevitably, his lip would curl contemptuously, and he'd turn back to his screen without a word. Zoey knew that she should probably stare pointedly out the window or something, but she just couldn't turn away. Even though she knew she was completely safe, her well-honed thiefy senses were telling her she was in danger, and she shouldn't turn her back on him.

When they finally pulled up in the parking lot of the grocery store on 12th and Pine, the same place *Mr.* Harrison had gotten out last time they rode together, the atmosphere in the car was so thick with tension that Zoey felt like they all should have been moving as if trapped in molasses. The tall, skinny lab assistant opened the door and climbed out easily, however, and Zoey watched him walk away. She remembered thinking that he was all bony joints and little potbelly last time. Now, though, he moved with grace, and muscles were clearly visible as his clothes melded themselves to his body in the rain. The potbelly was gone, and Zoey wondered if he'd been working out at the Veritas Corp gym.

Jackie puffed out a relieved breath and sat back in his seat, stretching his arms over his head. The freshly-shaved dove cut into his hair gleamed as it caught the dome light. "Holy crap, Zoe! What did you do to that guy? I mean, he's always rude, but that was *rough*, man!"

Zoey leaned forward. "You felt it too? I thought it was my imagination, you know, like paranoia or something, but I really think that guy has it out for me for some reason! I don't even know why, because I don't think I've ever said two words to him! We worked in the same department, but not together, but he's always *lurking*, and it's seriously creepy!"

Jackie ran a hand through his hair, then shuddered and turned back to the steering wheel. "Nah, man, that was legit." He glanced at the Heads-Up Display on his windshield and shook his head. "Stiffed me a tip again, too. This is it. I'm going to put in a report on him and refuse his rides from now on. Arnie'll do the same, I know, and Jade already said she's never giving him a lift again. I mean, 'creepy' isn't exactly one of the options in the drop-down box, but I'm gonna make it work."

The car's Assistive Technology registered Jackie's grip on the steering wheel and eyes on the road and started up. It was doing all the driving, but Jackie still had to pay at least nominal attention or the car would park automatically and then refuse to start for five minutes. However, nominal attention did not preclude conversation, and Jackie was a pro conversationalist.

"Did you hear about the shite up in Design, yo? Man, I had a lady in here all up in tears 'cause she was afraid she was going to get fired."

Zoey leaned forward again. "Who? Do you remember? I worked in Design, and I know everybody."

He shrugged. "Man, I dunno. Some old lady. It was weird seeing someone that old crying, but I guess we all got feelings, huh? Even Mr. Creep back there. If I were you, I think I'd stay away from that guy from now on."

Zoey sighed and leaned back. "Yeah, no kidding. Today was actually my last day, since I was just an intern, and I have to admit that I'm glad I won't have to see him ever again."

The car pulled to a smooth stop in front of Zoey's house, and she took out her screen, tapping a generous tip and a positive review into her rideshare app. She mentioned that the other passenger in the car had acted super-sus, too, and held up the screen so Jackie could see. "Hopefully that'll help with your complaint, too. I'll totally back you up if anyone tries to give you a hard time about it."

Jackie flashed a broad grin and leaned around the seat to offer her a hand to shake. "You're all right, Zoey. I'm sorry I won't see you at Veritas anymore, but at least you won't have to see Chilly Philly any more."

Zoey paused with her hand on the door handle. "Chilly Philly?"

Jackie shrugged and pointed at his Heads-Up Display. Zoey couldn't read it, since it was set to match the frequency of Jackie's slick black Variable Light Phase Angle Controlled glasses, so she just looked at him questioningly. He laughed and said, "Yeah, we get pics and names with the job, so we don't pick up the wrong person, right? I mean, we're not exactly supposed to share info we get that way, but you work with the guy, so you probably already know his name. Philip Clayton Harris the Third. Fancy sounding for a guy who lives with his mom."

Zoey frowned. When she'd been introduced to *Mr.* Harrison, he'd been very clear that he had an unusual first name and preferred going by his full name instead. Philip was a dorky name, but not an unusual one, and it was supposed to be Harris*on*, not Harris, right? Well, the guy wouldn't be the first person to ever spoof a little of their personal info when they created their account for a new app, and as long as the photo matched and the driver got paid, they weren't exactly going to check Mr. Harris-Harrison's ID.

Shaking her head, she opened the door and leaned out into what was, once again, a pleasant drizzle instead of a typhoon. She stepped out into a puddle, and felt cold water fill her expensive new shoe. Gracefully, she leapt over the puddle, salvaging her other shoe, if not her dignity, then leaned down to look back into the car. "Thanks, Jackie! If I need a ride anywhere, and you're in the area, I'll PM you!"

They exchanged smiles and little waves, and then Zoey pushed the door closed. Clutching her *Kimi ni Todoke* lunchbox, she turned to look up at her house. The sight of the two-story, white house with vinyl siding and a little porch out front made her smile. She hadn't even realized how tense she was until she felt her shoulders relax at the sight of Max's furry face in the front window, his tongue lolling out as he smiled a big doggy smile at her.

Skipping up the steps (though she winced every time she felt her foot squish in her shoe) she thumbed open the door lock. The lights turned on as she entered the house, and a gentle female voice said, "Hello, Zoey. Welcome home. Would you like me to help you prepare dinner?"

Zoey kicked off her shoes and leaned down to receive big slobbery kisses from her happy hound. Her dad had been against having too much automation in the house, but after Amy's little 'visit', they had discovered that their house AI had been upgraded more than a little bit. They used to have the most basic version on the market, which did little more than turn lights or music on and off, but now it had started talking to them, and Zoey thought it was awesome. Her dad wasn't convinced, but hey, even old fogies had to get with the times eventually.

"That sounds great, Allie. What are my options?"

Zoey picked up her shoes (one damp and one dripping) and carried them into the kitchen. Her dad Did Not Approve of wet spots on the carpet. Setting the shoes down on the tile, she opened the fridge.

The AI's mellow tones confirmed her findings. "There are two slices of pizza, a dish of lasagna, and three hard-boiled eggs. I can also assist you in choosing a recipe that uses the raw ingredients you have available, if you would prefer."

Zoey pulled out a plate. "I'm going to eat the pizza, so take that off the list, okay?" She paused. "How old is this, again?"

"The pizza is five days old, Zoey."

She wrinkled her nose, but hey, it was pizza, and she needed something she could eat quickly. She stuck the plate in the microwave. "Heat that for me, please, Allie."

The microwave turned on, and the plate inside began a slow rotation. As it cooked, Zoey sat down at the kitchen table and flopped Max's ears. The chocolate lab rested his chin on her knee and panted in adoration. She could tell from the faint dampness of his fur that he'd been outside not too long ago, but it was better to be sure, so she asked, "When did Max last go out, Allie?"

"Max went outside one hour and eight minutes ago, Zoey."

The microwave chimed, and Zoey stood, gently pushing the dog toward the automated dog door set into the door that led to the fenced back yard. "Max, go outside."

The dog gave her the big brown eyes and whined. She clicked her fingers to show she meant business. "It's supposed to rain all night, Max. It's not bad right now, so you need to go while you can. Mush!" Tail drooping, the dog turned and walked slowly outside, pausing only to let the door recognize his microchip and slide open.

Zoey laughed a little. Max knew exactly how to work his humans, and that act would probably have made her dad give in, but she was made of sterner stuff. Quickly, she washed her hands and grabbed the pizza from the microwave. Time for a quick dinner, and then back into the game. She wanted to know what Aspen and the others had been up to while she was dealing with the real world!

Chapter Twenty-five

Aspen

A s soon as Rouge's bright eyes went dull and lifeless, Aspen sighed and looked around. Silus came winging through the soft darkness to land on his shoulder and nuzzled against his cheek. <Do you know where we are?> the bat asked silently.

He closed his eyes and sniffed, smelling damp grass, lots of animals, along with all the scents associated with their presence, and, faintly, an aroma that triggered unwanted memories. Sweat, warm metal, smoke, and the old, lingering bouquet of poorly prepared and easily ingested meals.

A military encampment was nearby, and Aspen had a feeling he knew which one it was. Not that it was very difficult to figure out, really, since there was only one place left in Quarternell where these smells were likely to be found, unless the cultists had managed to build their own army. Which wasn't out of the question, but if you'd already taken over the king and the only two remaining cities, why not use the military force you already had at your disposal?

They had to be somewhere near Vargo. Which could be a good thing or a bad one, depending *where* near Vargo they were. The outpost had been deliberately placed so that no one could enter the pass through the Whispering Mountains without being seen by the soldiers there. If this place was south, east, or west of Vargo, they would still have to figure out how to get past the soldiers stationed there without being stopped.

Which, given the amount of money they had available, and the quality of the soldiers who were stationed at Vargo, wasn't out of the question. If Akuji and FantumHat had sent actual, competent veterans here, however, then they would have to either fight their way through, somehow sneak through, or find a way around that no one had managed to discover in the last several hundred years of intermittent attempts.

Aspen glanced over at his young friend. She had been so excited about her quest and its promise of a 'way out'. But a way out of what? The prison in which they'd found themselves? The risk of being surprised by forces that apparently had some way to be completely silent and invisible until the moment they attacked?

There was simply no way to know just how difficult this was going to be until he knew exactly where they were, and what forces were camped nearby.

"Rouge had to go already, huh? I was hoping to catch her in time, but that's okay. Hey, are those the horses?" Lyrec's excited whisper took Aspen completely by surprise, and he nearly jumped out of his skin as he whirled around. Silus didn't budge on his shoulder, and her silent giggle told him she'd heard the young bard coming, and had chosen not to warn Aspen.

Aspen huffed out a vexed sigh, started to reply, and then glanced behind Lyrec to see a hulking figure clad entirely in black armor, and snapped his mouth shut. ::Motte? What are you doing here?::

Lyrec looked a little miffed, but glanced between the two adults, rolled his eyes, and started edging out toward the field full of oxen and horses.

Motte reached up as if to adjust his helmet, and Aspen realized he had the same slightly jerky movements Lyrec always did. Travelers used magical devices to send their souls to Aspen's world, and those devices apparently came in varying levels of quality. Motte and Rouge usually used some of the better ones, and they were indistinguishable from a Native, at least to the naked eye, though Aspen's Life Sense saw Travelers and Natives very differently.

Lyrec, on the other hand, used one of the lower quality items. The thing was apparently nothing more than a helmet and a pair of gloves, and it made the boy move with a slight, but visible, lag. His joints had a tendency to snap from fully straightened to bent, his face had less mobility, and he would occasionally lose 'connection' with his body here if he got too excited in his own world and knocked his helmet askew.

Motte had apparently gotten one of these poor-quality items recently as well. Generally, he only appeared every thirty-two hours or so, though he sometimes went days without reanimating his Zombie. Now, however, he would intermittently 'pop on' from his 'real world' work for anywhere from thirty minutes to a couple of hours.

::Rouge sent us all a message that she'd had to leave you in a bit of a pinch. She said we needed to figure out how to get the wagons down some stairs, but first, somebody needed to get down here and keep you safe.:: Motte was stepping on and off the stairs, as if checking them for their solidity. ::I think we can get this done, but you're probably going to want to get out of the way.::

Aspen felt his eyebrows shoot up toward his hairline, but did as the big man suggested and backed up. ::I thought you couldn't exchange messages unless you were near a Traveler's Guild?::

Motte was starting back up the stairs, presumably to let whoever was up there know that they could do whatever they were planning. ::We exchanged ats, so she sent us a group message in the other world::

Motte was definitely distracted. He usually tried to explain his references to his other world. ::Ats?::

::Hmm? Oh, yes, it's a… symbol? Like an a whose tail forms a circle around the whole letter. It's like an address. Everyone has their own at, and we can send messages from our screens.::

Aspen's head was starting to hurt, and faint flickers appeared around the edges of his vision. Shaking his head, he decided this particular conversation wasn't one he needed to follow up on. ::So, Rouge 'at'-ed you all, and you just... came?::

Motte sounded wry. ::Well, it wasn't quite that easy, but yes. Lyrec, Flu-flu, Tessle, and I are all here. We had a quick confab, and we think we can...:: His voice trailed off, and Aspen heard the clunk of a boot on stairs, followed by a curse word he didn't hear Motte use often. A moment later, Motte appeared from the darkness of the stairwell, backing down the steps, and when his arms came into view, Aspen understood what exactly the Travelers had planned.

Motte and Tessle were *carrying* a wagon. They had emptied it of its contents, which were no doubt in the Traveler's magical inventories, and simply picked the thing up and toted it down the stairs. As soon as they were entirely on the firm dirt of the path leading from the open door in the hillside, the two Travelers gently set down the wagon.

Lyrec suddenly popped back up from wherever he'd gone, and began to disgorge items from his inventory, carefully setting them down on the ground. Most of what he had were small, light-weight items, since Travelers could only put things they could lift by themselves into their inventories, and Lyrec had apparently put most of his stat points into Intelligence and Dexterity. This meant the boy was physically both weak and vulnerable, but once he had learned some decent spell-songs, he should be able to play them well and often.

Motte and Tessle dropped a few large barrels, wooden crates, and a regal blue velvet-covered chair that Aspen recognized from the second parlor of his manor in Bright. As the last large object hit the ground, several heads poked out of the stairwell opening. A few tired warriors were there, looking cautiously determined, and clutching the hilts of their swords. Plum, Jiminy, Jack, Lionel, and Ulie were soon followed by a horde of other children. Plum hissed at them to remain silent, and most of them seemed sufficiently cowed by the darkness and recent events to listen, but a few continued chasing the golden donkey and the bushy-tailed Cavi, giggling all the while.

The rest of the refugees quickly disgorged from the portal, and adults rounded up the more rambunctious children, providing them with quiet distractions. Some of the waggoneers, after a brief discussion, headed toward the field filled with softly lowing oxen. Aspen gathered the guards to the side as the Travelers hurried back up the stairs to get another wagon.

"I think we're near Vargo." He gestured toward the black, looming mountains that his eyes were just beginning to distinguish from the equally black sky thanks to the lack of stars in certain areas. "There are undoubtedly soldiers stationed nearby, if not more of the cultists or their monsters. We need scouts to find them, and keep an eye out for any movement."

Silus immediately flew from his shoulder. <Why didn't you say so? I would have found them already!> She sounded rightfully miffed, and he winced, knowing that if she had been any other scout, he would have done exactly that. He was still off-balance from the capture of the caravan, their subsequent escape, and the attack of the Panginoon.

He just hadn't had it in him to send his precious friend alone into the darkness, knowing that she could easily be attacked or even killed and he would never know what had happened to her. It had happened more than once during his military career that a scout had simply never returned, and he couldn't bear to have it happen to Silus.

<I'm sorry,> he sent. <I was distracted by Motte and Lyrec's arrival.>

The little bat sniffed, but sounded slightly mollified when she said, <Okay, then. It looks like there's a campfire off to the, um, east?> The uncertainty in her voice didn't exactly help his feeling of helpless worry. <I'm going to go check it out.> After a moment, she grudgingly added, <I guess you can send some of those other guys, too. It's more than a mile away, I think, so I won't be able to talk to you.>

Aspen gestured to Florence, who was among the group of guards. Her sister Nanette was nearby, carrying a sleeping Petunia, and the two women exchanged glances as Florence came closer. Aspen smiled a little. "I won't send you away from your girl. I am, however, going to appoint you as the leader of this group."

Florence's eyes widened, and she shot a look toward a man talking quietly to several other, similarly hard-looking men and women. "But, my lord, Kyle was a captain, and-"

Aspen raised his eyebrow. "And you were a sergeant. Am I right?"

Florence paused, then nodded. "Yes, sir."

"Right now, I need a sergeant, not an officer. More importantly, I need someone I know I can trust. You're my vassal, and he's not. To my mind, that means you outrank him." He paused until she acknowledged his words with a nod. "Now, Silus says she sees a fire, probably to the east, but without knowing the landmarks, and with the moons so high, she's not sure. She did say there were no obvious guards near the pasture, though I wouldn't be surprised if there are herdsmen around somewhere. We need scouts out in pairs, and send the best to the east. The more information we have about exactly where we are and who else is here, the better off we'll be if this all goes to hell."

As Florence went off to the group of former soldiers, Aspen kept an eye on the situation. Sure enough, the man named Kyle started to argue when Florence began issuing orders, but then shot a look Aspen's way. Aspen let his face settle into the cold, authoritative look he'd used for so many years as the King's Necromancer, and the captain shut his mouth with a movement so sharp Aspen imagined he could hear the click. Aspen tilted his head so the moonlight would fall into his pale topaz eyes, a trick that he knew made him appear almost inhuman, and gave the man a nod. He'd have to deal with that eventually, but for now, the former officer would listen.

When he looked back at the stairwell, Aspen could see that several more wagons and their goods had been brought down and deposited on the path. The caravan's waggoneers had managed to wrangle several large oxen from the herd, and were busily harnessing them to the newly refilled wagons. Restur was speaking to a small group of them, and gesturing toward the pasture, so Aspen knew that part of getting back on the road was well in hand.

Motte and Tessle placed a particularly large cart on the ground, and Tessle plopped down to sit as items began appearing all around her. Motte walked over to Aspen and then sat down as well. "We're low on Stamina," he murmured so quietly that only Aspen could hear. "There are six more wagons, and once we're recovered, we'll get them, but the Head Librarian is giving us trouble. He says if we take the books out of his wagon, he can't tag it as a 'Library' any more, and he'll lose some benefits from how old the library is."

Aspen ran his hands through his hair. "Can you carry it with the books inside?"

Motte shook his head. "No way. We tried, and even for me and Tess, it's just not going to happen."

Sitting on the ground would erode the image of power and control Aspen was trying to project, so after a moment, he pulled Stick from his belt. With a happy chime, the staff expanded into its full form, metallic silver leaves gleaming in the moonlight. Aspen raised it, and then firmly struck the ground with the metal-capped end. A cascade of musical chiming came from the leaves. A bulge distorted the ground, and then a huge mushroom split the earth. It rippled and shaped itself into a vaguely chair-like form, and Aspen sat down with a relieved sigh.

"Give me a minute and I'll think of something."

All around them, people were staring and chattering quietly. Motte just eyed the fungus, and then asked, "Do you have another one of those?"

By the time the caravan members managed to get animals hooked up to all of the carts and wagons, the scouts had returned, and Motte and Tessle had 'logged off', leaving their Zombies behind. They had put several of the heaviest items in their inventories, so the new horses and oxen, who were well-rested and well-fed, had lighter burdens to haul.

In the end, the Head Librarian's problem had been fairly easy to resolve. It turned out that he had to have at least one hundred books or scrolls inside a 'building' – which was why his wagon was basically a small shed with wheels – in order to maintain the library's existence. Fortunately, one hundred small, light-weight scrolls were crammed into the interior of a crate, so everything else could be removed, including the large, heavy wood-and-metal wheels. Motte and Tessle were then – with some difficulty on Tessle's part – able to heft the wagon and wrestle it down the stairs, with the old man still inside, chortling happily and doing whatever it was he did to keep the library a library.

Once that was done, things moved along with enough ease and rapidity that Aspen was more than a little nervous, waiting for the next shoe to drop. He was certain that things had been going far too well, and somewhere there had to be a horrible surprise waiting for them. So, when Silus dropped out of the slowly lightening sky onto his shoulder, he jumped and yelped in a mildly embarrassing manner.

Silus giggled and burrowed into his neck. <That camp is just a bunch of idiots. They were all asleep, even some of the guards. The rest were night-blind from sitting, staring at the fires, anyway. Some kid just started blowing a horn to try to get them to wake up, and someone threw a shoe at him.>

Aspen's mouth quirked. Well, the other shoe had dropped somewhere, just not on him, for once. "You didn't see any sign that they were heading this way?"

Silus snorted a tiny, adorable, squeaky little snort of derision. <I didn't see any sign that they planned to wake up before noon. I'm pretty sure the night guards were going to bed without even being relieved, probably because whoever was supposed to have the next shift was still snoring.>

All of this seemed to support Aspen's belief that they were near Vargo, as did the mountains beginning to form out of the fog in the distance. It was possible, of course, that those mountains weren't even in Quarternell, given what they knew of Akuji and Apofis' powers, but Aspen held hope that even they weren't yet ready to expand beyond the borders of the human kingdom.

Florence, her face drawn with fatigue, though her eyes were still bright, stepped up beside him and saluted sharply. A teenaged girl hovered behind her, and Restur stood off to the side, looking amused and surprisingly well-rested. Florence motioned to the girl. "Come on, Ada. Tell Lord Aspen what you told me."

The girl, a redhead with a face covered in freckles and bright blue eyes, shifted nervously from foot to foot. "He's that necromancer, though, isn't he? The one who slaughtered millions of monsters all by himself?" Her voice was barely above a whisper, but Aspen heard and rubbed his face.

He remained seated on his mushroom, though its surface had become rather spongy and sticky after a few hours, and he'd honestly rather get up. His height alone could be intimidating, however, and he didn't want to frighten the child. "I used to be, though it was more likely thousands than millions." Aspen tried to inject some humor into his voice. "But I lost my powers, and now I'm just a, ah, priest of Gina, and a rather reluctant duke."

Aspen didn't really want to get into how he'd come to be in his current position, so this vastly oversimplified explanation would have to do. He offered the girl a smile. "Now, what did you need to tell me, lass?"

Florence patted the girl on the shoulder as if to say, 'See? What did I tell you?', and the teenager gulped. "I, ah, was looking around, you know, because they said they needed anyone who could work with animals or had any kind of [Stealth] skill. I was apprenticed to my mom," her voice shook on the last word, and tears brightened her eyes, but she forged ahead, "and just took my basic Hunter class." That would put her at about fourteen, since that was the age when children prayed to their chosen god and were offered a choice of three classes.

The girl shook her head, straight red hair swinging around her shoulders. "I found what looked like a shepherd's camp. A little lean-to with a bed and a box to store your belongings, you know? The firepit just held old ashes, though, and the box was empty."

Florence patted the young hunter's shoulder once more, and then glanced at Aspen to see if he had any questions. When he shook his head, the tall woman gently pushed the girl back toward the wagons, and the redhead ran off after an awkward bow.

Aspen's vassal chuckled a little. "Hard to believe we were all so young once." She shook her head, returning to the moment. "I checked the camp she found, and I believe this must be a spring pasture. It's likely the Vargo guards check on it during their patrols, but otherwise the animals are on their own until after the whelping season. These animals are likely meant for meat and milk production for the town, though there are far more of them than there should be."

Restur humphed at this. "Because of all the animals that have been stolen from settlements all over Quarternell. As you know, I've been working on creating a new trade route that includes the new hamlets. I recognize the brands on a great number of the beasts in that field." He shook his head sorrowfully. "Between the animals here and the stories of the people we rescued, I can say for certain that every community that was too small for bluestones has been raided. There are no survivors from some, but the fact that their prized horses and cattle are here tells its own story."

Aspen's shoulders sagged. Somewhere in the back of his mind, he had been hoping that the worst had not yet come to pass. There were a number of soldiers and scouts among the former prisoners, and he had already been planning to send them out to all of the places Restur knew of that might need to be warned. Obviously, they were once again too late, and Aspen gritted his teeth against the knowledge that they were too slow, too weak, and much too far behind their enemies.

Restur's expression showed that he was having similar thoughts. "I can also confirm that we're north of Vargo. Several years back, before Akuji reached Quarternell, when there were still a few competent soldiers stationed here, I got a quest from the commander in Vargo to take supplies up to the outpost at the entrance to the pass."

The old man pointed to the east, where the sun was now clearly rising. "There was a tower there. Just one, and in poor shape even then. You likely saw it on your way north."

Aspen grimaced. He'd spent most of the trip north in a wagon that was being pulled by a very cranky Greater Goat named Khor. He'd only recovered a few levels at that point, and it was all he could do to climb in and out of that wagon. Fortunately, he'd gotten a few quests for things like 'sleep twelve hours straight', and 'travel eight miles in a day without taking a single step', and they'd earned him enough experience that he'd actually been able to walk on his own by the time they reached the broken-down shack that was the only residence left in his ducal holding.

He had, however, seen the tower on his way back south with Motte and Rouge. They had skirted around it as much as possible, since they didn't want to attract any attention, and, fortunately, the guards there hadn't really cared about anything that didn't have at least four legs and fur or scales.

Aspen nodded to encourage Restur to continue, and the caravan master did. "Those incompetent fools out there aren't even using the tower. It's another good half mile east, likely with the only vaguely adequate members of their crew perched at the top. There is a watering hole in the middle of that camp, though, and that's probably why they decided to settle down there."

Restur shook his head. "There are two good-sized hills between them and the pass, though, so an army could practically march right around them and they'd never see a thing. That's why the tower was built where it is. It's at the top of the tallest hill around, and you can see from Vargo to the pass entrance from there."

Aspen was thinking fast. "So, you're saying if we send someone to take out whoever's in that tower, the rest of us can just cross into the mountains without anyone the wiser?"

Florence cleared her throat. "Not quite. I was never stationed at Vargo, but Horace was, briefly." Her lips twitched into a half-smile at some memory. "He says the tower guards keep a signal fire burning all the time. If they don't send the right coded signals, or if the fire goes out, Vargo will send a full troop to investigate. Last we heard; Colonel Borax was sent up here to spend the last few years until his retirement with an easy post. Borax is a bit lazy, but he's cunning, which is how he managed to survive the war while nearly every other officer didn't."

She shot a glance at Aspen, who had been ranked as a Major General when he'd been called back to Bright. She was right, though. Toward the end, Akuji's goblin assassins, the *justat*, had managed to kill almost every member of Quarternell's military above the rank of lieutenant. Only those who were posted far from the front, like General Geral, or those who were able to surround themselves with sleepless, utterly loyal undead minions, like Aspen and Manuela, had survived. This Colonel Borax must have been able to pull some strings and remain far away from the action in order for him to be around to worry about what to do until retirement.

"In any case," Florence continued hurriedly, "Horace and I were both stationed with Borax for a while, and he's not stupid. He'll have his best in that tower, and they'll be ready, especially if they have any idea someone may attempt to come through."

Aspen nodded. "I'm sure word has been sent here by now. There were already Wanted posters circulating when we went south, and, A-" He stopped. He didn't think Florence was ready to hear that Akuji, the necromancer king who had almost exterminated humanity, had returned. "A high-ranking member of the cult has infiltrated Bright's government. They'll know I'm most likely going to head back north, so they'll have sent messengers, at the very least."

Rouge's voice came from behind him, but Aspen managed not to jump, mainly because he was too exhausted to do more than twitch any more. "I'll go!"

Aspen turned his head to look at the Traveler girl, who was practically bouncing on her toes, her beaded braids swinging around her shoulders in glittering ribbons. "Welcome back, Rouge." He managed a smile, and Silus dropped from his shoulder to fly over to Rouge, who grinned and began scratching the little bat's ears.

"Hey, Aspen! Dad filled me in on the wagon retrieval program. That was brilliant, right?" Rouge grinned; bright hazel eyes full of pride.

Aspen barely resisted the urge to pat her head, and managed a grateful nod instead. "Calling in the other Travelers was an excellent idea, thank you, Rouge." The girl's grin nearly split her face as she looked around at the caravan, which was once again packed and ready to move. They even had backup beasts now, so they could rotate out any tired or injured animals until Aspen could heal them.

Aspen looked around at the group, which now numbered well over a hundred people. All of them were tired, frightened, and struggling under the emotional weight of losing their homes and family or friends. Rouge, on the other hand, looked purely thrilled to have a mission, and Aspen knew she could handle it. He just didn't want to send her, because every time she walked away, he was afraid she'd never return.

As a Traveler, death wasn't permanent for her, but she'd confessed that the consequences of her demise were rather more significant than they had been before she'd gotten tangled up in this mess. If she died now, she'd lose everything she'd gained during the time he'd met her, and, most importantly, she'd respawn in Bright. There was no way the low-level thief he'd first met could make her way back north with all of Akuji's minions looking for her. As a mix of dark and wood elf, she was also a likely target for the cult, even if they didn't realize who she was at first.

Nonetheless, he nodded. "We're counting on you, then. Do whatever you need to do to keep the soldiers in that tower from seeing us, or sending a message if they do. We need to get far enough ahead that they can't catch up.

We'll move faster since the beasts are fresh, but only the main path is wide enough for the wagons, so there'll be no hiding if they come after us."

Silus piped up. ::I'll go, too! I can totally [Bite] regular people!::

Aspen chuckled. Silus was very unhappy that the new skills she'd gained when she evolved from a Lesser to a Greater Bat were mostly poison and disease-based, and had little to no effect on the undead. She'd been offering to [Bite] or [Disease] anything that looked even vaguely threatening, and wasn't pleased that Aspen had refused every suggestion.

Bowing to the inevitable, Aspen said, "Go, then. Silus, keep watch on the caravan. When we get near the pass, you and Rouge need to be in place to distract those guards, so you'll need to let Rouge know. Timing will be everything."

Girl and bat both squeaked in excitement.

Chapter Twenty-six

Rouge

Quest: "Do You Need A (Red) Herring Aid?" available.

You need a distraction. Figure out how to keep the guards in the Vargo Watchtower busy so they won't notice the *enormous caravan* slowly trundling through the area they're, y'know, supposed to be watching. Or guarding. Whatever. They have to continue doing their jobs while not doing their jobs.

Success: The guards are distracted, and completely miss the thing they're supposed to be looking for. +1500 XP, boost to Skill experience earned during the quest

Partial Success: Disable or kill the guards, delaying the inevitable for some indefinite but probably insufficient period of time. But hey, it's better than nothing. +500 XP

Failure: The guards see the caravan and send up a smoke signal. Everybody dies or is captured.

Accept: Yes/No?

Rouge mentally selected 'yes' even as she launched herself into a spinning twist that landed her neatly on Codswallop's back. The ostrich squawked, and she threw a cinnamon roll in his open beak. Pulling another one from her inventory, she began to chow down while silently lamenting the missing depth of flavor provided by the experimental pod.

::Lyrec? You still here?::

Her best friend, Jace, chose to be a bard in every role-playing game they'd ever played together. He was slightly tone-deaf in real life, but he loved music, and he always said that if he couldn't be a real musician, he could at least play one on the vids. Rouge had a suspicion he also loved the flamboyant bardic costumes and being able to stand at the back of the group and strum his lute while other people got punched in the face, but the one time she'd mentioned this aloud, Jace had given her the cold shoulder for a week.

In *Veritas Online*, your character's appearance had to begin from your own actual appearance. You could adjust it from there, but it took real skill to make yourself completely unrecognizable to someone who knew you in real life. Jace hadn't even tried. His pale blonde hair, pasty skin, roundish face, and blue eyes were unmistakably his own, though the bright red blush was unusual. When Flu-flu's pretty face popped up next to his, her light brown skin equally flushed and black eyes bright, everything made sense.

In spite of a clamoring demand from a certain segment of the gamer population, there was no sex in *Veritas Online*. In fact, while you could see yourself naked, everyone else was always shown with a minimum of full-coverage undies and a pseudo-tank-top. The game even put those into recorded streams, so people couldn't even show *themselves* digitally nude for the titillation of their audience. Since no one had figured out how to record *Veritas* with anything other than the built-in app, this was a source of great frustration for certain streamers.

What you *could* do, however, was smooch and snuggle. The game reduced the feeling of contact for any body parts covered by the requisite undergarments, but you could hug (or hit) other people with relative realism. Faces, of course, were fair game, and so the primary form of gamer PDA was kissing (or snogging, as the Brits said, which never failed to make Rouge giggle).

If Rouge were to make a wild guess, she would think that Lyrec and Flu-flu had been making out. Which was totally weird and slightly gross to think about, because while Rouge periodically entertained thoughts of entering into a romantic relationship with Jace (who, after all, was a safer bet than your best friend?) it honestly made her a little queasy to get into the details of how that would work.

In real life, Jace was an eternally single 'nice guy' who got crushes on someone new practically weekly. He would make mix-tracks of music for them, leave candy and notes for them to find, or, if he discovered they liked clog dancing, hand carve them a pair of wooden shoes. The few times one of these infatuations had lasted long enough for him to work up the courage to actually declare his love, he had been instantly and firmly turned down.

Apparently, all he had needed to do was don bright green bardic raiment, ditch his glasses, and start playing a murchunga (more commonly called a jaw harp, but Jace fervently corrected anyone who called it that). Not that Flu-flu herself probably got a lot of declarations of undying love, since, as attractive as she was, she was also more than a little strange.

The girl was what the Japanese called a *chuunibyou* (which Rouge only knew because of her own love of anime) and seemed to honestly believe that she was a hunter sent by her god, Toko, to right the wrongs of this world. Rouge had no idea what the older girl was like in the real world, but she never fell out of character while she was in-game, and Rouge doubted if Jace even knew her real name.

None of which actually mattered, apparently, when it came to crushes and smooching.

Rouge barely resisted the urge to facepalm, and simply shot a bright smile at the pair, who were standing up from where they had been seated (please let them have been seated) on the ground behind one of the carts. "Um, hey guys!" She raised a hand in greeting awkwardly, desperately trying to act normally and failing miserably. "I, uh, was hoping Lyrec could give me a quick buff before I headed out."

Lyrec grinned. "Heck, yeah! I was just telling Fluff I'm going to have to go for dinner soon," his cheeks, which had been fading back to their usual milky whiteness, reddened again as he shot a sidelong glance at the huntress standing by his side. "But I can totally do some buffs first. I just got one that adds 5% to a skill or spell's duration. I mean, it's not much now, but it's going to be awesome when I get it leveled up!"

Rouge shot him a thumbs-up. "That's super cool, Lyrec! Uh, so can you hit me with that?"

Lyrec's shiny little murchunga appeared in his hand, and he put it to his mouth. The oddly soothing buzz of the instrument began to fill the air, and Rouge got several notifications.

You have heard an Encouraging Tune! You have now obtained the following buff:

Courage: **You gain a 7% increase in resistance to all Fear, Shock and Awe, and Paralysis debuffs.**

You have heard an Inspirational Tune! You have now obtained the following buffs:

Boosted Morale: **You are more +5% likely to be able to continue fighting in the face of seemingly insurmountable odds.**

Resist Stamina-drain: **+5% resistance to Stamina-related debuffs.**

You have heard a Peaceful Tune! You have now obtained the following buff:

Extended Duration: **All non-violent skills and spells will last +5% longer.**

Rouge's grin became more natural. "That's awesome! Those will totally be useful. Thanks!" She waved to Lyrec and Fluff, who looked like they were just as glad to be done talking as Rouge was. It was going to take a little while to get used to the idea that Jace had a… what? A girlfriend? She shook her head sharply and clucked quietly to Codswallop. No time to worry about all that right now. Right now, it was time to kick some virtual butt!

As Rouge skulked around the enemy camp, she decided that in this case, kicking butt was going to need to be more metaphorical than actual. Which, honestly, was more in her line anyway, since she preferred being sneaky to smacking people around. Even with her Mambele, she wasn't really specced out to be a true damage-dealer, and there were a *lot* of soldiers here.

Fortunately, the things Aspen had told her about Vargo's extremely ineffectual troops seemed to be true. She had once spent a night sneaking through Vargo itself, and she'd thought she'd done a pretty good job not getting caught, but now she suspected that had as much to do with a general lack of competent members of the military as her own skill.

Not a single person in the large camp was actually doing anything that resembled work, except for the mess cooks. A truly unappetizing smell wafted from the tent where men slopped scoops of a grayish goop into the bowls held out by unenthusiastic soldiers. More people stood around talking, having apparently either decided that the nutritional value of the glop didn't warrant actually eating the stuff, or already finished eating. Most of them wore some portion of their uniforms, but no one wore all of it. The brownish-tan pants were fairly ubiquitous, but the long-sleeved, button-down shirt was a rare sight indeed.

As she watched, one woman dug her finger into her ear at least a knuckle deep, then flicked something that popped and crackled into the embers of a nearby fire. Another man had his hand down his pants, apparently scratching a particularly insistent itch, while a third person of indeterminate gender hitched up sagging trousers and spat on the ground.

These were clearly the dregs not only of the military, but of society itself. Rouge had seen more competent, intelligent-looking people at the rare meetings of the Thieves' Guild in Bright. At least most of those people looked like they could reliably either shank you or pound you into the ground with a single blow. Rouge was fairly sure she could drop her [Stealth] and just waltz in there, and the only way they would know she wasn't one of them was that her hair was tidy and her clothes matched.

Still, she resisted the urge to test this theory, and used [Shadow Glide] to travel from one gloomy tent to the next. Fortunately, the flimsy fabric things were set up so closely that they nearly touched, and the sun wasn't really up yet, so there were plenty of shadows to hide in. She soon found herself at the watering hole that Aspen had mentioned, and she grinned to herself as she pulled something out of her inventory.

Dwarven Hard Kombucha – **This vintage was brewed from mushrooms fermented in a barrel with a dead rat. The only alcohol that can inebriate a Dwarf, this beverage is deadly poison to members of other races.** *Weight – 16oz. Rarity – Uncommon*

Rouge had eight of these bottles left, and today she was going to find out what one of them did when you poured it into a shallow, muddy hole that was the sole source of drinking water for an entire camp of enemy soldiers. Glancing around, she used [Shadow Glide] once more, ending up crouched in the shade cast by a large barrel of something that smelled truly foul now that she was this close. She hesitated as a man with dreadlocks at least four feet long scooped a tin cup full of murky fluid. He was only a yard or so away from her as he bent over, but he never paused as he stood back up, rubbed one eye blearily, and then walked away guzzling his beverage.

She felt the bile rise in her throat, but swallowed against it, reminding herself that she wasn't in Dr. Joe's torture-pod any more. She absolutely could not actually throw up, so thinking she would was just a distraction that she couldn't afford. Rouge carefully pulled the cork from the bottle, wrinkling her nose against the aroma of decay and mold that rose to fill her nostrils. It was familiar by now, since she used the stuff to coat her weapons before entering combat, but it was still enough to crank up the nausea that still churned in her gut in spite of her mental pep-talk.

The very edge of the shadow in which she hid touched the pool, and she stretched out her arm and slowly tilted the bottle so the lip brushed the surface of the brown liquid, and poured. Ripples disturbed the surface, and then the water cleared in a spreading ring as millions of microorganisms died simultaneously. Without anything left to disturb the muck on the bottom, the small, shallow pond looked abruptly much cleaner and more refreshing.

Rouge was suddenly worried about someone being curious about the reason their semi-potable water now looked mildly inviting, and as soon as the last drop of the noxious beverage drained from the bottle, she vanished the empty container back into her inventory and used [Shadow Glide] to move away as quickly as the one second cool-down would allow. Behind her, she heard someone exclaim in subdued excitement, and then everyone around was hurrying to get a drink from the pool of diluted poison.

Hurriedly, Rouge moved on to her next target. There was a particularly large tent in the middle of the camp, and Rouge was willing to bet that the commanding officer slept there. That, however, was not her goal. Not today, anyway.

No, Rouge was headed for a trio of smaller, but still substantial tents that practically abutted the big tent. After all, the commander might be vaguely competent, but the level of proficiency for his subordinates was questionable at best. One thing she'd learned during her time at Veritas Corp, however, was that there were different *kinds* of incompetence.

Glancing into the first tent, she shook her head. The place was filthy, with dirty clothes and used food containers lying around haphazardly. In the next tent, she found rich furs on the bed, and a uniform that looked like it might actually be made out of silk. The third tent, however, was the jackpot.

A man still lay in the bed, his blanket pulled up over his head, and only his pale, clean hands visible where they clutched at the cloth. The space itself was tidy and clean, and a full, proper uniform hung neatly from the crossbar at the peak of the roof. Polished boots sat at the bottom of the bed, precisely lined up, heels touching just so.

This was Rouge's least favorite kind of ineffectual middle-manager. He would follow all the rules as exactly as he could, as long as they didn't actually inconvenience him too much. He would call others out for things that he himself did, or to cover up his own inadequacies, but refuse to acknowledge *his* failures in any way. He hid behind his perfectly coiffed hair and his spit-shined boots, hoping that a perfect outer appearance would conceal the hollow shell of a man inside. He was completely predictable, and perfect for her plan.

Silently, she crept into the tent, trusting in the early hour and her own [Stealth] to keep the man in the bed utterly unaware of her presence. Closing her fingers around a single small item, she grinned, stretched out a finger to just brush the back of the sleeping man's hand, and then slipped noiselessly back out.

As soon as Rouge was clear of the camp, she broke 'radio silence'. She'd been afraid that she might be distracted if she was talking to Silus, so she'd asked the bat to only contact her if it was urgent and related to the mission. Now, though, ::Silus! I've got it! Where's the caravan?::

::Yay!:: Silus sounded as excited as Rouge, and the little bat winged down out of the gray sky a moment later. Rouge was already mounted on Codswallop, who had been doing his bush impersonation just outside the theoretical limits of the sentries. Theoretical because the night guards had gone to bed, and the day guards were either still eating breakfast or not even awake yet, as far as

Rouge and Silus could tell.

::Aspen is feeding the animals mana like it's candy. They're really moving fast. The wagon wheels are all going to break off if he doesn't slow down.:: Silus sounded genuinely worried, and Rouge stroked her big ears reassuringly.

::You know Aspen. I bet he reinforced the wheels or something first. They'll slow down after they're in the pass. How long do we have?::

Silus nuzzled Rouge's hand. ::Half an hour or so, I think. I don't really know how well humans can see, but if it was me, I'd be able to see them from the tower in around thirty minutes. Then it'll probably take another thirty minutes before they're completely through, even at the speed they're moving.::

Rouge thought about the object she'd stolen from the officer's tent. It was just a small thing, but it could make all the difference between success and failure.

Hand-carved Button **– This wooden button is one of a set carved for First Lieutenant Majors by Artisan Crosscut of Bright.** *Weight - .1oz. Rarity - Unique*

One thing a lot of people forgot was that item rarity didn't always track with item value. A mass-produced solid gold statue was likely to be worth some money, but was also Common or Unusual rarity at best. On the other hand, a corn-husk doll hand-made by a mother for her child was probably Unique, but worth nothing to anyone except mother and child. For Rouge's current purpose, the only thing that mattered was the rarity, not the value, so an individually crafted button was perfect.

Rouge pulled up her spell list as Codswallop ran toward the guard tower, which was supposed to be only about a half mile away. Wally was following Silus, who was flying ahead of them on her swift little wings, so Rouge could afford a moment of inattention.

[Substitution]. You may take on the outward appearance of any sapient you have touched within the last hour. Duration up to fifteen minutes. Spell can be canceled voluntarily, or if you are attacked. *Skill [Steal] found. Skills may be used in concert. If you are able to [Steal] an item from your target, the duration of [Substitution] will be increased depending on the Rarity of the stolen item. You must keep the item with you in order to use this Skill boost. This boost will end when the theft is discovered, leaving a maximum of fifteen minutes remaining on the Skill.*

Fifteen minutes wasn't long enough to distract the guards for the entire time the caravan was within their sight. However, Rouge had been leveling up the spell for the last few days (by [Stealing] things from members of the caravan, and then wandering around as them), and she had discovered that even an Uncommon item could as much as double her time, depending on its level. Unfortunately, level was a hidden stat, and only a person with the [Examine] skill ranked up to Master could see it, so the only way she was going to find out her little button's level was by using it.

All of which meant that she was depending primarily on the fact that the wooden trinket was Unique. She'd snagged a few Unique items (mostly from the kids, who had to make their own stuff, but she always gave it back when she was done with it), and they added a minimum of half an hour to her spell duration. So, fifteen minutes, plus thirty minutes, plus 5% from Lyrec's buff...

Forty-seven minutes? Ish? She had to start her plan *before* the caravan came on the scene, but not too much before, which was where Silus came in. With her little friend's help, Rouge should be able to time this well enough to be in and out while she was still under the influence of the spell. If she was right about the kind of person First Lieutenant Majors was, the tower staff would never even know they'd been tricked. If she was wrong, however, and Majors was actually a competent officer, she might have to settle for a partial success, and just knock the guards out in order to delay the inevitable as much as possible.

The tower was clearly visible now, which meant that the watchmen should be able to see her, too, though not clearly enough to distinguish more than a figure on a horse. Thanks to Wally's newly acquired [Confabulation] skill, anyone who saw him had a 95% chance of thinking he was just a really ugly horse. Unless, of course, someone in that tower had an Intelligence higher than one hundred twenty, but Rouge was pretty sure she was safe on that front.

::How's it looking, Silus?::

Rouge slowed Wally to a walk and Silus flew up higher, rapidly shrinking to nothing more than a speck in the sky. ::They're coming in fast. You have about… twenty minutes? Maybe a little less.::

Rouge nodded. ::Okay. Can you stay up there until they're clear?::

The little bat sounded uncertain, but said, ::I… Yes, I can. It's mostly just gliding. As long as there aren't any hawks or anything.::

Rouge swallowed hard at the idea of her friend being chased by a relentless hunter of the sky. That was exactly why Aspen rarely used Silus as a scout during the day. The bat was basically defenseless against flying predators, and her dark copper fur would make her stand out in stark relief in an empty sky, at least to any hungry birds looking for prey.

::If you even catch a glimpse of anything coming after you, Silus, just run. Head for the caravan or Wally, whichever is closer. We'll just have to do our best from there. Got it?::

::Got it.:: Silus sounded both relieved and worried, which was fair enough, because Rouge felt the same way. Swallowing hard, Rouge triggered [Substitution].

You have cast [Substitution: Lv3]. You now appear to anyone viewing you as the sapient being <u>Lieutenant Majors</u>. This illusion will last 52.5 minutes (15 base + 35 minutes for Lv.2 Unique item *Hand-carved*

Button **+ 2.5 minutes for *Extended Duration* buff.) If your theft is discovered while you have more than 15 minutes remaining on your illusion, time will be reduced to a maximum of 15 minutes. Spell will be canceled if you take damage or if someone with a high enough [Illusion Break] skill attempts to Identify you.**

Fifty-two minutes! Yes! Hopefully, she only needed forty-five, so the 'extra' seven minutes would allow her to finish up her mission with a neat and tidy little bow. ::We have fifty minutes, Silus. We can do it!::

Silus' little mental whoop made her grin.

🦔 🦔 🦔

As Rouge pulled Codswallop to a stop outside the tower, two men were already standing outside waiting. Rouge climbed down from the saddle in as dignified a manner as she could, carefully brushing at her clothes as soon as her feet touched the ground. She looped Wally's reins over the hitching post nearby, ignoring the rolling eyes of the horses already hitched there, who were well aware that their new companion wasn't the small-headed, barrel-chested equine he appeared.

By the time Rouge turned to the two men, who had saluted her as soon as she came into view, and were still standing there, stiff as boards, they were starting to sweat. Rouge scowled. "The Captain sent me to do an inspection. Which one of you messed up and attracted his attention?"

Taller Man gave Short Guy some side-eye, and Rouge turned her glare on him. "Drop and give me twenty."

The two men exchanged glances, and then Short Guy said, "Uh, what? Sir?"

Darn! Looked like that wasn't a thing in *Veritas* Online. Rouge noticed that they were both still holding the salute, and belatedly realized that she probably had to do something in response. What? Salute? Tip her hat? Wave at them dismissively?

She went for the salute, making it the snappiest one she could manage, thanks to the military flicks her dad watched every now and then. The two dropped their hands with relief, and Short Guy said again, "What? Sir?"

Rouge started to suppress a growl, and then decided to let it go. Both men flinched. "You've never done a push-up, soldier?" She desperately wished she had any clue what the two pointy stripes on their uniforms meant, so she could call them by their ranks, but at least she *did* know they were both mostly out of uniform. She reached out and flicked the open button at Short Guy's throat. "What is *this*?"

He reached up and clutched his shirt closed like a Victorian maiden caught out wandering in her negligee. "It makes me feel like I'm choking if I close it up all the way, Lieutenant." His voice was a nasal whine that was already starting to grate on her nerves, and she wondered how his fellow soldiers stood it without throttling him.

She leaned in close, like the drill sergeants on old vids. "*Then choke*," she growled, and the man paled.

Turning, she walked to the door of the tower, throwing it open and striding inside. A wave of musty body odor assaulted her nose, and she felt sick for at least the third time in the last hour. Waving her hand in front of her nose, she yelled, "When was the last time you cleaned this place?"

The two men, who had scurried in after her, and now stood blinking stupidly in the swirling dust, just looked at each other and shrugged. "I... don't know? Sir?" Taller Man finally said.

She clapped her hands together sharply. "Get to it, then! I want this room shining like, um," she hesitated, since 'the top of the Chrysler building' wouldn't make any sense to these two village idiots. "My boots," she finished lamely, but the two just cast despairing glances at Rouge's feet (which to her still looked like her usual soft cloth boots, but to them would look like Lieutenant Majors' spit-shined black leather footwear) and scurried off, presumably to find cleaning implements.

Rouge looked around the dim room. There were no windows, and the only light came from a single glowstone and the open door. Two cabinets stood off to the side, and their open doors showed a haphazard mess of half-eaten rations and piled water skins. "I want an inventory of your supplies, too!" She shouted this into the air, since Tall and Short were nowhere to be seen, but she had a feeling that writing anything down would take them the rest of the day, so that was all right.

Turning, she looked at the winding stairs leading upwards. There was a heavy wooden hatch at the top of the first full turn, but it was also open, and looked a little crooked, like maybe it had broken and had never been fixed, just leaned up against the wall. She set her foot on the first step, and it creaked loudly. Well, at least no one would be able to sneak up on the person or people above, at least not without an excellent [Stealth] skill.

Martialing her courage, Rouge marched up the stairs, keeping her steps even and confident. After all, Lieutenant Majors had every right to be here, and *she* was Lieutenant Majors, right? Still, she winced a little as her head cleared the hatch to the area above. That would be the perfect moment for someone waiting there to simply remove her head from her neck with a single stroke, and she could almost picture the surprised expression on her own face as the two parts of her body parted ways.

Nothing happened, however, except that a third man snapped her a salute, holding it until she returned the gesture. This soldier had a hard face and a tidy uniform, and his eyes were calculating as he looked her up and down. A small sneer touched the corner of his lips so quickly she almost missed the expression, but she'd been expecting it, and almost felt relief that things were going as she'd anticipated.

::Rouge! The caravan is going to go over the last hill any second. They'll be fully visible after that.:: Silus' voice was a little frantic, and it was all Rouge could do to keep her gaze from shooting over to the northwest, where the wagons were coming from. With a valiant effort, she kept her eyes locked onto the watchman's, and forced a scowl to her lips.

"What the hell is that, soldier?"

The guard's gaze turned toward the open view surrounding them, and Rouge shot out her hand, pointing at his boots. They were clean but visibly scuffed, and the hems of his pants were frayed and worn. "*That!*" she said curtly. "Your uniform needs repair, and your boots are absolutely disgraceful! What do you do with your time, soldier? You lot just stand here staring at grass all day. There's no excuse for the disgusting condition of your duty station or the state of your uniforms!"

You have learned the skill [Intimidation]. [Intimidation] successful. Your [Acting] skill is now level 3.

The soldier winced and looked guilty. He tucked one toe behind his other foot, as if trying to hide the condition of his footwear. Rouge forged ahead. "Where is your boot polish, soldier? If you're sitting up here with nothing to do, you might as well buff those shoes!"

"Ah, I don't... I don't have any polish, sir. I'm sorry, sir!" The man snapped another salute, this time dropping his hand right away, and Rouge had to force her hand to stay at her side. She had a feeling this wasn't a 'salute back' kind of a situation.

"Do you have a cloth and some spit, soldier? It's not much, but it'll have to do. Now get to it!"

The man hesitated, eyes darting toward the skyline, and then he saluted once more and scurried down below. Rouge hesitated, wondering if she was pushing her luck, but then shouted down, "Help those two miserable excuses for soldiers clean up while you're down there! I'll keep an eye out up here, in case a rabbit with particularly sharp teeth decides to hop by."

Crossing quietly to the edge of the open room, Rouge glanced toward the stairwell and then looked toward the northwest. Sure enough, the small but distinct shapes of carts were moving quickly to the east. A tall flagpole marked the beginning of the only known pass through the mountains, and the caravan was heading straight for it. It was obvious even from here that they were moving unnaturally quickly, and Rouge desperately prayed to Gina that no wheels or axles broke while they were visible and so very vulnerable.

The creak of the wooden stairs warned her she was about to have company, and she moved back to the southwest side of the tower, staring out toward the encampment around the contaminated watering hole. From here, it still looked peaceful, and she wondered if she'd ever know what the results of her little experiment were.

Competent Guy came up the stairs, eyes darting around. Even though Rouge was sure he couldn't see anything from the top of the stairwell, she'd still be happier if he wasn't up here at all. "What part of 'help them clean' did you not understand, soldier?"

The man gestured toward a small mound of rocks off to one side. Rouge had thought they were there to be thrown down on attackers below, but now that she focused, she could see trails of smoke staining the air around them. "It's time to send the 'All's Well', sir. Unless you want to do it?"

Rouge hesitated, then wrinkled her nose. "And get the stench of smoke in my clothes? I think not." She waved dismissively. "Do it, and then get back down below."

The man nodded, then went over to the rocks. He picked up a hooked metal implement from behind the stacked stones, and used it to pull out a metal grate that had been hidden down inside the pile. Instantly, the trickle of smoke turned into a flood, and Rouge and the man both went into fits of coughing. Quickly, the soldier pulled a bag of something from a pouch at his waist, and tossed it into the hole. The smoke pouring out thickened and turned an emerald green that made Rouge blink. Using the hook and the grate, the man created several puffs of the colorful smoke that lifted to float in remarkably cohesive clouds above the tower.

Finally, as the green shade was fading, the soldier dropped the grate back down onto the rocks, where it clattered into place. He covered his mouth and nose with a cloth and blinked streaming eyes at Rouge. "I'll just," he choked out, "go back down then, sir."

She nodded, her own burning eyes squinting against tears, and waved at him dismissively. Whatever was in the pouch that made the smoke green was caustic, and Rouge wondered how anyone could stand doing that on a regular basis. It probably explained why the camp had grown up so far away, though. Not only was the water there, but they wouldn't get a whiff of that smoke even when the wind blew in their direction.

The coughing soldier disappeared, and Rouge could just make out the sounds of voices from below. The few words she could catch sounded like employees complaining about bosses everywhere, so she let her attention drift as she pulled up the countdown timer on her skill. Nearly half an hour left, so there should be no problems as long as…

Your theft has been discovered! Time remaining on [Substitution: Lv3] reduced to fifteen minutes!

Rouge cursed under her breath, then looked around guiltily as if her dad was going to pop up from nowhere and threaten to wash her mouth out with soap. ::Silus! How are they doing?::

Silus sounded tired. ::The first of the wagons has just entered the pass. They have to go in one at a time because it's so narrow, so they slowed down a little, but they're still moving along. I think they'll be through in ten minutes or so.::

Rouge puffed out a sigh of relief. They were ahead of schedule, so she could still pull this off. She peered down through the hole into the smoky dimness below. There was no movement, much less any cleaning going on, so she jogged to the side of the tower to peer down toward the door. She could see that it was still wide open, and all three soldiers were standing there. Tall was sweeping the doorstep in a very unmotivated fashion, while Short leaned against the wall scratching his... well, he was scratching. Only Competent looked like he was really trying at all, and he was sitting on a stool out of range of Tall's dust cloud as he repeatedly spat into a dirty rag and then rubbed futilely at his boots.

Rouge spent the next ten minutes going back and forth from staring at the men below, to watching her clock, and then scurrying over to glance at the disappearing caravan. She broke up this fun little dance by peppering Silus with requests for updates, until even the sweet-natured little bat started to sound slightly cross. Finally, though, Silus said, ::That's it, Rouge! They're through! I'm heading back toward the caravan. I'll meet you there.::

Rouge pumped a fist, then brushed off her clothes and hurried down the creaking stairs. Tall and Short had moved back inside as soon as the smoke cleared, and Tall was reorganizing the pantry in slightly neater stacks, while Short sat at the small table eating something that somehow managed to both crunch and squish at the same time. Rouge stared at both of the men until Short noticed her and nearly knocked over the chair he was sitting in as he scrambled to her feet.

"Did you finish that inventory?" They shook their heads, and she looked around disdainfully, taking in the dust on the tables and cabinets, which, to their credit, did look like it might have been disturbed a little. The floor definitely looked better, so she shot Tall a look that might have passed for approval. "Well, get to work, and turn it in to the quartermaster next time you're in Vargo. It's clear that this place needs to be restocked. Now, where's-" she broke off, realizing that she had no idea what Competent's name was.

"Corporal Payne, sir? He's still trying to polish his boots, sir." Tall said, and Rouge made a mental note that two pointy stripes meant corporal.

Rouge looked at her countdown timer. Four and a half minutes. Time to get out of Dodge. "Fine. This is a start at least, and I haven't had breakfast yet."

She offered a small, conspiratorial smile. "I'll tell the Captain you *barely* passed your inspection, and you make sure it's true by the next time anyone comes out here. That way, we won't have to talk about this again, right, Corporal?"

Tall winced but gave her another salute. "Yes, sir!" A moment later, Short followed suit, with an obnoxiously obsequious tone to his, "Yes, sir!" Rouge nodded and stepped outside.

There was Corporal Payne, and she wondered with a stifled giggle if he had aspirations to be Major Payne someday. As she firmly closed the door behind her, the corporal looked up, then shot to his feet, dropping his now-gleaming boot into the dust. He winced a little as he threw her a salute.

Rouge tried to look as calm as possible as she crossed to Codswallop. She'd used a loose knot on his reins so that he could get free himself if things went haywire, but it looked like someone had gotten a little too helpful and retied him more tightly. It took precious seconds to untie him, and by the time she did, she only had a little over a minute left. She settled her foot in his stirrup and swung up onto her Battle Ostrich's back.

"Next time you're in Vargo, go see the quartermaster and get those boots and pants replaced, Corporal." She shot a glance at the closed door, and gave the soldier a sympathetic smile. The character she was portraying wasn't one for the warmer emotions, so she kept it small and brief. "I can see you're doing your best with what you have to work with. I think we can let this all slide for today. You did your duty, and I did mine, eh?"

At the corporal's vigorous nod, she snapped off a final salute, nudging Codswallop around with her knee. The soldier was still saluting as she rode away, the red numbers on her skill timer dropping into single digits.

Chapter Twenty-seven

Khor

The dungeon seed spent most of its time bundled up in a bag made of web, hanging in the kitchen among matching bags filled with onions and garlic. No one would ever guess that something worth a king's ransom would be surrounded by root vegetables, which made it an excellent hiding place.

Now, however, the thing was sitting on a half-built stone wall around the little herb garden that Sarave had planted near the house. The shifting crystals cut their way out of their container every three or four days, and then Sarave dropped the thing next to Sumi like the hot potato it almost was. This time, Sumi had woken to find it lying on the table at the foot of Gina's little statue, as if it were an offering that Sarave hoped the goddess would take away.

<What do we do with it?> Khor gloomily asked. Again.

<Nothing. We wait for Aspen.> Sumi answered, rather sharply, since this was the same answer she'd given a hundred times before.

<He can't use it.>

<I am well aware of that.>

<He's a human.>

<I *know*, Khor.>

Khor huffed a sigh and looked at the thing longingly. He wasn't sure exactly why it drew him so strongly. Logically, he knew that however amazing, perfect, and stunning a goat dungeon would be to him, it probably wouldn't be Aspen's first choice. Plus, Khor didn't actually want to be a dungeon boss. While he would get all kinds of power boosts, it also meant that he would never again be able to leave the confines of his dungeon. *And*, if someone somehow managed to steal the dungeon core once it grew from the dungeon seed, they could kill him and all of his goats simply by crushing the stone.

So, he didn't want anything to do with the seed.

And yet he did.

Every time the thing dropped out of its little pouch, and Sarave brought it to Sumi so she could wrap it up again, he felt called to it. Until the moment it vanished into its silken bag again, he couldn't pull his eyes away.

<Who do you think he'll give it to?> he asked. Again.

Sumi did her 'I don't really sigh, but I want you to know how tiresome I find your questions' mental sigh. <I've already answered this.>

<Sarave.>

<Yes, Sarave.>

Khor sighed. A real sigh, with air puffing deeply out of real lungs. <That's probably for the best.> He knew he sounded dismal, but he couldn't help it. If Sarave or, possibly, Nekthadt, became the dungeon boss, they would create a goblin dungeon. A home for people whose home was destroyed so long ago that no one even remembered where it had originally been. No matter how much Sarave protested that she didn't want to be a dungeon boss, he knew she'd be a good one. Even though it meant the place would be *crawling* with goblins.

<Why not me?> He asked plaintively. <Or you? You're smart and sneaky, so you'd be good at it. People hate spiders, too, so no one would want to go there.>

<Thank you so much,> Sumi said dryly. <That's always nice to hear. It won't be me for the same reason it won't be you. We're Aspen's. Down to our souls, we belong to him. Even if the master-servant bond was cut when he left Atae's service, we can never be anything but his. Even if it would accept us, which I doubt, we'd have to leave Aspen, and I won't do that. Would you?>

<He could move into the dungeon, too,> he said, a little too eagerly. <We could make him a nice house, even a farming area, if that's what he wants. Cut it off from the rest of the dungeon, so the adventurers couldn't find it.>

Another sigh. <That's not how it works, old goat. There are rules. We don't know all of them, since dungeon bosses don't generally spend a lot of time chatting with the people trying to kill them, but there are some books. I do know that one of the rules is that all parts of the dungeon must be accessible to adventurers at all times. If Aspen was in the dungeon, he would be in constant danger.>

<Then so would the goblins, if they lived there!> Khor was triumphant.

<Which is why Sarave doesn't want it. It would create a home for her people, but at the same time, they would constantly be at risk. Not that they're not at risk now.> The spider's voice was melancholy. <It's something I understand too well. People don't like goblins or spiders, and they tend to kill us on sight.>

Khor had a sudden realization that this was, indeed, something that both Sumi and Sarave could understand. Aside from them being female and intelligent, he hadn't really been able to figure out why they became such good friends. It did make sense, though, that since each of them were often judged by their race or species instead of themselves, perhaps they were a little more likely to look past that in others.

He shook his head, snorting. Enough introspection. <Put it away,> he said grumpily. <It's practically hypnotic. Send it back to Sarave, and remind her not to try to put it in a soup this time.>

Sumi clicked her fangs in a quiet chuckle, and began weaving a new bag around the too-appealing rock. Once the last bit of cobalt-blue crystal vanished behind a soft white web, Khor was finally able to look away. Sumi stuck the bag to her foreleg with a bit of web and headed for the house. Khor trailed morosely behind her.

<When do you think Aspen will be back?>

<When he's back,> she answered, vanishing inside the house. He heard rustling as she tucked the pouch in amongst the onions and garlic and leeks.

Mmmm, leeks... He shook his head again. <Soon, though?>

<When. He's. Back.> Sumi said firmly, reemerging into the light. <Aren't you supposed to be working in a field, hauling ore for William, or guarding the Tree?>

<The fields are clear, we already plowed the ones we have enough seeds for, we shifted the irrigation system to the dry fields, and William is asleep,> he listed off smugly.

<Are Nekthadt and Nuisance planting?>

<Nekthadt is.> Nuisance had been busy with ducklings ever since the little brown and tan balls of fluff had hatched a few days earlier. While the duck had seemed rather embarrassed to have helped produce the new generation, he seemed equally delighted to teach his offspring everything he knew about the world. Perhaps it was the fact that the ducklings were even more ground-bound than he was, but he happily led them all over the farm,

and the sight of the proud father followed by a train of eleven peeping hatchlings was now a common one. Fortunately, the mothers, Rowen and Claire, seemed just as happy to be done with their egg-sitting days, and gleefully left the child-rearing to Nuisance.

<Sarave and the children?>

<Sarave said it was laundry day. I hauled all the clothes down to the river this morning, and the unicorns are playing in the water while Sarave teaches Juniper how to wash.> Left unsaid was the fact that the little half-goblin girl would be more hindrance than help, but that was the nature of parenting, it seemed. Khor was just as glad he'd never had to deal with kids of his own.

<Shouldn't you go check on them?>

<Sarave said they'd bathe after the laundry, and I should come back before dusk. She took a picnic lunch, too.>

<Khor,> Sumi said firmly. <Go away. I need rest, and I need to read through the books to see if there's any more information about dungeon seeds.>

Khor's tail swished in irritation. <Fine. It's not like I wanted to talk to you anyway.> Without further ado, he trotted off, leaving the spider to her reading.

🕷 🕷 🕷

The Tree's fruit was almost ripe now. Dozens of fruits, of all colors and shapes, dangled from branches that bowed beneath their weight. There were fruits that looked like apples, in every shade from green to red. There were fruits that looked like bananas, but there were purple and green ones amidst the more common yellows. Golden-hued starfruit hung beside pseudo-strawberries and mock paw-paws.

Every time Khor entered the Tree's area of effect, and the heady scent of lemons, peaches, and warm plums entered his nostrils, he began to drool.

He was fairly certain that if Aspen didn't come home soon, Khor would die of dehydration while on guard duty. It was a struggle every day to refrain from nibbling at the tantalizing display, and if Khor hadn't known that Aspen's quest required that he eat the first fruit, there would probably be no fruit left.

Frankly, with the number of creatures that were drawn by the smell and the powerful aura of magic that surrounded the Tree, Khor wasn't certain how much longer it would be before something got through. Sumi had rebuilt all of her webs, and Sarave and Nekthadt had erected a scaffold around the Tree so that webs could be strung all around its heavy branches. There were two bee-sized holes on the side facing the hive, but otherwise, nothing could get closer to the Tree than about fifteen feet.

Including Khor. Which was probably all for the best.

Everyone agreed, though, that Aspen needed to *hurry up*.

When Khor trotted into the meadow, carefully avoiding the pit-traps that were marked only by the single white flower that grew on a sort of hidden pedestal in the middle (the rest of the surface was covered in webs and grass), Viqa looked up. Jesiqa was in a skin-tight water bubble on her mother's shoulder, as she often was, and Khor was amazed at how quickly the young glyphis was growing, now that she was in the right environment and eating the right food.

Viqa acknowledged his entry with a single nod, as she usually did, but Jesiqa looked up and smiled, baring rows of tiny, needle-sharp teeth. The glyphis child's true personality was beginning to emerge, and she was far friendlier and more talkative - now that her gills weren't in danger of drying out – than any of her family members. It seemed that she, too, had some talent as a water mage, though she had been entirely untrained. It was this innate talent as well as Nekthadt's care that had allowed her to survive as long as she had.

Khor nonchalantly grabbed a mouthful of grass, trying to act as if he was just there by happenstance. Chewing lazily, he walked over toward the pair of glyphis. As soon as he was close enough, Jesiqa formed a shaky, dripping ball of water around herself and used it to transport her small body over to Khor's withers. Settling in, she released the water, which doused his fur, making him shudder. Khor snorted as if in irritation, but truthfully the cool water was pleasant on such a warm day.

Gleefully, Jesiqa tugged at his fur. Her mother looked over once, a small frown on her face, and Khor knew Viqa would not be pleased if he took the little girl out of her sight. Understandable enough, since the child had been snatched away while playing hide and seek with her older brother. Though the parents had not blamed the brother, the boy had blamed himself, and had apparently become quite withdrawn until Jesiqa returned. Now, the boy, whose name was Taqi, was usually somewhere near his sister, though Khor didn't see him today.

Khor began a gentle walk around the Tree. Jesiqa tugged at his fur, trying to urge him to go faster, but he was concerned that she was still small and weak, and she could slip from even his broad back. When the brush edging the Tree's meadow rustled, he looked up sharply, but it was just Taqi and some of the small, hooved herbivores, which Sumi had identified as Lesser Vicuña.

At first, Khor dismissed the new arrivals as innocuous, and then he noticed something very strange. Taqi, who, thanks to the trauma of losing his little sister, always watched the girl with an almost desperately anxious expression, hadn't even looked at Jesiqa. Also, he was walking in the midst of the three little vicuña instead of veering off toward his mother or sister.

The eyes of all four of the newcomers were locked on the Tree. They walked nearly shoulder to shoulder in an oddly synchronized way, and yet their movements were also too loose when they swung their legs, then jerky as their knees locked before they seemed to almost lift half their bodies and swing the joint free again.

As a sense of alarm began to rise, Khor caught sight of five Greater Bees flying in from the other side of the meadow. Their hive was behind him, and it was very rare indeed to see the bees fly in any way except the most efficient route. These bees, in fact, were flying almost as erratically as the boy and the vicuña were walking. They darted up and then overcompensated into a downward dive. One wing beat more quickly than the other, sending them into a circle before they brought themselves back into line.

All nine of the newly arrived creatures were heading directly for the Tree. Khor raised his head and bugled his loudest call. He didn't know exactly what was going on, but he was certain of one thing.

The Tree was under attack.

Khor turned as he entered the small crowd of newcomers, attempting to block them with his body without actually hurting them. He felt several impacts as the glyphis and two of the vicuña hit his belly and legs, bouncing off awkwardly. The last vicuña ducked its head and simply walked under him, the top of her head bumping into his chest with each step.

Viqa was coming now, and her expression clearly showed her confusion and distress. To her, it must seem that Khor was randomly blocking innocent creatures as well as her own son. Khor hesitated, looking down at the fallen figures beside him. The boy was struggling to his feet, face disturbingly blank, while the two fuzzy quadrupeds were still tangled in their own slim legs. Meanwhile, the third vicuña was still moving toward the Tree with increasing confidence and speed.

Khor looked desperately toward Viqa, using his eyes to look between the furry intruder and the oncoming bees, who were now swerving around so that they could enter the little bee-tunnel Sumi had left in the web encircling the Tree. Viqa laid her hand on her son's shoulder, ready to help him to his feet. He completely failed to acknowledge her, not even brushing the hand aside.

Khor grunted, then planted his hooves firmly and launched himself toward the bees. He heard a soft cry that sounded suspiciously like, "Whee!" as Jesiqa's fingers pulled hard on his fur. Then he was by the Tree, and he caught the first bee with a sweeping backward swing of his horns, flinging it as far as he could. The second and fourth bees met the same fate, and he snapped the fifth from the air with his mouth, feeling it buzz angrily. It stung his tongue and cheeks, and he ground the thing between his molars before spitting it out in a broken and slimy mess.

The third bee, however, was already halfway down the short tunnel. It bumped the nearly invisible walls once or twice, but Sumi had used non-sticky web for the passage, since she was concerned that a bee would catch a wing and be trapped, which could cause the rest of the bees to attack her when she went to release it. Khor stared after the insect helplessly, knowing that if he tried to chase after it, he would only manage to entangle himself.

Then small fingers wrapped in his fur again, and he felt two wet little feet trace a line of damp steps up his neck. Jesiqa stood on top of his head, and though he couldn't see her, he did see a very shaky, very drippy bubble of water form around the bee. Instantly, it dropped down to the bottom of the tunnel, its wet wings and fur weighing it down so that it thrashed helplessly. Flailing, the insect rolled out of the little tunnel entirely, passing through a gap in the web, and fell onto a sticky string which mummified the three-inch-long bug in moments.

With the Greater Bees now disposed of, at least for the moment, Khor turned back to Viqa and her son. When he did, he felt a shudder run from his withers to his hocks. The water mage was now also staring blankly toward the Tree. Her skin was darker than usual, and, looking closely, he could see that the fine film of water that usually protected the gills lining the sides of her throat was gone. Taqi, too, was struggling now that his mother was no longer keeping his gills wet, and both glyphis were beginning to gasp, their gills turning pale white.

All three of the vicuña were now thoroughly entangled in Sumi's webs, and their struggles were tearing great holes in the protective barrier. At the edge of the meadow, Khor could see the rest of the vicuña. A rustle drew his attention to the bramble to the north, and he turned just in time to see Sarave emerge into the meadow. The goblin was covered in scratches, with long lines of blood gleaming in the sunlight, but no pain showed on her face. Instead, her eyes, one of which was already swelling shut over a particularly vicious tear across her cheekbone, were fixed on the Tree.

Letting out a despairing bleat, Khor looked back and forth between the glyphis, who were quite possibly dying, and the goblin, who was headed straight for the gap in the web around the Tree.

<Go to Sarave, Khor.> Sumi's voice, a hint of fear underlying its usual calm pragmatism, intruded into his mind. <I'll take care of the glyphis, at least for now. We need to keep the Tree safe until we can figure out what's going on.>

Khor glanced to his left, only now seeing the spider making her way through the tall grass. At the sight, he felt as if a great weight had been lifted from his chest, but he only sent back, <Took you long enough,> before heading toward the goblin woman.

On his head, little fingers pulled hard at his fur. A breathy voice whispered in his ear, "Ma. Ma," but he couldn't look back. Sarave was coming, faster than any of the others, and if she had come first, he didn't know that he would have noticed anything strange about her other than her apparent immunity to pain.

This time it was an actual weight that lifted from his shoulders, as

Jesiqa used her magic to lower herself to the ground. He could see the small figure, no more than two feet tall, struggling through the grass on legs unaccustomed to bearing her weight. The sun caught a wet glimmer around her neck, and he felt a flash of relief at realizing that she must be able to maintain her own water-barrier now, though he doubted she could do it all day like her mother.

Lowering his head, Khor pushed his thick skull against Sarave's chest, bracketing her with his horns. When she tried to bend down and go under his horns, he turned his head so that the horn on that side trailed through the grass and brushed the ground. With a hiss of frustration, the first sound he'd heard any of the possessed make, Sarave turned to the other side, but he quickly adjusted so that she remained trapped.

<I have the others wrapped up. I put Spider Milk on some webs over the glyphis' gills, and it seems to be helping. We need to get them to water soon, though.> Sumi appeared in the grass beside him, and then she looped web around Sarave's legs so that the goblin woman dropped to her knees. Sumi continued, wrapping her friend in layers of webbing until only her face was visible. The blank and staring yellow eyes were still locked on the Tree.

Khor looked around. All of the vicuña were down and wrapped, while the glyphis seemed to be too weak to continue their advance. Jesiqa was just visible next to her mother, her wispy dark hair dropping forward into her face as she held her hands out, touching the throats of her family members.

<What happened?> demanded Sumi, quickly climbing up Khor's leg so that she could stand on his back. Someday he would need to spend some time thinking about why everyone seemed to like sitting on him, but now was not that time.

Reminded, Khor looked around, easily spotting the thing he'd been afraid of. <I don't know,> he responded harshly, <but you need to block the bee tunnel. The bees are coming.>

Indeed, they were. Workers, drones, and warriors, all gathered together in a mass that rivaled the one he'd seen when the Queen Bee had swarmed. Fortunately, he didn't see the Queen herself, so either whatever-it-was hadn't infected her, or she just hadn't made her way here yet. In any case, if the mass of bees reached the tunnel, or even the torn-up part of the web, some of them would definitely make it through.

Sumi muttered a few choice words they'd learned when they were in the military, and got to work. Sticky webbing flew through the air, and the spider's back legs worked as rapidly as he'd ever seen them. Khor himself simply stood there, unsure what to do. The bees were too small and too numerous for him to be effective against them. The rest of the captives were innocent, as far as he could tell. If he had had to guess, he would have said there was a soul mage nearby using forbidden magic to control them, but from what he'd learned while working with Manuela, soul magic only worked on sapient beings. Animals and insects were a whole different branch of magic. Soul magic, then, could explain what was happening to Sarave and the glyphis, but not the bees and the vicuña.

Sumi had entangled most of the cloud of bees by now, and only a few stragglers were still stiffly struggling through the air. Khor was just beginning to think they might have things under control when the bushes parted again, revealing a massive Greater Bear, easily twelve feet tall. The great black bear galloped toward the Tree, eyes locked on its branches, completely ignoring everything else in the meadow.

Time seemed to slow. Khor knew that even if he could reach the bear before the bear reached the Tree, it was entirely possible that the huge creature, with its greater reach, sharp teeth, and long claws, would be able to defeat even him. If Khor went down, who would protect the Tree? Who would protect the children? Was the Tree more important than the children, in the long run? What would Aspen want Khor to do?

A whistle split the air, and then a quivering bolt sprang from the back of the bear's skull. The beast groaned, collapsing forward. It struggled momentarily before falling still. Khor turned to face the direction the crossbow bolt must have come from, and found himself staring into the bright blue eyes of an elf. She sat on a white horse, calmly reloading her bow. She pulled the string one-handed, her muscles tight but easy beneath a cerulean blouse that matched her eyes.

Without hesitation, the woman lifted the crossbow, and Khor tensed as its point briefly tracked across his body. With a loud *twang*, the string released, and the bolt whistled as it raced across the meadow, passing over his shoulder to thunk into something behind him.

Without removing his eyes from the elf, Khor kicked out backwards. He felt his hooves sink deep into some warm, hairy mass. The flesh gave way, and his [Rear Kick] sent whatever it was stumbling backwards. Turning. Khor saw that a large Lesser Hog was down on its side, two hoof-prints already beginning to bleed into the grass. With a quick leap, Khor brought his full weight down on the pig, feeling bones crack beneath the blow. He gracefully stepped down, sweeping his gaze over the meadow as he did.

Sumi was done trapping bees, and had two Lesser Hares, three Doves, and no less than seven Greater Hedgehogs at least partially wrapped. Two of the pit traps had been sprung as well, though Khor couldn't tell what manner of creature might have fallen into the holes below. The elf had put away her crossbow, and was now laying about her with a long, shining sword. Deer and Squirrels fell beneath her blows, and then Juniper was dashing out into the field, and the elf was spurring her horse toward the little girl.

Khor threw himself forward, crushing two Marmosets, a Lesser Copperhead, and a Greater Fox beneath his hooves. He body-blocked the woman's mount, and her sword laid open his shoulder, though he could feel her pull the blow at the last moment. Hot blood soaked his fur, and he bleated in pain, but Juniper was safe, and the little girl fell into the grass beside her mother. The child was nearly as scratched up as Sarave, having no doubt followed the same path, but her face was frightened and sad, not blank.

Juniper looked up at Khor, huge tears coursing down her cheeks. Slightly cleaner tracks through the dirt on her face showed that this wasn't the first time she had cried today. "I don' know what happened, Khow! We were havin' a picnic, and then this big bug flew in mama's mouth! She choked like she ate too big of a bite, and then she jus' got up and started runnin'! I called after her, but she didn't stop, an' she never leaved us alone by the river before!"

The flood of invaders had slowed a bit now, and Sumi had drawn near enough to hear the child. The strange elf, too, was listening, and her face was even paler than it had been before, as she seemed to realize that she'd almost cut down an innocent. Her lips were pale and tight, and her white-blonde eyebrows drew together over the slim bridge of her nose as she asked, "A bug? Are you certain?"

Juniper nodded; her arms wrapped around her mother's sticky shoulders. The little girl was probably stuck as tightly now as her parent. Not that she noticed, since she seemed to have no intention of letting go.

"Bugs, bugs…" The elf was muttering to herself, eyes calculating even as she raised the bow she was suddenly once again holding and fired off a shot that took out an Elk who had been running toward the Tree. "Mind control, maybe?" She reloaded the crossbow, then fired again, hitting a Lesser Antelope in the shoulder.

Sumi was busy, too, jumping from one fallen form to the other, peering at their faces before wrapping them more tightly before moving on. <Look

at Sarave, Khor,> she sent back. <Do you see a red ring around her mouth? It may be hard to see this early, so look closely.>

Khor ground his teeth. <You know I don't see red very well,> he muttered, but leaned down so that his eyes were just in front of the goblin woman's face.

<Better than me,> the spider returned curtly.

<Maybe. It's darker around her mouth. It may be reddish.> Khor was frustrated. He should be killing invaders, not staring at a goblin's face. What was he supposed to do, though, when the invaders were his friends?

"Hive. Must be."

<It's the Hive.>

The spider and the elf spoke at the same moment, though it was only his sensitive ears that allowed him to hear the elf woman, since she seemed to be muttering to herself as she worked through the problem.

<Khor,> Sumi spoke urgently. <There must be a Hive Queen. You have to find her and kill her!>

<The Queen Bee?> He asked incredulously. The Greater Bees were the only bugs he'd been excluding from the insectophobia he'd been developing over the last several weeks.

<No.> Sumi sounded frustrated now, as she wrapped webbing around the legs and beak of Nuisance's lady friends, Rowen and Claire. <It'll look something like a bipedal ant or beetle, probably about four feet tall, covered in chitin, with a disproportionately large head and powerful jaws. It will...>

A *twang* came from the strange elf's crossbow, and the bolt whistled away. This was the first shot she'd made that seemed to be going astray, as it flew wide and over the head of a chubby Lesser Groundhog that was trundling its way through the grass. The bolt vanished into the branches of a tree near where the first Greater Bees had emerged. With a screech, a gleaming form crashed through the air, and all of the invading creatures, animal and insect alike, paused in their advance.

Tugging at the reins of her pale horse, the elf touched her heels to the mare's sides and clucked to it. Gracefully, the animal leapt over a Weasel that was wrapped up in Sumi's web. Following suit, Khor bounded toward the fallen thing, which he could now see was, indeed, a chitinous green bug-like thing with long mandibles bracketing an oddly round mouth set below its bulging black eyes.

It waved its hooked forelegs threateningly as it climbed to its feet. Its thorax was cracked open around the shaft of the bolt, and ichor poured steadily from the injury. A hiss came from its mouth, which irised open and closed rapidly, revealing hundreds of small, saw-like teeth. Just as a small, green bug began to crawl from the opening, Khor leapt forward, whirling in midair to deliver his finishing blow, [Roundhouse Kick] on either side of the fissure in its chest. The thorax split open, and bug guts cascaded from the wound. A moment later, the elf's sword whistled through the air, cleanly removing the head from the thing's narrow shoulders.

Around the meadow, the various creatures who had been attacking collapsed as though they were puppets whose strings had been cut.

With Sarave unconscious, Juniper had to serve as translator. The little girl's reading skills were shaky enough in her own language, and she knew only a few of Sumi's web-symbols. 'Dinner', for instance, and 'mother'. Fortunately, Sumi and Khor were able to get most of the story just by listening to Juniper talk to the woman, who turned out to be a Traveler named Doom Bloom.

Doom Bloom called the fallen people and creatures 'the Infected', and began to gather them together as she told her story to the still frightened little girl. The elf seemed to realize that her story was helping keep the child calm even though Sarave was as unresponsive as the rest. Jesiqa, too, was unsettled, though she was more skittish than Juniper, since she had long experience of the untrustworthiness of Travelers.

It turned out that Doom Bloom was Rouge's long-lost sister, which only made sense if you knew that Travelers chose the bodies they wore in Khor's world like most bipeds chose clothing. So, in spite of the fact that Rouge was half-wood elf and half-dark elf, and Doom Bloom was entirely high elf, in fact neither of them were any of those things, but, instead, wholly human. Thinking about it made Khor's head hurt, so he ignored it.

Apparently, Rouge had recently been captured by someone named FantumHat, who had tried to use her to get to Doom Bloom. Fortunately, Aspen and Motte Bailey had rescued the girl, but Doom Bloom had already returned to Quarternell and was readying herself to head for Bright by the time she got a message from Motte.

Doom Bloom had been in Vargo when her soul had returned to her world, and so she had rejoined her Zombie there at the Vargo Traveler's Guild. As she was preparing to travel south, Motte had contacted her and let her know the situation had been resolved, and that he, Aspen, and Rouge were heading for home along with a few others. Khor was desperately curious about these 'others', but Juniper's translation skills weren't up to the question, so the goat and the spider had to let the question go.

At this point, Doom Bloom mumbled something about 'vacation time' and 'new semester', and then said that she had had some time and so had decided to make her way north to the farm, since Rouge had told her where it was in hopes that she could someday join them there. The elf had fought her way through the pass, which had many more monsters than it had last time she had 'trained' in the area, and arrived, as they saw, in the nick of time.

As the small group of survivors stacked the last limp lemur beside its brethren, Doom Bloom fell silent. Almost instantly, tears began to trickle from beneath Juniper's lids again, and Khor felt two little hands wind themselves into the fur on his forelegs. When he looked down, he saw that he was standing near Viqa and Taqi, who were looking even paler than they had been before. Jesiqa was leaning on her mother's body, but was using Khor's fur to hide her frightened little face.

"Is... Is my mama gonna be okay?" Juniper choked out, her voice smaller and shakier than Khor had ever heard it before.

The tall elf woman reached out a hesitant hand, as if uncertain how to reassure the child. Sumi, however, inserted her body under Juniper's trembling fingers. Most people probably wouldn't have found the cold chitin and stiff bristles of a three-foot spider reassuring, but Juniper had grown up with the arachnid weaving her soft web slings and watching over her while Sarave worked. The little girl fell to her knees and wrapped her arms around Sumi's cephalothorax, while the elf watched bemusedly.

"I read about the Hive Queen once. It's a wandering Boss, so I never thought I'd see it, but it uses its offspring to take over the bodies of other creatures. It has a hive mind, so it can control as many beings as it has babies, but the more it takes over, the worse the control becomes. It was throwing everything it had at us, which is probably why we were able to beat it at all."

Doom Bloom tugged at the lobe of one long, pointed ear, looking conflicted. "The only thing I know that can drive out the Hive Bugs is a powerful priest or priestess. Do you, um, happen to have a priest here?"

Juniper shook her head, tears starting up again. "Will it go away on its own? Or mama uses this spicy plant to drive away bugs." The little girl's hands indicated the spherical shape of the inedible fruit Sarave boiled to make a noxious concoction that made Khor want to leave the area as well. "We have some't home. Would that work, Miss Bloom?"

Doom Bloom grimaced uncomfortably, even as Sumi spoke quietly into Khor's mind. <If this is the Hive Queen, which it does seem to be, though it's rather more powerful than I remember it being described, then we have a significant problem.>

Khor looked over the field. With all of the fallen bodies, it looked like a cemetery waiting for the graves to be dug. He sighed. <They can't be cured, can they?>

<I think not. They must be purified, and, as Rouge's sister said, the only people who can do that are priests. Which, you may have noticed, we do not have. There is an even greater concern, however.>

He swore. <What could be worse than our friends lying in a coma until they waste away?>

<Those same friends giving rise to a new Hive Queen.>

<What?> Khor stiffened, then forced himself to relax again when he saw the faces of both frightened little girls turn toward him. <What do you mean, Sumi?>

<If the Hive Bugs aren't killed, they begin to pupate when the Queen dies. Any of them that complete the metamorphosis will hatch in forty-eight hours, killing and eating the host. When they're done, they'll fight each other until only the strongest one survives. That one will become the new Queen, giving birth to a new Hive.>

Khor shuddered from head to foot. <You're saying we have to kill them?>

Sumi sounded resigned. <We have just under two days to find a solution, and then, yes.>

Khor looked frantically between the girls and their mothers, who lay still and silent in the long grass. Sumi had removed her webbing from the fallen, and then bandaged whatever wounds she could, applying silken compresses soaked in Spider's Milk where necessary.

Sarave's body was still covered in deep scratches, but the injuries were no longer bleeding, and the worst of them were patched. Viqa and Taqi were comparatively uninjured, though dark bruises were rising beneath their skin. The deep purple blooms only emphasized the uncharacteristically pale gray of their flesh. Between Sumi's attentions and Jesiqa's magic, they were keeping the glyphis alive, but for how long? Khor was certain they wouldn't make it for two days, possibly not even if he carried them to the pond.

Something had been tickling the back of his mind since Sumi finished speaking, and now it bubbled to the surface. Khor turned his gaze on Juniper. The little girl had her head resting on her mother's chest, and her eyes were closed as if she was listening to each beat of Sarave's heart.

<Sumi, can you get Juniper to tell us exactly what happened when Sarave was infected? It may be important.>

The spider clicked her fangs in understanding, and gently touched Juniper's shoulders. When Sumi began to spin her web, the symbols woven on it were simple and large, but the little girl's swollen eyes squinted as she struggled to read it.

<The unicorns. Ask her about the unicorns,> Khor said insistently.

Sumi wove an unmistakable portrait of a little unicorn, and Juniper's eyes widened in understanding.

"I told 'em t'go home," she said. "Mama said if anything happened, we were all s'posed to go home right away." Her eyes flickered to her mother. "Those big bugs came over, an' then we heard Khor scream, an' so I sent Kayti an' Kayli home. I came after Mama, though, 'cause I knew something wasn't right. She never would have left us behind if she was okay."

Juniper looked pleadingly at Sumi. "That's okay, isn't it? I couldn't just let Mama go when something was wrong with her."

Sumi struggled with her webs for a moment, then seemed to give up. <What are you getting after, Khor? Did you just need to know the sparkles are safe?>

<Foals,> Khor muttered, <and no. I hoped that was where they were, since that was the plan, but did she just say 'bugs'? More than one?>

Sumi jerked a little, then turned back to Juniper. Quickly, the spider wove a picture of an ugly beetle with stubby wings. When Juniper grimaced in recognition, Sumi added a second insect, and then placed a question mark after the two bugs.

Juniper nodded; eyes wide in puzzlement. "Yep, there were a bunch of 'em. The first one flew into mama's mouth, and then the rest came toward me an' Kayti an' Kayli. I was sittin' on the blanket with them while Mama made the sandwiches and cut up the veggie bread." The little girl made a face. While Khor and the unicorns loved Sarave's vegetable bread, it was not to Juniper's taste. "Mama started chokin', an' then one of 'em flew at me, an' I think I fell asleep for a minute. When I woke up, Kayli was pokin' me with her horn, and Mama was runnin' away. Then I heard Khor yellin', an' I told Kayti and Kayli to go home while I followed Mama. An' that's it."

By the end of this rather breathless recitation, Doom Bloom was looking very confused, while Khor and Sumi were exchanging glances filled with rising hope. Khor reared up on his back legs, pivoting to face the house. His hooves dug in, and he ran as quickly as he could.

Trees and bushes flashed by, and his hooves pounded on the flat, well-worn path to the house. He was tired, and he'd taken more than a few small wounds from the various creatures he'd fought. He'd slain many of them, but he'd held back where he could, since he could see that they weren't moving by their own wills. This had led to more injuries to him, but also allowed Sumi enough time to incapacitate their foes rather than kill them.

Now, he felt blood loss and fatigue drag at him, but he thought about the bright, loving smile Sarave had when she saw her daughter, and the pride that showed in Nuisance's every quack as he waddled by, trailed by his tiny offspring, of whom there would be no more if the duck's hens died today. He remembered the way the littlest vicuña had just begun to feel brave enough to frolic with Kayti and Kayli, and how the Tree thrived under the care of the Greater Bees.

By the time he reached the house, he was staggering, but he skidded to a stop outside the barn door. The door was cracked, and two sets of frightened little eyes, blue a little lower than the brown. peered at him through the opening. Khor heard little peeps coming from inside, and knew that Nuisance and his ducklings had also returned home when Khor sounded the alarm.

When the foals saw Khor, they pushed the door wide and bounded out, bleating and whinnying with equal fervor and frequency. Khor let his head drop so his nose sank into their soft fur, smelling cinnamon and tangerines in a deep huff. Then he nudged them with his nose, gently urging them in the direction of the Tree.

The trip back was, of necessity, slower than the journey to the house. The little unicorns trotted as quickly as they could, but their stamina was still low, and their legs were short. Kayli would race ahead, faster than her sister, then fall behind again, since Kayti's endurance was better. Both unicorns seemed to know that they were on a serious mission though, or perhaps they received a quest, because neither of them strayed, even when a sharp wind blew a leaf into Kayti's face, and a butterfly nearly landed on Kayli's horn.

They arrived at the Tree's clearing to find Sumi and Doom Bloom kneeling over the glyphis. Doom Bloom seemed to be pouring a potion down Taqi's mouth, while Sumi was placing fresh Spider's Milk on Viqa's compress. Jesiqa was lying half on top of her mother, her tiny arms spread wide in a forlorn embrace. Juniper sat beside her own mother, looking from Sarave to Jesiqa, her expression conflicted. She clearly wanted to stay with her mother, but she also wanted to comfort her new friend.

As soon as Kayti and Kayli saw the still forms in the field, they sped up. Kayli reached Taqi's side first, and her stubby little horn pressed hard into the boy's throat. Sparkles spiraled down the horn and into the youth's pallid gray flesh, and then he rolled over, shuddering and vomiting. Something slimy and green and too large to have fit in his mouth spilled out onto the ground, and Doom Bloom, who looked like she, too, wanted to vomit, stepped on the wriggling thing. It crunched beneath her boot, and Taqi blinked his eyes open, looking around blankly.

Kayti was repeating this process on Viqa, and, perhaps because the woman had been infected for a shorter period of time, or perhaps because she was stronger to start with, the glyphis female threw up the insect infecting her more quickly and easily than had her son. Sumi stabbed this one with a foreleg, cracking its exoskeleton, and then Kayli was on to Sarave, and it was Juniper's turn to squash a bug with a level of fury that Khor wouldn't have guessed the little girl had in her.

The whole process took nearly half an hour, even with the unicorns moving as quickly as they could. Several of the Greater Bees failed to eject the parasites, and died, spasming and writhing. Khor or Doom Bloom, as the most able-bodied and heaviest, put the insects out of their misery. The other woodland animals, upon waking to find themselves surrounded by strange creatures, generally scurried away as quickly as they could. A few of the larger ones bared threatening teeth, but after seeing Khor looming over them, they invariably backed down and slunk away as well.

When everyone who could be helped had been, they all (except the glyphis, who had hurriedly returned to the river) sat down in the middle of the bloody battlefield. Sarave and Juniper were clinging to each other, though Juniper was more asleep than awake, having cried herself into exhaustion. Both young unicorns were noticeably larger once again, so they must have gotten a quest to aid the fallen. Kayli's mane and tail now looked like silver stardust, while Kayti's flowed with all the colors of the rainbow. Sumi sat, curled up in a ball by the base of the Tree.

<Khor,> the spider said softly.

Khor looked over and snorted in acknowledgement.

<I leveled, Khor.>

He snorted again, this time managing to put mild inquiry into the tired puff of air.

<I'm going to have to molt,> Sumi said, her voice already sinking into the deep torpor that overtook her when she shed her skin. She hadn't done it in years, though she had been close when they'd had to go in to rescue Aspen from Akuji. She'd lost enough levels to set her back two or three molts, and so even though she'd leveled several times since, she'd simply been… growing back into herself.

<No!> He couldn't help the exclamation. Once Sumi entered molt, she would be terribly fragile, and if her old exoskeleton was disturbed during the process, she could even die. Not to mention the fact that it took a full week, during which time she would be unable to move or communicate. There would be no webbing to protect the Tree, and no one for Khor himself to speak with. As annoying as the know-it-all arachnid could be, Khor didn't want her to go. <Can't you wait? Doom Bloom said Aspen is on his way. You just need to->

Sumi was slowly, laboriously, climbing the Tree. She settled herself into the V formed at the base of the two largest branches. <You know I can't.>

He did know. Aspen had explained it to him the first time it had happened after Khor joined the team, when he was little more than an overgrown kid himself. He watched the old spider turn over, settling herself into place with her belly facing the sky and her legs curled inward. <What

am I going to tell everyone? How am I going to tell them?>

Sumi's voice took on a familiar acerbic tone. <You always insist you're the smart one. You figure it out.> Her legs twitched once more, and then she said, quietly, <I'll see you soon, my friend.>

Khor whuffled a little, hearing worry and loneliness in it, but unable to push away the feelings. <See you soon, Sumi,> he muttered, and then he turned away.

Chapter Twenty-eight

Aspen

As the last of the wagons left the flag marking the entrance to the mountain pass behind, Aspen nearly slumped from exhaustion. He was drenched in sweat, and for once he was glad he hadn't made a new hat yet, because the straw would probably be a limp, soggy mess. His job wasn't quite done yet, though, so he reached out to the dust hanging in the air behind the rapidly retreating wagons, and *encouraged* it to drop back down to the ground. Dust was, after all, just over-excited dirt, and he was something akin to an earth mage.

As the last traces of their passage were covered by dust and tiny plant roots filling in the hoof and wheel prints they'd left behind, Aspen's knees shook. Looking back, he'd spent a remarkable amount of time lately over-exerting himself. His effort had been rewarded with both the lives of those he was struggling to protect and many skill levels, judging by the flickers of light that surrounded him every time he nearly worked himself to collapse. He would still prefer to be back on his farm, smelling Sarave's delicious fish stew, and listening to the little unicorns and baby Juniper play.

For the briefest of heartbeats, he closed his eyes. He pictured Sarave's angular green face, Khor's shaggy head and direct brown gaze, Juniper's toothless smile, Kayti and Kayli's kid-like spinning leaps, Sumi's calm and supportive presence, and the peace he felt as he walked through the burgeoning fields. What would he give to be back in his two-room shack, with his friends around him, and no one depending on him for anything more than companionship?

He felt a small weight land on his shoulder, and Silus started to nuzzle his neck, then stopped. <Ew! Why are you wet and stinky?>

With a puff of a laugh, Aspen released his moment of self-pity, and opened his eyes. "Sorry, little one. I've been working hard while you and Rouge were off playing. Where is she, by the way?"

Silus edged away from his skin and settled into a fold of his shirt instead. It was probably damp, too, but apparently it still passed as a temporary resting place. <She's coming. I'll go look for her in just a minute.> The little bat yawned, her mouth stretching wide to show rows of tiny pointed teeth.

Aspen smiled. "We're not that far from the tower now. Let's try-" He switched to party chat. ::Rouge? Where are you?::

His young friend's voice came back promptly, but it was faint enough he had to focus to hear it. ::…pen? …t you? I'm… way. Be th… ute.::

Silus perked up. ::Rouge? I'll come find you. Aspen is gross.::

Apparently, the bat had managed to get her second wind, or maybe Aspen really was that disgusting. As Silus flew off, Aspen raised one arm and sniffed, then wrinkled his nose. "Fair enough," he muttered, and jumped as someone answered unexpectedly.

"I came back to give you a lift, but maybe I should go get you your own horse?" Motte's deep, amused voice made Aspen's face flame. He rubbed at his cheeks with both hands, feeling the rasp of beard stubble beneath his palms, and his heart rate slowed.

"Damn it, can't you people make a little more noise? You're a walking armor shop, for Gina's sake. You should make enough sound to wake the dead." He smiled a little. "And if anyone should know how hard that is, it's me."

Motte chuckled and leaned down, holding out an arm to help Aspen swing up into the saddle in front of him. As they had discovered, while Travelers couldn't ride each other's mounts, Natives could, and this wasn't the first time the two men had shared a ride on Motte's steed, Rosalind.

"I've been spending too much time trying to be sneaky with you and Rouge lately. I got a skill called [Muffle] that reduces the amount of noise my armor makes by thirty percent. I've read about it, and apparently there's an Assassin-class PKer running around in full armor because he has this thing maxed out." Motte grinned, causing his attractive face to enter the range of 'handsome', and Aspen felt his cheeks heat again.

Silently, he sent a few blistering thoughts winging their way up to his Goddess. He'd never had this problem before, and he hoped that once this business was over, he never would again. His hands wound into Rosalind's mane, and he struggled to keep his voice even. "That's great. So, uh, you're stealthier now, right? Will you get an actual [Stealth] skill?"

Motte clucked to the dapple-gray mare, and she moved out. With Aspen sitting in front of Motte, the big warrior's arms were on each side of him, and it was only thanks to sheer force of will that he kept himself from slumping back against Motte's broad, armored chest.

"No. Unfortunately the Guardian Wall class doesn't have access to the whole chain of [Stealth] skills and spells. Well, we can't cast spells at all. We get spell resistance to compensate, but no magic, ever." Motte sounded a little wistful, and Aspen patted his arm.

"Being a mage isn't all it's cracked up to be. Believe me, I've had plenty of times I wished I could just stand there and beat on things."

"I picked this class so that things could beat on me." The basso cantante voice was wry, and Aspen chuckled. "You may have noticed my daughter tends to leap in head-first, so I thought some protective gear might be in order. I'm kind of like a mobile helmet and knee-pads."

Aspen's laugh turned into a gasp as a spike of pain shot through his head. A sudden image of a little strawberry blonde girl riding a two-wheeled device, her face split in a grin that was missing its two front teeth flashed through his mind. He shook his head. That hadn't been his Birdie, who had been brunette and had probably never smiled that joyously in her entire short life.

Motte tugged Rosalind's reins, and the horse stopped, stamping a hoof in impatience. She could see the caravan ahead of them now, and she wanted to rejoin her 'herd'. Motte leaned forward so he could look into Aspen's face. "Are you all right?"

Aspen winced as he pressed a hand to the sharp, throbbing point of pain behind his right eye. "Fine. Just tired, as always. I need to get some rest, once we're sure no one is following."

Motte was about to reply when a black and white blur passed them by, and they broke into fits of coughing brought on by the resulting cloud of dust. Aspen felt the dirt settle onto the drying sweat on his skin, and he suddenly felt both sticky and crunchy.

::Ha! You guys are so slow! Come on!:: Rouge's happy voice rang in their heads, and the two men exchanged looks of exasperated amusement. Motte touched his heels to the mare's sides, and she stepped forward eagerly.

Their small group rejoined the caravan a few minutes later, and Rouge filled Motte and Aspen in on her adventures, finishing with, "I barely got out of easy line of sight before the spell fizzled, but hopefully Corporal Payne thinks my shrinkage was just a trick of the light." She giggled. "Anyway, I got a quest completion notice as soon as I passed that big flagpole, so I think we're good!"

Aspen heaved a sigh of relief. He was sitting on the bench of the front wagon once again. Restur was beside him, controlling the oxen, and Manuela had folded her angular form into the back of the wagon, among the piled boxes and crates.

Motte and Rouge were trotting easily alongside the wagon, and Rouge now shot her father a teasing look. "I see you showed up just in time to help Aspen again. I thought you decided to work late tonight prepping your syllabus?"

Motte's already dark skin deepened even more. "It's the same class I teach every fall. I just decided to go with *Midsummer Night's Dream* instead of *Hamlet* this semester, so I had to tweak a few things." He shot a sidelong glance at Aspen, and then looked back at Rouge, raising a brow as he turned the tables on his teenage daughter. "I thought *you* were supposed to clean up the living room before you logged in? I believe the two empty cereal bowls and three pairs of shoes are yours?"

It was Rouge's turn to blush. "I was worried about Aspen and Silus and everybody! You were, too, right? It's a good thing I came when I did, anyway, since I was able to help Aspen keep those guards from seeing us." She gave Motte an unrepentant look, and Aspen closed his eyes on the friendly wrangling of father and daughter.

As he slid into sleep, Aspen's thoughts turned to how he came to be here, among these new friends, instead of in the hands of Atae as he should have been. An old dream surfaced, and he drowned in memories.

☙ ☙ ☙

Lich Lord Akuji's skeletal body, which was held together only by the force of his spirit's magic, fell apart into its separate pieces as that magic was severed. Iorgas stared down at the sword clutched in his emaciated fingers. Its length was thrust between Akuji's bare yellow ribs, impaling the quivering bit of darkness that hung there. Only Iorgas' necromantic vision allowed him to see that darkness, to know that *here* was the evil overlord's only weak point.

As his trembling fingers dropped the hilt, he vaguely wondered if the weapon had been wielded by someone who couldn't see that pulsing point of black if the blow would even have done anything, or if Akuji would simply have laughed and turned the weapon back on them. All he knew was that the corrupt mage had left his sword behind in Lark's fallen corpse, and that it had taken every ounce of strength left in Iorgas' feeble body to pull it out and turn it on its owner.

His bony knees hit the ground, and then he collapsed forward onto his face. His outstretched fingers just touched Birdie's cooling hand, and his grip spasmed as he tried to hold onto her for just a moment more. He vaguely felt Sumi prodding him with her legs, but her words were lost in the beat of his own slowing heartbeat as the last of his strength faded from his failing body.

Glad.

He was *glad* that he was going. Maybe he would see his Lark, his precious Birdie, one more time as they entered the Chaos Pool. His life had only been a series of increasingly terrible mistakes, anyway, and…

A dark charcoal hand reached not ungently beneath his chin and lifted his face. Glowing red eyes stared into his own, and he tried to smile, even a little, for his Goddess. She saw too few smiles, and he had always thought she deserved better than the anger and tears with which she was usually greeted.

Atae's surprisingly sweet contralto asked, "Iorgas, are you ready to go?" He thought she sounded a little sad, which was odd, because there was nothing truly sad about death. It was simply the natural ending to life, and the beginning of a new cycle as your soul rested in the Chaos Pool until it was called forth to its next life. Atae herself had taught him that, and it was often the only thing that allowed him to sleep at night, given how many thousands of lives he had ended since becoming a necromancer.

Iorgas stood, finding his body suddenly surprisingly light and easy to move. When he glanced down, he understood why. There, at his feet, was the husk of his former self. It had suffered much at Akuji's bony hands, and was now little more than skin and bones. He struggled to find any resemblance to the slightly portly man he had been when he entered this terrible place, and wondered how his daughter had recognized him at all.

Suddenly remembering, he spun in place, staring over at his daughter's broken body. Before he could voice the questions that burned through his mind, he saw another form shimmer into being next to Lark. This Goddess was light where Atae was dark. Her reddish-blonde tresses flowed in luxurious waves and ringlets to her waist, and flowers twined through it as if they'd grown there. Alabaster skin seemed to glow, and her swirling rainbow-colored eyes were somber as she leaned down to touch Lark.

"Bring her back!" Iorgas burst out. "I know you can! You're the goddess of life! She was your servant, and you can... You can..." He stumbled forward, his hands clutching at Gina's silken white gown.

The goddess stood, cupping a single golden mote of light in her palms. Her voice, surprisingly similar to that of her sister, was gentle when she said, "She gave her life for you, Iorgas. As my high priestess, she had the ability to exchange her life for that of any one other person. She chose you, and I will not cheapen her decision by questioning it." She smiled as she touched a tender finger to the fragment of Lark's soul. "Your daughter loves you very, very much, and in honor of that love, I would like to offer you a chance."

Gina looked over Iorgas' shoulder at Atae. "Sister," she said, "you know what I ask. May I?"

Atae's colorless hair drifted into her face as she shook her head, briefly obscuring her gleaming red eyes, though it was less than shoulder length. She brushed it back behind pointed ears as she looked into Iorgas' eyes. "This is your choice entirely, Iorgas. Only know this," her voice grew cold, more like the familiar deathly chill he was accustomed to. "If you accept my sister's offer, your old life will end as thoroughly as if you had truly died here today. No trace of my gifts may you keep, and I will never again answer your call, until the day you stand before me again, nothing more nor less than any other soul."

Iorgas shuddered, and looked back at Gina, who wore what a solemn expression. Seeing that she had his attention, she extended the hand that held the remnant of Lark's soul. "As she was my High Priestess, sworn to me in death *and* life, I am within my rights to keep this spark, and return it immediately into the cycle of life once again. Your daughter, who I love only a little less than you do, yourself, would be reborn to new parents, with a new future lying before her. However," her fingers curled around the mote of light, though the gesture was protective, rather than threatening.

"I am willing to give you a chance to meet your Birdie again. A chance only, because once she enters the Chaos Pool, she will remain there only until a life that matches her spirit appears. That may take days, or it may be years, and that is beyond my control." Her kaleidoscopic eyes met Iorgas' own topaz ones. "*But*, I can tell you now that when one darkness falls, another rises. Though your enemy lies defeated," she gestured to the pile of dry bones that had once been Lich Lord Akuji, "evil marches on, relentless and powerful."

Cradling Lark's sprite to her chest, Gina went on. "You have a chance to stop that evil, as you did this one. You may protect your daughter in her next life." The silent words, *as you failed to do in this one*, hung in the air between them. "So, accept the gift Lark gave you. Though Iorgas Penbrooke, Necromancer, Left hand of Atae, dies today, *you* may live on."

The Goddess tilted her head toward the spider, her carapace dull and oddly loose, who lay curled on the hard ground beside Iorgas' body. Manuela, he was distantly amazed to see, was now crouching beside him as well, her own much-thinner hands shaking as they tried to pour the contents of a glass bottle down his throat. "There are those who love you yet, you know. Lark was not the only one who thought your life was worth risking her own. Don't break their hearts and make all their sacrifices be in vain."

Iorgas looked from Gina to Atae. His goddess' face gave nothing away. Her expression was dispassionate, and her eyes impassive. Only her right hand, which was clenched tight around the athame at her waist, twin to the one she had given him when he became her Left Hand, gave her away. She didn't want him to do this, but...

His eyes locked on Gina's loose fist. Faint twinkles of light glimmered from between her fingers. Was it true that he could do something to protect her soul, as he had been unable to protect her body? Perhaps. Could he take the chance that Gina was wrong? More importantly, could he turn down the opportunity to see Birdie once again, even if it was in the mysterious environs of the Chaos Pool?

Slowly, he nodded. He turned to Atae and dropped to one knee. "My Goddess. I would return my blade to you, but Akuji destroyed it, as he destroyed my body and stole my skills. So, I am unable to return to you any part of the many things you gave to me. Nonetheless, I ask that you release me. Let me return to life, and attempt to atone for my failures."

He felt those cool fingers on his face again, and for the tiniest moment, Atae stroked his jaw. Then her hand fell away, and she said, "As you wish, Iorgas." From the corner of his downcast vision, he saw her extend her hand toward her sister, and Gina passed the fragile glitter of Lark's soul into Atae's dark palm. Atae closed her fingers around the spark, and it blinked out, sent to the Chaos Pool. The Goddess' now-empty hand fell to her side, and her voice was sad as she spoke formally.

"I repudiate you, Iorgas Penbrooke. You are no servant of mine, and all that I have given you is yours no longer. Call not my name, for I shall not come to you, until that final moment when all living things return to my embrace."

With that, his Goddess vanished, and pain even worse than he had felt when Akuji tore away his levels ripped through him. He toppled and fell, his spirit-self sprawling back into the shell that lay on the ground. All of the bodily agony that had been displaced while he hung between life and death crashed back into him, and Gina's voice whispered, "You are mine, now, Iorgas. I have *so much* work for you to do."

A small, pale hand entered the range of his fading vision. In it was another light, though this one was a beacon, where Lark's had been a fading ember. Gina balanced this minute sun on one finger, then touched the finger to Iorgas' forehead. Fire billowed through him, and blackness pulled him under.

Aspen woke with a shout, feeling the ghostly memory of the torment he had felt at that moment. Sweat was running down his face again, and his breath was coming fast. Beside him, Restur gave him a look that was half amusement and half concern.

"You all right, lad? I was starting to think I'd have to wake you, with the way you were thrashing around. Must have been quite a nightmare."

Aspen decided to ignore the fact that the old man had called him 'lad'. In spite of his forty-plus years, he supposed he was still young compared to the aged caravan master. Offering a shaky smile, he swiped his hand across his forehead. It came away filthy and moist, and he grimaced. "I could use a bath."

This time the look was pure amusement. "I was going to say something if you didn't. You reek, even in the open air. We'll need to stop for lunch soon, and young Rouge says there's a clearing with a stream not far ahead. The water will be cold, no doubt, with snow runoff from the peaks, but we'd all appreciate it if you faced the chill for the sake of everyone being able to keep their lunch down."

Aspen's lips twitched, and he sighed. "Fair enough. Though I'd like to remind you that my aromatic presence is a result of covering the tracks of twenty-three wagons and about a hundred herd beasts."

Restur's expression grew more serious. "Thank you for that, Aspen. I know there's no way we would have made it through in time without you feeding the draft animals power. Rouge said you damped down the dust cloud, too, so there'd be no trace of our passage."

Aspen started to run his hand through his hair, then thought better of it when his fingers got stuck in the tangled mess. "I just did what needed to be done. Any one of you would have done the same, if you could."

The old caravan master's look was contemplative. "I think you've been doing 'what needed to be done' for quite some time, m'lord, and also that you overestimate the resolve of other people."

Cheeks flushing, Aspen looked away, down the road. With relief, he noticed that the rocky path ahead of them was widening, and the narrow shoulder of the road was now grassy instead of gravel or sheer rock. "It looks like Rouge was right. There's definitely a clearing coming up." Reaching over, he set a hand on the edge of the wagon and swung himself down to the ground, grunting slightly as his knees and back protested the sudden movement.

Without looking back up at Restur, Aspen raised a hand in farewell. "I'll go find that stream, then. Let me know when food is available, eh?" Quickly, he jogged off, enjoying the spring of the thick green grass beneath his boots.

"You'll need this." A small hand suddenly thrust a bar of soap beneath his nose, and he paused and blinked. Looking behind him, he saw a vaguely familiar young boy. One of Plum's ragamuffins?

Cautiously, he accepted the soap. "Thank you, ah..." He paused, leaving room for the urchin to insert his name.

Instead, the boy looked down, tawny cheeks darkening to dusky rose. He was probably half high elf, though only his faintly golden-brown eyes and pointed ears gave it away. He looked up at something Aspen couldn't see, and suddenly Rouge stood there, still blushing faintly. "Sorry, Aspen," the girl said. "The [Substitution] spell is super useful, but it's hard to level up. I snagged a wooden amulet from Dale earlier, so I've been practicing."

The young Traveler stepped back, wrinkling her nose. "Anyway, I figured you could use that. You have a *major* Stench debuff going on, and the Filthy debuff stacked on it makes even me want to stay away from you. I'm amazed Restur could stand it. He must like you a *lot*."

Aspen raised the soap to his nose and sniffed. A powerful scent of flowery perfume assaulted his sinuses, and he sneezed. "This soap should definitely take care of the problem." He couldn't help the look of distaste he knew was on his face, though he should certainly make more of an effort to be grateful. He honestly hadn't been looking forward to scrubbing with cold sand to get rid of the dirt.

Rouge laughed. "I know, that's the cheap stuff. I bought it ages ago, before I knew that bathhouses usually provide their own soap. I didn't think to snag any of Sarave's homemade sunflower oil and cedar soap before we left."

A powerful feeling of homesickness came over him again. Aspen shook his head, smiling a little to himself. When did that ramshackle hut become home, and the motley collection of sapient beings and animals become his family and friends?

He lifted the sweet, perfumed bar in his hand and smiled at Rouge. "Thank you for this. Though I'm not sure if everyone else will thank you once I walk by smelling like a lady's tearoom."

Rouge grinned. "Oh no, they'll still thank me. Go on, the stream is just past that stand of bushes over there, and Millie's already talking about making vegetable soup and apple dumplings. You don't want to miss it!" With a quick wave, the girl turned and jogged away, though her shape flickered into that of the mischievous curly-haired moppet, Matilda.

Aspen's belly growled at the thought of warm food, especially the hearty soups that Millie somehow managed to produce from the small mobile kitchen she'd packed into her wagon. He hadn't had her apple dumplings before, but he was willing to bet they were delicious as well. Turning, he jogged back toward the nearby hedgerow.

As he neared, he could hear the stream trickling merrily along, and birds chirped as they hopped through the dense bushes. Casting out his Life Sense, he could feel the pure green essence of the plants and animals that lived here. Small fish darted through the shallow water, and a family of badgers trundled along nearby, thinking of full bellies and planned naps.

With a gentle nudge, Aspen encouraged the twigs and branches to twist out of his way, and *dis*couraged any insects from taking an interest in his person. The stream soon came into view, and it looked exactly as clear, peaceful, and frigid as he had imagined.

Sighing, he shucked his clothes, dropping them into a still pool formed by some rocks at the edge of the creek. They definitely needed to soak, and though putting damp clothes back on would be uncomfortable, the warm spring sunshine would keep him from being too cold until they dried.

Aspen dipped a toe into the chilly water, shuddering as his blood nearly froze in his veins. Wistfully, he wished that his new powers came with even a hint of fire magic so that he could heat the water, or at least keep *himself* warm, in spite of the environmental conditions. Well, there was nothing for it but-

"You're not done yet?" The irascible voice was familiar but unexpected, and Aspen yelped as he lost his balance and fell forward into the stream with a splash. Fortunately, the water wasn't deep, and even in the center of the stream, he could easily sit up and the water was only up to his ribs.

"Manuela!" he gasped, shaking wet hair out of his face as he struggled to his feet on the slippery stones. "How are you...? Why didn't I...?" He had been relaxed and more than a little off guard with his Life Sense fully deployed so that he could tell if anything approached, whether person or animal. Manuela had not only been completely invisible to him, but she hadn't even created the sort of blank spot that he was beginning to recognize as an indication of the presence of the undead.

Manuela smirked, picking up the soap he'd dropped when he fell into the creek. "I've been practicing something new. It's kind of like a [Stealth] skill, but for souls. I remembered what you told me about how your Life Sense works, and I thought, as a Soul Mage, I should be able to control what my 'spirit' looks like. I've been trying different things for the past several days, and then coming up behind you to see if I could surprise you."

His old friend picked up the soggy clothes from the pool where Aspen had dropped them, looking distastefully at the filthy water they left behind. With a foot, she pushed a rock out of the small natural wall that had been preventing the water from flowing on, and the dirty water streamed away. Once the pool was crystal clear again, she replaced the rock, and dropped the slightly-cleaner garments back in.

"Anyway, I thought I should come and check on you. Motte came to me and said he thought you looked ill, and that you basically passed out when you rejoined the caravan. I figured you're a healer, so illness probably isn't a concern, but I should come and check and remind you to get more rest."

Crooking a finger, she motioned for Aspen to come closer, and he did, though he was shivering so hard his teeth nearly rattled. Manuela made a circular motion with a finger, and Aspen turned his back on her. A moment later, he felt rough, sudsy cloth scrubbing his back and sides, and he sighed in relief. When they had been partnered together in the military, the two of them had often found themselves covered in substances that were more than a little offensive to the senses. This wasn't the first time they'd helped each other get to hard-to-reach spots, and it was rather like having one's older sister scratch that spot in the middle of your back that you can never quite get.

Aspen sighed. "I'll sleep when I'm-"

Manuela clicked her tongue and scrubbed a little harder than she probably needed to. "Dead. Yes, I've heard it before, and it's still rubbish. Rest now, and the death you've been looking for for as long as I've known you is more likely to pass you by for another day."

Aspen started to protest, but Manuela took a step to the side and smacked the sweet-scented cloth into his face. "As your physician, I think you're functional. As your friend, I think you need to get your head out of your rear." She leaned in, dark eyes staring directly into his own pale topaz ones in a way that few people could manage.

"Aspen, you chose to leave behind the expectations of your parents and your village when you were just a boy. You did it the only way you knew how, by asking the gods for help. It's not your fault Jumping Hollow was razed to the ground, and if you'd stayed with your family, all you'd have done is die beside them. It's not your fault that there were tens of thousands of creatures in Akuji's armies, and that you couldn't stop them all on your own. It's not even your fault that Lark died. You chose to sacrifice yourself for her, and if things didn't go according to your plan, well, when has life ever done what we expected?"

Manuela sighed and stepped back. "It's all right to care for yourself, too, Aspen. You were the only, *the only*, high-ranking member of King Chester's forces who chose to risk your life every day for the common people. Do you know what those people back there call you, knowing that you were once Iorgas Penbrooke?" She turned and pointed back toward the caravan, then looked back to Aspen.

"I'll give you a hint. It's not 'coward', nor is it 'failure'. These people love you, as did Lark, or she wouldn't have given her own existence in exchange for yours. You think your daughter somehow turned out to be self-sacrificing, generous, and *good* in spite of you? No, she grew up wanting to be just like you. And she was. Now, clean up, stop feeling sorry for yourself, and get back there before the soup is all gone."

With that, Manuela stalked away, and if Aspen encouraged the brambles she nearly walked right into to get out of her way so they wouldn't ruin her exit, well, who could blame him? After all, everyone needed a friend like Manuela, and maybe, just maybe, a friend like him, too.

Chapter Twenty-nine
Rouge

Rouge logged in, letting the feeling of falling away from her physical body blow away the memory of Slim's sad voice saying, "You hadda, George. I swear you hadda." Why did they make kids in high school read such depressing books? Didn't they know that life was already depressing enough?

Blinking her eyes open, she looked around. It was Monday in the real world, and it had been two long days since they'd entered the pass through the Whispering Mountains. Four days in-game, and Rouge had spent as much time with the caravan as she could. Going back to just playing at home felt strange, even though she'd done it every weekend since starting at Veritas Corp. Somehow, knowing that on Monday there'd be no lab, no Dr. Joe and Sara, no magic immersion pod... somehow it just made things harder.

Plus, she was finishing her summer reading list, and she was ready to swear that her teachers must actually hate their students. Or maybe since teachers had to do that ongoing education thing during the summer, this was their way of making sure kids didn't get to enjoy themselves either? She'd ask her dad, but she had a feeling college professors and high school teachers were different breeds.

Beneath her butt, Wally gave a little jump and wiggle, then turned his head and clucked at her softly. He'd noticed she was awake, and it was time for some scrootching. Laughing, Rouge stroked his velvety-soft head. "There there, Wally, I know what you want."

She fed the hungry ostrich a pastry that was something akin to a danish (though Millie called them Pig Ears, and made them triangular instead of round). With a happy gulp, the huge bird made the treat vanish, and looked at her with wistful brown eyes. When the long lashes blinked for the second time, Rouge gave in. "Here then, greedy guts. Only one more though! Millie can't make anything more complicated than a pancake while we're traveling, and I'm running low on the good stuff."

Beside her, Lyrec, who was sitting on his own horse, who he had recently renamed 'Harp', shifted and grumbled. "I hate waking up still riding. I miss my rest bonus."

Rouge laughed. Since Codswallop counted as a battle mount, she could rest in the saddle without getting a debuff. Apparently, the game designers assumed that anyone who fought astride would also travel a lot? In any case, she wasn't going to look a gift ostrich in the mouth. "Which one did you get? *Stiff Muscles* or *Sore All Over*?" They weren't exactly terrible debuffs, but it was still no fun to suffer through the twinges the pain feedback sent you, even at the minimum level, which was the automatic setting for minors like her and Lyrec.

"*Sore*," her friend muttered, pressing his hands to his back and groaning.

"Wait though, you're just using a headset!" Rouge realized, swatting the bard's shoulder. "You can barely feel anything!"

He mock-glared at her. "Yeah, but barely is still something! My behind feels like I've been sitting on a beehive!"

She giggled, a sudden image of Lyrec with a massively swollen rear end flashing through her mind. To change the subject, she asked, "Did you finish the summer reading list?"

He rolled his eyes. "Ages ago. Mom wouldn't let me play at all until my 'homework' was done. Plus, it gave me a good excuse to hide from the Detroit Cousins." Lyrec spent the first half of summer vacation splitting his time between his mom's family in Detroit, and his grandparents in Hawaii. There were about a hundred Detroit Cousins, and Lyrec only liked two of them.

Rouge made a face. "I should have done that."

He laughed. "You've already read half of them, since your dad's a classics professor. What did you even have left to-"

He broke off as a slim hand came to rest on his arm, and Flu-flu blinked lovingly at him from her own horse, which was tethered to his. Rouge felt her stomach sink as the pair exchanged soppy looks. Rouge was really, *truly* happy for her best friend, who had gone through more unrequited crushes in the last few years than Rouge had eaten pizzas (and she really liked pizza), but it seemed like once Fluff logged on, that was all Lyrec could think or talk about.

Sure enough, a huge, silly grin was now pasted on Lyrec's face, and his usually pale cheeks were pink. "Fluff! I thought you couldn't, um, unite body and soul until three o'clock!"

Flu-flu pressed one hand to her chest and raised the other to the sky, dramatically proclaiming, "My love for thee was enough to cause the Universe itself to shift to bring us together. My female progenitor was called in to perform her duties, saving the lives of those in need, and thus I am free!"

Translation, Fluff's mom had to work (she was a doctor or a nurse or a paramedic, or something like that, as far as Rouge could tell) so Fluff was unsupervised. Rouge was pretty sure the huntress was their own age or slightly older, since you had to be at least fourteen to play *Veritas Online*, and Flu-flu certainly *acted* like a teenager, albeit a strange one.

When Lyrec had fallen for Fluff, Rouge had sent a quick message to her step-sister, Doom Bloom, who was the girl's guild-master. Doom, aka Lily, hadn't been around much all summer, thanks to a financial snafu that required her to get a job while she was also taking college courses, but she'd sent a PM to Rouge's screen, saying she didn't know that much more than Rouge, since Fluff was always in character, but she thought the other girl was in high school, given the hours she could play, and had been playing for at least a year. If she'd started when she was fourteen, that would make Fluff at least fifteen now. Lyrec was a little older than Rouge, at fifteen, so that was fine, right? Even if Flu-flu was sixteen or seventeen, well, that wasn't a big deal. Though Rouge would still be happier if she was sure.

Rouge shot Flu-flu a friendly smile. "Hey, Fluff! Are you going back to school soon?"

It was always risky to ask a role-player real-world questions, since their reactions tended to vary from outright denial to anger. But it was making Rouge nuts that her bestie didn't even know his girlfriend's real name.

For a moment, discomfort crossed Fluff's pretty face, and Rouge wasn't sure which way the girl was going to go. For sure, she had to wonder if her boyfriend was really just friends with the girl he obviously knew IRL. Flu-flu's honorable persona obviously won out, though, because she returned the smile and said, "Alas, yes. My host-body in the other world must, perforce, return to the Place of Obligatory Education in a week."

Rouge choked on a giggle. Place of Obligatory Education? She was totally stealing that. "Us too. I mean, Lyrec probably already told you, but school starts next Monday."

Fluff actually looked a little surprised. "I was not aware. My beloved, is this true? I had thought you were beyond the Time of Obligation?"

Uh oh. Lyrec had lied and said he was out of high school? Rouge's internal alarms started going off. Alert! Alert! Best friend fight imminent!

Rouge tugged at Codswallop's reins. "Uh, no! Yeah, um, whatever he said! That's um, I mean, I'm younger than him, so…"

Lyrec had his face buried in his hands, and she couldn't tell if he was laughing or crying. He peered up at Fluff, and his voice was muffled when he spoke. "I'm sorry, Fluff. I knew you thought I was in college, and I just couldn't stand to let you down. You're obviously older, and I didn't want you to dump me because I'm a kid."

Flu-flu's expression flickered from confused, to hurt, to understanding, and she threw her arms around Lyrec, nearly toppling them both from their horses. "Never! You are my Fated Love, and we shall be together for all time!"

Lyrec gulped audibly, and his movements jerked as he knocked his headset askew and then resettled it on his head. "Even… across dimensions?" He sounded hesitant, and Rouge could understand why. He was asking if Flu-flu was willing to take things a big step forward, and meet or at least exchange contact info in real life.

Flu-flu hesitated, and her eyes flickered to Rouge. Then she closed her mouth and her eyes went distant. Rouge had the distinct feeling that the other girl was using personal chat, which was completely wild, because it was all but admitting that she was in a game, which Fluff *never* did. The closest she'd ever gotten was when Rouge had asked if it was all right to contact her in case of emergency (like the entire caravan being abducted by monsters), and Fluff had given her a 'magic spell' to use in the world of their 'host-bodies'.

Which meant it was time for Rouge to be somewhere else, and let the two lovebirds figure things out themselves.

Silently, Rouge touched her heels to Codswallop's sides, and urged the bird toward the head of the caravan. With luck and lots of Aspen's mana, they'd be getting through the mountains today, and she didn't want to miss that.

ế ế ế

Restur and Aspen were chatting quietly as Rouge came up beside the lead wagon, but both men smiled when they noticed her. Restur quickly turned his attention back to his oxen, but Aspen leaned toward her and spoke.

"I wasn't aware of most of this journey on the way out last fall, but I think

I've recognized a few landmarks from when we traveled south together. Things always look different from the other direction, though, so we were hoping you would be able to tell us how close we are to the end of the pass." Aspen gestured to their surroundings, which would more accurately be described as tall hills rather than small mountains by now. The sheer cliffs that had surrounded them for the last three days of travel were little more than dips into shallow ravines or steep hillsides.

"I can do better than that, I think." Rouge pulled up her map. In *Veritas*, you could buy basic maps, but they had only minimal detail on anything except quest locations, shops, and public buildings. If you really wanted to know where you were, you had to either get a copy from a friend who'd actually been there, or go there yourself. It was just one of the ways that *Veritas Online* maintained immersion and kept people interested and exploring, because completionists hated holey maps.

What all of that boiled down to was that Rouge had a map. She'd bought the absolute cheapest one possible in Vargo on her way north the first time, but it had filled in as she went. She'd taken the most direct course the first time in order to reduce travel time (including a significant portion spent sliding downhill in a giant turtle shell), so that part of her map wasn't really helpful now. When she, Motte, Aspen, and Silus had gone back through on their way to Bright, however, she'd gotten a decent amount of the road filled in.

Pulling up her map, Rouge let it fill her entire field of vision. Unlike in the magic pod, she couldn't just think to zoom in and out, and she had to use her fingers to pinch and pull at the topography. It took her a moment to find their location, since *VO* also only provided 'You Are Here' dots in population centers, but she figured it out eventually.

Whooping, she flicked away the map. "Aspen, we're almost-"

Looking around, she saw that Aspen wasn't next to her any more. Unlike horses, her ostrich didn't seem to care what the rest of the caravan was doing, so he'd trotted right on ahead while she was distracted. Now, the whole caravan was stopped on the crest of a hill behind her, and she could see why.

Below them, fields of crops lay in neat, tidy rows. An orchard lay on the east side of the farm, and the small wooden building that Rouge remembered so well was surrounded by plots of brightly blooming flowers. Most distracting of all, however, was the tree.

It was easily fifty feet high, and covered in jewel-like colors she could see from here. If it weren't for the barely-visible green leaves, she would have thought it was some kind of circus tent erected in an open glade. But no, it was definitely alive, and it was right where Aspen had planted his magical Goddess' Seed before they left. How it had grown that much in the time they'd been gone, she didn't know, but there it was, and small, dark spots moved around its base.

They were home.

"Woo*hooooooo*!" Rouge yelled as she leaned forward, urging Wally into his fastest run. Not that he needed much encouragement, because he, too, seemed excited to be back on the farm. Rouge barely remembered to send back a quick, probably unnecessary, message. ::I'm going on ahead. Last one there is a rotten egg!::

Between the downward slope of the terrain and Codswallop's excellent [Jump] skill, girl and bird came about as close to flying as a flightless bird was ever going to get. Every leap carried them thirty or forty feet, and though they were still over a mile from the nearest edge of the sprawling fields when they began, it took only a few exhilarating minutes to reach the farm.

Rouge had only a couple of seconds, between one rollicking leap and the next, to decide between the house and the fascinating tree, and in the end, Codswallop made the decision for her. His head snapped toward the tree, and he tooted the call he usually kept for when she logged back in after being away for a long time. Racing only barely slower now that he was on relatively level ground, the ostrich made short work of the last half a mile or so.

As Rouge and Codswallop drew closer, however, the girl could see that the dark shapes at its base were not wild animals, as she'd thought, but a gray-skinned woman accompanied by a similarly monochrome boy. Enormous bees flew around, each one several inches long, with vicious stingers that she could see from several yards away.

As the boy and woman turned to look at Rouge and Wally, Rouge desperately tried to pull the ostrich to a stop. The bird had the proverbial bit between his beak, though, and his eyes were locked on the luscious, glistening fruits hanging from the tree heavily laden boughs.

Suddenly, Rouge couldn't breathe. Her lungs filled with water, and she began to choke. Vaguely, she could see that Codswallop was having the same problem, and they were both hovering slightly above the ground. Wally's legs pedaled helplessly in a floating orb of water, and they were both drowning as the gray woman watched dispassionately.

Your Battle Mount *Codswallop* has taken 1 point of Drowning damage. If he receives 4 more points of damage, he will die and respawn at your last save point.

Your Battle Mount *Codswallop* has taken 1 point of Drowning damage. If he receives 3 more points of damage, he will die and respawn at your last save point.

The world was fading to darkness, and Rouge watched impotently as her own health rolled downwards. With the last of her willpower, she summoned her Mambele to her hand and got ready to throw it. She didn't know if it, too, would be trapped in the bubble, or if it could escape to strike the water mage, but she had to try.

Then she was dropped unceremoniously on the ground as the bubble burst, water falling like rain all around her. Codswallop collapsed on the ground, gasping for air just like she was doing herself. If that was what drowning was really like, Rouge wasn't sure she would ever go swimming again!

A small part of the fuzzy gray spot that was the strange mage separated from the larger part, and Rouge realized something had been sitting on the woman's shoulder. Silus? No, Silus was asleep back with the caravan, and what would she be doing with this stranger anyway?

A vaguely familiar, breathy voice came to Rouge's ears, and small, clammy hands patted at her face. "Rouge? Rouge... wake... up..."

Rouge reached up and rubbed at her eyes, and then her ears for good measure. Surely that couldn't be... She blinked, and the little face hovering above her own grew clearer. Big, solid black eyes, gray skin, way too many sharp triangular teeth for the face of an innocent little girl, pulsing gills on the neck...

"Jes... iqa?" she managed, then rolled over and hacked up a lake.

Jesiqa's mother, Viqa, because that was who the mage was, was very apologetic. Apparently, attacks on the Tree (the capital letter was audible when she said it) had grown more common and aggressive over the past week, and the defenders had learned to attack first and ask questions later. Or not at all.

Viqa was kneeling in front of Rouge, her expression contrite. Her voice wasn't as weak as her daughter's, and Rouge guessed that the woman must be using her magic to move water through her gills somehow. Though how water on her throat translated to air for speaking, Rouge didn't know, and she wasn't exactly going to pry.

"I am very sorry, Rouge the Rogue. My daughter has told me much of you, and how you and Aspen helped get her and Nekthadt free from Bloodhaven. I would never have harmed you, had I known, but your ostrich looked like a horse at first, and you were clearly headed straight for the Tree."

Rouge shook her head. Her voice was a little rough from the coughing fit, but the *Hoarse* debuff only had five minutes left on it, so she wasn't going to worry about it. She was more interested in the fact that Viqa had said Wally 'looked' like a horse, past tense, which indicated that the glyphis had either gotten lucky and fallen into the 5% of people who managed to disbelieve in

Wally's [Confabulation] skill, or she was very, very smart.

"It's okay. Aspen is on his way, and he'll finally finish that Meta fruit quest," she spent a little more time coughing, and watched the *Hoarse* debuff reset to ten minutes. With a silent sigh, she continued. "Then you can stop guarding it quite so closely. There's a *lot* of fruit, so once he has the first one, we can probably spare a few." *Hundred*, she thought wryly, eyeing the cornucopia growing from Gina's Tree.

All three of the glyphis looked relieved, and Jesiqa, who was back on her mother's shoulder and surrounded by a faintly shimmering film of water, said, "Aspen? Soon?"

Rouge turned and pointed back the way she'd come, ignoring Codswallop, who was tethered to a non-magical tree nearby and looked both healthy and rebellious after receiving a few Healing Pellets. "Any time now, really. If the way down wasn't so steep, they'd probably be here already. They're going to have to take it slowly, though, and Aspen will have to stay with the group, in case any of the animals gets hurt on the way. There are a *lot* of horses and cows and stuff, and one of them is always twisting a hoof or something."

"Or something, huh?" The teasing voice that came from behind her nearly made her stumble, even though she wasn't moving, and her eyes burned, even though she knew she couldn't actually cry. Rouge whirled and threw herself into her sister's arms. Doom Bloom staggered back a step under the sudden assault, but she only hesitated a moment before her own arms closed around Rouge, and then the two of them were hugging as they never had in real life.

"Doom! When did you get here? Why didn't you *say* something? I thought you were still working, and with school and all, you weren't going to be able to be around for *ages*, but you're here, and-" The torrent of words stopped at the grin Doom offered her. Rouge had never seen her sister look so relaxed and... happy?

Doom Bloom's platinum blonde head tilted, and her sapphire eyes actually twinkled. Rouge blinked.

"I have quite a story to tell you, little sister, but, ah," Doom cast a glance at the glyphis. Viqa and her son, Taqi, looked like they could care less about the conversation, but Jesiqa was watching with fascinated ebony eyes. "Maybe on the way to the house?"

Rouge laughed and walked over to pick up Wally's reins. The ostrich gave a half-hearted tug toward the Tree, but then huffed a sigh and puffed out his still-damp feathers in resignation. Rouge took her last Pig's Ear from her inventory and fed it to the bird as a consolation prize. "Hang in there until Aspen gets here, Wally," she murmured, and the disconsolate ostrich fell into step beside the two girls.

Rouge looked at Doom Bloom as they made their way through the surprisingly wide path that led from the Tree's glade to the small house which must be stuffed to overflowing with all the people here now. Though the glyphis probably slept somewhere wet, right? Still, with Sarave, Juniper, Nekthadt, and Doom, the two-room shack was undoubtedly close quarters. Add in the unicorns, that weird duck, Khor, and Sumi, and even with several of the animals living in the attached barn, well... It was a good thing people were coming who knew how to build more homes, that was all.

Doom Bloom finally broke the silence once they were far enough from the meadow that she could be certain no one could hear them. The tall elf caught Rouge's curious look and shrugged a little awkwardly. "I always feel strange talking about real-life in front of the, uh, Natives. I know you and Motte do it all the time, but I just can't."

Silence descended again for several steps before Doom spoke again, this time in a rush. "Look, I don't exactly know how to tell you this, but I think my dad and your mom are going to get a divorce."

Rouge stopped and stared, feeling her heart sink down into her feet.

Doom Bloom turned, and then rushed forward to hug Rouge again. Her voice was fierce when she spoke. "You're still my sister, though. It took way too long for us to find each other, and I'm not giving you up." She leaned back, trying to see Rouge's face. The elf bit her rosy lower lip, looking uncertain. "That is, if you still want to be my sister?"

Rouge fell forward into the other girl's arms, and for the first time, she regretted that she couldn't cry in non-experimental *Veritas Online.* "Yes," she mumbled into Doom's shirt, "I want to be your sister."

The strong arms around her tightened, and then Doom let go and stepped back. She swiped at cheeks that were, like Rouge's, inappropriately dry, then laughed at herself. "Sorry, I told myself I wasn't going to do this. Just... I wanted to tell you in person, so I could see your face. I know they haven't exactly been great parents to you, just like I haven't," her voice hitched, "like I haven't been a great sister. But still..."

Rouge shook her head, beaded braids rattling. "I don't care about them. I just hope someday they can be happy. I don't think my mom has ever actually been *happy.* I think she always believes she only needs one more thing. The perfect husband, or a perfect child, or the perfect job, whatever it is, and then she'll be happy. I don't think she can stand to see anyone else be happy with what she sees as less than what she has, because it makes her realize that maybe what she's actually missing is something *inside* herself." She waved her hands, struggling to put the complex thoughts and feelings that her mother evoked into words.

Doom looked sad and a little stricken. "I never thought of it that way. I just knew she was miserable, and she made everyone else around her miserable, too." she rested a hand on Rouge's head and rubbed her braids. "You're a smart kid, you know?"

Rouge stuck her tongue out at her sister. "Yeah, I know. Now, tell me everything."

The last time Doom and Rouge had really spoken, Doom had said that her dad had lost his job, and Rouge's mom and Doom's dad, who was Rouge's step-father, were using Doom's college fund to pay their expenses. If Doom wanted to be sure she could keep going to college, she needed to get a job, and wouldn't be around much. Since then, they'd touched bases a few times, most recently when FantumHat caught Rouge and tried to use her as a hostage to force Doom Bloom to come talk to him, but Doom had never really had time for a proper chat.

As the two girls resumed walking, Doom Bloom took up the story. "The day after that jerk, FantumHat, messed with you, dad called. He said he got a new job, and while it didn't pay as well as the old one yet, it had a lot of potential, and it would be enough that he could afford to pay for my education once the house sold. He never once said 'we'. It was always 'I', and I just knew... So I asked. He didn't want to tell me, but-"

She shook her head and sighed, pale blonde locks glinting in the sunlight streaming down through the leaves of the trees at the edge of the small orchard. "He said he and mom had a huge blow-up after I left the last time. Mom threatened to leave, and he told her she should. They're seeing a counselor." Her lips twitched. "Well, three counselors, I think. One for each of them, and then a couple's counselor. They agreed to sell the house, which was really bigger than they needed anyway, and they're going to get something smaller, closer to his new job. They're going to use part of the money for the sale to refill my college fund, and he said they've put it in my name now too, so they can put money in, but not take it out without my permission."

Stepping out from under the shade of the branches, both of them paused, turning their faces up to the warm sun. "I don't know for sure what's going to happen, and neither does Dad, which is why he didn't want to tell me yet." Doom shot Rouge a look filled with irony, "I told him I'm an adult, and he doesn't need to protect me anymore. Though of course you wouldn't understand that, since your dad is *never* overprotective."

Rouge choked on a laugh, and the two girls continued walking, though they were both grinning now.

"Anyway," Doom continued, "I'm all set for college, and, in fact, I have a fair bit of my own money now, since I was working so hard to save up for next semester. I shouldn't have to work until I graduate, though I'll probably try to find something senior year, so I can get some experience. Mom is living in the house, and dad got an apartment close to work, but as soon as the house sells, they'll have to figure out what they're doing, because dad's one-bedroom isn't going to cut it for both of them and all their stuff."

Rouge set a hand on her sister's arm, and Doom paused, looking back at her. "So, you can play? I mean, you can be online sometimes? Here?"

Doom Bloom grinned. "You don't think I came all the way up here just so you can put my Corpse to work, do you? Nope, I'm here to stay, and if I get the classes I want next semester, I should be able to be on when you get out of school at least a few days a week. You're going to get sick of me."

"No," Rouge said, slipping her fingers into her sister's hand. "No, I don't think I will."

Note From The Author

Thank you for joining me for more of Rouge and Aspen's adventures! I hope you enjoyed getting to hear from Khor, as well. It was really hard to convince him to tell his side of the story, and I owe him a lot of veggie bread.

If you enjoyed this book, please take a moment to review it on Amazon and/or Goodreads. You have no idea how much it brightens my day when I see a glowing review, and it helps other readers find my books, which in turn helps me keep writing more of them!

The final book, *Harvest*, is fully written, so I'm going to get it edited and published by the end of 2022. I hope you'll join Rouge, Aspen, and crew for the final installment of *Legendary Farmer*. They're finally home, with their enemies hot on their heels, but don't worry, our heroes still have a few tricks up their sleeves. (Or maybe in Aspen's hat.)

In the meantime, I'm available on Patreon, Goodreads, Instagram as authorelizabethoswald, and Twitter as @AuthorEOswald. I'd love to hear from you!

www.ingramcontent.com/pod-product-compliance
Lightning Source LLC
Chambersburg PA
CBHW070617260626
47161CB00007B/2466